Dancing
in
Concrete Moccasins

Amy Krout-Horn

Dancing in Concrete Moccasins
Copyright © 2016 by Amy Krout-Horn

ISBN: 978-0-9966634-7-2

Library of Congress Control Number: 2016944713

Dora's letter by Sage Sculli

Cover art by Carises Horn

For Gabriel, who brings out my best, my worst,
and everything in between,
and for all the urban Indians keeping it real off the rez.

Flight of the Glass Butterfly

The whole world appeared blue when she looked through its wings: the street light, the bare branches of a dying elm tree, even the sun. Lily Bordeaux could have shifted her eye in any other direction and everything could have been yellow or green or red. But yellow reminded her of cigarette-stained teeth, sharp and crooked behind thin lips. Green fives and tens and twenties folded in tarnished silver money clips paid for her mother Paulette's whiskey sours. Red, the worst color of all, crept across the whites of eyes like insect legs, ruined the bed sheets, and burned in Lily's cheeks. Only the symmetrical wedges of blue that crowned the glass butterfly's open wings could submerse her in their coolness. Like slices of clear winter sky, they numbed her and, for brief moments, delivered the blessed feeling of not feeling at all.

Her youngest brother Jack had given Lily the butterfly wind chime on a year that Paulette had forgotten her birthday, which was not unusual among the nine Bordeaux children, except for the oldest, who had the distinction of sharing a birthday with the baby Jesus. Jack had saved nickels, dimes, and the occasional quarter he found between the couch cushions and in Laundromat vending machine change slots. At a store where nothing cost more than a dollar, he purchased the gift and a card that appealed to a young boy's sense of humor: a grinning simian in a garish party hat. But "You look like a monkey and smell like one, too" couldn't minimize the affection he held for his adolescent sister. Lily had taught him the alphabet, made peanut butter sandwiches for him after school, and had chased down, throttled, and extracted an apology from a neighborhood boy who had jumped Jack.

"We're not redskins!" she had growled while she shoved the bully's face into a mound of car-exhaust-black snow as Jack, only a week into Kindergarten, wiped his bloody nose on a mitten.

On that day, he promised himself that when he got bigger and became a better fighter, he would protect her, too.

On a bent nail above the bedroom window, Lily had hung the chime and sometimes, even when the air was very still, she heard it tinkling in the darkness, like spirits seeking voice. Then Daryl came, the spirits grew silent, and Lily and the glass butterfly were alone.

***

Paulette Bordeaux and the Silver Spur Lounge had a long history together, longer than any history she had accumulated with her children's fathers, but no less turbulent. Despite the brawls, the drugs, and the recurrent police raids, she, like the other Indians, urban cowboys, and urban Indian cowboys, kept frequenting the dive in search of the magic elixir to heal the holes riddling her soul.

Fresh out of Stillwater and in violation of his parole, Daryl Chien leaned against the bar and cautiously scanned the smoky room. He had earned a lot of enemies while inside, almost as many as he had earned on the outside, and sliding onto an empty stool would have left his back to the door. A jealous husband and a broken beer bottle had once taught him the risk of complacency, a lesson which had cost him an eye.

"Buy me a drink, Chief?"

Daryl snapped his head around, his good eye squinting to find Paulette perched next to him. Her lips curled into something that resembled a smile.

"Where you from?"

He sized her up. She was heavier than he usually liked; an over-sized linty purple sweater ended mid-thigh, where black leggings, stretched to their limits, continued towards worn-out men's cowboy boots. A thick layer of foundation, much lighter than the bare loose skin of her neck, unsuccessfully camouflaged her age, masking what might have once been called pretty. A port-wine birthmark stained the hand that held a cigarette, and her hair, cut a few inches from the scalp, looked course enough to scour dirty dishes.

Red Lake," he said and pulled a lighter from his jeans, touching the low flame to her cigarette. "How about you?"

"Born on White Earth."

Paulette's family hadn't lived on the reservation since she was a child; Daryl's hadn't, either, but both thought the claim gave their city Indian status more clout, more native street cred, in an adversarial environment where it seemed everyone's identity was always in question. Without asking, he reached for the bar and slid a Newport from her pack. She didn't object.

"Some man gonna care if I buy you that drink?"

Paulette sneered, adjusting the sweater's V-neck just enough for him to snatch a view of wilted cleavage.

"Some woman gonna care?"

Daryl eyed her again. Better looking barflies buzzed around the pool table, but with less than an hour until last call, he weighed his options, and decided that, at least for the night, he didn't want to exert his energy on something more challenging, and that this one hovering beside him would have to do. He motioned to the bartender and pointed at

Paulette's empty glass.

The morning after her mother and Daryl's introduction, Lily woke to the aroma of bacon, onions, and fried potatoes. Her stomach rumbled to assure her that it wasn't just a pleasant dream. Who cooked breakfast on a Saturday morning? Not Paulette. Lily rubbed her eyes. A crisp spring breeze passed through the screen and the butterfly softly played its fairytale music, the sunlight stealing colors from its wings and splashing them across her bare feet as curiosity and hunger lured her from under the blanket.

In the kitchen, a stocky man with a crew cut, wearing boxer shorts and a thermal with a rip near the armpit, dished up hash for her younger brothers, who both stood, eager, undernourished, almost Dickensian, with outstretched bowls. Paulette lay in a snoring heap on the sleeper sofa. As Lily took a chair at the table, she watched him pick up the spatula and expertly flip the sizzling potatoes. She couldn't help noticing the odd way in which his one eye followed the task while the other stayed pinned to a charred spot of wall just above the stove. The stranger held up a plate of food and mouthed the word, "Hungry?"

Wary, Lily hesitated, but before she could answer, her brother Dave took it and set it in front of her.

"This is Daryl. He's Mom's new friend," he said, as he wiped his greasy mouth with the arm of his sweat shirt, then whispered behind his hand, "He's got a real glass eye."

Paulette often brought "new friends" home, but her children never saw most of them conscious until they rolled off the lumpy sleeper bed late in the afternoon, fumbled for their pants, and departed without bidding farewell. Some loitered for a couple of days, until the booze was gone. Dave and Jack's father had remained the longest, sticking around three months into Paulette's last pregnancy. Over the years, the Bordeaux children had seen men blacken their mother's eyes and listened to irate women, hunting for their husbands, pound the apartment door. They had even watched Paulette shove a couple of drunks, without boots or jeans, into the alley.

But in their chaotic collection of childhood memories, the most unusual event for Lily, Dave, and Jack occurred that morning. Daryl Chien had risen before noon on a Saturday and cooked breakfast. He appeared so alien to the others in the rogue's gallery of one-night stands and baby daddies, that he seemed almost … special.

As the weeks passed, he stayed, and continued to set himself apart from the herd. He found a full-time roofing job which paid cash, bought a truck that he let Paulette drive the kids to school in, and regularly put the skills he had picked up in the prison kitchen to use. When welfare checks and food stamps ran short, Daryl took up the slack. Although he liked his beer and the occasional shot of bourbon, he didn't puke or punch his fist through the wall or break the dishes, so it was all right. Often, he told filthy jokes that made Dave snort, confused Jack, and caused Lily to blush.

Paulette smiled more and drank less, and, for six glorious months, something that could have been mistaken for a functional family resided inside the four walls of the Bordeaux apartment. But a screw went mysteriously missing from the bathroom door knob and ,as if it had been holding it all together, everything cracked, shattered, and exploded like shrapnel.

***

One afternoon, around the time the screw disappeared, Daryl arrived home, unlocked the door, and dropped the key on the end table. As was his custom, he shuffled to the refrigerator for a beer, but, to his annoyance, there wasn't any left. In the far bedroom, he could hear Dave and Jack launching Match Box cars off of the cardboard ramps he had rigged for them out of a couple of pizza boxes. Slamming the refrigerator, he wandered down the hall to the back room and popped his head in, just as a miniature midnight blue Charger flipped and landed on a battalion of green plastic soldiers. He grinned sardonically as an image of his old man, the ex-Marine with a short fuse and scarred fists, flashed through his brain like a lightning strike and his tongue unconsciously darted to the toothless hole in his lower jaw. He still hated that son of a bitch.

"Hey, little Redskins! Where's your mom?"

"She's at the store," Jack said, and sent a silver Camaro speeding off a pyramid of phone books.

Dave simulated the sound of an explosion and leered up at Daryl.

"Did you break your eye today?"

The boys had a morbid fascination with the prosthesis and Dave found great joy in teasing Daryl about it.

"No, the old eye's okay, but you got a crack in your butt!"

Jack laughed as his brother crouched to pick up a dump truck, and the waist of his second-hand jeans gapped wide.

"Shut up, Jack-Ass," he yelled and threw the truck at the younger boy's head, narrowly missing an eye, but causing a bloody welt on the cheek below it.

Figuring that another Dave-on-Jack skirmish was about to ensue, and not really caring how it resulted, more severely injurious or otherwise, Daryl left the boys to their demolition derby and shut the door. Passing the girl's room, he noticed the butterfly twisting noose-like on its nail, the colorful wings dull in the late afternoon's dim light. He stopped. On the opposite side of the hall, from behind the bathroom door, he could hear the voice of the deceased Kurt Cobain wailing from her boom box and the sound of running water. Suddenly, the broken door knob leaked luridly into his thoughts.

They were the same kind of thoughts that had flooded him as he knelt on the curb of a side street next to the Lincoln someone had left unlocked. The kind that seized him when he tailed the man who had just withdrawn three hundred bucks from the ATM into the empty parking lot. Like a bottle teetering at the edge of the table, Daryl could have caught himself and prevented another crash, but he had always found a sadistic sense of satisfaction in the sound of breaking glass. Dark apparitions dwelled in the chip on his shoulder and whispered in his ear, "Take it, Daryl Chien. They owe you."

He grasped the broken knob and turned it. Startled, Lily spun around and hurriedly tried to cover herself with the towel she had been wrapping around her wet hair. The man's good eye lingered on her horrified face for a second before it followed a drop of water trailing down her throat towards the cleft between her small breasts. He smiled unapologetically, the motionless glass eye frozen as the other crawled over her body. He drank it all in: her smooth caramel skin, her firm thighs, the mane of thick brown hair, and her blue, blue eyes.

"Steer clear of white boys from Minnetonka," her mother had once told her. "They could turn out to be your brother."

When her kids prodded, Paulette revealed the last names of likely men, but the name of an upper middle class suburb was all Lily would ever know about *her* father.

She could hear her little brothers down the hall, smashing toy cars, and she stepped back until the clammy plastic shower curtain drifted out and stuck to her legs. Daryl moved closer, pressed a finger to his lips, and whispered, "Relax. Everything's cool. It's not like I'm your daddy."

Suddenly, he detected the faint scratch of a key in the front door lock and retreated.

"I'll get a new screw," he said, as he wiggled the knob, winked at her, and slipped out.

True to his word, Daryl fixed the faulty knob and Lily began to wonder if she had misinterpreted the bathroom incident. Had it been an innocent mistake? At the end of the week, when he received his paycheck, he offered Paulette rent money without her asking and brought home a video game system which he had bought from a roofing buddy who just happened to have one, reduced for quick sale, in the trunk of his car.

"You rock," Dave shouted when Daryl carried in the tangle of cables, cords, and controllers, and dropped it all on the couch next to the boys.

He hadn't forgotten Lily, either. Reaching into his coat, he extracted a scratched case and tossed the Smashing Pumpkins CD on her lap.

"Got that one?"

She shook her head, but stopped herself before any outward signs of excitement could rise to the surface.

"Like it?" he asked.

"I do. Thanks."

"Great. I'm glad. Now you owe me a favor."

Lily felt heat rush into her face as a cold wet, sticky sensation, like the shower curtain against her legs, shrouded her entirely. Daryl enjoyed the way she flushed, the way she squirmed, the way those blue eyes flew from him to the gift and back again, searching for the least dangerous place to land. And he savored it a few more seconds before yelling into the kitchen, "Want to go to the Spur tonight, Paulette? Lily'll watch the monsters."

Engrossed in the task of detaching the cable wire and hooking up their game, the boys didn't acknowledge his insult, nor did they notice their sister's shift from utter panic to distrustful uneasiness. Daryl dug his hands into the front pockets of his pants, his blunt fingers moving surreptitiously under the tar-spattered denim so that only the girl could witness what he was fondling. His mouth curled into a lipless smile, and then he ducked into the bathroom and locked the door. The sound of running water sent icy shivers through Lily as if she, rather than Daryl, was the one who had chosen the cold shower.

***

In the night, she awoke, again cold, again shivering. Someone had pulled the blanket off. Someone had lifted her T-shirt. Something heavy restrained her. Hot breath, reeking of beer, garlic, and cigarettes, assaulted her nostrils while a callous hand groped her breast. She tensed, a whimper growing to a scream, but the hand violently twisted as the other slapped down on her mouth, his voice hissing in her ear.

"Your brothers are next door. If you're not quiet, I'll show little Jack what it's like in prison after the lights go out."

Lily froze, paralyzed by the heinous suggestion, and by the suspicion that after an evening at the Silver Spur, Paulette was already blacked out. Once, as a toddler, while her mother slept, Lily had fallen down a steep flight of stairs, breaking no bones. Everyone speculated that it was because, as she bounced head first down the incline, she had gone limp. As a bony knee forced her thighs apart, the instinct, based in either self-preservation, or perhaps in total resignation, returned, and she lay like a corpse. She couldn't save her body, so she concentrated all her power, shrinking her spirit into a tiny pinpoint and hiding it so deep within herself no one could touch it. No one could take it. But as she tried to flee further inside her own mind, he whispered the words, the words he would repeat night after night, like a kind of cruel mantra.

"It's all right," he said, justifying the act for the sake of some tattered shred of his own conscience, as he stripped her of precious inimitable layers of innocence, "I'm not your daddy."

Daryl continued to pay the rent, continued to buy Paulette's drinks, continued to collect video games for the boys, while Lily continued to silently suffer his repayment plan. There was no point in divulging the truth to Paulette; Lily knew how she would react. Her sister Renee had set the precedent when their mother's last boyfriend had cornered the girl, unzipped his fly, and grabbed a fistful of her hair.

"Jesus Christ, Renee," Paulette screamed when her daughter told her about the assault. "You've been asking for it, jiggling around in those tight tank tops. What the hell do you expect?"

After that, Renee ran away to live in a boyfriend's basement apartment. She didn't love him and he didn't love her, but they both could provide something the other wanted, something the other needed. Lacking that kind of less-than-perfect option, Lily devised other means of escape, lifting money from Paulette's purse whenever possible, and hopping a bus to St. Paul.

"Better lay off the mac and cheese, Lil," Renee said one afternoon as they hid away in the dank basement and she sprinkled a line of grass across a cigarette paper, "You're chunky around the middle."

Lily rubbed her stomach, took the joint from her sister, and lit it. Drawing deeply, she held the harsh smoke for as long as she could and then blew it towards the low ceiling. Soon, a hazy cloud hovered around the exposed water pipes, and she felt numb enough to speak, numb enough for her ears to listen to the serrated ugliness of her own secret. Slouched on a square of moldy remnant carpet that didn't quite meet the cracked walls of the sad little room, Renee sat perfectly still, staring into her empty hands, until her baby sister had finished, and then she slowly shook her head. Neither girl cried.

"It's the same old shit," Renee said, her voice hard and acidic. "It's Paulette's same shit. It'll never change."

Her gaze dropped to Lily's belly again and her own churned as the sickening thought, enhanced by the inescapable paranoia of bad pot, closed in like a kidnapper's lightless, suffocating pillowcase.

"Listen, Lil. We're going to head out west this spring. Marcus' brother lives in Seattle. He thinks he can find him some construction work or a few guitar gigs. Come with us. Leave Paulette to clean up her own messes."

***

Winter arrived, encasing everything in ice, and Daryl's mind registered the meaning of the bump occupying the teenage girl's once flat stomach. He slid out one smoke gray dawn and did not return. In the selfish realm occupied by all children at one time or another, Jack and Dave sullenly moped about the video games he had promised. Paulette coped in her usual manner: she dowsed disappointment with an entire box of red wine. When she lurched briefly back into lucidity she berated Lily, who had just shrugged at the news and said, "Why should I care? It's not like he's my daddy."

"It smells like pot in here," Paulette snarled, swaying in the doorway of the girl's bed room, as drops of wine dripped from her plastic cup onto the carpet. "I'm not putting up with that crap in my house!"

Lily turned slowly, looked through dilated pupils at her mother, and then, without speaking, looked away. As Paulette started in again, Lily adjusted the volume so that the Stone Temple Pilots blasted through the ear phones and drowned out the tirade. Indifference had always enraged Paulette. Besides, she couldn't shake the gnawing suspicion that Daryl's departure had something to do with her beautiful young daughter and it further fueled her animosity. With a wet, gravel-coated shriek, she plunged into the room. The dropped cup landed beside the door with a sweet, crimson splash, but by some bizarre black magic, it managed to remain upright.

"Listen to me, you selfish little bitch," she screamed, ripping the head set off and slapping Lily's face with it.

The girl bolted off the bed, her fists balled, and their eyes locked, blue on black. Paulette's narrowed and her mouth twisted into a repulsive grin, spittle shining at the corners.

"Go ahead," she said, her foul fruity breath filling the space between them, "Hit me! Hit me, so I've got an excuse to throw your stupid ass out on the street."

The girl didn't retreat, but kept her fists at her side, her stare fixed on her mother as if daring her to look away first. When she finally spoke, her voice was emotionless.

"I'm pregnant."

Paulette's eyes fell from the girl, who still stood staring, and she staggered backwards, her shoulder blades thudding against the wall. The questions of how and why and who remained unasked because, by the expression on Paulette's face, Lily knew her mother had already guessed the answers. It was the expression she had when Renee sought her rescue, a hateful grimace filled with jealousy and accusations concocted from the sick belief that her teenage daughters weren't victims of violence at all, but, rather, her cunning competition. She could have offered the girls empathy. She could have told them that she, too, had known what it was to be violated, to be victimized. But no one had ever shown Paulette that kindness; not when, at thirteen, she squatted in the unheated bathroom of her mother's house and birthed the by product of an uncle's incestuous attack, not when a landlord had given her the option of a blowjob or an eviction, and not when three guys, dressed in Minnetonka High School letter jackets, dragged her into their van nine months prior to Lily's birth. Her daughters would have to learn the rules of survival as their mother had. Life had stripped Paulette bare of all tenderness.

"Are you going to get rid of it?"

Lily shook her head incredulously. Paulette knew that the cost of that choice was not in their means. Even if the money had been available, it was too late to free herself from the creature in her belly, the terrible little mass that she could now feel growing, moving, kicking in her womb, like a thriving parasite or a malignant tumor. She imagined it, with tiny stained teeth and one seeing eye, staring out of her as if she were a translucent cocoon, a transparent host the creature would quickly devour after its birth.

"I guess you got what you were asking for," Paulette said coldly as she shoved away from the wall and stumbled towards the door. "I'll take you to the welfare office on Monday. At least it'll mean another check."

Lily threw herself back onto the unmade bed, fished a chipped ash tray from under it, took the roach the tray held, and lit it. When she had smoked it so far the lighter singed her finger nails, she extinguished it between her lips and swallowed it with a swig of flat Pepsi. As her mind pried loose from a body she no longer chose to claim as her own, she glanced the butterfly's motionless wings, coated with dust, before her lids became too heavy and she spiraled and drifted far, far away to a stretch of fog-blanketed Pacific coastline.

***

"Seattle," she mumbled, when the Hennepin County nurse asked Lily what she was going to name the breech boy.

Through her post Caesarean section narcotic miasma, she had only heard the word going, and, later, when she read the name on the birth certificate, she could not dredge up enough feeling for the infant to attach more thought to it. She didn't care what the world would call him, for although the child had been blessed with Lily's features, when she looked at him, only one face, only one name, dominated her mind.

As if he knew and understood, Seattle would not accept his mother's breast, never cried when others bottle fed him, nor did he wake, the dawn she laid him with the note which said that she would not return, in a laundry basket. The baby would have to learn the rules of survival as his mother had. Life had stripped Lily bare of all tenderness.

***

"Too tender for the needle?" the Spokane dealer said. "Try this."

Lily set the tequila bottle on the discolored motel carpet and reached for the green glass one-hitter. Marcus dug an elbow into Renee's ribs and she rolled over, her eyelids at half-mast.

"Does she know what the fuck she's doing?" he slurred as he jabbed a thumb in Lily's direction. Renee watched as their newest connection flicked a lighter and her baby sister inhaled. She shrugged and wondered why he had bothered. He knew Lily smoked weed. Figuring that he must be drunk or high or both, she said, "Leave her alone, Marcus. You're not her dad."

The words penetrated the tequila and the dope, and, not knowing why, Lily flinched. The dealer rubbed at the acne on his hollow cheeks, coughed from some deep, decay-ridden cavern in his lungs, and offered her more. She took it, handing him the bottle of booze, all the time knowing what he really expected her to trade. When Renee and Marcus had passed out and the man, whose name Lily didn't know, had gone into the bathroom, she lifted the tiny foil-wrapped stash and one-hitter, and, stowing them in her bag with the bottle, she softly opened the motel room door.

"I'm going to Seattle," she said to no one as she swayed into the night, across the highway, and into the trees.

Clouds passed between her and the sliver of moon until she could no longer be discerned from the wind-whipped pine boughs. She wandered, floating lighter and lighter, as she murmured over and over, "I'm going to Seattle. I'm going to Seattle. I'm going to Seattle."

When she emerged from the trees, she found a footpath and followed it until it met the park's narrow access street. There, she melted onto a bench, suddenly feeling that her destination was too far, suddenly content to just lie upon the wood slats and stare at the only artificial light, high atop a pole across the street, flicker on and off. As her fingers fumbled blindly through her belongings for the heroin, her hand brushed against glass and metal. She pulled the butterfly from her bag, too. She filled the blackened glass bowl, smoked it empty, and then lay back again.

As she held the glass butterfly's string above her face, the breeze caught the chimes. It was one of the few possessions she had carried with her, though she had not taken it from her bag since they left Minnesota. It twirled in circles and turned her thoughts to Jack, to home, and finally, to Seattle, until she let go of the string and the butterfly fell with a small chaotic series of metal clinks into a silent heap. She reached for the tequila and finished the last inch of warm golden liquid, but her son's image wouldn't wash from her mind and for the first time, she saw him. Daryl's paralyzed stare, yellowing teeth, and thin bloodless lips were gone, and only Lily's own intelligent almond-shaped eyes, her long full lashes, and her mouth, like a small pink heart, shown through in the face of the child.

"He's mine," she said softly, her whispers lost among those of the quivering green needles.

She raised the butterfly from her chest. The whole world appeared blue when she looked through its wings; the street light, the bare branches of a dying pine, even the moon. She could have shifted her eye in any other direction and everything could have been yellow or green or red. But only the symmetrical wedges of blue that crowned the glass butterfly's open wings could submerse her in their coolness. Like slices of clear winter sky, they numbed her and, for this blessed moment, delivered the feeling of not feeling at all. Everything was so far away now, home, Seattle, the beating of her heart, and as it slid from her grasp, Lily Bordeaux knew this was the only way glass butterflies ever landed.

Pinch of Salt

When Jack Bordeaux spotted a Minneapolis police cruiser parked in front of the building, he spun around and walked back towards the corner. The bus still idled at the stop as the few sullen passengers climbed aboard, bound for their night shifts of emptying office trash, turning tricks, or peddling crack. Although he had just disembarked from it, Jack considered getting back on. But he realized, after shoving a hand into his pocket, that he had already dropped his last dollar in the cash box, and, without plans of needing one, hadn't asked the driver for a transfer. The bus roared away, the thick stench of diesel hanging in the cold air, as behind him, he heard the police car doors slam. He held his breath, it drove passed, and he forced himself to look at the cruiser's rear window. This time, the back seat was empty. He exhaled. Now he could go home.

The apartment door stood partially open, the smell of fried food and cigarette smoke intruding into the hall along with his mother's profanity, and Jack hesitated, clasping the book bag to his chest like a shield. The youngest of Paulette Bordeaux's nine children had learned the hard way not, intentionally or otherwise, to get between arguing alcoholics and addicts. If he forgot this lesson, the scars reminded him; the one on his shoulder from a sister's teeth, the one across his thigh from a brother's broken bottle, the ones he couldn't see in the mirror, but that mutated into the nightmares that robbed him of sleep.

Entering, the scene might have shocked Jack had it not been so familiar. His mother slouched on the sofa, the cordless phone still clutched in one hand, a glass of whiskey and ice in her other. Wild-eyed, his brother Dave paced the room, while Dave's girlfriend stood in the dining nook, a fresh bruise on her cheek, and dabbed at her mouth with a blood-spattered paper towel. Their whimpering daughter bounced on the battered woman's hip. They all stared at him as if he were an unwelcome stranger.

"Where the hell have *you* been?" Paulette said.

"At the university. I had a night class."

Unlike his siblings or his mother, Jack had graduated high school, applied to college, and laboriously waded through the bureaucratic quagmire of paperwork required for a non-reservation-born Indian to obtain tribal enrollment, in order to receive a tribal scholarship. He encouraged his siblings to do the same, but none had followed suit.

"Jackie's a big man on campus, Ma," Dave said, staggering closer and flicking the book bag with a middle finger. "Can't let us forget it, either."

He cocked his finger again, ready to land a second blow, but Jack dodged it and ducked into the dining nook. Dave whirled, tripping on his own feet. More blood rushed into his already flushed face and he snarled the usual insults.

"Half-breed punk piece of shit! Think you're too good for us real Indians!"

Although Dave and Jack shared the same paternity, something unique among Paulette's children, Dave's fairer complexion revealed their mother's mixed ancestry, and the Ojibwe genes seeming to have all manifested in Jack. Until Lily died, it hadn't really bothered Dave, but when she was no longer there to buffer his assaults on Jack, the empty space she left behind quickly filled with Dave's jealousies, both old and new. The obvious fact that Jack had been Lily's favorite didn't help. As a boy, Dave had secretly wanted their sister's attention, too, but almost never got it, unless he acted up, pissed her off, or made Jack cry.

"Knock it off," Dave's girlfriend whined.

"Shut up, Angie. Stay the fuck out of it," he screamed, waving a fist at her blond head.

Paulette shook the phone at Dave, threatening to call the cops again, and demanded that he leave the apartment. Just sober enough to know that he didn't want to wind up in the drunk tank this early on a Friday night, Dave lowered his hand. Ripping his jean jacket off the dining chair, he rifled through Angie's purse, grabbing some cash and cigarettes, before he muttered something about "bitches ruining his life" and stormed out.

Jack closed the door behind his brother and locked the dead bolts as Angie crumpled into a chair at the table. The baby stared up at her disengaged mother's bloody lip, fixated on the way it trembled. With the usual ambivalence she showed the younger woman, Paulette loudly rattled the empty glass's ice. It was a signal all of her children knew too well, and Jack took the tumbler from her.

In the kitchen, a large plastic bottle of whiskey stood on the counter among heaps of spilled flour, a dented metal mixing bowl coated with dried batter, and two pieces of cold fry bread abandoned on an oily paper plate. He pushed aside someone's attempt at dinner and poured a shot in the glass, filling it the rest of the way with ice and tap water, careful not to add too much. She had caught him once, and had accused him of stealing her booze. Jack rarely took a drink, less the time survived in Paulette's womb and the early years of baby bottles filled with vodka-laced Kool-Aid. But explaining the real reason for watering down the whiskey would have ended in a far worse beating, so at age nine, Jack had let her believe that he drank it. Mixing the concoction around in the glass with a paring knife, he dropped the blade into a pile of dirty dishes and brought her the drink.

"Where's Seattle?"

"In Washington, Stupid," Paulette snorted, in a fit of whiskey-soaked mirth.

For twelve years, the tired old joke had kept making the rounds in the Bordeaux family.

"Kid's in bed, I think," she finally said, as she put the glass to her lips and sighed a potent mixture of pleasure, relief, resignation, and bitterness

Jack checked on Angie, who had immodestly tugged up the bottom of her T-shirt to expose a blue-veined, milky white breast. She nursed the baby girl while herself nursing on the filter of a Marlboro, and her watery eyes followed the thin strips of passing headlights that escaped through the grimy slats of the window blind. He offered her some ice for her cheek, but she declined. He didn't ask what had happened. It was just some variation on the same tragic production, the characters playing interchangeable roles. Last week, Angie had performed the part of the ranting drunk, kicking Dave in the chest and cracking ribs. Earlier in the month, Paulette had inflicted claw marks on both of them as Dave and Angie wrestled her to the ground in a bar parking lot, all three cursing and spitting. They had pulled her off one of her ex-lovers, who had the misfortune of lurching in at the exact moment Paulette happened to be lurching out. With each new drama, Jack's pity couldn't quite balance off the loathing.

He opened the bedroom door, and Seattle looked up from the inflatable mattress where he sat with his back against the wall, ankles crossed. The boy laid the book he had been reading on the floor and smiled.

"Hey, Uncle. What's up?"

"What's up with you, little man? Why aren't you on *your* bed?"

They had shared one of the apartment's two bedrooms since Seattle outgrew the laundry basket and Paulette had set up a garage sale crib beside Jack's twin bed. In the family's rotating world of beds, rooms, and residents, the crib now occupied Dave and Angie's room, Seattle slept in the saggy twin bed, and Jack used the blow-up mattress. The boy pointed at a foul yellowish puddle marring the center of the blanket.

"Dave and Angie were fighting in the kitchen. The baby started crying. She kept screaming, but I guess no one heard except me. I went in and got her," he said, nodding at the movie poster of Wes Studi as Geronimo, taped to the thin wall between the rooms, "When I brought her in here, we sat on the bed and I rocked her, but she was really pissed."

Jack's muscles tensed, scenes from his own childhood rolling in his head: Paulette's laughter or her moans, or her curses tangled with a man's murmurs or his grunts and groans or his rage, a man who had bought Paulette drinks earlier in the evening, Seattle cutting teeth, feverish and bawling, Jack changing his filthy diaper, letting him gnaw his swollen gums on Jack's finger while, in the other room, Paulette and the stranger eventually pass out, the apartment grows quiet, and all the Bordeaux children within its confines, fall into a fitful sleep. Paulette was no longer the kind of woman the men at the Silver Spur Lounge bought drinks for, but the situation hadn't improved. The next generation had inherited her habits. Seattle's voice drew Jack back into the present.

"I tried to calm her down, but her face was red and pinched," he said, imitating the infant's scrunched expression. "Then she barfed all over my jeans, then all over the bed. Angie burst in here, yelling. Her lip was bleeding. She told me to stay the hell out of their room. She grabbed the baby and said I better clean up the mess before Grandma saw it. Then the cops came, so I stayed in our room, because I didn't want to get busted."

Seattle glanced at the stain then, embarrassed, turned to Jack.

"What kind of soap cleans up baby puke, Uncle?"

"I'll clean it up."

Jack stripped the thin fleece blanket off and found that the vomit had soaked through to the mattress.

He took the soiled bedding into the bathroom, scrubbed the spot, and hung it to dry over the shower curtain rod. Scrounging under the sink, he found some disinfectant and sprayed the mattress, not quite certain whether he was actually aiming at the newest stain or just wasting time on an old one. At some point or another, most of the Bordeaux children had slept on it when they were little, often two and three at a time, leaving the bed, like those who had tossed and turned on it, with nasty, permanent marks.

When Jack had enough money saved, he would move out, he would buy a spotless new mattress. He would buy one for Seattle, too.

"Sleep on the air bed tonight. I'll throw a towel down and crash here."

Seattle protested, but Jack changed the subject.

"Did you eat dinner?"

The boy shook his head. Dave's meltdown, and the subsequent visit from the Minneapolis PD, had canceled yet another meal. Returning to the kitchen, Jack disregarded the stale fry bread, searching for something more nutritious, but the groceries he had bought with some of his financial aid money earlier in the week were gone. Opening the refrigerator, he spotted a block of government cheese and a quart of milk.

He shook the carton, knowing there wouldn't be enough to wash down dinner, so using the same technique as he had on Paulette's whiskey, he poured the milk into a cup and turned on the tap. Like pancakes or French toast or anything involving white flour and a skillet, fry bread didn't reheat well, but he tossed it on a plate and slid it in the microwave anyway. Picky eaters went hungry in the Bordeaux household. Sometimes, all eaters did. As the bread hissed and popped, Jack looked into the living room, watching the wobbly flesh of Paulette's chin flop towards the lower terrain of sagging breasts and belly rolls. A loud gurgling rasp fell from her open mouth and startled, she jerked her head back for a moment, then let it sink to her chest again. As usual, she had lost the battle with unconsciousness.

Once, when Jack was a boy, he had asked her why her fry bread tasted better than Grandma Bordeaux's. Smiling proudly, she had told him about the pinch of salt.

"My mother taught me her recipe. She said never forget to add a pinch of salt. Then one day I was making a batch and I wondered what it would taste like if I added a pinch or two of sugar. When I told your grandma, she was really mad, asked me why I didn't think her fry bread was good enough. I guess we all have different ways of doing it, some better than others. Maybe each new generation improves on the old recipe."

The microwave timer beeped and Jack turned his attention away from where his mother slumped on the couch, the empty whiskey glass still locked in her fingers.

Seattle wolfed down the tough fry bread and American cheese, and suspiciously sipped the milk.

"This tastes kind of funny. Like it's got water in it," he said, and lifted the cup for examination.

"It's skim. It's good for you. Drink it," Jack said, as he spread a towel across the damp mattress and pulled off his sneakers.

The boy shrugged, then finished the diluted milk. He put the cup on the empty plate and picked up the book again. Since the sixth grader had read almost all the available materials his public school had to offer, Jack borrowed from the university library. Seattle hungrily plowed through written words faster than he could wipe out a pile of White Castle sliders, his mind growing as quickly as his body. Initially, Jack worried the collegiate level books might pose too great a challenge for the boy and suggested that he keep a list of words or concepts he didn't understand so they could discuss them, but the self-reliant twelve-year-old found a worn copy of Webster's dictionary at the Goodwill and talked Paulette into buying it for him. Seattle kept it close at hand as he devoured texts on the United States Constitution, Minnesota geology, and eastern philosophy, only referring to his uncle once to ask if Jack had ever considered practicing Buddhism. As of late, Seattle's most requested topics centered on Native America and he often delivered his new knowledge to the rest of the family.

"Traditionally, fry bread isn't a Native American food," he announced one evening as they all sat at the dinner table and his grandmother dropped another spoonful of batter into the pan.

Paulette looked up from the stove, wincing as if hot grease had spattered the inside of her wrist, and said, "Bullshit!"

"It's true, Grandma. Indian women learned about it from the white soldiers."

Never wasting an opportunity to weigh in on what was and was not Indian, Dave injected his commentary. He said that Angie's family, who had all emigrated from Norway, Sweden, and Finland, never ate it. Excited to be included in the debate, Angie nodded over-enthusiastically.

"I didn't know about it until I met you guys," she said.

Latching on to the flawed reasoning, Paulette said, "See, it's Indian."

Seattle glanced across the table at Jack, searching for support. Paulette glanced at Jack, too, her look as threatening as the night she had accused him of stealing whiskey. Jack shot a secret smile at his nephew, then looked at his mother as he spoke.

"Europeans introduced white flour to the indigenous diet."

As if the knowledge was a personal affront, Dave scowled.

"Thanks for putting it into college asshole terms for us, Jackie."

Their mother carried the platter of steaming fry bread to the table and threw it down in front of them.

"Well, it belongs to us now, doesn't it," she said, her voice cold cast-iron, as she cracked open two Old Milwaukee's. Taking a long drink from one, she gave the other can to Dave.

The boy now reserved most of his conversations for Uncle Jack.

"Did my mother know about Chief Seattle?" he said, lowering the book and peering up from the air mattress.

In the pit of Jack's chest, something heavy, something jagged, dug into his hidden, unhealed wounds as his sister's ghost flitted across the backs of his eyelids. On the night of her son's first birthday, somewhere in Spokane, the sixteen-year-old runaway curled on a park bench and died. She never reached her intended destination. Lily had never known about the Duwamish leader. For her son, Seattle, she existed only through fragments of his uncle's memory. Like Paulette's fry bread, Jack sometimes withheld ingredients of the story, sometimes adding others, trying hard to nourish the boy's need for the irreplaceable.

"Did she name me after him?"

Jack Bordeaux opened his eyes and turned to face Lily's son. As sirens wailed along Franklin Avenue, racing towards some other family's sorrow, he said, "Yes, little man, she named you after the chief."

And in the room's dim lamp light, Seattle beamed.

The Other Tribe

Barb StandingBull did not trust the government. And why should she? Like most Indian cynics, smallpox-infected blankets, broken treaties, and Wounded Knee topped a long, long list of reasons. Some said she was too angry, too intolerant. They talked about forgiving, forgetting, and leaving the past in the past. But every time she thought that maybe their accusations might hold a spark of truth, the phone rang and one voice or another out of Indian country would remind her of the nasty habit American history had of repeating itself. White-knuckling the receiver like a modern day war club, she would listen, the fire beginning to smolder in her belly. Corrupt federal officials striking deals with their tribal counterparts. Nuclear waste dumping on reservation land. Native vets with lost arms, lost legs, lost minds, losing their benefits. HUD houses without insulation in their walls. Pipes froze. So did the feet of the residents. Funds for Indian education disappeared. More kids dropped out. The words became kindling and the blaze burned hotter, burned higher, until her nerves felt like lines of lit gunpowder. So, as she took the form, attached to a clip board, at the Department of Public Health that morning, Barb StandingBull did not find it at all strange when she thought she tasted ashes.

A flu shot shortage had brought her there. No one else had the vaccine and she couldn't afford to miss any more work if some crude individual sneezed on her in the checkout line; diabetes had already caused her to use up most of her sick days. Walk-in patients packed the waiting room, a large majority of them clutching their jaws and hoping their name was next on the list for the student dentist's standard extraction. Sitting down on one of the metal folding chairs that had been set in the hall for the overflow, Barb balanced the clipboard on her knees and noticed the grubby wad of tape wrapped around the pen attached to it. She rummaged in her purse for one less likely to defeat the whole purpose of her visit. Across the corridor, a man and woman quietly argued in Spanish and the toddler on his lap whined. He frowned at the boy, then at the woman, as the baby she held let out a shrill scream. Annoyed, Barb pulled back from the noise, cracking her head on the cinder block wall. A hot rush of pain circling to her temples. The man abruptly stood up, unloaded the drooling child onto the metal chair, and slammed through the glass front doors, the frigid fall wind entering as he exited. Barb watched him as he dug a cigarette out of his coat pocket and struggled to light it. Then he smoked and paced, paced and smoked, his breath and the smoke becoming one in the cold air.

Shoving a pacifier into the baby's mouth, the woman hissed something threatening through her teeth at the little boy. Barb shook her head, suddenly thinking of the sign at the appointment window. It advertised reduced-rate vasectomies. Then she turned her focus back to the clipboard and strained to read what seemed to be unusually small print.

Name, address, gender, date of birth; she slowly penned the information on each line, checked each appropriate box, until she got halfway down the paper. Stopping, she read it twice and then a third time, making sure she hadn't missed something. Glancing up for a second, she scanned the light brown face and dark eyes of the woman holding the baby, as if she might understand Barb's disbelief. But her black, laser stare was targeted on the man, who now stood with his back to the door, shoulders hunched. She wouldn't understand, Barb thought, looking back at the paper. They had a category for Indians who spoke Spanish.

Hispanic/Latino, third in line under the heading Race, showed up after Caucasian/White and African-American/Black. Asian-American and Pacific Islanders took fourth position.

Last, and certainly what seemed like least, appeared a box next to a single word.

Leaving it blank, she felt the pen, pinched in her fingers, beginning to melt and she hurled it back into her purse. No one smelled the stench of burnt plastic invading her nostrils. None of them notice as she ripped the charred paper off the clipboard and threw it, along with a blackened twenty, on the counter. No one saw the little licks of flame flicker in her pupils as she walked to the end of the hall and entered through the door marked Foreign Travel. But the fire kept building.

As the nurse prepared the vaccine, Barb's attention was drawn to the space above the medical supply cupboards, where a collection of porcelain-faced dolls stood shoulder to shoulder, their lips pursed in identical fire engine red smiles. The one in the silk kimono wore the same expression as another with bright blue eyes and blond braids, and the one with the pointed wooden shoes grinned the grin of the one in the colorful fiesta dress. Scrutinizing someone's rendition of multi-culturalism, Barb glowered at the doll in fringed buckskin, beaded moccasins, and the generic goodwill smile.

"You're Native American, aren't you?"

Barb jerked her attention from the doll to the nurse but didn't answer. Disregarding the silence, the nurse wiped Barb's arm with alcohol, jabbed in the needle, and asked another question.

"What tribe?"

In the trash bin, in a reality separate from the nurse's sterile, white world, the alcohol swab ignited, burning away any trace of DNA. Barb imagined the waves of smoke rising from the discarded paper towels like little dark ghosts. All their wisdom, denied. All their history, rewritten. All the generations, before and after, erased. The United States government had condensed her people's entire identity into a word that identified nothing.

Barb StandingBull's teeth clenched, striking one another like flint, something molten rising to the surface from deep in her core. Hotter and hotter it rose. But just as it exploded from her lips, it transformed into ice.

"Other," she said, staring coldly at the confused nurse.

The nurse said something about not being familiar with that tribal nation, but Barb didn't hear her. She was already hurrying down the hall, bursting through the glass doors, plunging through the smokers' carcinogenic clouds. Barb rushed, a burning sensation creeping up and down her arm, her heart racing, and a cold perspiration covering her skin, until she reached the car. Jamming the key into the Mustang's lock, she flung the door open and fell into the driver's seat, faint and afraid of her mind's forming thought. Black type on white, white paper flashed on and off. Other. Other. Other. Her arm ached and throbbed, and the wildfire from which she could not run raged. What had the government nurse really injected into her body? Were these the side effects of some experimental drug? Had they, without her consent, administered something besides flu vaccine? Would she discover one day, like Aunt Mary and Cousin Tina had after receiving treatment from Indian Health Services, that she had been involuntarily sterilized?

Barb StandingBull reached under her coat and touched the skin where a hot welt had formed, catching her blurrier-than-usual reflection in the rear view mirror. No, she thought, squinting into the dark eyes straining back at her, not the side effects of their drugs.

She sighed and turned away from the smeared mirror. It was just the incendiary side effect of an American Indian living in America.

War Pony

"We need a new pony," Augustus IronHorse said, and slapped a section of Pioneer Press on the table.

Barb StandingBull raised a brow, sipped her coffee, and waited for him to go on, as, after years of cohabitation, she knew he would.

"Ours has a hundred thousand miles on it and the clutch's about gone," he said, as he sat down across from her, "It's time to trade."

She made a sound that could pass for either agreement or disinterest, brushed toast crumbs off the placemat into a napkin, and laid it on the plate. Each month, their 1996 Mustang demanded more nickels and dimes. Trading up was the only practical solution. But her concurrence with IronHorse's plan ended there. He rustled the paper open to a full page advertisement, his elbow knocking over a glass shaker. Oblivious of the spilled salt, he poked a finger at the page.

"Big Blow-Out Sale," he read. "This year's models must go!"

She swept the salt into her palm and tossed it over her shoulder, while he described the photo of the black GT, complete with chrome details and rear spoiler. Unimpressed, she cleared the plates, turning her back on Gus. She must gather energy for the inevitable argument, or, as they had nicknamed it after months of battle, the "cargument". He smoothed the paper and crossed his arms, his words of wonderment fogging the front window of some unseen Men-R-Us toy store.

"What a fine war pony."

Without comment, she ran a butter knife through scalding water and stabbed the blunt blade into the dish drainer. Grandma Daisy TwoBears had taught her the value of selective silence, for, like Barb, she had once fallen for a handsome long-hair who shared a similar condition to that of Gus IronHorse. Isaac TwoBears had been a Thunderbird man.

"I've always driven Mustangs," Gus continued, "mostly GT's. Wouldn't want a V6. Need the extra power."

Barb rolled her eyes, then tugged the stopper free. The water sluggishly gurgled through the old pipes. Opening a cupboard, she withdrew a prescription bottle and shook out a pill. She swallowed the diabetes medication, then pivoted to face Gus.

"Didn't you have a four cylinder once?"

She swore she heard the thump of a forehead against plate glass, as Gus, startled from his fuel-injected fantasy, jerked his stare from the newspaper photo.

"Well ... uh ... yes, I did," he said, silently cursing her consistently accurate ability to recollect his past.

At the dawn of his teaching career, while working in an American Indian Movement survival school, IronHorse had scraped together a hundred dollars and, without rear floor boards or a heater, braved his first Minnesota winter. Although thirty years had passed, Barb could still remember Isaac TwoBears comparable purchase.

***

"What the hell?" Daisy TwoBears had muttered on that long ago afternoon, almost spilling a bowl of peas off her lap as she leaned forward, squinting towards the west. Barb and her cousins quit stuffing pods into the burlap sack and gawked at her. Daisy never swore in front of her grand babies and shot "the look" at anyone who did, a look not unlike the one locked on the cloud of dust roaring ever closer.

Like a piece of prairie sky, the powder-blue Thunderbird materialized from the gray and rumbled to a halt in the yard. Isaac TwoBears jumped from behind the wheel, shaking dust from his braids. A crescent moon grin rose across his lean face as he spread his arms open.

"Which one of you little chickens wants to fly with Grandpa and his Thunderbird?"

Barb and the others raced towards him, all yelling, "Me, Okanna, me!"

He opened the driver's door and warned them not to cut their legs on the exposed spring in the back seat, and the excited children piled in. Daisy set the fresh green garden peas on a wood crate and crossed her arms, forcing Isaac to meet on her turf. He noticed her hair right away and approached cautiously. Most days, she combed the long black mane into a loose pony tail, sometimes weaving it into a braid. In the evening, when they were alone and amorous, it flowed free like a silk shawl. But that day it sat twisted and pinned at the nape of her neck in an ominous coil.

"Where did you find the money for that heap?" she hissed.

"I traded."

"Traded what? Your common sense?"

"No, some fire wood, a six pack, and ..."

He shot the bowl a quick look.

"And what?" she prodded.

"Ten pints of peas."

Her dark eyes narrowed.

"Who's pressure cooking those jars for you, TwoBears?"

She snatched up the bowl and stomped towards the house. He

followed at a safe distance.

"Please, Daisy Duck, don't be mad. The color, it reminded me of you."

At the screen door, she stole a sideways glance, wondering which color had enticed him, the blue paint or the brown rust.

"My moccasins," Isaac said, "the ones you sewed with light blue beads. The ones I wore on our wedding day."

She paused on the porch, a pause just long enough for him to catch a whiff of forgiveness in the August air, and Grandpa Isaac flashed an impish smile as he slid into the driver's seat. When Grandma Daisy returned, she still wasn't smiling, but she had changed into a clean blouse and her pony tail was fastened with her fancy silver barrette. Yanking open the creaking passenger door of what she would later nickname "the Rust Moccasin," she dropped into the faded seat next to her husband.

True to its name and minus a muffler, the Thunderbird flew the reservation's gravel roads with a bone-rattling rumble. Grandpa clicked on the radio and, surprised to find that it worked, twisted the volume knob higher. Barb and her cousins bounced and swayed to an old Gene Pitney tune.

"Only love can break your heart," Grandma sang.

They rode along, Isaac grinning, Daisy singing, the children giggling, until, out of nowhere, a lone storm cloud appeared on the horizon. As they sped towards it, Daisy stuck her palm out the window.

Isaac noticed the gauge, his brow furrowed, and he flipped the heater on, a burst of musty air exploding in Daisy's face.

"What are you doing?" she coughed.

"Car's running hot. This'll work."

Sweat beads soon lined Daisy's forehead as huge raindrops began to fall. They grabbed the window cranks simultaneously. But much to Isaac TwoBears' detriment, his rolled up on the first attempt. Daisy cranked and cranked, the rain pelting her as they drove into the center of the downpour, but not so much as a sliver of glass emerged. Finally, she turned to him, water and sweat dripping from her nose and said with deadly calm, "Where's the window, TwoBears?"

Meanwhile, the mixture of heat and rain brought a foul odor to their attention. Isaac glanced into the back, where his youngest grandson and namesake tearfully stared up at him and said, "I poop, Okanna."

With no better solution than to breathe through his mouth while he floored it home, Grandpa tried to convince Grandma to slide closer to him, but she ignored the idea, wringing out her hair and winding it back into the coil. Water puddled in her lap, ran down her legs, and rose around her feet, but she kept her look fixed on the windshield, the vein in her temple pulsing with the rhythm of the rain. Miserable over the ruination of his first pair of big boy underwear, Little Isaac howled inconsolably.

After the maiden voyage, Grandpa rummaged in the shed for his "Indian repair kit." Barb held the clear plastic in place while he applied the carpet tacks and duct tape. When the new window had been installed, Isaac TwoBears winked at his granddaughter and said, "It's got some flaws, but it's still a Thunderbird."

***

"Four cylinders or not, it *was* still a Mustang," Gus challenged. "A good pony. Never left me stranded."

"So what happened to it?"

Barb knew the story, but she wasn't about to let him off the hook.

"Horse thieves," he said, then added, "Probably a good-for-nothing Lakota swiped it."

"Oh, yeah?" she countered. "Well, only a dim-witted Cherokee would leave keys in the ignition."

Gus threw his hands up.

Okay, okay," he said, wondering how he could love such a sharp-tongued woman. "So what about this sale? We could go. Just look, grab a bag of free popcorn."

"You want to look at a brand new car. Is our money tree blooming?"

He frowned.

"Should I skip out back and pick some thousand dollar bills? Have you forgotten that I haven't worked in six months?"

Insulted, Gus pushed away from the table.

"I have a decent job. I'm not asking for a Mercedes. It's a Mustang. A stripped-down, manual transmission GT. No bells. No whistles. Just a basic Mustang."

"It's not only the sticker price," she fumed. "There's insurance, maintenance, gas!"

"We're paying for all that now. What's the difference?"

Barb shook her head in disbelief.

"I would say the difference would be about five hundred bucks a month."

Wadding the newspaper, he tossed it aside.

"I don't get it, Barb," he said, nodding towards the GT parked beyond the kitchen window. "Not once did you ever complain about the big engine or the price of insurance. When we picked it out, I don't recall you griping about miles per gallon. You loved that car. What's changed? Why are you so angry?"

She felt a crack form in the wall that dammed up the drowning darkness and the anger he had accused leaked faster and with more force. She gripped the edge of the sink, her knuckles cramped. Realizing how hard he had hit a nerve, Gus moved back, suddenly wishing he had the power to shift the conversation into reverse. But the cargument had taken a treacherous new turn towards an inevitable destination. Grasping the sink more tightly and willing the heat of her resentment to dry up the tears that threatened, she spoke.

"What's changed? I have, Gus. *I've* changed."

In her head, she could hear the doctor's voice linking diabetes and vision loss. She could hear the GT's fender crunching against the light pole. She could hear the jingle of her car keys as she hung them on the hook for the last time.

"Why am I so angry?"

Her throat tightened and she stopped. Stripped of her defenses, disarmed of her rebuttals about money and gas and engine power, Barb couldn't force the real words while damming the emotional deluge. Like a cornered wolverine, fearfully baring teeth, she struck.

"Are *you* blind?" she screamed, shoving passed Gus and slamming through the back door.

Too stubborn to use the white cane the social worker had suggested, Barb stumbled towards the indistinct outline of the old Mustang. She ran her hand over the hood, along the dented fender, to the door handle. Crawling behind the wheel, she pressed her forehead hard against it, until her thoughts traveled back to another time of loss.

The evening of Isaac TwoBears' journey to the spirit world, Barb had walked into the prairie grass behind her grandparent's house. There, she found Grandma Daisy in the Rust Moccasin, watching the sun set. Long ago, someone had removed the door and it lay on its side nearby, wild roses growing through the holes in the plastic tarp. Thin lines trailed the old woman's cheeks, like rivulets of rain across parched earth. A skinny tom cat laid on the driver's side. He purred, his green eyes contented slits, as Daisy absently scratched his head.

"Your grandfather and I made love in that back seat."

Barb blushed. Before she could recover, Daisy asked, "Have you ever made love in a Thunderbird?"

Her grandmother's blunt question rushed more blood into Barb's cheeks, as she thought of Gus, remembering their own passionate, yet awkward encounter. When they met, she had been a non-traditional thirty-something college student and he had been a divorced forty-something English professor. Although she had refused to admit her initial attraction, the afternoon IronHorse growled into the faculty lot in a fire red 5.0, beaming a rarely seen smile in her direction, first the car, then the man, had caught her fancy.

"I'm a grown woman, *not* a sixteen-year-old girl," Barb admonished, when a friend asked her what Gus drove.

However, later, during an after dinner drive, Barb's idea had brought them to the secluded lakeshore, her suggestion removed the T-tops, and her proposition had invited Gus to join her in the 5.0's back seat.

"Oh, that's right," Grandma Daisy said, the corners of her mouth curling, "your man loves ponies."

The residual sun light painted the tips of the prairie grass, as if the women floated in a golden sea.

"Your Gus is a good man, like my Isaac."

Daisy closed her eyes and saw her husband as he had been on that night, all those years ago. He had stood behind her on the porch and unfastened her hair, his long fingers gently running through it. Pressing his lips to her neck, he whispered that he would love her forever. Then he had taken her by the hand, and she followed him in the firefly light, all broken windows and rain clouds forgotten.

"My Thunderbird has powerful medicine," he said as he opened the door and she stepped inside. "Its radio only plays love songs."

And though the radio never sounded a note, as he caressed her she had heard Gene Pitney's song on the wind.

The old woman gazed up at her granddaughter as the cat leaped from the Rust Moccasin.

"A man needs a symbol," Daisy TwoBears said. "Our warriors painted them on their battle shields. They called on their power. Then those symbols were stolen. Thunderbirds and Mustangs became cars. Not even the names of our people were safe. Dodge Dakota, Jeep Cherokee. They make war with Apache and Black Hawk helicopters."

The tom crouched, stalking something in the tall grass.

"Your grandfather's Thunderbirds were modern warrior symbols. For him, it was retrieving some of our history, taking back something sacred, returning honor to it. For a time, I thought these old cars were a silly whim. But as we grew older and I grew wiser, I finally understood."

As the sun's last light disappeared, the old woman unwound her long black and silver hair. She drew a pair of sewing scissors from her pocket.

"Help me mourn, Granddaughter," she said, offering the blades.

It was the Lakota way, the way of a warrior's wife, and, with reverence, Barb StandingBull had accepted the scissors and cut through her grandmother's thick strands.

Barb leaned back in the Mustang's front seat and remembered the ceremonial manner in which Grandma TwoBears had laid the hair and a sweet grass braid upon the Thunderbird's dash. But dark thoughts began to drift over the memory, obscuring it like a storm cloud. She wondered if diabetes would take more than her sight?

Would it take her life, as it had Grandpa Isaac's? Would Gus mourn for her? Did he love her? The Mustang wasn't the only thing with worn wires and a faulty pump; most days, Barb felt like her body was breaking down, too. She wondered if Gus dreamed of new, sleeker, shinier women.

As IronHorse watched her through the kitchen window, he noticed her hair capturing the sunlight, and he thought of the day, years earlier, when she had peered over a copy of "Custer Died for Your Sins" and their eyes met. Those beautiful brown eyes flecked with green were like islands and he swam towards them, forgetting, for a moment, the struggles he faced as an American Indian teacher in the academic world. He forgot the bitterness of a failed marriage. He forgot that he was late for class. He had swum towards the security of those strong Lakota eyes. Even now, he could see the strength in them. Every day, she fought for it; fought the anger, fought the pain, fought the fear, and, most days, won the battle. But Barb StandingBull's adversary seemed relentless, and, too often, Gus felt helpless, recognizing how diabetes plagued their people as one of the twenty-first century's leading Indian killers.

As the disease waged war on Barb's retinas, Gus began to have a reoccurring dream. In the dream, he rides down their street on a fine horse, painted for battle. As he approaches, he sees Barb lying on the front lawn, one of Custer's Calvary men pointing a bayonet at her face. Gus nudges the horse, but they don't move. Again and again, he digs his heels into the animal's flanks, but the fine horse has deteriorated into a sway-backed nag, dying beneath him. Each time, Gus had awoken in a cold sweat and reached through the darkness, searching for Barb's warm skin. The fourth morning after awaking from the same dream, he went to the computer and entered Mustangs into the search engine, convinced that, somehow, he would ride in and save her.

I'm a fool, he thought, pushing the screen door open.

Barb watched a fuzzy shape stir in front of the car then heard the click of the latch as Gus opened the passenger door and got inside.

"I know why you're angry," he said. "I'm angry, too. Angry that I can't stop it, I can't steal back what's been stolen."

Her fingers tightened around the gear shift and he laid his hand on hers.

"There are some things that haven't changed."

Lifting her hand from the shifter, he clasped it between both of his own. "I love you. That'll never change. I promise."

The cargument had come to an end.

On the afternoon Cousin Isaac arrived to buy the '96 Mustang, they climbed in one last time. Gus shined the dash as Barb untied the pendant Grandma TwoBears had crafted. As she released it from the rear view mirror and touched the medallion, beaded in the traditional white, red, yellow, and black of the four directions, she remembered her grandmother's words.

"May you never lose your way."

She wrapped the leather laces through a ring on the end of her white cane.

I won't, Grandmother, Barb StandingBull thought, as she faced the west, and heard the low roll of thunder.

5

Trickster's Daughter

Desiree Stark wore a velvet dress the color of blood. The year before, her mother, Anita, had worn it, as, seated on a folding chair, her sunken stare had followed the circle moving round and round without her. The jingle dress dancers passed by, unable to hide their pitying little half-smiles. She had smiled back, her sallow face barely capable of concealing the skull beneath it, and smoothed her palm over the loose bodice where her breasts had once been. As more dancers passed, she pulled the ends of her head scarf, tightening the crimson silk around her bare scalp and causing the silver cones along the arms of the dress to rattle. Desiree stood by, stomaching what seemed like an endless stream of well-wishers, as they whispered their platitudes.

"Your mother is so brave."

"Isn't she strong?"

"What an amazing woman."

When Desiree couldn't stand it any longer, when she had bitten her lip raw to stop from spitting the accumulated bitterness like acid from an exploding car battery, she fled her mother's side. She couldn't help but loathe the way the cancer had seemed to erase Anita's past manipulations from everyone's mind. They obviously assumed that she, too, suffered from the sympathy-induced amnesia, but although Desiree's memories were sharp as razor blades, she knew better than to reveal them. It wasn't acceptable for a daughter to resent her dying mother for anything except perhaps dying. Therefore, Desiree, a seventeen-year under study to Anita's melodramatic lead, played the part of the devoted offspring. But that night, as her mother sat propped up like the Queen of the Dead, wearing the jingle dress in which Desiree had begged her permission to compete, and held court for her living subjects, the forced tears the dutiful daughter had reserved for the final act permanently evaporated.

Now, her mother's ashes lay beneath the silent frozen falls at Minnehaha and the dress, by default, belonged to Desiree. The shiny silver cones tinkled softly as she brushed a palm over the beaded velvet pressing against her breasts, and an electric feeling of having already won something crackled through her.

When the grand entry began and she entered the Mounds Park gymnasium, women who had once cursed under their breath at the sight of a contest powwow entry number attached to her mother's back, recognized the dress and cringed. Men took a second, then a third appreciative glance, as a more slender, more graceful, more beautiful rendition of the deceased jingle dance champion boldly returned their stares. Part ghost, part goddess, Desiree flowed through the crowd with her head high, glossy painted lips curled. It was *her* dress, now, *her* night, and as the beat of the drums swelled, she took her place in the dance circle, where the blood red velvet came alive with each fluid motion of her deer-like legs.

***

Once, while they were driving home from a Wisconsin powwow where her mother had won the three-hundred-dollar prize purse, Desiree had stuck her head between the van's front seats, and asked why she didn't have regalia like a lot of the other dancers' young daughters. Leonard Stark's face had lit up at the thought of his little girl joining the circle for the first time. He would hold a giveaway in honor of the occasion. As the broken lines of the highway flew passed, he calculated the abundance of fine, valuable items he intended to bestow, until the line solidified, the road began to slant upwards, and Anita spoke.

"We can't afford it," she said, as she worked a file against her acrylic-tipped nails, then added. "Your father lost his job."

The factory's lay-off had been voluntary, and Leonard would soon return to his supervisory position, but Anita's version stung nonetheless, and he shrunk back into the driver's seat. The Pendleton blankets and beaded hair clips of his imagined giveaway vanished along with yet another ounce or two of his pride. He had never felt quite worthy of his wife—a feeling that had served her well.

Desiree, despite similar scrutiny, did not suffer her father's inferiority complex, however.

"What about your prize money?" the girl asked pointedly.

The gritty scratch of the nail file stopped and the van grew uncomfortably quiet. Leonard sensed Anita winding up, and, out of paternal protectiveness, tried to distract her.

"Need to make a pit stop?" he asked, gesturing towards a pair of exit sign golden arches.

As was often the case, Anita ignored him. He shrugged and drove on, and a quiet funk descended upon them again. Leonard thought for a moment that maybe she had been deterred, that maybe it was over. But it was never over, not until Anita had verbally wounded her opposition—including her seven-year-old daughter—into a silenced, brow-beaten heap. Anita twisted suddenly, poking a finger into the girl's chest.

"Do you ever think of anyone besides yourself, Desiree? Or does the world revolve around you? I'm *not* raising you to be a spoiled brat."

The little girl had blinked, falling back against the seat, as if slapped.

***

With every step, Desiree's moccasins slapped the gymnasium's unyielding floor, as the circle made another revolution. Before tonight, only her father had ever seen these motions executed, when, as a girl, she had danced in their back yard, imitating Anita's style. The soles of her feet ached. It was an ache shared with all urban Indians who sought a Saturday afternoon sliver of traditional culture. But a Metro bus token doesn't go to any res, where toes might have a chance to feel the earth while you danced, so the center on Franklin Avenue has to be some long lost Lakota's Rosebud. Ojibwe show up at community college arenas, looking for a little Leach Lake. Powder Horn Park is no Keshena, but for a Menominee, living in the Little Earth housing projects, it might keep the ancestral homesickness at bay. For Desiree, the pain traveling up her calves, had nothing to do with a need to mentally meld the Mounds Park Middle School into Mille Lacs. Anita's craving for contest powwows had, many summers, taken the Stark family to the reservation where she and her daughter were enrolled. For Desiree, it was about the fulfillment of a wish.

***

"Listen," Anita had said, clutching Desiree's arm, "These are my wishes."

The hoarse whisper and bony, long nail tipped fingers digging into her skin like a hungry crow seizing a piece of meat jerked Desiree awake in the chair beside her mother's hospital bed. Although Anita had not been lucid in days, Desiree's first impulse was to pull away, but the terminally ill woman's uncanny strength kept the girl pinned.

"My jingle dress …"

Desiree relaxed, the urge for escape diminishing, replaced by a mounting anticipation. Anita's morphine drip registered a soft click.

"I want you …"

The young woman's mind raced ahead, and she pictured the crimson velvet, the gleaming silver, and the cut glass bead flowers. Desiree admired her reflection from every angle in imaginations mirror, relishing her inheritance as an only daughter.

Then, as if a stone had been hurled, her mother's voice caught up.

"I want you to make sure that I'm cremated in it."

The image crashed into a million slashing shards, the woman slipped out of consciousness again, and Desiree had torn free, Anita's nails leaving behind bloody scratches.

***

The dancers circumnavigated the drums again and Desiree noticed a handsome young grass dancer. His regalia, not unusual enough to prevent him from blending in, disturbed Desiree with its subtle oddness. He wore many black feathers, which swung from his roach where the other grass dancers' single feathers hung. This didn't distract, however, from how undeniably magnificent he was, and, as she drew closer, she swayed her hips more noticeably.

A sly smile of recognition played upon his lips. The girl looked stunning in the dress, as stunning as her mother had looked, and the stranger's gaze swept over the collaboration of crimson and silver, memory reminding his fingertips of the velvet's softness, the neck line's tiny hidden hook, and the way the zipper glided so easily downwards to the small of a bare back. Yes, he knew every inch, every fold, every elegant line, so well. Any lingering doubts about whether or not his memory might be lapsing into tricks vanished when Desiree returned his smile, the tip of her tongue flicking, for a second, to the corner of her glistening mouth. Their eyes locked, sealing her identity. *She* was the daughter.

He gestured to the mirror board in his hand, inviting her to view herself in its glass, but she couldn't pull her gaze from the mysterious grass dancer's sculpted body, smooth skin, and dark, hypnotic eyes. The black crow feathers fused with the thick strands of his long hair as if a shift in shape was incomplete, as if a bird spirit could not quite be contained beneath the flesh of a man. Caught between the sensual slow burn of sexual attraction and an icy tingle of fear, Desiree lowered her eyes past the mirror to his waist, where lengths of ribbon, yarn, and fringe dangled, their tips brushing his muscular thighs. Among them, hidden between the satin, cotton, and acrylic, the girl saw something startling. She blinked, sure of what she saw, but baffled as to why she was seeing it. Who was he? What was he? Alarmed, she lost track of the drum's rhythm and stumbled. As she did so, the young man closed the space between them and caught her arm, pulling her from the circle and through the crowd. Behind Desiree and the stranger, a blade of switch grass drifted free, but no one noticed it land on the gym floor. No one noticed how it faded away, like a wisp of smoke in the wind.

***

Their seduction had been mutual. Anita had batted her spidery lashes, black with mascara and liner. The beautiful grass dancer hadn't been able to hide his confident smirk as he pointed his chin towards the setting sun beyond the powwow grounds. Raising a brow, he asked the question; nodding, she answered it. When Anita again saw the sun, its light sliced between the musty drapes of a Rapid City motel room, branding hot trails across her naked body. The door stood open; the enigmatic young man was gone. On the tangled sheets, a black feather and a bone-dry blade of switch grass lay beside her, but when Anita moved her fingers to touch them, a rogue wind swirled into the room, lifting feather and grass, and spiriting them out the door. For some inexplicable reason, she sprang from the bed in a desire to catch them, but, like her young lover, the feather, the switch grass, and even the wind, had vanished.

In the weeks that followed, their anonymous encounter had swum like a surreal water color through Anita's dreams, but the rigid plastic stick, its accusing pink tip protruding above the wadded tissues, eventually solidified waking reality's consequences. Whatever realm in which she and the grass dancer had made love, from whatever shadowy corner of ancient legend he had returned, was far, far away from her parent's tiny bathroom. Anita slouched on the edge of the tub, face in hands, eyes dry, wheels turning. *How can this be? I'm too young, too pretty, too clever.*

Like the lovely maidens in the stories the old ones told about carnal cravings and trickster's talents, Anita recognized none of her own character flaws. For her, the ancient stories existed only as quaint childhood myths, without validity or contemporary value. Before Anita's Grandmother had "found" Jesus, she had spent many Minnesota winter nights remembering the tales of Nanabozho and his escapades to Anita and the other grandchildren, but after Grandma had nailed the painting of the Madonna to her bedroom wall, she clucked her tongue, saying, "Those are silly pagan myths. Full of the Devil."

Once Jesus and his mom had ousted Nanabozho, Anita soon forgot about tricksters.

So Anita sat, locked in the bathroom. Her head buzzed with plans, sketched, then erased. Finally, her brother's annoyed demand that she "give up the john" shook a solution loose from her twisted tangle of calculations. She made sure the pink stick was hidden at the bottom of the waste basket, checked her makeup in the mirror, and unlocked the door.

"You're dating Lenny?" her brother asked a few days later, dumbstruck, amused, and more than a little dubious. He had spotted his buddy's old Firebird at the Dairy Queen. His baby sister, in painted-on black jeans, a push-up bra, and a plunging neck line, had crawled out of the passenger side.

Leonard had been surprised, too, when Anita suggested they go grab a Blizzard, then catch a movie at the Cottage View Drive-in. Since junior high, he had been stealing anxious looks at the girl through the thick lenses of his glasses. She had often stood, with her hands on her hips, at the edge of the basketball court, and yelled their mother's orders at her older brother. As she grew up, the guys whistled, whispered crude suggestions, and fist-fought each other for her attention, but Leonard had always hung back. He was too shy to speak. He couldn't imagine actually talking to the nimble dancer that spun through his dreams, jarring him from sleep, a rhythmic throb pounding between his thighs. To him, Anita was as untouchable as the delicate china figurines arranged on the lace doily atop his mother's dresser.

"Not for your big clumsy hands," he had been told, again and again.

But as the new moon's blackness fell around Leonard and Anita and a fierce gun battle raged across the giant screen, his fantasy had run her fingers down his arm, along his waist, to the zipper of his jeans. He froze, afraid that if he reached for her, he would feel the brutal sting of a woman's slap. Not for your big clumsy hands, Leonard. But Anita had lifted his palm, sliding it beneath her shirt, under her bra. His breath caught. Then lower and lower, across her belly, she directed him, until everything he had always wanted, but never imagined he would have, lay open and waiting for him.

***

"What do you want?" Desiree asked, the twinkle in her eye telling the grass dancer that she was open to any answer.

Some conquests were too taboo, even for him. He moved back from the young woman, who leaned against the brick wall of the deserted hallway.

All his oddities had made him no less desirable to her; the warning sirens of her intuition only managed to fan the flame higher. Desiree stepped closer and pressed herself to him, staring at his face, challenging him to look at her. She lowered her voice to a husky whisper and her warm breath caressed his neck.

"What do you want, Grass Dancer?"

She wove her fingers around a blade of switch grass at his waist and tugged it loose.

"What are you going to do, now?" Desiree asked.

***

"What are you going to do now?" Anita had asked, hands on hips, as if she were back at the basketball court, needling her brother.

Leonard flinched. Hadn't she given him permission? Hadn't she said not to worry? Apologetically, he dared to look at her. This had not been part of the dream. But she was so beautiful, even in all her indignation and contempt. He took her in his arms, choosing not to notice the way her body grew rigid at his touch.

"We'll take care of it," Leonard said with assurance. "I have some money saved."

Anita's body softened slightly and she let him kiss her. Soon it would be over. Leonard had said the words she had expected. He would give her the money, perhaps a ride to the clinic, and then she would be free.

But Anita had not calculated Leonard's character into her equation, and when she came home the next evening and found him sitting at the table with her mother and father, she knew it was too late to refigure it. Her parents, though uncomfortable with Leonard's announcement, had nodded and smiled, relieved that he had a good die cast manufacturing job and that, under the circumstance, he wished to marry their daughter.

***

"I'm here to see someone's daughter," the grass dancer said as he held Desiree's wrist firmly and snatched the blade of switch grass.

"I'm someone's daughter," she purred, and ran her nails lightly over his palm.

"You are," he said. "Indeed you are."

***

The day Desiree Stark arrived in the world, a stranger had hosted a giveaway. He had shown up at the Franklin Avenue Indian Center, where he presented fine Pendleton blankets to the homeless alcoholics loitering outside and left finely beaded earrings, silver bracelets, and turquoise money clips for the director of the art museum. Thrilled with their presents and stunned that the handsome young man with the black feathers in his hair could afford to be so generous, everyone forgot to ask his name. Small, precisely handwritten cards, attached to each gift, stated that the items were to celebrate a birth.

Across the river, in St. Paul, Leonard's mother had come to the Ramsey County hospital bearing gifts, too.

"Thank God," she declared as she peered at the nursing infant and heaved a relieved sigh. "She looks like Anita."

Leonard smiled, accepting his mother's thinly veiled insult along with the wrapped packages. Anita offered her mother-in-law the swaddled baby girl. Desiree looked up at Leonard and then looked at the woman that held her, and contorted her round face, as if she had just tasted something sour, something bitter. Leonard felt the sting of tears. This delicate, precious gift belonged to him, this tiny life whose head rested like a sweet peach in the palm of his huge chapped hand, whose little toes only reached the crook of his arm. He had not known love could be this big.

"Open your gifts, dear," Leonard's mother urged. "The large box is for you and the small one is for Desiree."

Anita offered the woman an obligatory smile and began to tear the pink paper apart. When the boxes were open, she pulled a tissue-wrapped bundle from each and laid them on her lap.

"Careful, honey," the older woman said, as she jiggled Desiree, who had begun to fuss. "They're breakable."

Anita removed the protective layers to reveal a painted ceramic doe and a spotted fawn. Astounded, Leonard suddenly felt himself teetering between a happiness he had never known and a profound sorrow, with which he was all too familiar, not wanting to plummet into either emotion. How many times as a child had he longed to touch them, to peer inside the small round hole in the ceramic belly of the mother deer? To see what was inside? How many times had he reached for them, only to have his hands feel the hot rush of pain inflicted from a fly swatter, a leather belt, a wooden spoon? His mother couldn't hide the pride in her voice.

"They're a family heirloom. They belonged to Leonard's grandmother, then to me. Now, they're yours, my dear."

Anita offered a chilly nod and sat the ceramic deer on the bedside table. She had seen bric-a-brac like these at garage sales and at Goodwill, mass-produced inexpensive stuff from China. They weren't ugly, nor were they beautiful. They simply were a reminder of what she imagined her future with Leonard would be: dull, common, without luxury. Suddenly, Anita snatched the figurines from the table, hastily wrapped them in the wrinkled tissue, and shoved both into the larger box.

"Here," she said, pushing them towards Leonard. "Take these home—so nothing happens to them."

He hesitated, the fears of his childhood whispering the warning that he was just a bed width away from his mother's admonishing blows. With impatience, Anita moved the box closer and frowned. Finally, he took it. Since the wedding, performed in a church at the demands of his mother, and, at the demands of Anita's mother, before her daughter's belly bump began to show under the bridal gown's fitted off-white lace, Leonard had been trained to jump at the sound of another woman's loveless voice.

"Take them, Leonard," Anita ordered.

Later, in the shadowy parking ramp, as he walked towards the car, he struggled to pull the car keys from his pocket. The box tipped, the lid lifted, and one of the figurines fell. It hit the concrete with a sickening crack. Out of habit, Leonard cowered. When he had unlocked the door and climbed behind the wheel, he held his breath and tore away the tissue paper. Swallowing hard, he forced himself to look at the two broken pieces of ceramic lying on the seat beside him, his boyish question finally answered. Even though he had always known the truth, the ache swelled inside his chest anyway. The mother deer was hollow. Taking the fawn, still nestled in its protective pink tissue, Leonard cradled it in his huge hands, and wept.

***

The grass dancer continued to grasp Desiree's wrist as he raised the mirror board, and, unable to look away, she peered into the crystal-clear glass. Her alluring reflection, scarlet lips pursed, keen eyes shining, flawless complexion, peered back.

"Striking, isn't she?" he said, as he tipped the mirror from side to side in a mesmerizing manner.

Desiree's reflection shifted like a rectangular pool of rippling water, the winds of an impending storm churning it. In the distance, she could hear the tinny rhythm of jingle dresses. The sound grew louder, becoming less metallic, less sharp, until only a dry hollow bone rattle roared in her ears. Desiree screamed. In the dancer's mirror board, a familiar, emaciated face grinned. Then, still smiling at Desiree, the woman raised bird-like claws, and tightened the knot of her crimson head scarf, a crimson scarf that matched a blood-red velvet jingle dress.

6

The Red Meat Eaters' Society

The office window wouldn't open. The wood had swollen from more than a half century of winter snows and spring rains, and though Gus IronHorse pushed, extreme irritation the fuel of his force, it didn't budge. What could he expect after a decade of dedicated service to the university, an office with a functioning window? He supposed that relocating from one of the few non-air conditioned buildings left on campus was completely out of the question, too. Was eighty-five degrees a normal Minneapolis spring temperature? He wiped his brow with his shirt sleeve.

"I don't believe all those intellectuals and their hype about global climate change, do you, Mr. Vice President?" he said, mimicking a rather convincing drawl, as he gave up on the stubborn window and turned towards his teaching assistant.

Jack Bordeaux looked up from the pile of essays and raised a brow in a considerate, yet comical expression.

"Of course not, Mr. President. And about that air flow problem we're having, let me call the Pentagon. Our buddy, the defense secretary, will launch an attack."

"Attack the window?"

"No, Mr. President, let's not give in to logic."

Gus chuckled, then said, "All right, I agree. Logic is elitist. Let's invade Belgium. They have marvelous chocolate and fancy waffles."

Jack rose from the small corner table that served as his desk to give the window a shot. With a grunt, he shoved the warped frame upwards until it issued a high pitched squeal and opened just enough for a warm breeze to blow the heap of graded papers onto the floor. Gus retrieved them.

"Ah, youthful vigor wins again," Gus said, and slid the essays into a file cabinet drawer marked American Indian Literature.

"Well, that's that, kid. You're done for the day."

Jack packed his books and pens, and slung the bag over a shoulder. His day was far from finished. After a four o'clock ethics lecture and a three-hour night class, he'd catch a bus to Roseville. The ride allowed time for a power nap, then he'd work at a retail chain, unloading and stocking electronics, until dawn.

Somewhere, in between it all, he might grab a Red Bull and a bag of chips, and call it dinner.

"Care if I take the last of this?" he asked, nodding to the coffee maker.

"Help yourself," Gus said. "It's not very fresh."

"As long as it has caffeine."

Jack emptied the muddy liquid into a travel mug.

"Yeah, Barb's taken sugar, red meat, and beer away, but she still lets me have real coffee." IronHorse chuckled.

Over winter break, when Professor IronHorse had invited him to dinner, Jack had learned of the dietary restrictions Barb StandingBull attempted to implement upon her reluctant companion. Jack had eagerly accepted the opportunity to sample Barb's famous Four Directions Chili. As the trio sat around the IronHorse/StandingBull kitchen table, and Jack and Gus dug into the steaming bowls of soup and hot corn bread, Gus asked, "There's meat in this, right?"

Barb threw him a mildly perturbed look, saying, "Of course, dear. Con carne, just the way you like it."

Gus blew on a hot spoon full.

"Good. Jack and I are members of the He-Man Red Meat Eater's Society. Aren't we, kid?"

Squeezed between his boss' question and the etiquette he sensed he should show the cook, Jack concentrated on a piece of corn bread for a long moment, and then said, "This is the best chili I've ever eaten. Best corn bread, too."

A lovely smile spread over Barb StandingBull's face. She understood why Gus had such a fondness for the young man whose charm didn't sacrifice his genuine modesty. She also detected a vulnerability not unlike that which endeared IronHorse to her.

"Thank you, Jack. You're welcome in my kitchen anytime."

When the meal was over, as Jack washed the dishes, Barb divulged the chili's secret recipe.

"Do you like turkey?" she asked, as she towel-dried the stock pot and placed it on the stove.

He said that he loved it. Thanksgiving had been the only time his mother had ever cooked it, but she'd discontinued that inconsistent ritual about five years earlier. Since then, the closest thing he'd eaten came as the overly-processed center of deli sandwiches. Barb nodded, lowering her voice so that Gus, who had gone into the living room to hunt for a book he wished to loan Jack, couldn't overhear..

"I figured you did. Especially after your third bowl."

Jack didn't fit the pieces together immediately.

"We have to keep that old goat's arteries unclogged somehow," she whispered. "Augustus says turkey shouldn't be ground. Believes that it's 'a crime against nature' and that a turkey burger is an 'abomination'. So, with the right amount of cumin powder, Tabasco, and tomato sauce, I feed him what he thinks he wants: red meat."

Sauntering back into the kitchen, thumbing through the paperback, Gus, self-proclaimed leader of the He-Man Red Meat Society, sat back down at the table, oblivious to their snickering. Barb winked at the young man who, under different circumstances, could have been her son. He gave her a covert thumbs-up, which, on his departure, awarded him a grocery bag packed full of Four Directions Chili, corn bread, chocolate chip cookies, raw veggies, dill dip, and a block of jalapeno cheese. Barb StandingBull put an arm around Jack's shoulder as he left, and said, "Thank you for making Gus' job at the university a little easier. You're a great help to him."

For some reason, Jack couldn't reply. Maybe it was because usually no one expressed that type of gratitude towards him. Perhaps it was because he suddenly had this aching feeling that obligation was about to drag him away from a version of home, the version about which he had, since he was a boy, dreamed. But in Jack's boyhood world, five-star sit com family values had never been able to transcend the television's screen. In Jack's world, mothers had never been successful lawyers or doctors or cookie bakers. They never met their children's mistakes with wise words and a home-cooked meal. In Jack's world, most mothers, at one time or another, had required the services of a pro bono attorney. In Jack's world, children's mistakes ended with fists rather than feasts.

Barb StandingBull's sincere, delicately maternal tenderness, threw him into unfamiliar territory. He stood in the circle of front porch light, and as Augustus IronHorse wrapped his arms around Barb's waist and laid a cheek against her hair, Jack watched, in fear that if he were to speak, he would fall apart and beg them for asylum. But someone across the river, waited for him, someone who loved him, who, Jack knew, appreciated him, and who counted on him.

So finally finding words, Jack said, "Thank you for the food. My nephew, Seattle, he's an eating machine."

Jack's brown eyes lit up the way, Gus had noticed, they always did when he spoke of the boy. Jack went on, "I took him to one of those steak places for his birthday, an all-you-can-eat buffet. The kid threw down so many wings and meatballs, hit the dessert bar so many times, I thought we might get banned for life."

Barb patted Gus' hands and said to Jack, "Sounds like he should be offered junior membership into your Meat Eater's Society. Please, next time, bring him with you."

"I'll do that. Thanks," Jack said, as he stepped outside the porch light's glow. "Better run. I'll miss my bus. Got to get home to Seattle."

Gus and Barb simultaneously thought to offer up a lame joke about it being an awfully long ride to Washington, but neither said anything as the young man, wearing too thin a jacket for the frigid December night, hurried up the dark street, through the snow.

***

"Man, it's hot in here," Gus said, scooping up an empty file folder from his office desk and fanning his face. "You still burning the candle at both ends?"

Jack stopped, his hand on the door knob.

"Is there any other way to burn it?"

Having survived, much to his amazement, his own grueling journey through the twenty-somethings, Gus understood and nodded empathetically. While in graduate school, juggling fifteen credit hours, Gus had pumped gas, waited tables, and unloaded grain sacks off of freight cars, the task which had forever established his hatred of heavy lifting and ravenous rats.

"Have you thought any more about the offer?"

Jack reddened and directed his attention towards the floor. He knew what Professor IronHorse was talking about, but still asked, "About the barn?"

"Yes, it's yours if you want it."

The younger man shifted his weight from one foot to the other, but didn't look up as he said, "Can I get back to you on that? I mean, it's not that I don't appreciate it. It's just that ...."

Sensing discomfort and understanding the reason behind it, Gus said, "Hey, kid, no problem. There isn't any rush. It's there if you need it, but if you don't, that's cool, too."

Jack thanked him, mumbled something about being late, and, with a lingering self-conscious expression, he ducked out of the office, another hot gust of wind slamming the door behind him.

***

The winter night that she met Jack Bordeaux, Barb StandingBull had laid awake, listening to Gus snore peacefully while she fought not to do what she always did in those wee hours of the morning while insomnia and anxiety plagued her. Gus groaned, rolled over, and yanked the blankets off of her. She sighed. She wasn't winning this battle. She slid on slippers, wrapped up in a fleece robe, and quietly left the bedroom. Without flipping on the light, she entered the kitchen. Nearly blind women didn't need light to brew a cup of herbal tea. As the water heated, she sat at the table, massaging her temples, thoughts whirling through her mind like dust devils.

"What's the story there?" she had asked Gus earlier that evening, after Jack had left their house.

He told her about Jack's sister and her abandonment of Seattle, the heroin overdose, Paulette Bordeaux's version of mothering, and the college student's plans to liberate his nephew.

Sensing Barb's assumptions, Gus, a passionate backdraft flaring in his voice, had added, "That's not why I hired him. He's a brilliant, strong-willed kid who has a real shot at surviving all the shit, a real shot at doing something good for our people. He's one that's going to make it."

"Some do," she had said, taking Gus' face in her hands, gently kissing his lips. "Some do."

The kitchen light switch clicked.

"Can't sleep again?"

Barb sighed. Gus massaged her shoulders as he said, "Which of the world's problems are you wrestling with tonight? The Inuit's melting ancestral land? Drowning polar bears? How to convince Alaska's governor to ban aerial wolf hunting?"

The tea pot began to whistle and Gus lifted it from the stove, poured a cup, and dropped in a tea bag, setting the cup in front of Barb.

"It's a cold night. Thought your worries might have an arctic theme."

Barb slid her palms around the mug, appreciative of the warmth.

"No," she said. "I've lost sleep over those already. I'm sure I'll revisit them some other night, though."

"So what has my beautiful blind bedmate crashing cups and tea pots around at three o'clock in the morning?"

She reached a fuzzy foot from under the table and gave his shin a soft kick. "I wasn't *crashing* around. I'm stealthy."

She tasted the tea, then said, "I was thinking about Jack and Seattle."

He sat down beside her, rubbed the stubble on his chin, and sighed heavily. Over the years, her midnight musings had proliferated into their participation in an anti-nuke protest rally; produced eloquent letters, addressed to senators, representatives, governors, and the White House, on what she deemed the "environmental holocaust"; and ended in checks paid to the order of wildlife defense funds, Indian-operated health clinics, and local animal rescue organizations. The latest bout of insomnia had ended with a ten-year-old Labrador retriever and two cats taking up residency in their house.

"The neighbors are facing foreclosure," she had said, when Gus voiced his displeasure at arriving from work to find Finnegan, the dog, in Gus' usual spot on the sofa, a layer of saliva coating the remote. "They have nowhere else to go."

He soon discovered that he was allergic to cat dander and that Finnegan's arthritis required costly veterinarian appointments each month, but Augustus IronHorse fell in love with the new family members anyway, almost as much as he had fallen in love with their tender-hearted savior. He couldn't find fault; after all, he, too, had been one of her rescues.

"Jack and Seattle?" Gus said. "What about them?"

Finnegan hobbled into the kitchen and laid his slobbery chin on Barb's leg. The old dog had learned that, some nights, she ate graham crackers with her tea. "Sorry, handsome. I don't have any sweets tonight."

She patted his head. The dog sighed and departed the kitchen, his nails registering a slow soft click along the hardwood as he ambled down the hall to the bedroom. A moment later, Barb heard the familiar sound of Finnegan laboriously hoisting his stiff joints onto Gus' side of their bed. Gus heard it, too, and groaned.

"Did he just …?"

"Uh-huh." Barb grinned. "Guess I'll be sleeping beside two old dogs again."

"You could go out and sleep in the barn," Gus said.

Her face lit up, and she excitedly grabbed his hand, saying, "That's it! Of course! Why didn't I think of it?"

He began to argue. The barn, which really wasn't a barn at all, but rather a second garage at the rear of the double lot, wasn't a suitable place for anyone to sleep. The previous owner had built it to house his classic '57 Chevy, "The Majestic Lady." At his wife's demand, he had included an apartment above the garage to house his not-so-majestic mother in-law. Before the apartment was finished, however, divorce had separated the guy from all three of his ladies.

When Gus bought the property, he discovered a barn owl had moved into the vacant red building. Although the owl stayed only a few months, then flew off in search of a real barn, the name stuck.

"No, fool!" Barb said, laughing at the notion that he actually thought she might curl up in the unheated, uncarpeted, unfurnished apartment. "For Jack."

At first, Gus wasn't keen on the suggestion and cited several reasons why the plan wouldn't work.

"Your cousin still hasn't made good on his end of the deal."

Barb said she would call Isaac again and remind him that the price of the Mustang he had bought from Gus had included his offer to help with some of their fix-up projects.

"Construction business is slow right now. He should have some spare time," she said optimistically.

"What if Jack isn't interested in living in his boss's back yard?"

"We'd give him his privacy."

Again, Gus sighed.

"What about *my* privacy?"

She shrugged and said with an impish little grin, "I suppose you'll just have to give up your nude sun bathing."

"Seriously, Barb," he said, annoyed at her flippancy. "Do you think we're prepared to become landlords?"

She swallowed some tea and then said, "In this case, I wouldn't use the term landlord. That's too impersonal."

"What would you intend to call yourself? 'Mom'?"

The comment, in all of its truthfulness, made Barb bristle. As her biological clock wound down, she had always thought it would get easier, but a birth announcement in the mailbox or women in her yoga class cursing their stretch marks or some bad actress screaming her way through delivery on the Lifetime channel could still twist a tender regretful part of Barb's heart. The closer she crept towards menopause, the more irritated she became at herself when that longing forced feelings of feminine inadequacy. What was the definition of motherhood? Did her ability and desire to nurture make her a mother or were women, like Paulette Bordeaux, who succeeded in the obstetrical task, the only ones worthy of the title?

"Maybe," Barb softly said, as though if the notion was uttered too loudly, it might draw ridicule. "Would it be so wrong, me wanting to mother him?"

Gus ran a hand through his hair and leaned back in the chair. There was only one correct answer, despite what implications came of it, so he said, "No, not wrong. Jack and Seattle have been cheated when it comes to female nurturing, but I don't want to see you set yourself up."

"Set myself up for what?"

Disappointment," he said. "Jack may turn down our offer."

"We can make it real affordable, so that money isn't a deciding factor."

"Yes, but there's other issues ... issues of trust."

Her brow furrowed.

"Why wouldn't he trust us?"

"It's the old adage, 'If something sounds too good to be true.' When you grow up never knowing when the next shoe's going to drop, you learn to be suspicious of compassion, you question other's kindness, and sometimes you back away from a good offer, simply because receiving anything that you haven't had to struggle for is so outside your comfort zone that you'd rather wait until you think you've suffered enough to have it. Only then do you think that you might be able to trust it."

"Some might call that paranoia," Barb said.

"Call it what you like. When I was Jack's age, I called it survival."

Although over the years IronHorse had dropped most of his shields when it came to Barb, on occasion he still emotionally pulled back. She never fulfilled the prophecy that, since boyhood, he hadn't been able to shake. She stayed, coaxed him from the dark corners of his mind, and loved him harder on the other side.

"How can you love me?" Gus would say.

"How could I not?" Barb always replied.

She stood, placed the cup in the sink, and folded the robe more tightly around her chest.

"I understand, but I can afford disappointment. That's a small price to pay. Let's offer it to him and I'll accept whatever decision he makes. Can we, Gus?"

Beyond the kitchen's warm comfort, a bare branch came alive in the icy wind, tapping the side of the old house, as if impatiently marking time while awaiting an answer. It had taken more years than Gus would admit, but he was slowly reprogramming, allowing himself, on certain rare occasions, to embrace the idea of hope. Despite the powerful familiar urges from his past, he suddenly grabbed a hold of the thought that maybe, just maybe, it wouldn't take Jack Bordeaux almost fifty years to break free from his cagey tendencies.

"When I return to the university after winter break," he said, "I'll ask him. All right?"

The night grew still, the tapping ceased, and, as the furnace kicked in, Finnegan began to snore. Barb threw her arms around Gus and covered his face with kisses, which, although he tried hard to refrain, caused him to grin like a silly school boy.

***

Gus had just started sorting through the student emails cluttering his neglected in-box when Jack burst back into the office without knocking. The younger man clutched a cell phone, and, in a voice, monotone with shock, yet barbed at the edges with rage as sharp as razor wire, he spoke.

"Professor IronHorse, I need your help. Can you drive me somewhere?"

Gus, who had asked Jack a long time ago to drop the formality of addressing him as "professor" when they were outside of the classroom, was taken aback at the abrupt return and the unnerving way Jack seemed to be functioning in a sort of alarm-based automatic mode that precluded anything as casual as first names. Regardless, IronHorse nodded, logged off the computer, and grabbed his car keys as Jack threw the cell on the desk and shoved the window closed with such force the glass rattled violently in its frame. Gus picked up the cell, intending to hand it to Jack when he spotted the text message still frozen on the screen, and though he was only vaguely versed in Generation Y's abbreviated techno language, Gus understood this transmission perfectly.

"This is for emergencies only. Got it?" Jack had instructed when he purchased the cell phone for Seattle. "No texting your basketball buddies or some little girl you've got a crush on."

The boy had blushed at the mention of girls and crushes, but promised he would do as his uncle asked.

"Don't let Dave or Grandma see it, either."

Jack's brother wasn't above pawning his nephew's stuff, and, as Jack had learned at age fifteen when his bicycle went missing, neither was his mother. On nights that Jack had to work, he always made sure that Seattle kept the cell on vibe, in his pocket.

"But don't hesitate to call or text if you need me. Okay?"

Leaving the boy in Paulette and Dave's hands tied his guts into an acid-soaked knot, but the alternative didn't seem much better. No job meant no money. No money equaled no deposit. No deposit translated into no new apartment, an apartment where he and Seattle could escape their family's never-ending drunken drama. So Jack went through the motions of lugging boxes and unpacking computers, all the while dreading the sound of Seattle's ring tone.

As Gus IronHorse roared down Cedar Avenue towards Franklin, the ring tone that had stopped Jack cold like a stone planted in a flowing river of students continued to buzz in his brain. The men didn't speak until Jack pointed at a rundown apartment building. Gus pulled in front of the No Parking sign, and said, "Go get him. I'll be right here."

Jack looked at the older man as if to say, "Are you sure?" Gus nodded, and said, "Go get Seattle, kid."

For years, Jack Bordeaux had kept all the ugly family secrets—that is, until he met Gus IronHorse, because, despite Jack's typical wariness, there was something about the college professor that he trusted. So as an unusually warm April wind blew a crumpled Star Tribune page across the car's hood, Jack jumped out with the certainty that his mentor would still be there when he returned. IronHorse watched as a younger version of himself, full of a familiar rage and purpose, loyalty and love, shoved the front door open and disappeared inside.

Barb picked up on the first ring. With his concentration glued to the building, searching for movement behind the iron barred windows, Gus spoke quietly.

"I need you to do some things."

"Name them."

Shadows darted across the broken blinds of a ground floor window and he paused until the length of his silence disturbed her and Barb said his name. Apologizing, he resumed.

"Please call Isaac. Tell him the barn job needs to be started ASAP. Make up the guest beds. Try to reach your friend who works for Child Protection."

She broke in, concern registering in her tone as she asked, "What's going on, Augustus?"

On the sidewalk, an Indian kid with a Cleveland baseball hat and jeans sagging low enough to see most of his black boxers swaggered up to the car. He pushed up his designer shades and tapped on the window.

"Hey, brother, need a hook-up? I can get ya some smoke. Some rock. Maybe a little ice?"

Gus scowled at the dealer and shook his head, mouthing the words, "Get the fuck out of here"

The kid shrugged, kicked the car's fender on his way by, then shuffled on down the street.

"Gus, tell me what's happening," Barb's "don't jerk me around" tone punched through the cell's earpiece.

"Jack and Seattle," he said as he fused his gaze back between the bars of the window, his heart pounding as the same misshapen shadows appeared against the blinds. "I'm bringing them home tonight."

For a split second, he glanced the drug dealer in his rear view mirror, a boy not much older than Seattle, only a hand full of years younger than Jack, and Barb's words whispered from the corners of his memory.

"Some do make it," she had said. "Some do."

At the other end, Barb heard him draw a long breath, as if he were about to dive to the bottom of a deep pool.

"I'm bringing them home," he said again, then added, "They've got nowhere else to go."

7

Save the Man

Paulette's scissors lay on the dining room table, as if she had spent the afternoon engaged in a sewing project. In order to supplement her income, she often accepted piece work, and occasionally even finished it. But the sewing machine still sat on the floor in the corner beside a stack of unhemmed pants. The tiny beads she stitched onto belt buckles, earrings, and barrettes didn't litter the carpet under her chair. The strips of raw hide and dyed porcupine quills, used for crafting hat bands, weren't anywhere to be seen, either. Only the scissors, blades slightly apart like the sharpened beak of a famished stainless steel bird, occupied the otherwise empty dining room table, and, as if it had been hunting the apartment for the makings of a nest, the riveted hinge held a long dark strand of hair.

Jack found his mother at the kitchen sink, tossing dirty dishes around as she searched for the drain stop under the crusted knives and forks. Mumbling a stream of profanity, she didn't acknowledge her youngest son's arrival. The sound of cracking glass and chipping ceramic didn't faze her, either. The mechanical movements and unintelligible seething surged on without a skipped beat. Jack almost issued a warning that she might cut her hand, but then remembered why he had come home. In the shadows of the hallway, Seattle stood. As the boy moved into the dining nook's dim light, Jack felt a thousand hot metal wires constrict around his gut, and he swallowed hard. For a moment, Jack's eyes lingered on the red outline of a familiar handprint marring Seattle's cheek, and then his glance darted to the swollen lip, the scratched and bruised forearms, finally halting to stare at what the child held in his locked fist. Jack blinked, as if it might erase the image from his brain, but it fused with others from the past, the question Seattle had once asked, echoing on a playback loop in Jack's memory.

"Why did they cut their hair?"

Jack had turned his attention from the library study carrel that distant afternoon to his nephew, who held an open book. The page contained a grainy black and white photograph. A caption stated that the somber faces belonged to new arrivals at the Carlisle Indian School. At the dawn of the twentieth century, the government concluded that decades of costly warfare and the forced removal to reservations had not solved their "Indian problem", so with the pressure of eastern social liberals, the concept of "Kill the Indian. Save the man" was implemented. But it wasn't men they sought as subjects for their sociological experiment. Through coercion, intimidation, and force, the children were stolen, herded onto cattle cars, and shipped east to Pennsylvania. Those that escaped were hunted like animals. Those that continued to speak their native tongue were beaten. Those whose bodies survived the epidemic illnesses often committed suicide when their hearts could no longer bear the homesickness.

Jack had seen pictures like it before: the drab uniforms, the hard-sole boots, the boys' and girls' cropped hair. Everything familiar had been stripped away, right down to their names, replaced with that which white society deemed civilized and Christian. Taking the book, Jack noticed an uncanny resemblance between his nephew's expression and that of the Carlisle students. What biblical name would they have chosen for Seattle? Jonah, Ezekiel, or perhaps, Levi? The university library suddenly felt chilly, like many ghosts had entered the room, and Jack shivered as, one by one, they all passed through him.

Seattle leaned on the back of his chair, and asked again, "Why?"

The pained look that had chiseled his nephew's face in the library that afternoon, the afternoon on which they both had vowed to grow their hair long, was there now, and though Seattle refused to cry, Jack felt his own tears form.

Suddenly, Paulette whirled around. A spray of soapy water flew off the wooden spoon she held, hit the wall, and left an arch of droplets like the forensic blood spatters of a multiple stabbing.

"I told you to stay in your damn room," she bellowed.

Seattle didn't budge, his focus locked on Jack, who stepped between the boy and the woman. In a voice too composed for what was boiling within, he said, "Seattle, go pack some clothes."

Paulette dropped the spoon and glared at Jack. "What the fuck do you think you're doing?"

Jack stepped towards her, every cell in his body yearning to hurt her, but he heard the boy draw a startled breath, and resisted.

Seattle's voice shook. "Please don't hit Grandma."

Jack winced.

"We're just going to talk. No worries, okay, buddy? Go ahead and pack. Grandma and I will be fine."

Seattle hesitated, afraid of the way Jack's monotone voice and trembling hands didn't align, but, trusting in Jack's history of nonviolence, the boy finally retreated to the bedroom.

In the kitchen, Jack lowered his voice to a whisper as he backed his mother up against the counter, and said, "Don't say anything because there isn't justification for what you've done. There never has been. All of us are grown, so you turn your hatred on the next generation?"

Vehemently, Jack shook his head, and his long braid whipped around and struck Paulette. "No, you've inflicted enough damage. You're done. I'm finished with you."

"You think you can just snatch Seattle? Don't you think the state will have something to say about this? I'm his guardian. I have rights," Paulette hissed.

He laughed, like someone teetering on the edge of sanity. "Rights? You have rights? The right to beat him? The right to expose him to human garbage, like the piece of shit who raped his mother, my sister?"

Paulette closed her eyes in resistance to the onslaught, but Jack's landslide of resentment was gaining momentum, and there wasn't anything left inside him that could barricade it.

"How many times have we found you laid out naked on the bathroom floor, in your own puke? Do you know how old Dave and I were the first time we saw you black out? I was three, Mom. I was three years old. Dave and I sat on the floor beside you and cried until Lily came home from school because we thought you were dead!"

Jack flipped his forearm over and exposed the record of cigarette burns.

"Every last one of us have the scars from your dry drunk rages. But that's nothing compared to what you've done to our minds. Do you even know where all your kids are, Paulette?

She started to open her mouth, but he told her to shut up.

"I'll tell you where they're at. Lionel's in Sioux Falls. Last time I heard, he's homeless. Tim's out in California dodging child support on his kids in Wisconsin. Shawna's on her third husband. This one's an abusive cop. Ronnie's got six kids with four different men. Clayton's doing fine. That's probably because he doesn't have contact with you anymore, but in case you give a shit, he doesn't beat his wife or his son."

She shifted uncomfortably, the counter edge digging into her spine, but he continued to push.

"Renee's back in Saint Paul, but her prison record is making it tough to support her kids. Her meth habit doesn't help, either. Oh, yes, and then there's Lily."

The name stuck in Jack's throat, years of grief threatening to drown him in its undertow, but he treaded harder. *He* was Lily's only voice, now.

"Don't tell me about your rights. You've never owned up to any of your wrongs."

He moved away then, Paulette's sweet, boozy breath nauseating him, and went to pack his own belongings. She followed, winding up for her rebuttal, but Jack spun on her. Gripping her fleshy shoulders, he backed her into the living room, shoved her onto the sofa, and, without a word, turned and walked away. She began a loud litany about how hard her life had been, how ungrateful all her "little bastards" were, and how she was going to kick Jack's ass, but, despite the threat, she didn't move.

Jack emptied some books out of a cardboard box, and threw in as many clothes as would fit. Having already stuffed his backpack, Seattle dropped the overflow into a plastic Walgreen's bag. When you didn't have much and could travel light, escape was easier. Their ancestors had known it; now they did, too.

"Where are we going, Uncle?"

"Someplace better than this."

Solemnly, the boy nodded. He had never slept a night outside this room. Jack laid his hand on Seattle's head, his voice scraped hoarse by emotion.

"I'll take care of you, little man. I promise."

They took their meager possessions and vacated the oppressive room, a room that had once belonged to Lily, the room where Seattle had been conceived.

Paulette lumbered to her feet as they passed and tried to grab Jack's arm, but he shook her off, hustling Seattle out the front door. Breathing heavily, she followed them, the sunlight blinding her as she ventured outside.

"It was just a God damn trim, for Christ's sake," she hollered. "The kid freaked out over a God damn trim. What was I supposed to do?"

From the car, Gus IronHorse saw Seattle emerge through the apartment security door, Jack not far behind. A large disheveled woman with a sweaty red face and bare feet stumbled out behind them, flailing her hands and cursing.

"Paulette Bordeaux, I presume," he said under his breath, as he swung open the door and got out of the Mustang.

Jack pointed Seattle in Gus' direction and the older man popped the trunk, took the boy's bags, and loaded them inside. Though he tried, Gus couldn't stop his gaze from drifting towards the child's head or the sickening way in which the sight dragged him back.

***

"Augustus," his mother had said that distant afternoon, when he had returned home from middle school, to find her and Lieutenant Trigg waiting. "We have some good news."

Ever since she had married Randall, at the Army officer's demand addressed only as "Lieutenant Trigg" or "sir", Gus' mother had delivered a variety of "good news." First, she announced that they would be moving from North Carolina, away from Gus' beloved grandfather. They relocated to a Texas Army base, where he discovered that most of the kids at his new school had seen too many John Wayne flicks and weren't fond of "Injuns." Soon, though, his mother came with more "good news."

"We're moving to California. Isn't that wonderful?"

He allowed himself to hope for the wonderment of which she spoke, but, upon their arrival to the west coast, Gus learned about a new variety of racism.

"Lettuce pickin' wetback," the ninth grader in the locker room spit as he pummeled IronHorse. "Keep your filthy hands off our white girls."

There was no use explaining that he wasn't Latino, or a migrant worker, or that the cute redhead in the cafeteria had smiled at him first. Besides, carrying on a reasonable discussion with a boy bigot's fist in your mouth wasn't a possibility.

Not long after his introduction to Hispanic/white relations, his mother announced that she and the lieutenant were expecting.

"I hope the baby looks like Randall," Gus overheard her confess to another Army wife. "Gus is so dark. Maybe this one will have pretty skin."

As hoped, the baby girl's complexion matched her father's fair Irish features, but the wish backfired, for often, as they strolled to the market, passersby mistook Mrs. Trigg for the child's nanny. But Gus' mother, in awe of her daughter's beauty, rarely noticed, and soon, another creamy skinned infant was born to Lieutenant and Mrs. Trigg; this time, a son.

Like the warning tremors along a fault line, when the half-siblings arrived and the house grew smaller, Augustus IronHorse sensed a shift, His mother and Lieutenant Trigg began having strident discussions about what to do with "your kid", and though Gus had never instigated a fight, Trigg regularly reminded his wife of her son's "violent distendencies." As their arguments grew more boisterous, then suddenly stopped, his mother's final piece of "good news" arrived.

"Randall has generously offered to send you to an exclusive boy's academy," she said in an octave reserved for fabricated enthusiasm. "Your grades are good, but we feel that you need to learn more—"

Her eyes darted to the Lieutenant, who took the liberty of completing his wife's thought.

"Discipline," he said. "You are not stupid, Augustus, but you require a stricter set of guidelines. You lack the proper motivation and commitment that it takes for one to succeed."

As if he himself were the elevated bar to which Gus was expected to reach, Trigg pulled his shoulders back and lifted his chin a bit for effect. Mrs. Trigg looked admiringly at the father of her lovely light children, and said to Gus, "It is our hope that by sending you to Hill Crest, you will not end up like—"

On cue, the lieutenant finished. "Like your father," he said coldly.

Augustus had little recollection of Jimmy IronHorse, but his mother had filled in the blanks. According to her, he was a lazy, irresponsible, violent fool, whose volatile temper had landed him in the only suitable location for a man so disdainful: prison. But back in North Carolina, Gus had once heard Grandpa IronHorse point out that Jimmy wasn't distasteful enough to stop her from marrying him or having his child.

"Hill Crest is in Idaho," his mother chimed, as if Idaho were something akin to Disneyland.

"Are we moving?" Gus said, already guessing the answer.

She didn't bother starting the sentence this time, deferring to Trigg with a nervous flutter of her hand.

"No, the academy is residential. You will live there during the academic year and visit your mother during summer break."

Augustus locked an incredulous stare onto his mother, but, instead of meeting her son's look, she busied herself with some invisible dust on the arm of the sofa.

Lieutenant Trigg informed him that arrangements had been made with the head master, a retired Army captain, and that an academy representative would meet him at the train station next week. The boy need not pack much; the Hill Crest military-style uniforms would be provided.

"We need to get that hair cut, though," Trigg said pointing a finger and frowning as if he had discovered that the neighbor's bulldog had taken a dump on the front lawn again. "Your mother lets you run around looking like a sissy. That won't fly at Hill Crest."

Thirty-plus years had not erased Lieutenant Randall Trigg's smug smile from IronHorse's memory. He could still see the man's pale blue eyes glinting with sadistic glee as he told the barber to give Gus the "regulation cut." The electric clipper's whine still buzzed in the back of his brain, mixed with the low self-satisfied drone of the male voices. The men had joked and slapped each other on the back, and subconsciously reveled in their small victory for the "white man." Gus remembered how they all chuckled when Trigg paid the barber, and then said, so that his rapt audience wouldn't miss the line, "Come on, Chief Crew Cut. Let's go!"

When Trigg made a cigarette stop at the PX, Gus stayed in the car. The California sun beat through the rear window and felt unusually hot against his raw shaven neck, sweat stinging the numerous razor nicks. As he waited, rubbing the back of his bare scalp, Augustus had come to some crucial conclusions: he would not cut his hair again, he would not go to Hill Crest, and, perhaps most significantly, that his dislike of Trigg paled when compared to the feelings he harbored about his mother.

On the trip home that day, the lieutenant had done something odd, as if, in his misguided manner, he were attempting to forge an awkward bond with his wife's son.

"Want a Marlboro, kid?"

Wary of a trap, Gus hesitated.

"Go ahead," Trigg said and slid the pack closer. "I'm not going to tell your mother. You're fifteen, for Christ's sake. You're a man."

Gus waited another second or two, still unsure of Trigg's motives, but then slid a cigarette from the pack. Trigg pushed the dash board lighter until it popped, took it and touched the red-hot coil to the end of Gus' Marlboro. The boy drew on it, coughed a little, and tried again. Trigg laughed and said, "You'll get the hang of it."

The lieutenant flicked his filter out the window and clicked the radio on. A Doors tune came on, Jim Morrison unleashing a primal scream. Disgusted, Trigg snorted and then cranked the dial.

When he found Elvis crooning about a teddy bear, he leaned back and whistled the melody with nostalgic satisfaction.

"Who knows, Gus. Maybe I'll buy you your first beer, too, before you ship off to Hill Crest."

"All right, sir," Gus said, consciously adjusting the tone of his voice so as not to sound like an over-eager, needy child.

For a few unspoiled moments, Gus had almost convinced himself that Randall Trigg wasn't as bad as he thought, that maybe the lieutenant wanted what was best for him and that Hill Crest was a place where a boy could learn the principles of manhood, but then Trigg added, "An Indian's got to learn to drink. Right, Chief?"

Augustus IronHorse rose before the sun the next morning, and, as he silently lifted fifty dollars from Trigg's wallet, stuffed a pack of Marlboros into his knapsack, and jumped the back fence, guilt did not chase his heels. Neither did the lieutenant nor Mrs. Trigg.

***

Paulette Bordeaux staggered off the front step towards the car and Gus intercepted her as Seattle crawled into the Mustang's back seat.

"Who the hell are you?" she said with enough acidity that someone less familiar with her kind of woman might have taken a step back. Gus stayed put. "Are you a damn social worker?"

He shook his head, calmly folded his arms, and leaned against the car.

"No, Ms. Bordeaux, I'm not a social worker, but I know one over at Child Protective Services. I can call her, if you like."

She gave Jack a contemptuous look and demanded, "Who is this clown? You drag some stranger into our family business? What's wrong with you?"

"Just go inside," Jack said. "We're leaving. I'll come back for the rest of Seattle's books later."

Paulette grunted, then spit, narrowly missing her own big toe.

"The hell you will!" She shook a fist at no one in particular, shouting, "I'll throw the shit in the dumpster."

A sudden, soothing shroud of apathy fell upon Jack, he opened the car door, and shrugged.

"Suit yourself."

Fuming, Paulette took a step towards the car, but Gus cleared his throat, saying, "Go inside, Ms. Bordeaux."

She spun and thrust a crooked index finger at him, her voice shrill. "I'll get your license plate number. I'll call the cops."

"Be my guest," IronHorse said. "In fact, let me dial it." He withdrew the cell phone from a pants pocket and hovered a finger over the keys.

"While I'm at it, why don't I give HUD a call, too? You probably have Section Eight, don't you Paulette? They might be interested in how many people you have living here. Jack tells me he pays you rent. Like I said before, I'm no social worker, but I'm fairly sure the state would frown upon such arrangements."

Her face flashed crimson-crazy, devoid of any embarrassment, and she lunged at him.

"Don't threaten me, you son of a bitch!"

Gus sidestepped the attack and Paulette fell against the car, the fender slowing her fall, before she landed on a patch of brown, litter-strewn lawn. IronHorse extended a hand and offered her help, but she told him where to go and what to do to himself when he got there, so he climbed into the car and started the engine. She heaved herself up, grabbing a crushed fast food container off the ground, and ,as the Mustang pulled away, she hurled it. The trash slammed against the back window, and a ketchup coated chunk of hamburger bun tumbled out and slid down the glass like a bloody appendage.

Seattle clutched the severed ponytail, touched the nape of his neck, and tasted the coppery taste of his split lip. Would he ever see his grandmother again? The thought brought a convoluted jumble of relief and sorrow and guilt. What if he hadn't sent the text message? What if Jack hadn't shown up? Four beers after Seattle came from school, Paulette had suddenly exploded, saying that he looked like a "faggy little girl." She insisted that he needed a trim. When he protested, tried to explain, and, finally, tried to run, she laughed and said it was "just hair." Was it? Maybe if he hadn't fought back, hadn't pushed her away, she wouldn't have slapped him so many times, grabbed him by the arms, or thrown him against the wall.

Hearing Paulette's savage scream, Seattle peered through the smeared car window, and, for a moment, their eyes met.

"You ungrateful little bastard! You're all ungrateful bastards," she roared over the Mustang's engine.

The boy looked away. No, he thought. It's not just hair.

On the freeway, rush hour brought the cross-town traffic to a crawl. The leaden silence grew heavier, until Jack pointed to the compact discs stacked in the Mustang's console. "Do you mind?"

"No," IronHorse said. "Go ahead."

Jack selected one and slid it into the slot. Recognizing the song, Gus turned up the volume, and Jim Morrison delivered the lyric, "Women seem wicked, when you're unwanted."

From behind a sardonic half-smile, IronHorse said, "A brother from another mother."

8

When Women Dance

Finnegan cocked his head towards the screen door and sniffed the warm air. It was going to rain, the kind of rain that brought thunder. The old Lab didn't like thunder. He wasn't fond of vacuum cleaners, either, but Barb had explained, as she dragged the noisy machine up the stairs, that Seattle was coming. Her announcement brought Finnegan happy anticipation, which lessened the horrible anxiety. Let the vacuum roar and the thunder roll. The boy with kind, gentle belly rubbing hands, was on his way. Sensing something out of the ordinary, the cats scurried to the front door, stood on their hind legs, and peeked out the window. In the distance, the dog heard a low rumble. Thunder? No, not yet. Tilting his head, floppy ears strained, he panted with recognition. It was the rumble of a Mustang's engine. Time to sound the alert. Like the waving wand of some mad maestro, Finnegan's tail wagged furiously as he issued a series of excited whimpers, and then, accompanied by the meowing felines, gave a booming baritone bark.

Barb emerged from the kitchen and smiled at the animals' exuberance.

"Good babies," she praised. "Seattle's going to need lots of love."

She unlocked the door and let the four-legged welcoming committee out onto the porch, where Finnegan performed his endearing arthritic little back leg dance, shifting from one paw to the other.

Gus pulled the car into the driveway and shut off the engine. Turning towards Seattle, he asked," Ready for some sloppy dog kisses? Looks like the animals are happy to see you."

Seattle had met Augustus, Barb, and their furry family members a few months earlier, when he and Jack visited their South St. Paul home for a Super Bowl party. Though the boy loved football, and the tailgate style dinner rivaled his birthday buffet, it was Finnegan and, as Gus called them, the "Twin Tigers," that the boy most enjoyed. Despite Seattle's lack of experience with pets, he and the animals took to each other as if they were old friends.

Gus opened the car door and one of the cats flew off the porch, jumped into his lap, used the center console as a bridge, and leaped into Seattle's arms. Disgruntled at the obvious upstaging, Finnegan let out something akin to a howl. The swollen lip stung, but Seattle smiled for a brief moment anyway. IronHorse climbed out of the car, slid the seat forward, and Seattle gently urged the cat to exit.

"Okay, okay, Finnegan. He's coming," Gus said with good-natured firmness when he saw that the dog was assessing the porch steps and considering whether or not his stiff old legs would make it.

Barb knelt and draped an arm around Finnegan's neck. Though age had weakened his back half, his front half still possessed surprising strength, and when Seattle unfolded from the car's back seat, she strained to keep the Lab from launching off the top step. The boy's blurry figure moved up the walk towards the house, and Barb released her hold as Seattle squatted and accepted the dog's greeting. Finnegan sniffed intently, first at the boy's swollen lip, before licking Seattle's entire face. He hugged the retriever, pressed his cheek to Finnegan's neck, and, as though the dog's affection had provided reason to finally drop a heavy shield, the boy sobbed into the shiny black coat. Barb placed a hand on Seattle's back, and, as she did, something soft fell onto the splintered porch floor, and brushed against her bare foot. Her fingers reached to identify the fallen object. As her right hand traveled across the rubber band and through the long strands, her left hand rested between the boy's slender shoulder blades, and Barb recognized what was missing. She brought it to her nose and breathed in the faint smell of some sweet shampoo, shadowed by second-hand cigarette smoke. Grieved by the question of who could do this to a child, Barb pressed her lips to it and kissed the tail of hair.

"Seattle," she softly said. "I'm glad that you're here. I'll keep this safe for you."

He raised his tear stained face from the dog's scruff, and, seeing what she cradled in her hand, said in a gritty whisper, "Thank you."

***

At twilight, they gathered in the back yard. Barb carried a small garden trowel, Jack brought IronHorse's tobacco pouch, Gus carefully held the ceremonial pipe, and Seattle clutched the jagged bundle of foot-long dark brown hair. Barb knelt, Seattle kneeling beside her. Near where lavender iris had begun to bloom, she turned over the soft, black earth, and when the shallow hole was dug, she took a red flannel prayer tie from her pocket and laid it inside. She then looked at Seattle. Blankly, he stared at what he held. He stared for a long time. first at the hair, and then at the spot of disrupted ground, until, at last, unable to lay it in its resting place, he offered the hair to Barb.

"Are you sure?" she asked.

He nodded and draped it across her lap, and, as she tenderly arranged the strands in a circle around the prayer tie, Seattle closed his swollen lids. He could hear the sound of the trowel scraping earth and the sound of Barb's voice whispering a Lakota prayer. As he listened, his thoughts turned deeply inward, towards something — someone — that he rarely allowed himself to contemplate. Seattle's thoughts turned to his mother.

**

At midnight, as the storm approached, a gust of cool wind blew through the upstairs window. In his sleep, Seattle sighed peacefully as it caressed him and left tear-like raindrops on his bare shoulder. Lightning lit the night, illuminating the bent snapshot that, earlier, he had removed from his pocket and leaned against the table lamp. Suspended in time, the blue-eyed young woman cast her gaze down and away from the camera, as if she didn't feel pretty enough to be photographed. Regardless of her hesitancy, the picture had captured her eternal beauty.

The wind blew through the room, grabbed the picture, sent it swirling, and thunder shook window glass, but, undisturbed, Seattle slumbered, safe within a dream, a dream of a turtle, white owls, and women dancing.

**

In the blackness, their talons scratched against the cottonwood's bark, and though she did not expect to be able to see the source, the unsettling sound caused Barb StandingBull to look up at the branches of the massive tree. Veins of lightning lit the night and, for an instant, she caught a glimpse of many pairs of huge, unblinking amber eyes set in ghostly-white faces. She stiffened, something very cold running its finger along her spine, and terror, not only of what she saw, but that her blind eyes were seeing it, gripped her. Another brilliant flash, this time much closer, and she blinked, but the glowing round eyes above didn't close. A dream? Yes, I am dreaming them. They are here, in the dream, with me.

But the grass was wet against her feet, the smell of ozone was too heavy, and the continued clicking of talon on tree and the eerie inquisition, "Who? Who? Who?" echoed far too clearly.

As the storm gathered strength and the wind wailed through the cottonwood, ruffling the feathers of the spectral chorus, a young woman appeared from behind the tree's immense trunk. She wore the dress of the ancient ones: deerskin adorned with porcupine quill work of traditional Ojibwe design. Her unbound hair draped over her shoulders to her waist where a belt of deer's teeth rode low around her hips. She walked towards Barb, and the wind tossed the young woman's dark brown mane like a veil across her piercing blue eyes and rattled the belt's pine needle-stained teeth. Though Barb had never before seen her, she recognized the lovely young woman, so youthful she might still be considered a girl, and she whispered her name. But the young woman only smiled and opened a hand to reveal what she had carried on the passage between worlds. In her palm, a small turtle sat, his head thrust defiantly forward. Barb stared at the creature who fearlessly stared back, until a remarkable glow filled the turtle's eyes and beams of white light shone from beneath its shell. The light grew brighter, until it was almost blinding as the reptile drew its head and legs inwards, towards the source. Barb could feel her heart beating, slow but strong, and, knowingly, the young woman nodded. She then closed her fingers around the turtle and the light vanished. When she again opened her hand, the animal, too, was gone. In its place sat an intricately painted rattle, the top half crafted from turtle shell, the lower, cinched rawhide. Another flash of electricity ripped through the sky to expose the crimson outline of a heart painted in precise strokes on the shell's center. Sunray-like lines of white pigment extended from its red borders.

The young woman cupped the ceremonial object and shook it in a slow steady rhythm. As she did so, the rain fell with greater force, the wind wailed with more ferocity, and suddenly Barb became aware that her own hands were no longer empty. She offered what she held to the young woman, who accepted it. For a moment, their fingers met, Barb shuddering at the inconceivable sensation. The young woman then pivoted on her toes and began to dance, her feet keeping time with the rattle, and, as she moved around in a small circle of her own making, she looked over her shoulder and gestured for Barb to follow. Rain fell in torrents, drenching their hair and the hair which the younger woman lovingly grasped, hair identical in color and thickness to her own, and they danced. It soaked the white cotton of Barb's nightgown and splashed in muddy puddles around her bare feet, and they danced. Lightning reached from the heavens and touched the earth around them, and the women danced. They danced and danced, until the rain became a pane of blurred glass between them. Then the young woman and the owls fused with the water and the wind, and, with the force of their departure, Barb StandingBull collapsed.

Somewhere, far away, a dog was barking. Someone was shouting Barb's name. Her lids fluttered open, but all she saw was darkness. Suddenly, strong arms lifted her from the soggy earth, where she lay, curled up like a sleeping child.

"Barb! Wake up," Gus yelled, fear pinching his words into a voice much higher than his own.

He shook her and something fell from her fingers into the wet grass.

Struggling away from him, she searched for it, but he grabbed her again, pulling her to her feet. He half carried, half dragged her towards the back door, where Finnegan continued to bark and howl. Gus deposited her onto the kitchen floor, ran to the bedroom for Barb's blood glucose meter, and frantically shoved a test strip into the machine. He punctured Barb's fingertip with the lancing device. Sure that she was suffering a hypoglycemic episode, he held his breath and waited for the abnormally low result that he expected

Ever since the doctor had replaced her oral diabetes medication with insulin injections, and a pre-dawn scare had required the paramedics, who had administered intravenous glucose to a listless, semi-conscious Barb while she belligerently attempted to fight off what she had perceived, to be "flying monkeys," Gus had lived in fear of night hypoglycemia.

But the number that came up put Barb in perfect range. Though the reading squelched a common anxiety linked with diabetes, other worries surfaced. Was she sleep walking? IronHorse had never known Barb to nocturnally wander and when he asked, she shook her head.

"I'm cold," she said.

Finnegan laid at Barb's feet and cleaned the spattered mud from her ankles, while Gus found towels and a robe. He stripped off the ruined nightgown, rubbed her dry, and wrapped the robe around her shivering body. Gently, he toweled her rain-soaked hair.

"What were you doing out there?"

Barb's dazed expression wasn't based in bewilderment; she knew what had transpired. She simply couldn't find the right words. Something sacred had happened, something magic. Once, a Lakota elder had told Barb that their people had, before the arrival of Christianity and the English language, possessed secret words, known only to the wisest medicine people, words uttered only to relate the greatest aspects of their mysticism. Somehow, Barb sadly knew that this story would have best been told in that ancient lost tongue.

IronHorse dried his own hair. Sitting across from her, he took Barb's cold hands and said, "I woke up and you weren't there. Finnegan was at the back door, going crazy. I searched the house and couldn't find you, and it scared the hell out of me. What happened? I thought you were gone."

She squeezed his warm flesh and promised herself to always remember the smooth comforting way their palms fit together, as if they had once been a single being whose divided halves had fused again. Her time before Gus seemed like a hazy dream in which she was a different woman, a woman Barb now barely recognized. That woman had embraced self-loathing like a religion. Once, she had drawn those to her who would support the belief, and when they made their offerings of crumbs, she graciously collected them while reciting her creed, "I'm starving. I'm still starving. But this is more than I deserve." When that woman met Gus, she tried to convert him, but he refused to love her any less than completely, and, soon, a more beautiful Barb had been born. Love had that power to carry someone from one life to another, from one world to another, from one reality to another..

"I wasn't gone," Barb said in a hushed breath. "I don't think that anyone ever really is gone, just ... elsewhere."

"What do you mean?"

"I was two places, Gus. Out there," she turned her head towards the door, "and somewhere else, too. Something happened while I was in those places. If I try too hard to explain it, whatever is supposed to come of it, won't happen. It's wakan. It's sacred. That's all I know. Maybe, when I understand why it happened, if I ever understand, I will be able to talk about it. Until then, just trust me."

The rain stopped and the steady blup blup blup of water dripping from the eaves into the rain barrel slowed, and a lone tree frog began its chant.

As Gus stroked Barb's fingers, something Grandpa IronHorse once said, emerged. "We don't always have to go seeking a vision; sometimes it comes and it finds us."

"I do trust you," Gus said.

***

In the indigo of early dawn, when all but the morning star had faded with the departing night, Barb heard a familiar scratching, and, still drowsy, she crawled from beneath IronHorse's protective embrace. In the kitchen, she found Finnegan pawing at the back door, as was his morning ritual, and she unlocked the screen. She stepped out behind the old retriever and stood at the edge of the cement patio, breathing in the clean, green smell of the rain-washed world. Where spirit owls had perched, ruby-breasted robins now stirred. Grandma Daisy had taught her that the robins are the first winged ones to greet the day and the last to bid it farewell. Her grandmother had taught her many things: how to hand-stitch a hem, the right time to plant potatoes, which spiders could live in the corners of the closet and which ones must carefully be escorted outside, and the words to old Lakota songs. Grandma Daisy had also taught her about the naji.

"White folks call them ghosts. They like to scare each other with stories about them and how they haunt your house, rattling chains and breaking dinner plates," Daisy TwoBears had told her grandchildren. "I don't know about those kind of naji. I just know about our kind."

"What do our naji do, Kunsi?" Barb had asked.

"When they make a visit from the spirit world, it's for something important. Sometimes, there are things they need to do here before they can be peaceful in that other place. They want to help someone they love, someone who is still here in this world, and only the naji has powerful enough medicine. So they make a visit and bring the pejuta wakan, the sacred medicine."

As Barb stood, breathing deeply the sweet perfume of fresh blooming lilacs, Finnegan came to her side. He whined softly and pressed his damp muzzle against her leg until she squatted and asked, "What is it, dear one?"

The dog opened his mouth and dropped something at her feet. As it landed, it issued a soft, but strangely familiar sound. Barb reached into the wet grass and retrieved a rattle. a rattle with a painted heart and white lines, a rattle made from a turtle's shell.

"Pejuta wakan," she told the dog. "It's pejuta wakan."

9

Run, Rabbit, Run

Jack Bordeaux awoke with a sense of urgency, uncommon for a Saturday morning, and, for a moment, he couldn't remember where he was. The bed sheets were much too crisp and clean, and the mattress was far too comfortable. As he sat up and squinted through the room's muted light, everything came back to him, but recognition only triggered a greater wave of dread. The previous day, when Seattle's text message had thrust him into an instinctual series of actions, and they had ended up here, at Gus and Barb's, so many details had been left up in the air, but now Jack felt them all hailing down upon him. Where would he and Seattle go? They couldn't stay here permanently. What about school, for Seattle and for him? What about his job?

Jack pulled on jeans and a T-shirt and opened the bedroom door. Across the hall, where Seattle had retired the night before, the door stood ajar, and Jack felt relieved that the boy still slept. Since Seattle's infancy, they had always shared a room, and Jack had worried that the boy might feel uneasy, alone in the unfamiliar surroundings. He had told Seattle to wake him if he needed anything, but the night had passed without incident. Sometime during Jack's deep slumber, he had been roused for a moment by Finnegan's barking, but then remembered what Gus had said about the Labrador's fear of storms, and had fallen back to sleep. Quietly, Jack pushed the door open a little and saw the boy, head buried under the comforter, sleeping peacefully. Jack closed the door, and went into the bathroom, where Barb had piled two sets of towels on a wicker shelf. He took the pink set, and left the green for Seattle. Back at home with Paulette, they were lucky to find a clean towel of any shade; the family linen closet, when it held anything, contained a threadbare collection of mismatched stuff that included a stained Bugs Bunny beach towel and a couple of pale blue ones that had made their way home from a hospital emergency room. The fluffy facecloth, decorative liquid soap bottle, and basket of potpourri had the unsettling effect of reminding Jack of the chaos from which they had escaped and that this was only a temporary address. He splashed cold water on his face, combed his hair into a ponytail, and mentally organized a to-do list while brushing his teeth.

***

Paulette couldn't find any toothpaste, so she attempted to rinse out the bad taste with a slug from a mostly empty bottle of mouth wash. She grabbed a damp towel from the shower curtain pole and wiped her lips. As she threw it back onto the rod, a faded terry cloth face grinned a buck toothed smile at her, the bubble above its head demanding, "What's up, Doc?" It had belonged to one of the kids; which one, she couldn't remember. Was it Seattle's? No, it had been there longer than that. Maybe Renee or perhaps … had it been Lily's? As the cold water ran, Paulette stood at the sink, locked on the obsessive thought that if she could dredge the memory of to which child the towel had belonged, the answer would free her from Jack's accusations. She closed her eyes, the haggard face in the mirror a distraction from her quest to prove to herself that she did remember, that she did care, that she wasn't a bad mother, but, try as she might, the memory wouldn't surface. The damn ragged thing had belonged to them all, at one time or another. What did it matter?

Suddenly, a chilly wet sensation soaked the front of Paulette's pants. The sink was overflowing and water splashed onto the linoleum, drenching her socks. She fumbled for the faucet, shut it off, and yanked the towel down, hurling it in a wad, into the spreading pool of dirty water.

"God damn it!" she hissed.

She shoved her hand into the sink, which caused more water to rain over the edge of the vanity, and dug around the drain until she hooked her fingers on something. Ripping it free, the harsh white light revealed a tangled mass of dark brown hair.

***

Gus IronHorse wiped his hands on the dish towel that hung from a belt loop on his jeans, and turned the sausages.

"Someone's awake upstairs."

"The smell of breakfast will do that," Barb said, slid a spatula under a pancake, and gave it a flip.

The stairs creaked, and judging the sound against their respective sizes, she said, "Pour some java, please."

Jack soon appeared and Gus greeted him, offering him a seat at the table and the mug of fresh coffee.

"Did you sleep well, kid?"

"I did. Seattle, too. He's still sacked out."

Although the dark circles and the lines of tension on Jack's face didn't give him a well-rested look, Gus didn't press. Some things were too heavy for one night's sleep to lift. He unplugged the electric fry pan, placed the lid over the browned sausages, and sat down with Jack. Barb took a cookie sheet full of golden pancakes and placed it in the warm oven before joining the men. A moment of awkward silence ensued until she cleared her throat, and said, "Listen, Jack. You probably have a lot on your mind. It all happened so quickly, without the three of us having a chance to discuss anything, but the important thing is that you and Seattle got out. Don't second-guess your decision; asking for Gus' help was smart, and we're honored that you trust us."

Above them, floor boards squeaked and Finnegan lumbered to his feet, panting excitedly. Gus patted the dog's head and said, "Don't you try to climb those stairs. Your buddy will be down in a minute."

Not wanting Seattle to overhear, Jack lowered his voice. These details were adult responsibilities.

"I'm sorry. I didn't want to involve you. That doesn't mean that I'm not grateful for all of this. I just wish I could have avoided dragging anyone else into our family's mess, but I needed to get Seattle out of there."

Don't apologize," Gus said. "You didn't drag us into anything. You just asked for a hand. Sure, this was all off the cuff, and we didn't have time to make a plan, but don't forget, I had already offered to rent you the barn. That offer still stands. Granted, it needs some work, but Barb's cousin, Isaac TwoBears, is a carpenter, and he owes me a favor. Do you know your way around a tool box?"

"With instructions, I'd probably do all right."

Gus grinned. "Me, too. Isaac's a pro. He can give the orders, and we can pound the nails. What about Seattle?"

"He's really bright, loves to learn new skills. He would like hanging with the guys, building stuff, talking sports. It would be good for him."

Though Jack didn't say it, he knew it would be good for him, too.

"Until the project's finished," Barb said, "you guys can stay upstairs."

"What about rent? We can't stay here for free."

She frowned and shook her head. "For now, you are house guests. Guests don't pay rent. Don't offend us by arguing this point. When the barn's done, then we'll sit down and discuss it. For the time being, please pick up after yourselves, wash your sheets and towels—laundry room's over there—throw a couple of bucks towards groceries once a week, and we'll call it even. Is that acceptable?"

Little by little, Jack could feel the urgency that he had awoken with lessening, and he nodded, saying, "Better than acceptable."

***

Paulette clutched the fistful of hair, unable to accept what she saw. It hadn't been there when she turned on the faucet; of that, she was sure.

Where had it come from? It was too long, too straight, and too light-colored to have fallen from her permed salt and pepper head. Dave wore his in a military styled buzz cut, and his girlfriend Angie, a natural blond, had taken their daughter for a visit to her parents in Fargo last week. The hair could only belong to one of two people: Seattle or his mother.

Paulette's legs melted, she sat down hard on the stool lid, and the wad of hair fell onto the ruined beach towel.

When Jack heard Seattle shout his name, he thought that perhaps the boy wasn't sure which towels to use. Jack himself had hesitated when he saw the perfectly folded piles, thinking that they might only be decorations.

Jack excused himself and climbed the stairs. As he reached the top step, he froze, so baffled at the sight of his nephew, he almost lost his balance. From behind Seattle, ethereal morning light framed him in golden warmth, his face a blend of utter confusion, amazement, and joy. Cascading from Seattle's head, over his shoulders and down his chest, lay long, beautiful, dark brown strands of healthy hair.

He gently tugged at either side to demonstrate, that, indeed, it was attached, that it was real, saying, as he ran his fingers through it, "How?"

Stunned, Jack could only shake his head. Upon closer examination, he noticed that Seattle's lip still bore a cut and a purplish bruise marked his cheek. Except for the miraculous mane, the proof of Paulette's attack on her grandson was still evident.

"When I woke up, it was there. Like it never was cut," Seattle said, and then pointed at the bed. "The picture was there, too. It was on the pillow beside me. It was the first thing I saw."

Jack looked at the snapshot resting on the quilt. It was the only one the boy had of his mother.

"I thought about her yesterday, when we buried my hair, while Barb was praying, I thought about my …."

It was a word that had always felt like a piece of broken tooth, something that belonged to Seattle, but because of trauma or neglect or some inexplicable weakness, had cracked loose. Though he wanted to spit it out, doing so was the ultimate act of admission, the admission that reattachment was impossible. So often, the only reason he found himself saying the word at all was to explain her absence, which generated awkward moments, filled with nervous teachers, well-meaning guidance counselors, and curious classmates. No one ever met Seattle's eyes. They quickly moved on, ignoring the jagged hunk of tooth. Although he, too, rushed beyond it, he knew, without a doubt, that eventually a stranger's question would force the word loose again.

"Your mother?" Jack said quietly.

The boy nodded and said, "I dreamed about her last night. She was flying through a storm, between lightning bolts. White owls were flying with her. I saw her dance, and she had a turtle in her hand."

***

From the far off hidden murky marshes of her memory, suddenly Paulette remembered. Lily's face floated forward into conscious thought.

Paulette's youngest daughter had run home from the Indian center that far-off winter afternoon, clutching it to her chest like a baby doll.

"It's my gift. You're not getting it," Lily had yelled as she burst into the apartment, a breathless Renee, straggling in behind her agitated ten-year-old sister.

Paulette had sent the girls over to the holiday carnival, where local merchants had donated refreshments and gifts for the community's underprivileged children. No kid left the party empty-handed; each donated box of crayons, shop-worn stuffed animal, or basketball had a sticker with a number printed on it, the children drawing miniature candy bars with corresponding labels from Santa's bag. Renee and Lily had giggled behind their hands when they saw the fat Indian man in the rented red suit. They didn't know his name. On the frequent occasions that he turned up at their apartment to drink with their mother, they just called him Two Ton. When Renee and lily's turn in line came, he winked at them, and, in a fake booming bass, reserved for the mythical character, said, "Hau! Hau! Hau! I'm Santee Sioux Claus. Have you girls been minding your mama?"

Lily had nodded between nervous giggles, but Renee rolled her eyes and said, "Hell, no" which caused her younger sister to crack up. Two Ton's cheeks, already permanently alcohol-reddened, took on the deeper shade of his shoddy costume, and he muttered something about them being "little shits" as he handed them the bag and they each dug out a piece of chocolate.

"Catch you later, Double T," Renee said, as she and Lily hurried off to the table where elf-hat-clad women were matching the children's numbers with a gift.

As the line to the table moved forward, Lily spotted it, a thick cylindrical package, wrapped like a giant Tootsie Roll, curly ribbon fastening each end. She didn't have a clue what might be inside, but the shape intrigued her, and she knew right away that it was the one she wanted. She had saved the chocolate for Jack, and she glanced at the number on the wrapper. Seven. Wasn't that a lucky number? A sacred number? She couldn't remember, but, in case there wasn't any magic attached to it, she decided to conjure some of her own, and began the chant of hopeful children and desperate gamblers. Under her breath, Lily whispered, "Seven, seven, seven, seven. Come on, seven," wishing so hard, her head hurt. As each kid in front of Lily reached the table, her heart beat a little faster, until only Renee stood between her and the giant Tootsie Roll present. Her sister handed her empty chocolate smeared wrapper to one of the elves, and, after what seemed like forever, received a square box, adorned with a green bow. Lily's hands shook as she held up her candy bar. The elf woman smiled.

"Don't you like chocolate, sweetie?"

"It's for my little brother. He's home with chicken pox."

"That's nice," the elf absently said as she scanned the rows of gifts, searching for the number seven.

Lily held her breath and chewed the inside of her lip. Seven, seven, seven, she thought, her nails digging into her sweaty palms, as she bounced on her toes. Then it happened, like a slow motion dream sequence: the elf woman picked up the giant Tootsie Roll, turned it over, looked at the sticker, and laid the magical bundle in Lily's hands. Before Lily could stop herself, she let out a joyous squeal and the kids in line behind her, laughed. The elf woman grinned—the girl's enthusiasm was contagious—and said, "That's great. I'm glad you're happy with it."

"It's just what I wanted," Lily said. "It's what I wished for. Thank you."

"You don't even know what's inside, stupid," the boy behind her mocked, but Lily ignored him and ran off to unveil her good fortune.

She found a row of empty folding chairs in the back of the room and sat down and propped the giant Tootsie Roll on her lap. Though she was eager to see what wonderful surprise lay beneath the reindeer-covered paper, she paused for a moment, just to savor the scintillating sensation of providence. Renee, much too boy crazy for age twelve, had taken off for the gym, where some tough-looking teenage guys were shooting baskets. Lily didn't notice that someone had sat down next to her.

"There must be something real special under that paper," a soft, matronly voice said. "Seven is a sacred number, you know."

She peered up to find an old woman hunched over a cane, one arthritic finger pointed at the numeral.

"I thought so," Lily said in amazement. She had never seen someone so ancient. Snowy wisps of hair barely covered the woman's scalp; deep lines crossed her forehead, fringed the corners of her eyes, and framed her thin lips. Purplish veins shown through the age spotted skin of her hands, and when she smiled, Lily saw that most of her teeth were missing. But the old woman's eyes still sparkled with a keen clarity and an attractive warmth that drew the girl in with its promise of kindness. The old woman raised a sparse white brow and said, "Shall we see what's inside?"

Lily carefully slipped the ribbon from the ends of the package, slid a fingernail through the single piece of tape, and unrolled the bundle. The old woman folded the discarded paper and ribbon, stuffing them into a canvas shopping bag she had hanging around the crook of her knobby arm. When Lily revealed the bright beach towel, the old woman gave a barely audible whistle and said, "Ah! Look at that, a rabbit. Do you know about rabbits?"

Assuming that she was referring to the cartoon character, Lily said that she did. But the elderly woman continued, saying, "Rabbit's heart beats very fast because he knows someone is always about to chase him. Fox chases him, Bobcat chases him, Eagle chases him. People chase him, too. They all want Rabbit. So his heart races as fast as he does, and his head is full of fear. Some of us have a heart like the rabbit, but I think the turtle's heart is best. It beats slow and strong, for a very long time. Do *you* have a turtle's heart?"

Lily cast her gaze down at the smiling rabbit. Living in the Bordeaux house, she was much too familiar with the animal's kind of anxiety, and the old woman's question only quickened the pace. Ashamed, Lily pulled her jacket closed, suddenly afraid that the woman might notice the rapid quivering beneath it, and mumbled, "I have to go."

Hastily, the girl wadded up the beach towel, sprang off the chair, and ran.

As if a sandbag had been dropped on her chest, Paulette sighed heavily. She had never really mourned her daughter's death; instead, she had done with her grief what she did with any emotions that she thought might exhibit vulnerability. Her sorrow at the loss of a child, like all the other disappointments, fears and anxieties in her life, converted into rage. Had she been born a man, Paulette Bordeaux could have carried the fury into a boxing ring or unleashed it in the jungles of Vietnam, but fate brought only pregnancy, with no provisions that society deemed suitable for a woman to release all that anger. No title belt or Medal of Honor for an alcoholic Indian woman with nine unplanned mouths to slap. Paulette hadn't chosen motherhood; it was a consequence of spontaneous, sometimes horrible, acts committed by her and upon her, and the children served as tarnished souvenirs, constant reminders of a million bad decisions. But what would she be without them? Had she ever had aspirations of becoming something else? If she had, she couldn't recall anything now. Perhaps she had always known her destiny and had simply laid down and met it.

The invisible weight kept pressing as if something strong and persistent was trying to crack Paulette open, but she pushed back, her breath short and rapid. She laid her hands above her left breast, forming another layer between herself and that which she believed was an external force, but the feeling only grew more intense.

Hauling herself off of the commode, vertigo swept through her and she grabbed the edge of the vanity, coming face to face with the woman in the mirror.

"You need a beer," Paulette told her.

She had been telling that woman the same thing for years. She had told her that the night they buried Lily. With the apartment full of family, macaroni casseroles, and cigarette smoke, Paulette had slipped out the back, a six pack under her coat, no clear destination in mind. She wandered until she came to the entrance of what locals called Cockroach Park, where she found a dark area under some trees and dropped onto the ground beneath one. She unzipped her coat and took out the remaining cans of beer, with no recollection of having drank the other three, and sat them gently on the grass beside her. Popping the top of one, she took several long drinks until the can was almost empty.

"Hey, slow down there, Sister."

Paulette jumped, her eyes trying to make out the source of the male voice. Before she could object, a man squatted on the ground beside her and said, "You don't want to end up like those two Indian dudes who got thrown in the trunk of a Minneapolis cop car, do you? Better let me help you out with those."

He yanked a can from the plastic ring and popped it open. Paulette still couldn't quite see him, but he had the sour rancid odor of an indigent alcoholic.

"Do you think the pigs would pull that shit on some loaded college boys over in Dinky Town? Fuck, no! I thought that beating up drunk Injuns bullshit ended with AIM, but I guess some fascist trends never go out of style."

He laughed a deep emphysemas laugh, until it broke into a rattling cough. He worked something vile to the surface and spat it on the ground. Paulette caught a whiff of cigarette-tinged breath and rotten teeth. Though repulsive, he seemed harmless enough, and Paulette said, "I heard they're going to sue the city for police brutality."

"Cool! Hope those poor bastards clean up," he said, and took a couple of bent cigarettes from a pocket. "For the beer."

In the dim light of a lit match, she reached out and accepted the trade, and, as she did, she caught a glimpse of him. He wore a dark stocking hat tugged down over greasy shoulder-length hair. A jagged scar, beginning somewhere under the hat, ran just beyond the hairline and across his forehead. Even in the dim match light, the yellowish skin betrayed a failing liver. He pinched the flame out. They sat, smoking in the night noises of the city, until Paulette heard herself say, in a stone flat tone, "I buried a kid today."

The man blew a long smoky breath, and replied, "That's a rough one, Sister. They're supposed to bury us, not the other way around. What happened? Booze?"

"Smack."

"Fuck. How old?"

"Sixteen."

"Boy?"

Paulette took a swallow and another drag on the cigarette.

"No, a girl."

The man had followed Paulette several blocks before she had turned into the park. He knew most of the homeless women in the area; she wasn't one of them, but she seemed like she would share her six pack with a down and out brother. Sliding back the stocking hat and scratching the scar, he muttered, "I got a kid. About … twelve. I don't know, maybe thirteen. His mother took him to New Mexico. Won't let him near me. Says I'm too big a fuck up."

Paulette chucked the last beer at him and said, "Here's to great parents."

She struggled to her feet, leaning heavily against the rough bark of the tree. As she started to walk away, she heard him open the can and say, "At least my kid ain't dead."

On her way home that night, Paulette stopped on the Franklin Avenue bridge and watched the dark swirling river below, something calling to her, "Jump, Paulie, jump" and for a long peaceful moment, she handed herself over to the idea. No more responsibilities. No more anger. No more anything. So simple. Climb over the rail. Take the leap. Swallow the ice-cold blackness.

"What the hell are you doing out here, Paulie? Get your ass in the car!"

She turned to find her mother yelling out the window of a beat-up Buick, Paulette's brother at the wheel. She glanced back over her shoulder. The river would always be there. She climbed into the back seat of the Buick. Her mother pivoted and shoved something at Paulette.

"Take him. He's been screaming all night."

Seattle's tear-stained face peered up at her from the wad of blanket. Saliva ran from the teething baby's mouth and he stared at his grandmother with a disgruntled look, as if to say, "What are you going to do now?"

"We both could jump," she had whispered. "We both could just jump."

Seattle found her thumb, clutched it, fiercely gummed it, and grinned gratefully up at her.

***

When Seattle walked into the kitchen, ran a hand down the pony tail draped over his shoulder, and grinned, Gus IronHorse blurted the first thing that popped into his head.

"Holy shit!"

Barb began to admonish Gus' language, until Seattle moved closer, took her hand, and laid it on the reason for the spontaneous reaction. Her jaw dropped, and she repeated what Gus had just said, added an apology, and then said it again. Suddenly, Barb StandingBull wove all the threads together: the dance, the turtle rattle, the mysterious growth of Seattle's hair, and she began to laugh and cry at the same time, until she shook. Timidly, Seattle put his arms around her, seeming uncertain if the show of affection was appropriate. Barb responded with her own embrace, and, for a long wonderful moment, they found themselves flooded with feelings their lives—motherless and childless—had disallowed them. She straightened the pony tail, arranging it in the middle of his back, and said, "I have something for you."

She exited the kitchen and returned a minute later. Gus didn't recognize what Barb held, but Jack's breath caught when he saw it.

"My dream," Seattle said, as she laid the turtle shell rattle in his hand.

"Mine, too," Barb replied, though both seemed to know that it had been much more.

Noticing the painted symbol, Gus said, "Turtle's heart beats slow and strong."

***

Paulette's heart drummed so hard she thought she could hear it echoing in her ears, and she leaned against the toilet tank, unsure if the dampness soaking her back was the perspiration of the ceramic or her own. The weight of everything she had done and everything that she had yet to do, everything she knew now she must do, squeezed, until she felt as if the next breath might not come. But it wouldn't stop her; of that she was quite sure and "quite sure" was a state of mind in which Paulette had seldom found herself. She struggled to her feet, and, without changing her wet clothes, she took a slip of paper with an address scribbled on it, an address she hadn't considered visiting until this morning. Along with the slip of paper, she tossed a few items she knew she would need into a purse and slung it onto her shoulder. A weird tingle traveled down her left arm. Paulette ignored the sensation, determined to follow her decision to the end of the line. There was no turning back. Today was the day. Today, Paulette Bordeaux would make things right.

10

Chain Link

The racket began early in the afternoon, just as Desiree Stark began to doze on a lounge chair in the sunny back yard. Prior to the disturbance, she had opened the macroeconomics text to the assigned chapter in hopes of catching some rays while prepping for her most challenging college course, but the tantalizing mix of cool breeze and intense spring sunshine quickly caused her thoughts to wander and an unplanned nap soon followed. The high pitched whine of an electric saw and the loud bang, bang, bang of several hammers crashed through the peaceful moment, causing Desiree to wake with a jerk that sent the book, pages down, onto a patch of moist dirt beneath the chair. She grabbed it, but dark smudges had already formed on the paper. That hundred and fifty- dollar textbook wouldn't have much resale value.

"What the …?" she snarled as she hoisted herself off the lounge, stomped to the chain link fence at the rear of the property, and squinted down the alley towards the source of the noise.

It was coming from the interior of what her dad's friend, Gus IronHorse, called "the barn." The building's garage door stood open, a pick-up truck full of plywood, two by fours, and sheets of drywall backed in front of the entrance. From within, male voices, mingled with the rise and fall of laughter, emerged over top of the tools' tumult. Immediately, she recognized the truck's door logo: Isaac TwoBears, Building and Remodeling.

Desiree blushed, as she thought of her and Mr. TwoBears' introduction.

***

One balmy evening last summer, Gus IronHorse had invited her father over for a beer on the back patio. Leonard had asked that Desiree call him if she was leaving the house, so that he could return to watch the boys, but as Desiree dialed she noticed that, as usual, he had forgotten his cell phone on the kitchen counter. The twins, Oscar and Owen, oblivious to anything but the game controllers and high definition television, didn't budge when she ordered that they go get their dad. Dressed in club attire, Desiree hadn't expected to have to face Leonard, who would undoubtedly object to her six-inch stiletto boots, faux snake skin spandex micro-mini skirt, and black leather and lace corset. The ensemble would reveal her plans for the night, derailing the lie she had formulated earlier, when her father said he'd be up the alley for a while.

"I'm going to the movies with some girls later," she said, pouting and putting on her daddy's little girl face, the one to which Leonard could not say no. Please don't stay at Mr. IronHorse's too long."

Even as out of touch with most things as Leonard Stark was, Desiree knew he wouldn't confuse a "movies with girlfriends" outfit with a "man hunter" ensemble.

"Get your asses down the alley and get Dad," she snapped. "I have to leave."

Oscar, the fraternal twin who most resembled their deceased mother, turned, grinned at his irate sister, and shot her a middle finger. Owen, Leonard's little carbon copy, laughed and said, "Bite it, Dezy."

She issued the usual empty threats of bodily harm, but the boys had already glued their ears and eyes back on the big screen, leaving her no other choice than to deal with her father's disapproval as she always had in the past: smile, agree, and then do as she pleased. She preferred avoidance over disobedience because she, despite her lack of respect for Leonard, liked to harbor the notion that she was a decent daughter.

Slamming the back door behind her, Desiree tip-toed across the yard, the spike boot heels sinking into the soft earth, until she reached the locked gate at the rear of the property. She jammed the key into the padlock, untangled the attached chain, and stepped into the alley as a pair of headlights swung into the narrow corridor at the opposite end of the block. She froze, startled at the sudden appearance of a rarely seen vehicle in the pathway, and, as it approached, she stepped back, pressing herself against the chain links, but the truck stopped beneath a streetlamp behind Gus and Barb's house. Somewhat relieved, Desiree moved away from the fence and took a few tentative steps in that direction, as a man, whom Desiree guessed to be in his early thirties, exited the cab. He stopped and offered a wary smile as she approached and said, "Hi. Are you a friend of Gus? I'm Desiree, the girl next door."

She winked and followed it up with her patented "don't you think I'm sexy?" giggle. When the truck lights had first exposed her in the alley, Isaac TwoBears had sworn he saw a dog—no, not a dog, a coyote—crouched along the fence, lips pulled back from its sharp teeth in what looked like a grin. He had blinked, and when he glanced again, the young woman was there. Jail bait, he had thought, a thought which now solidified as he took a closer look.

"I'm Barb's cousin, Isaac," he said, then added, so that she would know he considered her too young. "Are your parents acquainted with Gus and Barb?"

Desiree smirked, taking note of his expensive snake skin boots, designer jeans, and black silk blend T-shirt. He wore an onyx and turquoise ring on his little finger, but no wedding band. *Good taste. And he has money.*

"My father's here, having a beer with Gus," she said, then ran her hands down her hips, and whispered, "Your boots match my skirt. They'd look hot together on the dance floor. I'm hitting a club later. Interested?"

"You may be right," Isaac mused, glancing at the micro mini. "But I don't wear mine that short. It attracts negative attention."

Desiree reddened, completely thrown by his response. So that's how he wanted to play it, make her work for it. She supposed that a man with his sex appeal could successfully execute a move like that. He was, undoubtedly, an alpha male. In her opinion, she, too, held a dominant position, and though she had grown accustomed to an easy hunt, she would simply have to change her strategy.

"With thighs that nice, you should reconsider," Desiree ventured, expecting, but not receiving, her desired reaction.

Suddenly, Isaac remembered Grandma TwoBears' warnings about tricksters and their mischief. "They can take many forms," she had said. "Some believe they come as spiders, others say on the wings of the crow. Many think it's coyote that delivers the lessons we humans have such trouble learning, but I think trickster uses all those shapes, and many more.

His grandmother had smirked, her eyes sparkling in a way that had made young TwoBears think that she might possess the powers of which she spoke, and then she said, "The stories say that sometimes, Old Trickster turns into a handsome, and extremely charming, young man so that he can lure foolish girls. But don't forget, Grandson, there are plenty of foolish boys, too."

He rolled his eyes at his gregarious pursuer and said, "Listen, Girl Next Door, why don't we tell Daddy that you're here because honestly, honey, you're strutting your stuff for the *wrong* audience."

With that, Isaac TwoBears had grabbed a carton of Heineken from the truck bed and left Desiree standing in the alley, scarlet-faced and speechless.

***

"That figures," Desiree said under her breath as she gave the truck a second glance and plucked a piece of grass off the econ book's cover. "Pompous ass."

She turned away from the alley, prepared to retreat into the quiet of the house, but sudden movement at the barn's entrance caught the corner of her eye. A tall, long-haired young man walked to the rear of the truck and pulled a wood plank from the bed. Stopping to prop the two by four against the tailgate, Jack Bordeaux noticed a young woman peering at him through the chain link fence and he waved. She smiled and returned the gesture, a friendly exchange between neighbors. She continued to watch him unload supplies, her nose sniffing something subconsciously desirable in the air, as, with appreciation, she assessed the way his faded jeans fit and the defined lines of his arm muscles through the University of Minnesota T-shirt. She hoped this very fine-looking male wasn't connected to Isaac TwoBears, but she feared he might be a younger brother or, at the very least, a cousin. He was every bit as striking as TwoBears, perhaps more so, and, by her best guess, considerably younger than her nemesis, too. How could she meet him without running into that loathsome Isaac?

Jack sensed that the girl was still staring at him, but didn't turn around to confirm it. This kind of attention had always made him uncomfortable, and though he often caught women watching him as he entered college classrooms or found them smiling up at him from their tables as he passed them in Starbucks, he had never grown accustomed to his good looks, nor the obvious appreciation the opposite sex had for them. At least the fence and several yards of alley prevented this one from starting an awkward conversation full of single-sided flirting. Chain link really is a wonderful invention, he thought as he hoisted the lumber onto his shoulder and walked beyond reach of Desiree Stark's intentions.

She had been about to coax him to the fence, beyond the reach of Isaac TwoBears, with a mundane inquiry about the carpentry project, when Oscar trotted out the back door, onto the patio, Desiree's ringing cell phone in his hand.

"It's Dad," he yelled.

Pivoting, she glared at the boy, "Answer it, stupid."

He frowned and didn't comply, saying, "You told me not to answer your phone anymore."

The cell quit ringing and Desiree glanced back over the fence. The cute carpenter had gone back to work. Sighing, she walked to the patio, tossed the textbook onto a table, snatched the cell, and, as she pressed the number, berated Oscar until Leonard picked up. Her voice shifted to sweetness. Her weekend plans were contingent on another of his handouts, so until fifty dollars lined her pocket, daughterly charm must prevail over sibling loathing. Oscar attempted a getaway, but Desiree grabbed his shoulder before he could escape. He squirmed and she gave the fistful of Timber Wolves jersey a vicious jerk.

"Yes, Dad. Laundry's in the dryer. Dishes are done. See you soon. Love you, too," she said, before dropping the smart phone next to the book.

Exhaling, Desiree's tone twisted and panic hinted through her anger.

"Dad's off early. He's on his way home. Go throw the stuff in the sink into the dishwasher. Tell Owen to put the towels in the dryer."

Oscar protested, but she reminded him of the fact that she had caught him and Owen trying to disengage the adult content filters on their father's lap top. As before, Oscar insisted that Owen had master-minded it. Since their accidental conception, the twins had brought a strong sense of pride and happiness to Leonard, but, like their mother Anita, Desiree had viewed their unexpected arrival into the world as a dreadful twist of cruel fate. Upon Anita's death, Desiree had picked up their mother's merciless, often malicious, maternal role.

"I don't give a shit which one of your dirty little minds cooked up the idea. The point is I busted you both."

She released her grip and the boy darted for the door, his sister's sickeningly sunny ultimatum trailing after him.

"Dad doesn't have to know," she sang in a voice as deliciously diabolical and delicate as an arsenic laced chocolate cherry. "Tell Owen not to forget the fabric softener."

When Leonard came through the door from the attached garage and sat his lunch box on the kitchen counter, Desiree announced, "There are some men over at Gus and Barb's house. They're doing something to that building on the alley."

He raised a bushy eyebrow above the frames of his thick glasses, and said, "Really? Did you see Gus out there?"

She shook her head. "No, but I saw Isaac TwoBears' truck and heard all kinds of power tools—saws, drills, hammers, all that stuff."

Leonard smiled at the idea that his daughter thought a hammer was a power tool, and gave her a peck on the forehead before he walked to the patio doors and cocked an ear to the east. The enticing sound of a hacksaw echoed down the alley. Leonard Stark couldn't resist the lure of a do-it-yourself project, potential male bonding, and, presumably, a cooler of cold beer.

"Oscar ...Owen," he boomed. "I'm heading to Gus'. Maybe hammer some nails. Want to come?"

Desiree smirked. *Bait taken.*

***

Blood seeped through the shirt that Jack held around his hand. Embarrassed, he looked up at Isaac who nudged the offending tool with a boot toe and said, "Damn linoleum cutters! I've lost more skin to these damn things."

Isaac squatted and asked if he could look at the cut. Jack pulled the ruined shirt aside. Though the blade had sliced cleanly below the thumb, leaving all flesh attached, the laceration was deep enough to cause a lot of bleeding. Having worked in construction for many years, TwoBears was no stranger to this kind of injury, and always kept a fully-stocked first aid kit in his truck.

"Apply pressure," he said, springing to his feet. "I'll be right back."

He returned a minute later, having taken the stairs of the garage apartment two at a time. Ripping open the kit, he grabbed some rubber gloves, cleansing wipes, butterfly adhesive strips, and assorted bandages. Jack smiled, amused at Isaac's serious expression and first responder-like efficiency, saying, "Am I going to live, Doc?"

Isaac chuckled. "Sure, a few of my patients make it."

Jack removed the shirt again. The bleeding had slowed. Gently, Isaac wiped the wound clean, then applied the strips to close the cut. Both men knew that stitches would have been ordered had Jack seen a doctor. Unwilling to join the rest of the uninsured at the Ramsey County Emergency Room, he felt grateful for Isaac's modest medical knowledge.

As TwoBears finished bandaging the wound, Jack tried to remember if anyone, besides Lily, had ever shown concern or care for him like this before. Only one name materialized from the recesses of Jack's memory, and the memories that came with it, caused him to wince. Isaac noticed and, laying a gloveless hand on Jack's forearm, said, "I didn't mean to hurt you. Sorry."

Jack shook his head, suddenly disquieted by the way Isaac's voice and touch took on a familiarity that fused with the reminiscence, spiraling his thoughts deeper into the past, until Jack focused on Isaac TwoBears, but saw only Madesio DeMarco.

Somewhere, quite near, a crow cawed its humorless laughter.

11

Crossroads at the Spoonbridge

At age sixteen, Jack Bordeaux met Madesio DeMarco, and the lingering doubts that Jack had been grappling with since elementary school drifted away on the soft sweet notes of Madesio's acoustic guitar. Jack had followed the music that reached through the open window of the apartment through the door, down the low-lit hall, to the chipped cement steps at the back of the apartment building. Madesio sat on an old kitchen chair, eyes closed, classically-trained fingers dancing over the six strings of a well-worn Washburn. Air-brushed images of unfurled flags adorned the instrument's top: Puerto Rican for his mother, and Kenyan, the symbol of his father's ancestral homeland.

Sensing that he might interrupt something sacred if he were to speak, but unable to resist neither the beauty of the sight nor the sound, Jack quietly took a seat on the cement at the musician's bare feet. When the song ended and Madesio opened his eyes, Jack exhaled the breath that, though unaware, he had been holding. In a tone as smooth and rich as his music, DeMarco said, a smile playing upon his lips, "Ah, an audience."

He lifted his arm from the guitar and made a grand sweeping gesture, and Jack's gaze followed, passing quickly over the dumpsters' overflow, the weed-entangled chain link fence, an abandoned motorcycle, its front wheel missing, a prostitute teetering on high wedge heels through a pool of street light on the opposite side of the adjacent avenue, and then returned to Madesio's jovial face.

"Welcome to Urban Decay Auditorium."

Jack nodded, fumbling to find something clever to say, but was too nervous to deliver anything witty, so finally he said, "You're really good. Where'd you learn to play like that?"

"My mother," he replied, as he sat back and gently laid the instrument flat on his lap. "She played for me, while I was in her belly ... at least, that is, until it got too big. Then my dad played for us both. So, you see, it's in the blood, man. I was destined to be a starving guitarist."

Once more, Jack searched for the perfect response, but only managed a smile. The handsome musician offered him a hand, saying, "I'm Madesio."

They shook, Jack strongly aware of the guitarist's callused fingertips against his skin, Madesio strongly aware of Jack's intense, espresso-colored eyes. The eyes, like the fingertips, lingered a fraction of a second beyond a typical introduction, until a woman's voice called from the third floor and Madesio called back, "*Si, Si*, Mama."

"I got to go. Mama's freaking out. She's afraid we're going to be late for Mass," he said, shaking his head as he stood and slid the guitar strap onto his bare shoulder, "She's catholic. Devout with a capital D."

Despite the distraction of recognizing the dilapidated kitchen chair as one from the Bordeaux's mismatched set, this time, Jack rebounded. "Pious with a capital P?"

Madesio flashed his unforgettable smile, rewarding Jack's only comment with a laugh, and said, "Amen, friend. Amen."

***

For Jack, the nights that followed were restless with thoughts of Madesio spinning with tornadic force, a quiver, both pleasurable and painful, like something alive in his belly, and a longing so intense it bordered upon madness. Jack could no longer avoid nor deny the direction to which his desires lead him. For several years, he had been standing at a sexual crossroads, sure that straight, the path of least social resistance, would only end in self-loathing, but despite Jack's inner voice whispering the map he must follow, he had postponed forward motion, and waited for an outward sign. Now, the sign had come. A beautiful seventeen-year-old musical prodigy pointed the way.

Three tortuous days later, Jack heard a faint knock at the apartment door, and, expecting to discover Dave, yanked the door open with an irritated jerk, saying, "Lose your key again, shithead?"

Madesio grinned at him and said, "I don't mind 'shithead', but I prefer 'dumbass.'"

Taken off guard by the young man's presence, and embarrassed at his own boyish blunder, Jack felt heat rush to his face. He apologized and explained who shithead was, which just made Madesio shrug and say, "I got a shithead brother, too. He's over in Iraq, getting his balls blown off so the rich folks can keep pumping foreign oil into their Hummers."

It was a trait that Jack would come to love and hate in DeMarco, the jarring manner in which he could take a conversation from trivially light to disturbingly heavy in the same sentence, leaving your wings clipped and plummeting towards the rocks, only to swoop in and soar back towards the heavens. The sensation could be exhilarating, but after long stretches with Madesio, Jack could sometimes feel the adverse effects of a kind of emotional altitude sickness.

"I borrowed my mom's car and I'm heading to a coffee house over by Loring Park. Want to hang out?" he said, shifting the guitar bag on his shoulder, the shine returning to his tone.

Jack tried to dial down his enthusiasm at the invitation, but DeMarco couldn't miss the broad smile on Jack's face or how quickly Bordeaux shoved a pair of boots on, snatched a jacket, and bolted out the door.

The young men drove the back streets, Madesio explaining their destination with vague references that Jack thought he was interpreting correctly, but lack of experience told him his intuitions might just lie in wishful thought. The late model Celica squealed as Madesio cranked the wheel and parallel parked beside a row of small storefronts. When Jack climbed out and dropped change in the meter, he caught site of the gay and lesbian bookstore on the narrow street that ran beside Loring Park, and something vibrated in the pit of his stomach. Madesio grabbed his guitar and swaggered up the sidewalk, just ahead of him, until they reached a cluster of bistro tables beneath a colorful awning. The calligraphy letters, painted on the front window read: Pot O' Gold. Under the letters, an image of a coffee pot with a wavy rainbow rising steam-like from its spout, depicted the shop's logo. Madesio gave Jack a crooked smile as he nodded towards the signage, saying under his breath as he opened the door and stepped inside, "That's what you get when a couple of gay Irishmen open a coffee house.

Still unsure as to whether DeMarco's comment indicated comfort with his own orientation or just a live-and-let-live attitude towards the proprietors and their target market, Jack played it safe and remained silent. Madesio wound his way through the tables, making his way towards the counter, where a middle-aged man with thinning red curls grinned with recognition and shouted, "Hey, Maddie. Long time, no see, youngster. Where you been hiding?"

"I was in last week, oldster. Thomas said you were home, nursing a cold. Feeling better?"

"With Thomas's magically medicinal chicken soup and hot toddies, that virus didn't stand a chance. Like my sainted mother always said, 'Marry a cook.'" He chuckled, turning his sparkling blue gaze on Bordeaux. "And you must be Jack. I'm Patrick Kennedy."

Madesio blushed, shooting a cautionary look at Kennedy, but the fact that he had mentioned Jack to Thomas, who shared all gossip with his partner, manifested like the proverbial middle-of-the-room elephant. Unless Bordeaux was far more obtuse than Madesio gave him credit, the older boy's crush now seemed transparent. Jack's cheeks bore the same crimson glow as he nodded and held his hand out to Patrick. Flustered, DeMarco slid the guitar bag from his shoulder, offered it to Jack, and pointed to a separate room off to the right of the counter, saying, "Could you grab a table? I'll bring the coffee."

When Bordeaux had disappeared into the private meeting room, Madesio shook his head in panic, leaning closer and lowering his voice so only Kennedy could hear over the noise of the other customers.

"Shit, Patrick! He doesn't know … and, well, as far as where he's at … my gaydar may be way off."

Patrick nodded, his amusement manifesting deep dimples, and poured Sumatran blend into two ceramic mugs adorned with the shop's rainbow logo. When DeMarco laid cash on the counter, the older man shook his head and pushed the money away, saying, "Listen, kid, we've all been there and it's scary as hell. You're asking yourself, 'Is this guy the one, or am I about to become another hate crime statistic?' But take it from one of your adopted gay daddies, Jack, at the very least, is extremely bi-curious, but my bet is that you're his first crush."

DeMarco's brow raised. "Are you sure?"

Patrick rolled his eyes, laughed, and pointed out the front window. Madesio glanced through the glass and saw a statuesque blond, decked out in full drag. The older man smirked, saying, "Jack followed you into a coffee house with Roberta perched out front in her pleather mini skirt. Yes, Maddie, I *am* sure."

The younger man sighed and said, "You're right. Bobbie would frighten off most straight boys, wouldn't she?"

"All of them except for the ones who like to pretend that all girls sport size fifteen stiletto pumps and Adam's apples."

DeMarco picked up the mugs and gave Kennedy a grateful look before joining Jack.

As the afternoon flew by, they did not address the elephant, but rather allowed it to exist as the third occupant at the cozy table for two, somehow managing to maintain a surprisingly high level of comfort, until Thomas McCormick arrived and caused his rendition of a stampede. Unlike his partner's third generation Irish status, McCormick had grown up in Dublin and still possessed a brogue that some found difficult to decipher. He burst into the room like milky-skinned mayhem, a man of slender six foot-and-a-whisker stature, graceful and energetic, his wild shoulder length hair circling his handsome face like some abstract dirty blond frame. He swooped in, planted a kiss on Madesio's cheek, and announced, to both boys' horror, "My Pattie said I should pop in and meet your new sweetheart."

DeMarco tried to kick Thomas, but missed the mark. Turning towards Madesio, McCormick continued as if Jack couldn't hear his exaggerated whisper.

"Good job, Maddie boy! He's *very* cute." Thomas gestured towards the guitar leaning against the wall. "Play a love song for him. No one with a soul can resist the power of an acoustic serenade. The guitar is an aphrodisiac, you know. The night I met Patrick, we went to my loft, and I played for him. Do you want to know what song?"

Neither boy answered, but McCormick continued, a devilish glint in his eye. "U2," he coyly confessed. "All I Want Is You."

Jack's gaze fell to his empty cup, leaving Madesio to wonder if this would send Bordeaux running for the nearest bus stop, but despite his down-cast eyes Jack remained, a slight smile playing at the corners of his mouth.

Later, they sat in the car, staring at the Minneapolis Sculpture Garden's pond, their focuses fixed on Spoonbridge and Cherry, while Madesio spoke. "So … now you know."

Jack couldn't respond, the tremor in his stomach traveling to his sweaty hands. Madesio tensed, but continued.

"Are you pissed? Freaked out? Are you straight?"

No one had ever asked Jack the last question, and his pulse quickened, not from fear, but with the adrenalin rush that preceded an inevitable free fall. He turned to face Madesio and shook his head.

Madesio's expression softened, the tension draining away. "Does anyone else know?"

Jack shook his head again. His hands still trembled.

"Are you afraid?"

"No," Jack said, so softly that Madesio almost couldn't hear the words. "It's just that … I've never had …."

DeMarco rested a hand on Jack's shoulder and finished the sentence. "A boyfriend?"

Jack nodded, the sensation of Madesio's fingers sending sparks throughout his body. DeMarco unveiled an irresistible smile and asked, "What are my chances at being your first?

Twilight fell around them. The guitarist's strong fingers pressed against the nape of Jack's neck, he leaned closer, and their lips touched. As a little boy, Bordeaux had loved to peel the paper from broken crayon pieces, arrange them in artistic patterns, leaving them on summer-baked sidewalks. As Madesio's tongue found his, *he* felt like all those melted bits of red and brown.

12

Pursuits

Desiree fluffed her hair and closed in on the barn's entrance. For the time being, the sound of power tools had ceased and she could hear Leonard chatting amiably with Gus IronHorse , and the sound of the boys playing basketball at the front of the house, but she couldn't detect anyone else inside the garage. Where had Isaac TwoBears gone? His truck still stood parked in the alley. Where was the handsome young reason for her impromptu visit?

Gus noticed her and smiled, saying, "Hey, Desiree. What did you bring us?"

She glanced around the garage, and then, with apparent disappointment, said, "Thought you guys might want this."

Setting the case of warm beer on top of the cooler, she dropped into a lawn chair, prepared to wait for the return of her prey. Leonard took note of his daughter's short cut-offs and tight knit halter top, and, as he often did, vented his frustration in the form of an audible sigh. He wanted to believe that her gesture held no ulterior motive, but the clothing indicated otherwise. As soon as the foot falls on the stairs brought Jack into view, Isaac close behind, and Desiree's face took on a disturbingly impudent air, Leonard cast aside any further assumptions that her act was altruistic.

"This is Leonard's daughter," Gus said to Jack, pointing with his chin in the young woman's direction.

Ignoring Isaac, she sprang from the lawn chair and offered Jack a manicured hand. He nodded towards his injury.

"Just cut open my thumb."

Never missing a beat, she reached out and cupped a bare shoulder, lightly running the fuchsia nails across Jack's skin as she released it.

"I hope it feels better soon," she purred. "In the meantime, if there's anything I can help you with … let me know."

The insinuations hung like heavy musk, and Jack Bordeaux felt heat racing across his face. Sensing the young man's discomfort, Isaac grabbed a cold bottle from the cooler and unfolded another lawn chair.

"Have a seat."

Isaac gave him the bottled water, and, before Desiree could make a move, sat in the only remaining vacant seat. She threw an evil glance TwoBears' way, but he just grinned and said, "Sorry, Girl Next Door. I've been working all day and need to take a load off. That's cool, right?"

"Not a problem," she said, bending into a low squat, the frayed denim riding up higher, as she turned to Jack. "Got your cell? I'll put my number in it for you."

Isaac had noticed the outline of a phone in Jack's back pocket when they descended the stairs, and he felt the indecisiveness he'd encountered time and again as he waited for Jack's response.

"Don't have it on me," Jack said with a shrug. "I'm pretty forgetful when it comes to my phone. I miss a lot of calls."

Isaac felt the situation tip slightly in his favor, but the white lie didn't deter Desiree for long. She reached down the top of the halter, fished a smart phone from between her breasts, and, with a few quick clicks of a vicious-looking acrylic nail, brought up her contacts.

"Give me your digits."

Like a carnivore-cornered rabbit, the side of Jack's mouth twitched as he tried to soften the sting of guilt his conscious was feeling at the approach of another fabrication, but escape seemed more desirable than ethics. Desiree flashed a victorious look at TwoBears as Jack recited, and she unwittingly entered, the number of Minneapolis's most popular gay nightclub. Isaac TwoBears smiled to himself and his instincts joyously hollered "fake, fake, fake."

***

Barb StandingBull trusted her instincts about people; they had on only the rarest occasion, failed. Upon meeting Desiree Stark years earlier, she had kept distance between herself and the girl. Even as a child, Desiree seemed to emanate a kind of danger. At first, Barb reasoned that her feelings derived from the negative interactions she had experienced with Anita Stark, the mistress of passive aggression and cutting commentary. But although the mother irked her, the daughter elicited a much stronger, less explicable emotion. It was a feeling akin to that of hearing a strange singular sound in the dead of night, without ever knowing its origin. Following Anita's death, Barb had offered help to Leonard and the boys, but despite an urge to sympathize with the girl's loss, she resisted, her inner voice warning that the result of reaching out might end in a nasty bite.

As Barb crossed the backyard, a picnic basket full of sandwiches and condiments over one arm and her white cane in the other hand, she heard Desiree's false laughter drifting from inside the garage, and she stopped. The fine hairs at the nape of her neck rose, and the primal wariness that the girl unleashed kicked in. Suspicion told her that Desiree's interest in the men's project lay with Jack, and a strong maternal protectiveness shoved aside the apprehension.

Sure enough, Barb could just make out the fine figure of the Stark girl, circling around the young man. She cleared her throat and said, "Could you take this, Jack?"

More eagerly than Barb would have expected, he rose from the lawn chair, relieved her of the basket, and set it on the work bench.

"Hello, Mrs. IronHorse," Desiree said, her voice clipped, but frosty sweet.

The girl knew better, but it was a jibe she had picked up from her mother, who had never missed an opportunity to remind Barb of Gus' ex-wife and how fabulous Anita thought she was.

"I simply cannot understand why Gus would separate from such a beautiful brilliant woman," Anita Stark had mused on meeting Barb for the first time. "Did you know she has a Master's degree in library science? She's in charge of overseeing the University of Wisconsin's entire system."

Barb StandingBull had wanted to respond with, "Did you know that Gus found her in bed with his cousin?" But rather than taking the poisonous bait, she had kept the information to herself, as Anita asked the question that would become her standard greeting during their subsequent meetings.

"So when is Gus going to marry *you*?"

At first, Barb had explained that they were happy with their current situation and had no nuptial plans, but Anita had only used the information in future attempts to make Barb feel inferior to the former Mrs. IronHorse. She particularly relished these opportunities when she had spectators to her mean-spirited inquiry.

"He *still* hasn't put a ring on your finger?" she would say, her voice laced with pseudo shock as she peered around at the other women present. "I wouldn't put up with that. Would you, ladies?"

Finally, one day Gus had inadvertently given Barb the counterattack she needed to silence her nemesis. Soon after, at an evening gathering of women who got together to do bead and quill work, Anita threw down the usual gauntlet, eager to vampirically feed off of Barb's discomfort, but StandingBull had only smiled, paused, and then said, "I suppose I *could* just get knocked up ...tie him down with bootie laces ..."

Some of the women giggled, others looked at the floor with flushed faces. Barb had looked right at Anita, and finished.

"... but I find that kind of entrapment contemptible, don't you?"

Barb StandingBull nodded at Desiree, thinking, Let that battle end with her mother.

"Would you like some lunch?" she asked the girl. "There's plenty of sandwiches."

Desiree grimaced, as if Barb had just offered her something from the bottom of a dumpster, and said as she lightly patted the bare flesh of her perfectly toned midriff, in hopes that Jack would catch the comment, "No, thank you. I'm watching my figure."

Unruffled by the obvious posturing, StandingBull shrugged.

"All right then."

Suddenly uncomfortable in the older woman's company, Desiree decided that, with Jack's number saved in her cell, her mission had been accomplished, and she would make her exit. She couldn't figure out why Barb StandingBull rattled her, as if the woman's almost visionless looks could see through her, spying something that even Desiree herself could not sense.

"I have to leave," she said, slinking passed Barb, but turning around as she left the garage. "I'll call you later, Jack."

Occupied with a ham sandwich and a bottle of mustard, Bordeaux barely proffered her a glance.

"Thanks for the beer, honey," Leonard called, but she didn't bother to answer.

One of the striped cats appeared from beneath a lilac bush and hissed at Desiree as she passed. The girl locked her stare on the animal, baring her teeth ever so slightly. The cat growled, recoiled, ears laid flat, and darted back beneath the safety of the flowering bushes.

With Desiree gone, the overall mood seemed to shift from cautious to carefree, and, listening to Leonard Stark laugh and joke with the other men, Barb dished coleslaw onto plates and searched for some speck of his pleasant personality that could link his daughter to him. She could find none. Desiree was an off-putting combination of Anita and some unknown variable absent from Leonard's genetic code. Oscar, Owen, and Seattle came running into the garage, the twins launching themselves at their dad's sturdy, brick house frame. With a broad smile, he wrestled a boy under each of his muscular arms, saying, "Chill! Your old man's too tired for WWF."

The grubby boys wiggled free when they spotted the sandwiches and chips.

"Are those for us?" Oscar said excitedly.

"Ask Barb," Leonard said, then teased. "I think she made them just for the workers."

Owen's face lit up, brows raising atop the frames of his thick glasses, inheritance from his near sighted father. "We've been working on our jump shots. Does that count?"

"Of course it does," Barb said, genuine affection warming her tone. "I would never deny three future NBA players lunch."

Jack watched Seattle and the twins grab food and cans of soda, strongly aware of his nephew's light-heartedness. For a moment, something caught in Jack's throat, and he swallowed a long drink of water before it had a chance to let loose an ill-timed emotional response. How long had it been since Seattle played with other children? Jack had no recollection of the boy ever bringing friends home to the Bordeaux apartment, but then, remembering his own dismal youth, he could understand Seattle's lack of companionship. No kid wanted to bring their peers into a shaky environment filled with uncertainty. What if Paulette had one of her afternoon "headaches"; the ones that caused her to scream, "Turn down the fucking TV"? What if Dave and Angie were fighting again? What kid wanted to come hang out in a cramped bedroom shared with an uncle? What twelve-year-old boy wanted to spend time with the kid who had only a stack of borrowed library books as entertainment? The realization hit Jack like a left hook to the heart: before today, he had been Seattle's only friend. The simple scene of three boys, a basketball, and bags of potato chips made him feel that regardless of all the questions concerning his and Seattle's future that hung in the balance, the choices Jack had made for them thus far were beneficial.

Isaac watched Jack's face shadow, then brighten again, and TwoBears felt greater fascination. The obvious bond that Bordeaux had with his nephew revealed a depth of character that surpassed anything Isaac had witnessed in a man. At thirty-four, Isaac needed more than just sexual chemistry, more than just physical magnetism, and though TwoBears supposed that he had at least a decade on Jack, the younger man seemed to possess what some would call an old soul. For some men, Seattle would be a relationship deal breaker, but for Isaac, who had for some time imagined the contentment of a family life, the prospect of a man with a child was appealing.

Jack looked up and caught Isaac's dreamy gaze. Both men fidgeted, Jack shifting on the lawn chair, Isaac suddenly in need of the bandana in his pocket. Wiping his forehead, Isaac cleared his throat and said, "Seattle's a cool kid. Does he like baseball, or is he just into basketball?"

"He likes baseball. Watches it, doesn't play it. We're not really from a Little League kind of family, if you know what I mean."

Isaac took a bite of three-bean salad and nodded empathetically. "We should head downtown and catch a Twins game sometime. I did work for a guy who paid me in tickets," he said. "Great seats, right behind home plate."

TwoBears, a less-than-lukewarm Twins fan, had accepted the payment without much enthusiasm, and had continued to repeatedly kick himself for having not insisted on cash, but now, as the tickets became a potential date with Jack, and time to get to know Seattle, he smiled inwardly at the wise way the universe sometimes unfolded.

Gus watched the scene between them and wrinkled his brow. The sparkle in TwoBears' eye made IronHorse wrestle with whether or not he should share his suspicions with Barb, who, engaged in a conversation with Leonard about which tomatoes should be planted in patio pots, had probably had missed the enamored undertones in her cousin's voice.

Collecting the leftovers and, under Barb's radar, scarfing the last two macaroon cookies, Gus loaded the picnic basket back up, all the while leaning toward the wise idea that he and Barb should stay out of whatever might happen. After all, Isaac and Jack were grown men. He had great fondness and admiration for them both, and could easily picture them in a relationship, platonic or otherwise. By the look on Isaac's face, Gus sensed that he desired more than Jack's friendship, and, for the sake of both men, IronHorse hoped that his wishes were in the realm of possibility.

He hefted the picnic basket off of the work bench, swearing as he realized its weight, "Damn, woman! You shouldn't have hauled this out here by yourself. It's only a quarter full and it still weighs a ton."

Barb frowned and said to Leonard, "He thinks that my visual impairment has weakened my arm muscles."

Grabbing the white cane, she bid Leonard goodbye, gave Isaac's shoulder a pat on her way past, and followed Gus to the house. In the kitchen, IronHorse put the basket on the table and turned to leave, but her whisper stopped him.

"Are Isaac and Jack hitting it off?"

He chuckled. Nothing got passed this woman.

"Isaac cornered me earlier," she said, pulling the bowl of pasta salad from the basket and sliding it into the refrigerator. "He wanted to know all about Jack."

"Not my business. Not yours, either."

"I know. I know ... but wouldn't they make a great couple."

"Not our business," he reiterated, throwing her a useless warning glance.

As he pushed open the screen door to make his escape, he could almost hear the match-making wheels grinding away in Barb's busybody brain.

At dusk, the men flipped off the power tools and called it a day. Another afternoon's effort and the apartment would be ready for its new occupants. Happy to rid himself of some of the clutter in his garage and basement, Leonard offered Jack his pick of the Stark's extra furnishings and Jack gratefully accepted.

Would you and the boys like to stay for dinner?" Gus asked. "I'm firing up the grill." With a sheepish grin, Leonard took a sudden interest in a faded red paint spill on the garage floor, mumbling, "Thanks, Gus, but I'll have to pass. I've got a date tonight."

Oscar made wet, exaggerated kissing sounds, and, to heighten Leonard's horror, announced, "Dad's going to get some."

"Where do you learn that crap?" he said, his cheeks crimson.

"Dezy," Owen said. "She says it all the time."

Gus stifled a laugh, saying, "That's great, Len. I'm happy for you."

Many years before Anita Stark's untimely death, Leonard had developed a crush on Maggie Gustafson, a divorced computer technician, who worked in the die cast plant office, but Leonard's moral code had never allowed him more than appropriate lunchroom chats with the short, rounded woman with the pretty laugh and shoulder-length blond curls. Maggie, whose only means of expressing her mutual attraction had been through her homemade gingerbread cookies, which he had discovered in his work locker at least once a month for the last five years, was thrilled when he finally approached her in his endearingly awkward manner and asked her to dinner and a movie.

The twins darted towards home ahead of their dad, out of earshot, and as Leonard turned to follow them, Gus smirked, saying, "May Oscar's prediction come true, my fine friend."

Stark made a motion with his mitt-like hands as if throwing aside the idea, but his toothy smile indicated otherwise.

***

"Could you give me a hand with the rest of the tools?" Isaac asked Jack when they had finished dinner, and Barb, Gus, and Seattle had found a movie they all could agree upon.

Finnegan lumbered to his feet and followed the two men, but reconsidered when he reached the back door and heard Seattle calling for him. The old Lab yawned, licked his chops, and tottered off towards the family room. Isaac raised an eyebrow.

"I used to be Finnegan's favorite, but I guess that's the usual story," he said, walking out into the cool night air. "Tossed aside for a younger guy."

Detecting an opportunity, Jack asked, "Women troubles?"

"No," Isaac responded without hesitation. "Men troubles."

They reached the garage and Jack began helping him load the power tools into the truck bed.

"What about you? Have anyone special in your life?" TwoBears said casually, though the moth wings in his chest wouldn't rest and the ground no longer seemed firm under his feet. "That Stark girl seems more than a little interested."

Out of the corner of his eye, Jack snatched a glance of Isaac. He liked his face, the thin lines carved from years of work in the summer sun, expressive brown eyes full of warmth and sensitivity, and the small hump on the bridge of his nose that made Jack think that he must have broken it at some point. Isaac was handsome in a rugged, yet oddly refined way. Though his hands were a little chapped, the nails were clean and manicured, and while the jeans he wore showed signs of wear and tear, the faded T-shirt bore the Tommy Hilfiger logo. Throughout the afternoon, Jack had caught the scent of a sandalwood cologne when Isaac passed; he hadn't wanted to make comparisons, but Madesio had always worn sandalwood oil. At some point, Bordeaux had stopped loving DeMarco, and the heady sent had turned acrid in his nostrils, the memories it evoked bitter to his brain.

A soft breeze lifted the sandalwood from Isaac's skin, and what had become fetid once again seemed fragrant. Jack breathed in the earthy smell, and then spoke.

"I'm single, and Desiree Stark isn't even close to my type. Of course, she'll figure that out when she tries to call me and reaches the G Street Club."

Isaac broke into a fit of raucous laughter before saying, "No shit? That's the number you slipped her? That's clever as hell!"

Jack leaned a forearm on the side of the truck bed as Isaac slammed the gate closed and looked at TwoBears' face illuminated by a street lamp.

"Would you like my real number?"

Isaac grinned, retrieved a phone from his front pocket, and entered the digits Jack recited.

"If I call this, will there be some closeted dude at the other end, telling me that Jesus will help me resist my sinful homosexual urges?

"Am I that devious?" Jack mused. "Guess you'll just have to call the number to find out."

Playing along, Isaac poised to dial as Jack pulled a silver Samsung from a back pocket, but before Isaac's fingers reached the touch screen, Jack's cell began to ring the tone reserved for unknown callers. The sound echoed menacingly up the alley and, like a sudden bone-chilling fever, shook loose Jack's optimism.

~13~

Sacrifice

Pulling the wrinkled sheet of paper from her bag, Paulette Bordeaux mumbled the address and the driver nodded. She labored up the stairs and dropped a handful of change into the machine, asked for a transfer pass, and turned into the aisle as the double doors slammed shut and the bus lurched forward. She stumbled, but caught hold of a grab bar at the last second. She spotted an empty seat at the back, next to a young man with sandy blonde dreadlocks. Engrossed in the *Twin Cities Reader* personals section, he didn't look up as she sank heavily into the space and wiped sweat from her forehead.

The pungent scent of patchouli and body odor assaulted Paulette when he turned the newspaper page, and the nagging nausea that had plagued her all morning undulated through her. In a little more than a rasp, she said, "Could you open the window?"

Without answering, he pushed the release mechanism and slid it open. Warm wind raced in and flapped the paper like the wings of a frenzied bird. Wrangling the unruly pages together, the man folded them into a smaller, more manageable square, and continued to scan the Women Seeking Men section.

Had Paulette Bordeaux not taken the slip of paper containing the address from Frenchie, life might have stayed on its crooked, yet familiar track, but months earlier, when her cousin dropped by with "dirt on an ex," Paulette had taken the bait.

"I was up on the northeast side last week," Frenchie had said as Paulette poured coffee into a mug and set it in front of one of the few members of the family who had quit drinking. "My youngest lives on Pierce Street now. Nice neighborhood. Not all white. Not all black. A few Mexicans. A few Indians. Less crime than the south side. She likes it."

Paulette gave an unenthusiastic nod before she pried the cap off her Coors. Frenchie had a subtle way of always working something into their conversations that implied she and her children held positions of socioeconomic and moral superiority. Usually, a positive comment about her children would be followed up with a question about one of Paulette's brood, a carefully chosen question that would guarantee a far less impressive response. Frenchie never inquired about Jack, as the university student was her malcontented cousin's only possible source of parental pride, and, though Frenchie's four remained incarcerated and employed, none had attempted higher education. On that afternoon, however, she moved on without bringing Paulette's kids into it.

"I was at a station, pumping gas, and who do I see coming out of the store and getting into his truck?"

Paulette's memory slowly sifted through a jumbled collection of men as she made a feeble effort to match names with faces. Except for one, she cared nothing about them; they were as irrelevant to her now as worn out shoes, lost pocket change, or empty bottles.

Frenchie leaned across the table, wrapped her hands around the cup as if suddenly chilled, and lowered her voice. "Daryl," she said. "Daryl Chien."

Instantly, everything inside Paulette began to tighten until it felt like hot tar poured into her that was quickly solidifying around her lungs, around her brain, and, most rapidly, around her heart. In over a decade, she had not heard that name spoken aloud, and like dark Ojibwe jeebik, its black magic seeped into Paulette's soul.

"Have you invited Jesus Christ into your life?" the bubbly young woman inquired as Paulette Bordeaux faltered down the bus steps and squinted at the afternoon sun.

Breathing heavily, she looked at the woman as if her words held no meaning. Still flashing her used car salesman grin, the woman shuffled through her pile of pamphlets.

"*Espanola*?" she asked, adding a second tri-folded piece of glossy paper to the one she had already waved in Paulette's face.

"I got my own religion," Paulette mumbled, snatching the brochures anyway and stuffing them into her bag. "I'm going to the temple right now.

The corners of the woman's mouth dropped ever so slightly, and, as if she were a theological authority, she said, "You must be Jewish."

Paulette's heart beat against her ribs like a caged animal driven to captivity-induced insanity, and she mopped her brow with her shirt sleeve. Again, she narrowed her eyes at the sun; a hazy halo that only she could see encircled it.

"Going to make a sacrifice," she muttered, moving away from the woman, whose unnaturally white teeth had vanished a bit more behind shiny pink lips. "Going to take his heart."

"Are you feeling all right, ma'am?" she asked, but Paulette didn't answer, and the woman did not persist. Since committing herself to the urban ministry, she had become acquainted with the physical and behavioral signs of the chronic alcoholic: permanent reddening of the cheeks, the skin's yellowish tinge that indicated a failing liver, excessive perspiration, and the incomprehensible thoughts of a toxified brain. Paulette Bordeaux exhibited them all. The sidewalk evangelist watched for a moment longer as the Indian woman trudged a zigzag path to the corner, turned, and disappeared behind a hedge of over-grown spirea, before another bus load of sinners in need of salvation arrived. Again, she slipped the happy mask on and positioned her pamphlets for proselytizing.

Stopping in the shade of the spirea, Paulette peered again at the address scrawled in her cousin's almost illegible hand, and the blue ink numbers swirled and blurred as if she were reading them from the other side of a fish bowl. She rubbed her lids and held the paper closer, until she was just able to decipher the digits; committing them to what memory she had left, dropped it among the fallen white spirea flowers. So close now to the place, to the person, to the point, where all her love and all her hate intersected.

Shuffling laboriously onward, she didn't notice the loud scuffing sounds her feet made as they dragged along the concrete; her mind was focused on the number of the house and its one unique detail.

"I followed him to a gray two-story with an old claw foot bathtub on the front lawn. It had flowers planted in it," Frenchie had said, and Paulette had not been able to wrap her head around the thought of Chien, or anyone associated with him, caring for a bed of plants.

She turned at the next corner and scanned the rows of houses on the opposite side of the street, her already struggling heart beating harder as she spotted the gray wood siding and the antique tub halfway up the block. She shoved a shaking hand into her bag and inconspicuously arranged a worn wooden handle into a more accessible position. As she moved closer, the three digits that had been printed on the paper came into view as silver metal nailed to a post on a leaning front porch. The street was quiet, the house's gravel driveway empty. Paulette hesitated beside the tub. She could vaguely remember one of the many houses and apartments that her family had rented when Paulette was a girl having one like it, a deep cast iron monster that had had only one working cold water faucet. On the rare occasion that the gas bill had been paid, they had boiled water on the stove, added it to the bath, and Paulette, along with her two sisters, would quickly jump in and wash before the warmth disappeared. She considered the dead geraniums. Although the weather was mild enough, no one had replaced them. Paulette's brow creased. Her sister Marcella had died in a car crash outside of Fargo. She no longer spoke with Claire, who, decades earlier, had found her husband and Paulette sprawled on Claire's kitchen floor, drunk, naked, and guilty as hell. Claire hadn't even called when Lily died. If the Bordeaux's were able to hold on to anything, it was a grudge.

From behind the overgrown hedges, the porch's floor boards groaned, and a little girl with fluffy pony tails on either side of her round, milk-chocolate-brown face appeared at the top of the steps. She was perhaps nine or ten; her tummy, still plump with baby fat, peeked under a black cropped shirt announcing, in fake pink rhinestones, that she was a Diva in Training. Popping a bite of Oreo into her mouth, the child wiped her fingers on the leg of her capri pants before assessing Paulette suspiciously, and then asking, "Are you here to see Daryl?"

Paulette paused, unsure of how to answer. The girl's unexpected presence had obscured the single focus of the mission, and Paulette became acutely aware of the liquid beads crawling between her shoulder blades and down the middle of her back. She assessed, adjusted, and then asked, "Is your mother home?"

The girl shook her head.

"Not yet. She will be soon."

Paulette felt time and opportunity quickly slipping through her fingers, and she took a step towards the porch as her hand groped for the top of the purse. She didn't know whether or not this child would be considered a credible witness, but at least the girl's mother was gone. The milky mixture of Paulette's thoughts told her that if she was going to finish what she started, she had to act now. She tried to offer the girl a friendly smile, but only managed something that more closely resembled a wince as she asked, "Can I talk to your dad?"

The girl's expression turned belligerent and hateful.

"Do you mean Daryl? Because if you do, he's not my dad!"

"Damn right I ain't."

The child whirled as the storm door creaked open, and Daryl Chien emerged. Though his hair had turned a sooty gray and his belly road low over his belt buckle, Paulette would have recognized him anywhere. His static glass eye seemed to fix its gaze on her face like the laser scope of a high powered hunting rifle; his living eye was as cold as death.

"What the fuck do *you* want?" he said, and squeezed the little girl's shoulder, his fingertips crawling towards her budding breast.

The girl stiffened, her eyes flashing fear and revulsion, and Paulette's fingers locked around the wooden handle. For a moment, the little girl's image seemed to shift in Paulette's vision, and when she pressed her eyes shut for a split second, and then opened them again, Paulette Bordeaux not only saw the plump little girl beneath Daryl's intrusive grasp. She saw Lily. She saw herself.

"This is for you," Paulette told her, the breath labored. "Now go in the house."

Confused, the child pulled free, but did not leave the porch, instead retreating from view behind the hedges that had originally hidden her. Daryl folded his arms across his chest and leaned against the porch's rusty wrought iron support. He spat onto the sidewalk, and said, "I got nothing to say to you, Paulette. You should leave before this gets ugly."

"I got nothing to say, either, you son of a bitch!"

Everything slowed, as if all their movements were trapped in clear thick glue: Paulette drew the knife from the bag, Daryl's face registered bemusement as she lunged forward, the weapon clutched in both hands above her head, a guttural scream howling from her very depths, and then, as if an invisible weight had fallen from the heavens, Paulette dropped to her knees. The knife fell to the sidewalk, spun, and landed in the green tangle of hedge. Gasping, she slumped onto the bedraggled lawn, and her hands clawed at her chest.

Daryl looked at her as if glancing a dying animal in his rear view mirror, and then he turned, went inside, and slammed the door.

From behind the dense green hiding place, the little girl laid on her belly and stretched an arm off the porch edge. When her fingers brushed the cold sharp metal, her heart beat fast with thoughts of the space between her mattress and headboard where she would conceal it until Mama went to work again, and Daryl came into her room and wanted to play the "special game." For now, she buried her new secret beneath the rotting cushions of the abandoned sofa at the end of the porch.

Inside the house, Daryl Chien looked at the phone, briefly considered dialing 911, and then looked away.

14

Ties That Bind

"Is she going to die?"

Seattle's flat voice, lowered to a whisper, reached from the darkness of the back seat of Isaac TwoBears' club cab where the boy's face pressed between the passenger side head rest and seat belt. The question landed in Jack's right ear like a black wasp, his body grew instinctively wooden, and a long silence followed before he said in a chillingly similar tone, "I don't know."

The truck roared off of 494 onto 35W as they sped towards downtown Minneapolis, and Seattle sat back and watched as they plunged into a surrealistic pool of halogen light that spilled across the freeway before another stretch of blackness swallowed them. He didn't know what to feel, any more than Jack knew how to answer the question, but somehow, knowing that he wasn't alone in his unknowing gave Seattle quietude, as fragile and ephemeral as an insect's wing.

Too soon for the feeling to take root, the truck veered off 8th Street, idled in front of the Hennepin County Medical Center, and Jack and Seattle climbed from the warm interior out into a night that had grown cold and damp. Isaac departed with Jack's promise that he would call if they needed anything. Pausing on the sidewalk, they watched the tail lights until they disappeared, and then Jack grasped his nephew's shoulder. Before they had left South St. Paul, he had given the boy the option of staying behind, but Seattle had only stared at Jack with a disarming stoicism, shaken his head, and said, "We're family. I'll go."

Now Seattle turned and looked at his uncle with the resigned gaze of the very old, an aged man whose life had shown him far more sadness than he had ever thought possible, and his look said, "I'm ready. Are you?"

Jack Bordeaux nodded once, and, with his hand still touching Seattle's arm, they walked through the hospital's entrance and approached the front desk. The receptionist offered a tired half-smile, and asked if they were there to visit a patient. Seattle nodded, and Jack said, "Paulette Bordeaux."

The intensive care unit's lounge was scattered with the anxious, the exhausted, and the grief-stricken: a woman hunched in a couch corner and murmured into a cell phone about discontinuation of life support, her eyes closed as she methodically worked both temples with fingers and thumb; a priest in a black shirt and white clerical collar huddled at a small table with a gray-haired man, rosary beads encircling his fist like a blessed pair of brass knuckles; sleeping beneath a large jacket, a little girl stirred and the old woman, whose lap served as the child's pillow, patted her back and softly sang a line from a Vietnamese lullaby. Jack searched the unfamiliar faces until he spotted Dave. Angie sat next to him, cradling their daughter. Renee, flanked by her kids, had dragged an armchair beside Angie. Ronnie, her teenaged son awkwardly holding her hand as she cried, had managed to perch her obese body on a couch arm. Ronnie hadn't seen Jack for over a year, and she hauled herself up when she saw him, crushing him in a desperate embrace, her sobs shaking them both.

"It's bad, Jackie," she said as he gently freed himself from her grip. "It's really bad."

Ronnie sank back onto the couch arm and dug into her purse for more tissue, until she found a fast food napkin and blew her nose loudly into the wrinkled paper.

"The fucking doctors won't let us in to see her," Dave said, his mouth contorting into a thin line as he bit his upper lip.

Renee shook her head, saying, "That's not true. We just can't all go in at the same time. Shawna and Clayton are with her right now. He seems to be the only one of us who can understand all their medical lingo. I still can't believe Clayton showed after all the time he's stayed away, but I'm glad he's here"

Jack nodded, and then asked, "Did anyone reach Lionel or Tim?"

"We called Tim," Ronnie said. "But none of us has a number for Lionel."

Speaking the homeless Bordeaux sibling's name reopened the flood gates, and Ronnie's son skulked off in search of more tissue.

The priest and his elderly companion departed, and Seattle grabbed their empty chairs to add to the circle, offering one to Ronnie and the other to Jack. Seattle squatted on the floor with his cousins. Renee slipped another piece of nicotine gum into her mouth, and then, turning to Jack, said, "She's been in and out of consciousness, but she keeps asking for you—and for Seattle."

In another family, in another place, on another day, this information might have meant something, might have caused a swell of immense love, or urgency, or it might have even caused a sense of superiority, but Jack only felt ice water pouring into his chest, drowning his heart. The cold ran through him, chilled the bones, and drained in the form of a single shiver.

When he spoke, the voice sounded cold, even to him. "What happened to her?"

Angie had gotten back from Fargo early and found the apartment empty. The police came to the door an hour later, asking for a member of Paulette Bordeaux's family.

Dave said, "Ambulance picked her up outside a house on Pierce. Some little girl called 911."

"What the hell was Ma doing on the northeast side?" Jack asked.

Paulette didn't venture too far from the apartment, her usual destinations limited to either a liquor store a few blocks away or the Walgreen's located beside it. Once a week, Angie drove her to the grocery. When the idea to socialize occasionally still hit her, the Silver Spur and Paulette's cronies were a five-minute bus ride down Franklin Avenue.

"We thought maybe that's where you and the kid were. Thought she might have gone to find you," Dave said.

Jack shook his head and said, "Not even close."

"Where are you staying?" Angie asked. "Dave told me that you took off."

Jack had no intention of sharing that information; no one who still resided under Paulette's roof needed to know. Before an awkward pause formed, the doors that separated the critically ill from their families swung open, and Shawna, followed by Clayton, appeared. Without greeting, Shawna headed straight for Jack, waving her hands.

"She's awake. You need to get in there right now."

Jack's gaze moved from Shawna's house-on-fire expression to Clayton's unreadable mask, and said, "What happened?"

Clayton motioned for Seattle to follow, and Jack and the boy entered through the swinging doors as Clayton directed them through the corridors and explained the situation as best he could.

"She had a heart attack. The doctors say it was mild, as far as heart attacks go, but she fell. Her hip is broken in three places. They did angioplasty, took care of the blockages, but the hip is going to need surgery when she's stabilized."

Clayton stopped a few feet short of the next doorway, and said, "She's in there. I'll be in the chapel. Come find me when you're done."

He slapped Jack on the back, saying, "It's good to see you, little bro."

"You, too, man," Jack replied, as Clayton retreated down the hall.

He looked at Seattle, who nodded an affirmation to the unasked question, and they quietly entered the hospital room.

Paulette lay flat, her eyes barely visible through puffy slits. Her face was doughy and pale. A tangle of bags filled with liquids hung from a pole attached to a monitor, the bags' contents slowly traveling to a firmly taped port in her wrist and a second site in the crook of her arm. Only the rhythmic beep of a heart monitor disrupted the silence. As Jack drew closer, she stirred, the slits between the discolored lids widening. Paulette tried to lift a hand towards the fuzzy figure she thought, she hoped, was her youngest child, but something halted the movement.

"Ma'am, you must not pull at the I.V. tubing," the aggravated nurse had warned. "If you don't leave them alone, we'll have to restrain you."

As the first faint flutters of consciousness brought the realization that she, not Daryl Chien, faced death, the idea that this failure should be her final failure possessed Paulette, and she had torn viciously at the medical tethers that tied her to life.

The HCMC nurses, whose career choices were rooted in saving lives—wanted or not—had slipped the padded bands around her wrists and fastened them to the bed rails. One of them injected something into the port of the IV tubing, and a warm melted wax feeling ran into Paulette's veins. Soon, all thoughts flew from her mind like wind-strewn ashes. When again she awoke, the faces of children and grandchildren hovered above her, two at a time. As she slipped in and out of darkness, the faces changed, but did not transform into the two, that suddenly, she knew she must see. From beneath the layers of ambiguity, the cogent idea rose, and in a voice so brittle it required the faces to move within inches of her cracked lips, Paulette spoke their names. With each pair of faces that appeared, she repeated the condensed request that the utterance of the names implied. Jack, Seattle. Jack, Seattle. Her attempts came as little frail wisps of sound entwined with shallow breaths. Now the ones she needed came into focus, and the less plausible idea that she had somehow manifested them entered her mind.

"Jack?" she whispered. "That you?"

He leaned closer to his mother, but he didn't touch her, saying, "Yes, it's me. Seattle's here, too."

Paulette peered over his shoulder at her grandson. The yellow outline of a bruise that her hand had inflicted still marred his cheek. She looked away, but before she did, her eye caught a glimpse of the long dark ponytail that, for a moment, swung from behind his arm as he moved around the end of the hospital bed. The sight triggered an unpleasant tingle along her nerves and thrust her into a state, like a lucid dream, where the real and unreal have no discernable edges. What had she done? What had she *not* done?

Paulette's vision seemed to glaze over, her lids beginning to draw closed, and Jack wondered if they should leave, but her head jerked and the slits reformed, while her left hand pawed at the sheets, searching for some part of her son to hang on to, as she sensed they might escape before she could say what she needed to say.

"Don't go," she said, with great effort. "Need to tell you."

Jack sat in one of the chairs beside the bed and rested an arm against the rail, still keeping his fingers clear of Paulette's touch. Seattle sat beside him, and discreetly slid the chair back so that his uncle blocked the view of his grandmother. The boy hadn't expected to feel pity, but the sallow hue of her skin, the intrusive lines running into her arms and into her nostrils, the audible indication of her beating heart, and, most of all, the restraints, roused his sympathy. He didn't want to cry for her, but despite his best attempts, tears threatened. He wouldn't let her see them.

"Daryl," she whispered. "I saw him."

Jack's stomach lurched, the taste of bile assaulting the back of his tongue. Was this why she wanted them here, to hurt, to turn the knife deeper, to destroy? Surely, she wasn't going to use her fragile state as a shield, as an excuse to reveal the too-cruel truth? Was she going to tell Seattle that the monster was his father? Before Paulette could find breath to utter another sound, he spun from the bed, and grabbed the boy's arm.

"Go back to the waiting room. Now!"

Confused and alarmed, Seattle rose to leave, the chair almost tipping over with the momentum of the exodus, and disappeared before Paulette could argue. Jack whipped around to confront her, sharp, steely hatred radiating from every line in his face, as he said, "You are not ever going to tell him. Do you understand me? Never! That miserable fuck is a rapist, not a father."

Paulette shook her head with as much strength as what her limited amount and the oxygen tube would allow.

"No, no, no."

His mother's pathetic wail froze him in place. Were those tears?

A nurse, clad in light blue scrubs and running shoes, arrived at the commotion. The man, a few years older than Jack, his arms covered in tattoos, gave his patient a concerned look and then narrowed his gaze through his round wire-rimmed glasses to assess her latest visitor and said, "It's time for you to leave, sir. You being here has upset Ms. Bordeaux. Please go."

With no intention of arguing, Jack started to leave, but Paulette cast an anxious glance towards him and then to the nurse, pleading that her son should remain, and that her agitation wasn't his fault, until, reluctantly, the nurse approved, checked the monitors and lines, and left the room.

When Jack again looked at her, he could still make out wet trails marking his mother's cheekbones, and he inhaled deeply, letting the air linger for a moment before the audible release. Like a man observing himself from a point outside his body, he acknowledged the numb spot where feeling for her should have been. From that oddly objective place, he wished for a glint of compassion to replace the numbness, wished for the reaction he imagined a "good son" would have at the sight of his mother's pain, wished for some semblance of attachment to reconnect him to her, but the place within his heart, the place reserved for the woman who had given him life, remained empty.

"Daryl," Paulette began again. "I found out where he lives. I went to put a knife in him. I went to kill him."

Jack stared blankly at her for a moment before the gravity of the confession hit him and his eyes darted to the door. Had anyone else heard? Was Daryl Chien dead? Was his mother a murderer?

"I wanted to do it for Lily, for Seattle, for all of us," she said in a ragged whisper. "But I failed."

A strange mixture of relief and disappointment washed through him, and, briefly, the empty space within Jack, though not filled, felt diminutive twinges of some undefined emotion. Suddenly weary, he wilted into a chair, slumped forward, and rested his forehead on the bed rail.

"The others don't need to know. Just you, Jack."

He looked up at Paulette and nodded. The weariness grew.

"You and Seattle have a decent place to stay? Will you make sure he gets to school?"

He said they did. He said he would.

I'm glad," she said, as her lids began a slow crawl towards her craggy cheekbones.

When her eyes were closed, he stood to go, but halted as a slurred whisper rose from the hospital bed.

"Tell the kid … I'm sorry."

When he was sure that she slept, Jack left, the weight of his weariness pressing upon him like the gravity of an alien world. He found Seattle in the chapel with Clayton. The boy thumbed through a Gideon Bible. Clayton sat, head bowed, eyes closed, hands folded in prayer. Jack sat beside him, and he raised his head, unclasped his hands, and looked at his youngest brother.

"So?" he asked. "What's going on with Ma? You look like you've been hit by a bus."

"Just tired, man," Jack said, unable to meet his brother's stare. "Ma wanted to know that I'm going to do right by Seattle."

You can handle that?"

Jack caught Seattle's expression, and said, with far more conviction than he thought his spirit capable of at that moment, "Absolutely."

Years before, Clayton had made his escape when he married the daughter of a Unitarian minister. The couple left the city and set up house outside of Stillwater. With the encouragement of his wife, he had sought refuge among the members of his new family and broke ties with Paulette. He couldn't argue that the Bordeaux side had much to offer his children; it certainly hadn't granted him much more than a strong desire to create an opposite universe from the one that he had been raised in. His choice had come with a price, though. In cutting off contact with their mother, he had lost touch with his younger siblings, a fact which, as he studied the lines of fatigue that etched Jack's face, caused Clayton guilt.

"Listen," he said, getting to his feet, as he pulled on a St. Croix Trucking cap. "I've got to head out, get home to Jenny and the kids. I'm leaving for the east coast early tomorrow morning. Got a dozen drops in Jersey next week. Money's good, but it's hell on my back. Hate being away from the family so much, too. Every time I come off the road, it seems like the kids are three inches taller and ten years smarter."

A wistful smile played across Clayton's mouth, and then he said, "Can I give you guys a lift somewhere?"

For a moment, Isaac TwoBears' offer came to mind, and though Jack would have liked to see him and reap the soothing calm that the man seemed to create, he heard something in Clayton's tone, something that indicated Clayton's need was greater than Jack's, something that made the choice seem obvious.

"Sure, we could use a ride."

"You can take that Bible with you," Clayton said as Seattle got up to go.

The boy looked at the book in his hand and then at Clayton. With a shy smile, he laid it back on the chair where he had found it, and said, "Someone else can have it."

***

Seattle spent the ride back to South St. Paul lost in thought, his uncles' voices rising and falling like unintelligible white noise humming outside the range of his concentration. Why had Jack demanded that he leave his grandmother's bedside? What had they said to each other after he left? Had they argued? Jack had seemed so angry after Paulette mentioned someone called Daryl. Who was Daryl? Though he didn't think he had heard the man's name before, something about it felt almost like a fragment of memory, a memory that hid inside of him, but didn't belong to him. This strange phantom memory hadn't been there until he heard the name, and though he wished that he could exorcise it and rid himself of the sick little swirl of fear that spun in his belly, he somehow knew that what had been unleashed was there to stay.

Seattle felt the oppressive drain, wringing out his last droplets of energy, until sleep overtook him and merciless dreams mimicked reality.

He stands beside Paulette's hospital bed. Her lips move, but he cannot hear what she is saying. He leans closer and her bound hand catches his wrist. Her vacant stare feels like it penetrates his flesh and he winces as her lips again form a word and he recognizes it.

"Daryl."

Seattle recoils from her, only to find that he now wears the restraint locked to the bed rail bars. Her other wrist, though free from the opposite rail, still wears the cuff. The cuff attaches to a long rusty chain that runs down onto the white hospital tile, out the door, and into the thick shadows of the hall. In the distance, the sound of slow, heavy footsteps echo, each one fused with an ominous clatter of dragging metal links. Seattle fights to tear away the tie that binds him, but he can't break it. The one attached to the chain, the one attached to Paulette, one who is somehow attached to him, too, is coming.

15

Sword of Vengeance

Rukiya Walker couldn't sleep. Anticipation, has it had done for a week now, kept her pupils dilated as she stared through the darkness at the bedroom door, and kept her chubby brown fingers wrapped around the knife handle. Beneath the thin cotton sheet, she waited, silent and still.

***

Silent and still, Paulette Bordeaux waited for the night nurse. The flesh and bone that connected to her new plastic and steel hip ached relentlessly, and she breathed a small sigh of relief when the nurse appeared beside the hospital bed with a hypodermic syringe of Demerol in hand. She smiled at the middle-aged woman with badly permed gray hair and crow's feet at the corners of her kind green eyes. Paulette liked this one. Last shift had included a fresh-out-of-nursing-school twenty-something who had chided Paulette when she requested more pain medication, saying, "The orthopedic doctor wants you weaned off that so you can begin physical therapy soon."

At the shift change, Lorna arrived, Paulette assessed her, and decided to ask again.

"Of course, Lorna had said when she had scanned the computer med log. "You can't heal if you are in pain."

Now, as dear Nurse Lorna and the narcotic delivered on their promise of relief, Paulette drifted in and out of wakefulness, dreams, and the odd spaces in between.

***

Rukiya felt herself drifting towards unwanted sleep, and poked the knife tip into her thigh. Mama had gone to work the nursing home graveyard shift hours ago. These were the nights when Daryl came to her room, the nights when he brought her treats that Mama said she could no longer have because she was a "fat girl," the nights when he, in return for grape soda, snack cakes, or frosted cereal with tiny marshmallows, asked her to do things that Rukiya knew were nasty.

She had loved sweets ever since she was a baby, back before Mama caught Daddy with that "ten-dollar whore." Before the divorce, Daddy used to sit on the front porch, Rukiya in his lap, with a big bowl of ice cream covered in chocolate syrup. He would take a bite, then offer her a spoonful, until the bowl was empty. Daddy loved sweets, too, but when the "ten-dollar whore," whose name was really Sharice, had a baby, Rukiya only saw Daddy on the weekends, and the new baby shared Daddy's ice cream on a different front porch, way across town. So on that very first horrible night when Daryl sat on the edge of her bed and held out an ice cream sandwich, in the few minutes while she ate it, before he guided her sticky hand towards his ulterior motive, she felt like someone's special girl again.

Over time, Daryl's visits brought fewer cookies and more threats.

"Your mom don't need to know about this," he would say. "Unless you want her to know what a dirty, sneaky little pig you are. Do you want that, Kiya?"

But then the Indian lady had shown up, and Rukiya Walker had seen the same hatred in the woman's eyes as the hatred the girl had in her heart. Only she and Daryl knew why the woman had come that day; she had told Mama about the lady's collapse onto the sidewalk in front of their house and how she had remembered what to dial during an emergency, but Mama didn't need to know the rest. When the ambulance had arrived, Daryl had claimed not to know the woman, but Rukiya knew who she was: she was her savior, the angel for whom she had been asking the old white man in the sky, and just like those pictures in the Sunday school books, her angel carried a "sword of vengeance."

Now, as the girl heard the distinctive creak of the loose floor board outside the closed door, she gripped the handle more tightly and felt the faint sting where the knife point had punctured her skin, and a nervous, almost maniacal smile twitched her lips. The Indian angel the old white man in the sky sent had failed, but Rukiya Walker would not.

***

Paulette Bordeaux felt like an angel hovering above a hospital bed that contained a woman whose face she had seen in mirrors countless times. Was she dead? No, she could still hear the steady beep of the heart monitor, and she could still see the rise and fall of her own chest in the bed below. No, this wasn't death, but the tangibility, the solidity that connected her to all her senses didn't seem dream-like, either. This was some other kind of existence, some other plain of consciousness, a place where Paulette found herself feeling free of all that pained her, all that confined her, all that limited her.

She began to rise away from the sleeping body, and although it didn't seem as if she controlled the movement, she wasn't afraid. She knew that she would return to it when she was done. The room vanished beneath her, and for an increment of time so brief its passing could not be measured, Paulette's senses registered nothing, and then this new and powerful form of herself landed within a room draped in midnight, except for milky lines of moonlight that penetrated window blinds and illuminated a child's empty bed.

***

When he entered Rukiya's room, Daryl's eye, with its failing night vision, mistook the wadded comforter for the child, until he reached the empty bed and his rough hand squeezed only cotton and fiber fill. Irritated, he flung it onto the floor, and sat down hard upon the mattress. He would wait. She would pay.

***

He will pay, Paulette thought, all the sharp edges of her hatred for Daryl Chien ripping through the barrier of her present world and his.

"You rotten fuck," she growled. "This time, you're a dead man."

But Daryl Chien didn't even flinch, didn't even move, and as Paulette attempted to reach for his throat, she didn't move, either. Only her loathing had perpetrated into her mysterious space, along with the old suffocating hopelessness, that, at its worst, made the next breath seem optional.

***

Like deliciously sweet music, Daryl detected the sound of rapid breathing. An anxiety-filled aria that rose from somewhere in the field of his glass eye and pleasurably heated his blood. Always the cunning predator, he poised, stone-still, and allowed the girl's fear adequate time to steep. A minute ticked in his brain, and then another, before he heard the breathing move slowly closer, but he didn't move. Why spring when the prey delivered itself?

Paulette watched the child rise from the shadows, the knife appearing too large and awkward, as she lifted it with both hands over her head. Panic gripped Paulette; the girl possessed neither the strength nor the proper method to deliver a mortal wound, and nothing but death was an acceptable outcome. With focus and a concentration, Paulette had never known, she suddenly felt something—no, some*one*, enter her ethereal form. It felt like youth, and physical strength, and fear, wrapped in an intense hatred, and it flowed through Paulette's arms and legs until she was moving beyond the limitations that had prevented her previous attack. The new energy fused with her own and moved towards, and then into, the child. With eyes much clearer than her own, Paulette saw a hand, their hand, small and chocolate-brown, shift the knife. Paulette could smell the salty stench of body odor and feel the greasy residue of unwashed hair as their left hand grabbed a fistful, jerked the man's head back, and, with the force of three, Lily, Paulette, and Rukiya, slashed their sword of vengeance through Daryl Chien's throat.

***

The Minneapolis PD's homicide investigation fizzled quickly: the homeowner/girlfriend had a legitimate alibi; the child, who had been found by the mother, wrapped in a blanket on the living room couch, her nightclothes free of blood, had slept through it all. They found no signs of forced entry, no signs of struggle, no footprints, no hair samples, no fiber samples, or tell-tale DNA; only a corpse and a kitchen knife so immaculate of fingerprints it was as if human hands had never touched it.

Blood of a Stranger

Society's morbid fascination with brutality created a media frenzy around Daryl Chien's murder, and for weeks Jack couldn't turn on the local news, pick up a paper, or carry on casual conversation with anyone attached to the Twin Cities' Native American community without a sickening, yet satisfying, sensation shooting through his gut as his mind waged war upon itself in a battle between what was logical and what seemed ethical. Though Jack tried to use discretion about the subject when Seattle was in earshot, the worry lines and the way his jaw moved as if he were grinding gravel between his teeth revealed too much to such an observant boy, a boy who harbored a question.

After their visit to Paulette's hospital room, Jack had walked around with a feeling akin to that of hearing the vicious growl of a large dog behind him without knowing whether or not that animal was safely on the other side of a chain link fence. Had Seattle forgotten the mention of Daryl's name? Was the boy even curious? Would he ask the ugly question, and if so, then when? But many busy days followed: he registered Seattle at a St. Paul school, prepared for college finals, worked thirty hours, and helped Gus grade papers. Somehow, he thought that all the basic activities of life might act as a buffer, and perhaps the looming question would be forgotten, but news of the murder erased all the quiet comfort of their minutiae, and, one night as he sat on Gus and Barb's patio, toiling over a calculus equation, Jack Bordeaux turned to find that the fear that had stalked him for weeks was about to jump the fence.

Seattle cleared his throat as he pushed the screen door open and joined Jack on the patio, old Finnegan at his heels. The dog ambled out into the yard, just beyond the cement, and slowly lowered himself onto the ground with an exhausted huff. Seattle dropped into the lawn chair next to his uncle, and, without prelude, met Jack's eyes.

"Who was Daryl Chien?"

He held his nephew's gaze only for a moment before the weight of it pushed his own pained look back to the textbook balanced on his knees, as if it might reveal a cleaner, neater answer amongst its lines of letters and symbols and numbers. Didn't some believe that numbers are the true language of the universe and that all solutions could be discovered through them? But Jack, at his finest mathematical hour, could only be considered an average student, so with deliberate slowness, he closed the text. Truth was the only acceptable answer.

"He was a friend of Paulette ... a long time ago, when I was a kid."

"A friend?" Seattle asked. "Like a boyfriend kind of friend?"

Jack nodded.

"Was my mom," he hesitated, rubbed his palms on his jeans, and then continued, "was she alive then? Did she know him?"

Jack flinched. How quickly the boy's apparent perceptiveness had taken them to the point he feared most, but perhaps ripping the bandage off fast, exposing the wound sooner rather than later, could bring them closer to a healing place.

"Yes, your mother knew Daryl."

Seattle noticed the scalding bite of his uncle's voice when he spoke the man's name, and he felt the chain he had seen in his dream, pulling him closer to what he somehow had known since the night at Paulette's bedside, but needed to hear someone say aloud.

"Were Grandma and he still 'friends' when I was born?"

"No."

"Were he and my mother still 'friends'?"

Jack clutched the arms of the patio chair in an attempt to quell the rage that threatened to lash out upon an undeserving victim. He breathed in, the faint scent of lilacs catching him off guard and reminding him of things more beautiful, things alive, of renewal.

"He was never her friend."

For a moment, a veil fell across the boy's face, as if the course that he had so carefully plotted through this labyrinth, suddenly had lead him into a wall of briars.

"But aren't I his ...?

He laid a hand on Seattle's arm before the boy could gain the courage to finish the question, to utter the word, to seal the connection.

"Yes," Jack said, never breaking the physical bond between himself and the child he loved beyond measure, beyond calculation, "you are."

They sat like that for a long time, Jack's hand seeming to be the only thing holding the boy's body to the Earth, as all the letters, symbols, and numbers that calculated the very meaning behind his own existence raced around Seattle's mind, transporting him inside and outside of himself, backwards and forwards in time. When Seattle again spoke, when he again moved, the absence of feeling Jack heard in his nephew's words only caused him to grasp more tightly.

"My mother must have hated him. Must have hated me, too. I don't blame her. No wonder she left me. I come from someone bad, something bad. I'm bad."

He broke then, his body shaking, an agonized guttural sound rising from the deepest depths, depths no child should have to delve. Jack dropped to his knees in front of the boy and pulled him close. Seattle fought, screaming, "No one wanted me to be born. No one ever wanted me. She should have had an abortion," but Jack's strength never wavered.

"No," he said, repeating it, chanting it over and over like a prayer. "I wanted you. I love you. I want you. I've always loved you. I'll never leave you, Seattle. I promise. I'll never leave you."

Jack shut his eyes, another memory floating from what seemed like a bottomless, icy well of disillusion and regret.

Jack had just settled his five-year-old nephew on the couch with a spoon and the cardboard can of commodity peanut butter, and tuned the television to the horrible shrill voice of the red Sesame Street puppet that Seattle loved so much, when someone pounded urgently on the Bordeauxs' front door. Jack turned the volume down and waited for whatever crisis the knocking implied to disappear. They were there alone and the last thing he needed was a run-in with one of Paulette's obnoxious bar buddies, or, worse yet, the Minneapolis PD looking for one of Paulette's obnoxious bar buddies. Eventually, the knocking ceased, but an anxious voice replaced it.

"Jack, it's Madesio. I know you're there. Open the door. Please."

The obvious distress in his voice brought Jack to his feet and had his fingers sliding the chain lock and dead bolt open before he had given himself even a second to consider whether or not the source of his young lover's anxiety might actually be in the hall, too. His teenage lack of prudency had cost Jack nothing, though; only Madesio stood slumped against the door frame, his guitar bag and a knapsack on the floor beside him. Jack saw his ripped shirt, the bloody dish towel he had pressed to his nose, and the abnormal angle in which Madesio's shoulder tilted, and grasped the uninjured arm to guide Madesio inside, where he slumped onto the couch next to Seattle.

The little boy's eyes widened and then wept. Why were grown-ups always fighting, always hurting each other? Why was everyone so angry? Who would want to beat up Uncle Jack's best friend? Seattle liked Madesio; he had taught him a song about a magic dragon, and they had sung it together while Madesio played guitar. Maybe Dave had punched him. He said that Madesio was a "fag," and even though Seattle didn't know what that word meant, he knew that Dave hated anyone who acted like one.

Madesio mussed the boy's hair and said, "Don't cry, Jackie Paper. I'm okay. Just a few bumps and bruises."

Despite great apprehension, Seattle offered him a smile. He liked it when Madesio called him the name of the boy from the magic dragon song. If Seattle ever met a rascal like Puff, he'd love him, too. Besides, "Jackie" sounded like a version of Jack, and though he was no magic dragon, Uncle Jack sure came closer than anyone else. The boy noticed that his uncle held Madesio's hand, like he had done when Seattle had tripped on the sidewalk and skinned his knee, and he felt glad that they both had Jack to make them feel better.

"Maddie's right. He'll be fine," he said, though he didn't sound like he really knew for sure. "Would you go to our room for a few minutes? I need to talk to him alone."

"And get him some Band-Aids?"

"Yes, I promise. I'll make sure he's all bandaged up," Jack said, tapping on the boy's knee that still held a curled adhesive strip.

When Seattle closed the bedroom door, Jack turned to Madesio and they had fallen into each other's arms as he brushed a hand over Madesio's hair and demanded, "Who did this to you?"

"My old man."

The sickening dread had planted itself in both their bellies the night before, when, as they kissed in what they thought had been a vacant stairwell, Madesio's father had come out of the shadows, back early from his band's uptown gig. The boys had slipped off the landing into the adjoining hallway, unsure if they had been identified or not, frantically hoping that the homophobic patriarch of the DeMarco family had, in such poor light, not witnessed their passion.

"He told me I'm a fucking abomination, a freak. He told me decent black men don't do that kind of shit, said it must be the nasty-ass Puerto Rican coming out in me."

Madesio choked on a sardonic laugh.

"My mother took offense. She hadn't minded up to that point. Hadn't said a fucking word as he dislocated my shoulder. Didn't make a move as he put a right hook in my face. But don't disrespect her parents' homeland. She just sat there, making the sign of the cross, and saying that if I would go to mass with her more, I would understand what an evil person I am."

Jack held him in silence as he spoke, an ugly voice in the background of Jack's thoughts whispering, "It's not hate that beat this beautiful human being, it's your love."

"They threw me out," Madesio said. "I called Pot O' Gold; Patrick's on his way. Go grab your shit, man. We're liberated."

He leaned away, and looked at Madesio, confused and terrified, and said, "What do you mean?"

"Just that," Madesio said, his voice taking on a sharper, cooler vibe. "Don't you want out of this place? It's not like your mother gives a shit about you."

Jack tried to let the truth of the statement move him from the ripped sofa cushion. A familiar tenderness sifted into Madesio's tone. "Come on,

Jack, I want us to break free, love each other, stay together."

DeMarco touched his face, lightly brushing his thumb over Jack's lips and saying, "No one loves you like I do."

Though his mind still kept him loosely held in place, the emotional and physical swell created whenever Madesio touched him swept him from the couch and into the dining room.

"Hurry," Madesio said. "Patrick will be here any minute. We're going to crash at their house for a while, until we can find jobs and get our own place."

Jack stopped short at the sight of Seattle. Without the young men's notice, the little boy had returned and hidden under the scarred dining table to listen. He lifted the child to his feet and held him at arm's length, as he met a wild-eyed stare. Signaling impending tears, the boy's mouth began to quiver.

"What did you hear? Everything?"

Seattle nodded, and before Jack had a chance to say anything, the child threw himself at the older boy, clinging so tightly to Jack's neck that he had to struggle for his next breath.

"Don't leave, Uncle! Please, please, don't leave me."

Tears and snot and peanut butter soaked Jack's T-shirt as he tried to extricate himself from the hysterical boy, but Seattle gripped more tightly, until finally Jack gave up and wrapped him in his arms. If he were to leave, who would care for the child? Paulette would keep him alive … probably. Dave said that the kid was a giant pain in his ass. The others never came around. They had their own problems. Who loved Seattle the way that he did?

He picked the boy up and carried him to the couch, where he continued to cling to Jack, his face buried in his shoulder. Madesio's stare had grown wintery and his words followed suit, as the sound of a car horn caused him to stand and snatch his bags up with a violent one-handed jerk.

"Last chance, Bordeaux. Is it me or the kid?"

Jack's tormented expression pleaded, but, as he had too often witnessed during the handful of months that he and DeMarco had been lovers, Madesio's mood had flipped with hair-trigger quickness, and the thin line about which poets pen and singers sing now lay like an impenetrable wall between them. With a final odious huff, a dismissive shake of his head, and a slam of a door, Madesio DeMarco had exited Jack's life.

The young man, barely beyond boyhood himself, held the child he had chosen, as he took in the lavender lilacs, the old sleepy dog, and the windows of the garage apartment that would soon be their home. His choices had brought them here, and though resentment threatened at his emotional edges, he shoved it back, disallowing it to take shape in the form of a sharp reminder to Seattle of where he was and who had brought him safely there.

When the boy's emotional storm abated, Jack sat back beside him and said, "You are my nephew, my sister's son, my blood. When I look at you, I see Lily's hair, the shape of her mouth. When you do that crazy laugh that sounds like a donkey, I remember the silly things I did as a little boy just to hear her laugh that same laugh. You are so much your mother's son, from the way you use your hands when you're talking about something that excites you to the way you like to eat your tomato soup with potato chips crushed on top of it."

Seattle glanced at his uncle and saw so much sorrow that he had to look away.

"I miss her, Seattle," Jack said. "For me, she lives on in you along with all the other incredible things that make you unique, make you special. For me, that's all there is: my love for Lily, my love for you."

"What about him? What about the part of me that's him? How could you love that?"

Jack paused, pushed out a tattered breath, and said, "No one is ever all good or all bad, Seattle. Life just isn't that black and white. People seem to spend a lot of their time in the gray area."

Though it was almost inconceivable, Jack muscled the only memories he had of Daryl Chien, and tried to imagine him as a boy, as an innocent child, as someone who might have harbored the vulnerable sensitivity and eager mind of the boy who sat beside him on the patio.

Seattle rubbed a fist back and forth over is swollen lids, and asked, "So you think even Daryl had a little good in him?"

"Whatever potential he had for it," Jack replied, tapping a finger against the boy's chest over his heart, "is going to grow strong inside someone like you."

The twin tigers, Siegfried, his brother Roy close on his heels, appeared and rubbed affectionately against Seattle's leg until the boy scooped Siegfried onto his lap and scratched behind his ears. Finnegan lifted his head and began to pant with the anticipation he always exhibited when *his* boy was doling out love to the cats. Unwilling to wait his turn, the Lab lumbered to his feet, mounted the patio, and stuck a huge wet nose under Siegfried's belly, rousting the indignant feline and drawing a faint smile from Seattle as the dog laid his bulky head on the boys lap and looked up at him with what could only be called adoration. Roy stuck his head under the chair's armrest and butted Seattle's hand when he tried to rub Finnegan's ears, which resulted in the cat receiving an unwanted slobbery Labrador-style face washing.

"Are my four-legged children out there with you?"

Barb's soft voice came through the screen door like much-needed fresh air, and Jack wondered if she had heard any of his and Seattle's exchange. He found himself hoping that she had, as he mentally flailed around, unable to grasp hold of the best way to close the conversation, at least for tonight. *I'm so tired. I cannot do this.*

"Yes, Barb," Seattle said. "They're all here."

"Of course," she said, opening the door and tapping her white cane down the cement stairs. "You're there. Where else would they be, but with their best friend?"

When her cane reached the edge of the patio, its tip brushing across the grass, she swung it wide to the right and located her favorite place to sit: a weathered wooden rocker next to a massive terra cotta pot that, in summer, held rosemary, basil, and chives. She rested the cane against the pot, sat on the faded blue seat, and slowly began to rock, a soft soothing creak echoing from the old chair's wooden joints like a sweet lullaby.

"Animals know goodness when they see it. People, they can fool each other sometimes, but animals know. I think it goes way back to the time that the elders tell of, a time when the people and the animals spoke the same language. Somewhere along the line, humans began to forget that sacred tongue, but the animals remember, and they know when they've met a two-legged who really wants to, really tries to, understand them. And if that person is respectful, and listens with more than just his ears, they will teach him to remember."

Siegfried cautiously approached the rocking chair and sprang onto Barb's lap. The cat circled twice, and then curled into a purring ball. She stroked the animal while she spoke. "Understanding, and the words that go with it, can be hard to find sometimes ... even between those who speak the same language."

She slid a bare foot off the patio and raked her toes through the fragile spring grass. "Love keeps leading us to try, though, doesn't it?"

On the roof of the barn, a mourning dove cooed, the lonesome sound surrounding them as they sat in their silences for many moments, letting the truth of all the words hold them together.

17

The Crow and the Coyote, the Lily, and the Guitar

The oily-black crow that stood on the coyote's back seemed to stare at Desiree Stark as she craned her head and peered into the mirror at the supple flesh just above her hip. The coyote stared, too, and the creatures grinned in a way that seemed both sociable and sinister. They had lived there, in permanent ink, ever since the night that the mysterious grass dancer had shared the revelation of his mystical mirror. Desiree had fled from him, the jingling dress making her feel like a belled kitten cloaked by the shadow of a hungry raptor, until she reached her car. Safely inside, she had driven, without direction, without a conscious destination, finally finding herself in uptown Minneapolis, the vehicle idling at the curb outside a tattoo and piercing boutique. The shop's door had been propped open; a buxom woman sporting a tiny tank top and cropped platinum blond hair leaned against it, smoking a clove cigarette. When the girl got out of the car and the woman saw the beaded moccasins, the jingle dress, and the girl's glazed expression, she raised a triple-pierced brow, shoved the rest of the cigarette into a coffee can full of sand and butts, and motioned for the girl to enter. It was strange, but the tattoo artist had certainly seen stranger.

"Ink or metal?" the woman had asked, as she stepped behind the counter and pointed to the price listings posted on the wall.

"I want a tattoo," Desiree said, though she hadn't known why.

The woman pulled a large book from below the counter.

"Prices vary on ink; it all depends on what you're looking for."

The woman began to flip through the book, figuring this one for something tribal, or the usual butterfly "tramp stamp."

"I don't think what I want will be in that book," Desiree said, and the woman closed it, her curiosity sparked.

"Did you bring your own sketch? 'Cause that'll probably cost you more … that is, if it's something I want to take on."

Shaking her head Desiree leaned closer and said, "No drawing, but I'll describe it."

Without knowing what words would next fall from her lips, Desiree Stark had told her in detail, and the woman skillfully sketched the ominous-looking bird, that appeared to be transforming from a coyote, rather than sitting on one. When the metamorphic image was finished, the artist turned the pad for Desiree to see, and the spooky girl grinned a disturbingly similar grin to that of the penciled pair, nodding with approval, saying, "Trickster … yes, yes, I am trickster, too."

The following morning upon waking, Desiree had felt an itching, burning discomfort and had risen to find them staring back at her in the mirror, but she had no recollection of how they had gotten there. Regardless, she loved the tricky twosome, and found herself pulling aside clothing to glimpse them whenever a mirror was available.

"Where's Unktomi, the Lakota spider trickster?" her friend, Bonnie KillsTwice said when she saw the tattoo. "He's a bad-ass arachnid."

Now, as Desiree ran a finger lovingly over her crow and coyote, she thought of spiders, tricks—and Jack Bordeaux.

***

"That's an interesting tattoo," Isaac TwoBears commented. "Both the content and the location."

Caught off guard, Jack began to shift positions so that the arch of his left foot wasn't in view, but then stopped, lifting the foot onto his right knee and casually running the perspiring Corona bottle across it. Omission wasn't a good foundation for a new relationship.

TwoBears flipped the rib eyes and rotated the ears of sweet corn, then he leaned against the deck rail and said, "Seems like that would be a pretty painful place to get inked."

The topic seemed too heavy for their first date, but Jack felt safer, more secure, more relaxed, than he had in a long time. With the sound of crickets, and Lake of the Isles a block from Isaac's cozy bungalow, the night breeze carrying the green scent of fresh water to mingle with the aroma of charred meat and mesquite smoke, Jack's mood elevated, and the inclination to tell this thoughtful man the story took hold.

***

In the days after Madesio DeMarco's departure, Jack had, with diminished senses, let time wash over him, his sight fading all colors, his ears muting any music that escaped into his deliberate silence, food tasteless on his tongue. But these strange impairments that allowed him a respite from life didn't disturb him, only the absence of physical feeling frustrated him because the mental torture was all consuming. In vain attempts for relief, for reconciliation, or perhaps reprisal, he dialed DeMarco's cell and left cloying voicemail messages until the mailbox was full. When the messages went unanswered, he phoned Pot O' Gold, and

Patrick and Thomas sympathetically informed him that Madesio needed space. But when Jack showed up at the coffee house and pleaded, the proprietors escorted him into their office and offered the jilted teenager some raw, honest advice.

"I'm sorry, kid, but it's over. You have to get on with things and forget about Maddie," Patrick said.

Thomas set an espresso on the desk beside him, but Jack ignored it, saying, "I love him. Why would I want to forget him? I just need to talk to him."

Thomas McCormick pushed aside the coffee and sat on the desk's edge, a less benevolent, more intense look darkening his face as he spoke.

"You may not want to forget him, but you sure as hell should."

Patrick Kennedy's fingers nervously grasped the hot drink that had been intended for the boy, and he took a scalding sip, as Thomas and he glanced at one another, neither one wanting to proceed, but both knowing that it would be necessary. He replaced the demitasse and sighed. Though every new day brought another few strands of red hair lost forever to his brush, after-hours raves had been exchanged for quiet early dinners at home, and visits to the health club served to remind him that there probably was a knee replacement in his future, Kennedy wouldn't return to the awkward years of teenagers for all the dark roast in Sumatra.

"Madesio moved out of our place yesterday. He left with a young guy with an Augsburg College sticker on the window of his Lexus and a downtown one-bedroom apartment. Do I need to go on?"

Thomas patted Jack's shoulder and said, "I'm really sorry, kid. We've all been through it. First love is a bitch."

Feeling like a foolish child, Jack had left them, and wandered through Loring Park despite the falling snow that clung to his hair and melted into icy tendrils that ran down his bare neck. The snow deepened on the sidewalks and surmounted the tops of his tennis shoes, soaking his socks, but Jack had walked on, feeling nothing of the outside world and everything of the inside one, until he saw a fuzzy outline that resembled a bus, and boarded it. Jack didn't see the man with an electric blue and lime green stocking cap that looked like the Nordic version of a court jester's hat. He didn't smell the diesel exhaust or the wet wool or the odd salt and chemical de-icer mixture. He rode and rode, tuning out the sounds of plodding snow boots, the clink of coins tossed into the change box, and the off-tune singing of a woman wearing earbuds, until only he and the driver remained. As they slowly made the turn-around to start the route over, the driver shouted, "Hey, buddy. Did you miss your stop?"

Jack shook his head and the driver shrugged. Eventually, after another twenty minutes of desensitized travel, Jack briefly focused on a pawn shop. He forced his hand to pull the cord, the bus halted, and he exited. In the pawn shop's grimy front window stood a row of used guitars: a shiny black electric bass, a child's classical with some strings missing, and a beat-up Taylor acoustic. Standing outside, staring at the instruments, all the songs Madesio DeMarco had ever sung rose to a deafening, distorted level in Jack's head, until he wanted to scream, break the plate glass, and smash the silent trio. But, in the end, he had walked away; some musician had left them behind, too.

Somewhere, near uptown, with frostbitten fingers and toes, Jack Bordeaux stumbled into the tattoo and piercing boutique. The woman with the platinum blond cropped hair and the triple pierced eye brow had smiled and said, "Ink or metal?"

***

For many moments, Isaac TwoBears considered the dark brown guitar with a white lily's green stem entwined through its strings, then said, with deepest sincerity, "Losses."

Jack could still remember the exquisitely beautiful pain that the fresh tattoo had created, how each stabbing step towards home had released another lock on his emotional shackles, how each twinge brought him a little farther back into the physical world.

He sometimes reflected on his actions during that time, regretting the pitiable way in which he had chased after a ghost kind of love, those cold phantom fingers that had still clutched his heart, long after the retraction of DeMarco's warmth, knowing now that that stage of grief is called denial. It had gripped him before, when Renee had come back from Spokane carrying a plain wooden box full of their sister's ashes. Scowling, Jack had demanded how anybody could know that was really her, insisted that a mistake might have been made, that the girl found in the park could have been someone else.

"It's Lily, Jack. I'm the one who had to identify her body," Renee yelled, anger erasing any conciliation.

Jack had railed, called Renee a liar, and shoved their grandmother away when she tried to comfort him. Denial had culminated with a transfer of pain that day, too—Jack's fist through a closet door. Unlike the regret he experienced every time a cold autumn rain placed the dull ache in the once-broken knuckles, the pain of the lily and the guitar receded, only leaving behind an intricate work of art.

"It's beautiful," Isaac said in a voice that enticed Jack fully into the moment, invoking thoughts of honey, and smoke, and crushed red pepper. Their eyes met, the look lingering just long enough to allude to where their evening might lead.

***

Far across the river, Desiree's dark eyes bore an angry glint as they strayed from the tattooed tricksters to the cell phone that lay silently on the floor. A fake number; a move right out of her own playbook, but if Bordeaux and Old Man TwoBears thought that fooling her ended the game ....

She kicked the cell. It slid, hit the wall, and cracked, dislodging the battery.

Of course, she had accepted that her strategy must change. Her feminine wiles couldn't win this one, and for Desiree Stark, the main objective, as it always had been, was to win. Her mother had instilled the almost obsessive competitiveness in Desiree, and had exhibited, on several occasions, that there is more than one way to obtain a victory. Years earlier, Anita had first demonstrated her point with a switchblade. As she crouched next to a Chevy with Oklahoma plates and stabbed the tire, she whispered to her eight-year-old daughter, "That Ponca bitch shouldn't have smiled at me when they handed *her* the fancy dance prize purse. Now, she'll have to spend that money to get her uppity ass back to Tulsa."

Anita Stark had taught her daughter another applicable lesson: hell hath no fury like a woman ignored.

"Don't you mean scorned?" Desiree had asked, the first time she heard her mother use the line.

Anita had laughed, and said, "For some women, disdain trumps apathy, but I disagree. Love me, hate me, but *never* ignore me."

Impossible to ignore, Desiree glanced at the crow and coyote again, and ran her hands over her skin, the flesh feeling strangely hot, as if a fire burned dangerously close.

18

Where There's Smoke

The spider observed the young woman through the multi-faceted vision of its tiny black eyes. For weeks, its web had hung in a corner of the window, cleverly hidden behind a dusty dream catcher, allowing the spider time to learn that the fragmented image spoke not only of how it saw the world, but about the young woman's identity. She was many, within the body of one, and though she seemed not to know this, the spider knew, and it waited and watched, as it sensed a vibration in the night air. For Desiree Stark, revelation was coming, carried from the darkest depths of the Mystery on shiny black wings.

Sprawled across the cool sheets, naked and bored, Desiree listened, with increasing resentment, to the sound of laughter rising from the patio below. Oscar, Owen, and their sleep-over guest, Seattle Bordeaux, hooted and hollered, as Leonard told the boys another one of his patented corny jokes. Maggie Gustafson, Leonard's constant companion these days—or, as Desiree liked to refer to the short, plump woman, "the Swedish Meatball"—giggled the loudest, and Desiree crammed a pillow against her ear. Everything about the happy family scene below, from her father's dimpled, squeaky-clean girlfriend right down to the fucking s'mores, made her want to stick a finger down her throat. Of course, while Leonard lit a wood fire in the adobe chimney at the edge of the patio, the Meatball had asked Desiree if she wanted to join them for "some roasted treats," an invitation that she had flatly declined, adding, as she let her look travel to Maggie's prominent middle-age muffin top, "I watch what *I* eat."

The insult hadn't landed with the force that Desiree had wanted it to, and the Meatball had just smiled and babbled on about how a girl with such a lovely figure need not worry so much. Desiree had retreated upstairs, before the annoying woman pulled a mental muscle in another lame attempt to win approval, something she had already accomplished with Oscar and Owen through chocolate chip cookies and some damn thing called "taco casserole."

The aroma of roasted hotdog and marshmallow caused Desiree's stomach to growl, but she would dig in the dresser drawer for a role of old breath mints before she would join the current subjects of her disdain. Not all the members of her shit list were frolicking around the Stark's backyard, though; she had overheard Seattle say that Jack had gone somewhere with his friend Isaac.

Smug bastards, Desiree thought, and hurled the pillow aside. The rising anger and frustration made her feel caged, not only within the stuffy bedroom, but within her own body; something pushed from the inside, wanting out. Her mind felt too full; thoughts that she recognized as her own, and others that she could not place, spun madly with a kind of mental friction that seemed to scorch the interior of her skull.

Below, the yard at last lay in silence, the boys having moved on to their sleeping bags and video games in the basement. Leonard and Maggie had gone to the living room sectional for a romantic comedy and some discretionary dry humping. For a moment, the quiet seemed too quiet, and Desiree felt a little tingle of anticipatory fear. All at once, as if it had simply materialized there out of the ether, a crow stood in the window sill. Desiree stared, and the crow stared back, until she averted her eyes, suddenly self-conscious of her nakedness. She waved her arms at the unusually large bird, but it only bobbed and weaved, cawing in a manner that sounded much too much like laughter. She rose from the bed, the heat racing from her head down her spine and through her limbs, until her fingers and toes felt like the tips of smoldering matches.

Shifting from foot to foot, the crow cocked his head and watched with a glowing sense of pride as everything unfolded. The spider dangled on a silken thread to gather a closer look, too. The thing inside Desiree that wanted out tugged inwards and pushed outwards, the force so violent and sudden Desiree sensed a kind of simultaneous death and birth. Her arms drew inwards and her legs felt as if they were shrinking beneath her. The long hair that usually brushed down her back to her waist changed into a feathery down-like feeling that seemed to cover her entire torso. Her mouth, her nose, her eyes, all took on an unfamiliar elongated feel, and, although she wanted to, she couldn't scream. She tried repeatedly, until a piercing "caw" escaped from her. She froze, so terrified of the sound and what it signified that she couldn't wrap the mind that was still so clearly her own around this altered reality. The voice that she suddenly heard in her head had frightening familiarity.

"You truly *are* my daughter. I, too, enjoy the feel of a crow's skin, the shiny black feathers, the intelligent eyes, very attractive, not to mention how wonderful flight can be when fleeing the scene of some mischief."

Desiree slowly moved what had been arms just moments earlier, lifting herself onto the dressing table chair, and peering into the mirror, she saw the truth. What *am* I? She thought.

"My progeny, an old legend born anew while everyone was busy forgetting and ruling magic out of the world," the crow replied with haughty superiority. "Now come, my gorgeous girl-child, do you not have a score to settle?"

Desiree glimpsed the crow on the window sill in the mirror's reflection, and for an instant its shape undulated and the form of a man sitting with one leg crossed casually over the other smiled and winked.

"Recognize me now, my dear?" he teased, as he twirled a blade of switch grass between long slender fingers. Then the image shifted, and a crow again perched, breast feathers fluffed, wings spread.

What does he want from me?

"Let us fly into the night and see what tricks a father can teach his precocious princess, shall we?"

Why now? Why not before, when I was a child?

"Everything in its own time. Your time arrived tonight. You have come into your power. It's your choice to do with it what you will," the crow answered, and preened a feather from its wing.

Desiree walked along the edge of the dressing table, the crow aspect of her being admiring the shiny, colorful necklaces and bracelets that spilled out of her cedar jewelry box, and hopped onto the sill beside the creature who claimed to be her father. Was it *really* all so strange, this black-winged confessor, appearing to confirm what she had suspected since their first encounter in the dance circle? Somehow, hadn't she always known that, in the Stark family puzzle, she was the piece that did not quite fit? The acquisition of power was the ultimate game-changer, was it not? Without knowledge of how long her new ability might last, she decided that she shouldn't squander precious seconds, so Desiree nodded her glossy black head at the crow, and the fat spider that sat beside him, turned, and flew out the window, into the night.

Despite its newness, flight seemed natural, and Desiree landed easily upon the giant cottonwood branch that shadowed the barn. The crow soon arrived, the spider balanced on its feathery neck like a bizarre bareback rider, and they too, positioned themselves on the great limb.

"Intriguing," the crow said, when he saw the flashes of deviousness running through Desiree's thoughts. "Only *my* girl could possess such guile."

No one had taken residency in the garage apartment yet; in order to comply with city code, the electrical system still required upgrades. Only a few pieces of the Stark's cast-off furniture occupied the rooms within: a floral print sleeper sofa that had been replaced by a "more masculine" leather model; a pair of white wicker night stands, also discards of Leonard's fragile male ego; and the small dinette set that had been in their kitchen until the twins were born and the family had outgrown it. Through the bare kitchen window, with a crow's keen vision, Desiree surveyed the round wood veneer table and ladder-back chairs. The sight triggered an unwanted thought, a thought so detached and incongruous to this moment, to these motives, and to the malaise that had delivered her here, that she spread her wings and flapped from the tree, refusing to permit a silly, sentimental memory derail her from exacting her revenge. She lit on the exterior stairway, beside a lower garage window, and her odd companions joined her.

"Oh, look," the crow commented, as he nodded at the three-inch gap. "Mr. IronHorse has conveniently left this window ajar for you, darling."

The space was much too small; she couldn't hope to squeeze through. The crow hopped over and poked its beak through the opening.

"One could lose precious plumage attempting to cram through there. That is … if you're going to give it a go as a bird."

The crow grinned wickedly, and once again Desiree Stark felt pyre-like heat building inside her.

When the fire of transformation subsided, Desiree flexed eight long, nimble legs, scurried across the step, up the wall, and onto the window ledge.

"Some creatures eat their young. Did you know that, little daughter?" said the crow sardonically, as its hooked beak nudged Desiree. "But I'm *not* hungry, and besides … I find you more amusing than edible."

Desiree glanced around and wondered what had become of their silent spider companion. Perhaps the crow had no appetite because he had already dined. Before she could further contemplate the notion, the fat black spider dropped down on a silky strand, and came to rest next to her. The crow rolled its bottomless black eyes.

"Tsk! Tsk! My own daughter thinks no better of me than that? Our web savvy friend is here to assist us in your mission of mayhem. The cunning criminal kills the accomplice only *after* the crime has been committed. Honestly, Desiree, are you completely hopeless?"

The words slashed at her pride with a cold savagery that she had only ever experienced from Anita, and the pain thrust her thoughts back to the place from which she had, just minutes before, escaped. Her mind took her upstairs, to the relinquished table and chairs, and the memories that were attached to them.

"She's hopeless, Leonard," Anita had snapped. "This is a total waste of my time and my sanity!"

She shoved away from the table, scattering the multiplication flash cards. Dumb-struck, Leonard and a tearful Desiree were left to figure out how the little girl would pass the elementary math class. Patience and a tolerance for imperfection were not among Anita Stark's strong points, so after several minutes of ripping cards from the deck with a motion that grew increasingly vicious with each wrong answer, and several accusations that Desiree wasn't trying hard enough, she had made the snap decision that her child's mathematical ability was beyond improvement. Drying Desiree's face with a napkin, Leonard pulled a chair next to hers, and said, "You are the smartest girl I know, and you're certainly not hopeless. Learning the multiplication tables takes time. It says it right here on the cards."

He picked up the laminated learning deck and chose one. He pointed at the number, the symbol, and the next number with a large blunt finger.

"See," he said. "Ten *times* ten, that's a lot of time."

She had smiled at his silly joke, the same jape that he made each evening of the many evenings that they sat at the round table, Leonard calmly working through the deck, Desiree memorizing the correct answers until, at last, she had mastered the skill. One night, Leonard had returned from the plant late to find his daughter's multiplication final, complete with gold star, upon the place mat at his usual spot. From her own chair, Desiree grinned. It had been one of their proudest moments, one of their happiest memories.

"Isn't that touching?" the crow said, its voice like an oily pollutant, invading and clouding Desiree's recollection. "Your dearly departed mother was always impressive in her practicality. Didn't you end up at a community college, love? The high school marks were a bit sub-par by university standards, were they not? Perhaps if your interests had been more upon studies, and less upon the opposite sex …."

The crow performed an excited jig, and cawed maniacally.

"Sex as sport; that fine trait can be attributed to both your mother and me. By the way, did sweet Anita ever come clean? Does poor old Leonard know that he's not the baker who put the first bun in her oven? Nonetheless, that's a dastardly deed for another day. In you go then!"

And with that, the crow, with a quick, sharp shove of the beak, launched Desiree through the open window. As with flight, natural instinct took over before she hit the cement floor, and she caught herself upon a rudimentary web that the silent spider had constructed. She waited, not certain of the next move, or what she might accomplish while in such an insignificant form, until the spider carefully spun its way towards the workbench, and Desiree followed. They crept over wrenches, around a neat row of paint cans, and over top a dented copper tea kettle full of assorted nuts and bolts, until they discovered the dark cramped cubby hole, hidden behind a drill bit set, for which the spider had been looking. That was where the most necessary item lay. That was where they came upon the box of matches.

Little flames of excitement danced in Desiree's tiny eyes. Wouldn't Isaac TwoBears be frustrated when he hears that all his handy work had turned to ash? Won't Jack and that sad puppy dog-eyed nephew of his be disappointed? She imagined that, eventually, after adding the stress of cleaning up the damage, Gus and Barb would feel that the Bordeaux boys had worn out their welcome, and ask them to take up housekeeping somewhere else. No one would get hurt; just annoyed, impatient, and entertainingly pissed off, the goals of any good trick.

"Come out, come out, wherever you are," the crow sang, and although the sing-song sound sent cold prickles through her, Desiree emerged from the pigeon hole. "I can't very well expect you to strike an Ohio Blue Tip with those eight skinny legs, now can I?"

The mutating blaze exploded within her again, and as it melted and fused all the particles of her being into a shape that she herself could not predict, a realization rose out of the chaotic conception. Desiree had command over neither her shifts, nor her shapes. The stifling heat rescinded and she felt the cool cement floor beneath bare human feet. The crow tapped a grating, rapid rhythm against the window, until she grudgingly gave it her attention.

"That's right, my observant offspring," the crow mocked. "You are but a piece upon my game board, a tantalizing tool within my bottomless bag of tricks. When I said that the power was yours, well … I lied. It's true, you do possess the switch, but only *I* can flip it."

In the sooty darkness of the garage, naked and chilled, Desiree suddenly forgot what had provoked her into this ever-more freakish fiasco. The crow became unnervingly still, its shiny onyx stare boring into her like drops of hot tar, as it said, "Revenge. It's what drew me. It's what transformed you. It's why we are here. Now, prove that you are worthy of being called my daughter!"

Something hardened within Desiree, and she hatefully seized the matches, a crushing compulsion to rise to her winged father's challenge shoving her blindly forward.

Look, Son," the crow said to the spider that now sat upon the window ledge. "She *is* one of us after all."

Desiree jerked her head towards the pair, and for a moment, she saw the familiar face of the grass dancer alongside that of a young boy, a few years older than Oscar and Owen, with a round, full face and eyes that resembled her own. And then she blinked, and the images shifted back into a crow and a spider.

"That's right, dear," the bird quipped. "Say hello to your little half-brother! Your mother wasn't the only lusty young lady to whom I've granted my special gift. This little fellow is what they call a chip off the old block. We have a wonderful time together."

In a gesture that might have been construed as affection had it not appeared so sinister, the crow clutched the spider with its clawed foot.

"Wouldn't you like to be a chip, too, Desiree?"

She paused, and a distant memory surfaced from the recesses and pinched that tender place she had once had for Leonard. The day her parents had brought the twins home, Desiree had watched with envious silence, as her daddy sat with an infant boy in each arm and remarked upon their resemblances.

"Owen has my funny ears, and Oscar has been cursed with my big goofy toes," he had joked, but the pride shining through the light-heartedness had made Desiree feel like a dissimilar interloper whose features now excluded her from this new and tightly-knit circle of paternal admiration.

Though Leonard had never stopped reminding her that she was "his special little girl," the genetic die had been cast, and she gradually adopted Anita's stance on Leonard and the twins: all three were symbols of misfortune. For Desiree, their mother's untimely demise seemed only to emphasize the point.

With steady fingers, she took a match from the box. She could be part of something greater, something more powerful. She would show those who had excluded her from their circles that she did not need their fragile forms of family or friendship. She did not need their warmth. She could light her own fire. The crow smiled, and Desiree struck the match. For an instant, she watched the flame consume the blue tip, and then, touching it to the neat rows of wooden sticks, she set the box ablaze.

19

To Light a Fire

Isaac set a stoneware plate piled with steak, roasted corn, and a leafy green salad tossed in his signature cilantro vinaigrette in front of Jack, and then settled himself on a plush floor pillow on the other side of the low, narrow Japanese-style table. Pouring some cabernet into Jack's glass and then his own, he raised the crystal stemware, offered up a sensuous smile, and said," To pleasure."

The surroundings attested to the fact that TwoBears strove for satisfaction of all five senses. The custom kitchen, which he had designed and remodeled, included handsome glass-front cherry wood cabinetry, with an impressive collection of Hopi pottery arranged atop the cupboards, a stainless steel six-burner range of which any gourmet chef would approve, and granite counters lined with bottles of high-quality olive oils, vinegars, and cooking wines. Isaac's refrigerator always contained his must-have splurges: imported cheeses, fresh herbs, organic wasabi almonds, mangos, and bars of dark chocolate. The kitchen opened onto the living/dining room, an eclectic blend of Asian minimalism and American man-cave comfort. The sectional sofa promised to swallow up anyone who reclined on it to watch a Sunday afternoon Vikings game on the big screen, while the delicately carved, black lacquered end table beside it featured a pair of hand-painted white egrets. A watercolor of a pierced sun dancer shared wall space with a shelf that held a piece of African Kente cloth, a jade Buddha, and an antique carpenter's level. The heady scent of Nag champa incense rolled from a brass holder shaped like a dragon, and Isaac's favorite playlist drifted from all corners, filling their space with an inviting ambiance.

No one could feel anything but good here, Jack thought. He lifted his glass, and said, "Yes, pleasure."

Their crystal softly clinked, and, in the background, Adele's soulful voice sang of setting fire to the rain.

The smooth way the younger man handled the sexual overtone quickened Isaac's pulse, and he felt himself growing hard. Dinner could wait. Setting the wine glass down, he jumped up from the pillow, and said, "Come on. I want to show you something."

"Really?" Jack said, letting a look linger just south of Isaac's inlaid belt buckle. "I'd like to see whatever you want to show me."

They moved into the hall; halfway between the living room and bedroom, Isaac had hung a shadow box which he had built to protect one of his most prized works of art, a nineteenth-century beaded pipe bag. The condoms were in the bedroom, his desired destination, but the nuisance memory of Barb StandingBull's encouragement to "take it slow" stopped Isaac for a moment, allowing Jack an out, if he wasn't quite ready to play out the scenes that kept popping in and out of Isaac's head like a peep show.

"I was on a demolition job, tearing down an old house out in White Bear Lake, and we ran across boxes of rotted books that had been left in the crawl space. As I was hauling one out, it broke and this fell out with all the junk," he said hurriedly, as he gestured at the sacred artifact safely displayed behind the spotless glass. "I suppose, from an ethical standpoint, I should have inquired, but I decided that if no one had cared any better for it than that, they did not deserve to have a piece of our culture."

While Isaac had been admiring the shadow box's content, Jack Bordeaux had been admiring the shadow of stubble along TwoBears' chin and above his lip. He had been taking in the curve of his ear and the tiny inlaid turquoise and silver stud against the soft brown lobe. His eyes had drifted back to the wall briefly, but had then returned to appreciate the strong sinuous cords of Isaac's neck.

"So you took what you wanted. Nothing wrong with that," Jack said, his voice a confident growl.

He captured Isaac's face in his hands and pressed and eager mouth to his lips. The conflagration of their first kiss unleashed a rush of heat so intense it felt as if the baked air of a brush fire swirled around them. With Jack as the initiator, all cautionary notions went blissfully up in smoke. For a breath, Isaac's eyes widened with euphoric surprise, then slid closed as his tongue responded to the delicious sensation of Jack's teeth quickly pulling at his lower lip, and he tangled his fingers into Bordeaux's long ponytail. Fervor drove them against the wall, Isaac's muscular thigh pleasurably pressed between the younger man's legs, as Jack kept him pinned, his mouth trailing to Isaac's throat.

Uncharacteristic to Jack's previous encounters, he asserted his mounting desire, empowered and unafraid of the way this man made him unashamedly hunger for complete physical and emotional nakedness. Isaac TwoBears was the shelter and the storm, the first lover with whom Jack had ever sensed he was both safe and sexually set free. His hands found Isaac's silver belt buckle, and grasping it, the question came short and hot against the other man's ear.

"Yes?"

The self-possessed, self-employed, self-motivated Isaac TwoBears, savoring this new, very rousing role in which he found himself, said in an urgent, pleading gasp of pure pleasure, "Yes, yes ... yes!"

Jack unclasped the belt and unbuttoned Isaac's jeans as Isaac tore away Jack's shirt. Shoving the denim down Isaac's thighs, Jack squatted, running the warm, wet tip of his tongue just above the waistband of boxer briefs. He could feel Isaac's erection push against his throat, and the loose khaki shorts he wore suddenly felt unbearably imprisoning.

"Get up," Isaac breathlessly urged. "The bed's in there."

TwoBears kicked the jeans off and left them on the floor. Stripping his shirt off, he tossed it somewhere near the bedroom door as they rushed towards the California king. In the muted light of dusk, a subtle scent of mesquite smoke drifting through the window, Isaac threw the sand and sage colored comforter aside, and they fell together into the turquoise green sheets. They shed their remaining pieces of clothing, all the while caressing, tasting, and breathing in each other's scent. Jack relinquished his earlier control, and Isaac fervently took charge. Though taller and heavier than his lover, Bordeaux allowed himself to stay pressed beneath Isaac's sinewy, muscled body, and the crush and grind of their hip, caused both men to grow more brazen as each moved ever closer to their combustion point. Hovering over Jack, Isaac's lips sucked aggressively at his ear lobe, and Jack felt the sensation travel to his loins like wild fire. TwoBears freed the ear lobe, and whispered, "What gets you off?"

Jack felt the heat of Isaac's hand as it slid between their bellies, finding, grasping, and then languidly stroking his stiff, sensitive flesh. He then searched through the sultry darkness until his teeth found a hardened nipple, and Bordeaux moaned. Smiling, Isaac worked his tongue unhurriedly down his young lover's ribs, circling the navel and flicking lightly across a hip. He paused then, and the anticipation of what both men wanted rose like waves of heat from sunbaked concrete, until he could no longer contain desire. Isaac's mouth covered Jack, and a thousand licks of fire swept over them.

Later, when both men were spent, they returned to the table, sprawled naked upon the floor pillows, and fed each other pieces of steak while they finished the bottle of wine. Rapturous post-orgasmic bliss ran through them like a drug, everything heightened by their lingering ecstasy, everything electrified by the unspoken promise that their night together, was long from over.

Cutting a bite-size chunk of ribeye, Isaac offered it to Jack, who took it from his fingers with his teeth. He chewed, a juicy grin spreading across his lips as he said, "Damn, this is even incredible cold. I proclaim you Grill Master."

Isaac took a long sip of wine, and then offered Jack another morsel.

"I love carpentry, but cooking is my secret passion. I'm a closet foodie."

"Fabulous in the bedroom and the kitchen," Jack teased, licking his lips with great exaggeration. "You're quite the catch, Mr. TwoBears."

"Taste this, it's one of my specialties."

Jack opened his mouth and accepted a fork full of salad greens, and then fell back, as if in a swoon, declaring, "I'm in love."

Both men paused, a brief uncomfortable moment hanging between them, until Isaac poured the last of the cabernet into Jack's glass, and said, "So ... what do you want to be when you grow up?"

Bordeaux had a year left at the university, and he had often thought that when he was finished he would study for the LSAT. Jack leaned on an elbow, and glanced at Isaac; few members of his family, excluding the very quizzical Seattle, had ever inquired about his life aspirations.

"I've considered tribal law," Jack said. "But I think it could be one of those careers where, after years of attempting change within a broken system, you end up as a bat-shit-crazy vigilante. Lately, I'm leaning towards elementary education. I've grown up poor and under-appreciated, so I figure that I'm already psychologically cut out to be a teacher."

"It's a noble profession, shaping the young minds, though I think it probably has a fairly high bat-shit-crazy risk factor, too."

"True enough. I've heard some of Gus' classroom horror stories, but, if it weren't for a couple of great teachers, Gus included, I could have been just another unfavorable American Indian drop-out statistic. I want to pay that forward."

In the background, a song faded, and another of Isaac's favorites began. Jack closed his eyes, smiled a broad grin, and moved his head to the rhythm, saying, "Best Zeppelin tune ever."

"No argument there," TwoBears said, as "Tangerine" transported him back several decades. "I have one of my best childhood memories attached to it."

With so few pleasant childhood recollections, Jack suddenly wondered what TwoBears' upbringing had been like, and he urged him to share the story.

"Money had gotten really tight, and my dad couldn't find a job, so, when he heard about an opportunity in Alaska, he left my mom, my sisters, and me here in Minneapolis, and went to work the pipeline. He was gone over a year, and when he came home, I remember Mom slipping and sliding down the driveway, and them falling into a snow bank. They didn't care who was watching; they just kept laughing and kissing and crying. That night, I woke to this song, and it really drew me, so I snuck out of bed. The Zeppelin album was playing on the turntable, and my parents were dancing. The way they were holding each other, with their eyes closed, swaying, it seemed magical, even spiritual. I knew it was their private moment, and that I should go back to bed, but seeing them lost in such a loving state, made me feel so happy, so safe, I couldn't pull myself away."

Jack lowered his gaze to the cigarette burn scars on his forearm as he struggled to relate, Isaac's story suddenly seeming like emotional hieroglyphics, and though he tried to hide his envy and resentment, some spilled over into the tone of his question, as he asked, "Are they still married?"

"Yes," Isaac smiled. "They've been together for forty years."

"I think my parents were together for about forty days," Jack said in an attempt at humor, which, when he heard it, only sounded sardonic. "You're lucky that your parents had their shit together."

Isaac shook his head, chuckled, and ran his fingers through his short dark hair.

"Don't be fooled; it wasn't all love songs and slow dances. About six months after that Zeppelin night, we found out about my little half-sister in Anchorage. I do believe that's when the "Tangerine" album mysteriously ended up on the living room floor in three pieces, along with a couple of broken dinner plates, and a smashed institutional-size jar of dill pickles."

"Sorry, man. I didn't mean to twist a warm family memory into something Bordeaux-tainted."

"No, every family has its own brand of dysfunction. They worked it out, stayed together, and, on a hot day, you can still detect the faint scent of garlic and vinegar rising from the carpet. I tease my mom about it. It couldn't have been a coincidence that she chose to create a pile of glass shards and such a phallic condiment right at my dad's feet. Seems like a pretty clear message to me."

Jack laughed, and then, shifting to a more serious vibe, cautiously inquired, "Do you want that, Isaac?"

"What? Vlasic-scented floor coverings?"

"No," Jack said. "Stability."

TwoBears exhaled, sensing that he must tread carefully if he were to head the direction that Bordeaux had taken the conversation.

"Isn't that what most people want, a "Tangerine" moment?"

Jack nodded, and, to the relief of both men, the song ended. As the first few notes of the next selection introduced the beat of a G-Street Club favorite, Jack raised a brow.

"Really, TwoBears? Lady GaGa?"

Isaac shrugged, saying, "What can I say? I proudly embrace some of the stereotypes. There's a dream catcher hanging from my rear view mirror, I own a pair of moccasins, and I saw "Rent" at the Ordway ... twice."

"Any rainbow stickers?" Jack teased, rubbing the bottom of Isaac's foot with a big toe.

"No stickers. I have a jean jacket with a beaded rainbow shield across the back."

"Awesome!" Jack laughed. "Two stereotypical birds, one stone … fucking clever!"

Isaac rolled closer, propped himself on one elbow, gave Jack his best "fuck me" stare, and sang, "I want your leather-studded kiss in the sand."

20

The Nature of Nurturing

Fire licked at the tips of Desiree Stark's fingers, singeing the painted nails black, and she hurled the flaming box into a plastic bin half full of newspapers and cardboard. Gleefully, the crow threw its head back and cawed. She couldn't have chosen better kindling. But the expected inferno did not ensue. The previous night's rain had swept in the open window, soaking the piles of recyclable paper. Only clouds of smelly black smoke billowed from the container, causing Desiree to cough as the garage quickly filled with the choking substance. Through the rain's entrance, the acrid odor exited, and the crow, the spider again on its back, launched from the sill and made their escape. Trickster had no time for those whose dirty deeds ended with such disappointment.

Pawing at her eyes, Desiree tried in vain to locate the crow through the thickening smoke. She drew in a raw breath, and rasping, she called out, "Father! Help me!"

But no shift to safety came, only more layers of suffocating smoke, and the wretched realization that he had abandoned her. Dropping to her hands and knees, the gritty cement scraping her skin, Desiree crawled alone through the darkness, towards what might be a way out. She must deliver herself from her own fire.

The table and chairs drifted into her light-headed thoughts, along with a sense of odd relief that they, unlike her, were impervious to the consequences of her folly. Her hands found a door jamb, and she groped for locks and latches as consciousness seemed to float further from her reach, and a long-forgotten, bitter-sweet memory resurfaced.

She had placed the cake in the center of the table, and Leonard had lit the birthday candles. They were alone; Anita always seemed to have other plans on this day. That afternoon, Desiree had walked to the grocery, the contents of her piggy bank stuffed in her pockets, and purchased the Pillsbury mix. She phoned Grandmother Stark, who had initially refused, but eventually instructed the seven-year-old. By Leonard's return from work, a single layer chocolate cake, complete with a rudimentary frosted message, waited for him. His tears welled when he saw Desiree, her broad smile missing a front tooth, and the thin, sweet lines of icing that read, "I love Daddy."

As the smoke swirled around her like a deadly cocoon, and all her worlds collided and crumbled, Desiree Stark felt herself falling, and whispered, "Dad … help me."

***

Leonard sniffed, and then, lifting his head from the couch's armrest, craned towards the patio screen door, saying, "Do you smell smoke?"

Maggie unwrapped from his embrace, sat up, and breathed in deeply.

"Yes," she said, wrinkling her nose. "It reminds me of when my dad used to burn garbage in our farm's trash pit. That's not good. Whatever's burning shouldn't be."

Certain that he had extinguished the clay chimney's embers, Leonard felt assured that he wasn't the cause, but the pungent stench wafting through the night air triggered something primal, something protective, something purely paternal.

"Would you go check on the boys?"

Maggie stood, straightened her blouse, and headed downstairs. He trusted Owen, but Oscar had a defiant side, and though Seattle seemed a respectful and gracious kid, Leonard knew that the boy had been subjected to way too much destructive behavior. Maggie returned a few minutes later to say that all was well, and that Oscar had requested some of her "killer nachos." Leonard raised his brows and frowned.

"It's all right," she said as she entered the kitchen and took a cheese grater from the drawer. "He asked very nicely … even said please. What can I say, Leonard, the boys have their father's irresistible charm."

"I'm going out back," Leonard said. He passed Maggie, gave her rear end a playful squeeze, and planted a kiss on her cheek. "That smoky smell is getting worse."

Crossing the yard, Leonard detected motion just beyond the chain link fence and spotted a pair of dogs laying waste to a neighbor's trash bags. The animals moved from the shadows, revealing their true identities, and Leonard stark froze. The larger coyote quit tearing at a fried chicken carcass, and turned to lock eyes with him; the intensity of its shrewd stare causing a chilled sweat to rise on the man's thick neck. The wily creature held the gaze for a moment longer, and then threw its toothy jaws open in a yipping howl. Lifting its filthy muzzle from the plunder, the smaller coyote joined the eerie requiem. Leonard wondered if more lurked nearby and would answer their call, but when the pair fell silent, the only sound that followed was the slow creak of door hinges. The larger coyote growled, nipped at the other's hind leg, and they fled into the darkness.

The noxious smoke rolled down the alley, and, suddenly aware of its origin, Leonard sprinted to the gate, shoved it open, and whirled to witness his greatest fear.

She lay face-down on the ground, her upper body in the gravel entrance, her legs still inside the partially opened door. The senseless sight propelled Leonard with a speed and agility that the slow, maladroit man had never before known. He was scooping his daughter into his arms and carrying her away from the smoke that, though lessening, still reached from the garage's interior like the murderous tendrils of some evil entity, before his mind had time to catch up and question it all. When he had deposited her gently onto their lawn, she gasped and began to cough until she retched. Her lids fluttered, and, seeing Leonard's panic-stricken face, she tried to speak, but more fits of harsh hacking choked back the words.

Through the kitchen window, Maggie saw the unsettling scene, and ran outside, the couch blanket in one hand, her cell phone in the other. Leonard took the star quilt and wrapped it around the naked girl as Maggie dialed 911. In between deep painful hacks, Desiree mumbled something about tables and chairs and needing the fire department, but no ambulance. Leonard held her close, saying, "Desiree, sweetheart, you need medical attention!"

As if the words carried an additional burst of oxygen to her lungs and brain, Desiree forced back the overwhelming urge to cough, and, with strength founded in a deep sense of dread, insisted, "I do *not* want an ambulance. I'll be fine!"

Maggie had the phone to her ear. It rang once … twice. Something pleading shown through the young woman's protest. What was the girl afraid of? In the darkness, Desiree's hand found Maggie's and squeezed, not in a threatening way, as the woman would have expected, but in a way that expressed true urgency. Maggie's intuition told her that the urgency involved a secret, a secret Maggie was being asked to keep. She owed this girl nothing; Desiree had never missed an opportunity to insult her. The woman was well aware of the one-sided turf war waged against her, including the cruel little nickname she heard often whispered under Desiree's breath,. Maggie had met the girl's late mother, and, at several of the plant's Christmas parties, observed Anita's intolerable tendencies towards the members of their gender. She had been the quintessential "mean girl" and Desiree's primary role model. Always calculating this, along with the immense impact of losing a mother, Maggie made allowances when it came to Desiree's rudeness. More importantly, she knew that Leonard Stark adored his daughter, and Maggie Gustafson adored *him*. Anything that hurt Desiree would most surely land a thousand times harder blow upon her devoted father.

It was a risk. The girl could have smoke inhalation, though her years as a volunteer EMT told Maggie that every fresh breath the girl took seemed to improve her situation. The phone rang a third time, an operator answered, and she went with her gut.

"Fire," she said, when asked the emergency, and then repeated the next question, her eyes focused upon Desiree's face. "Is anyone hurt or inside the building?"

Desiree shook her head. Maggie looked challengingly at her, and Leonard's expression darkened. The girl shook her head again.

"No," Maggie said, praying that she had not horribly underestimated Desiree Stark's potential for immorality as she pressed the phone's end button.

Maggie expected Leonard to balk, but he had grown strangely silent, as if locked in deep concentration. The fact that they had not seen the girl descend from her room, though they had a clear view of the stairs, her nakedness, and how she ended up sprawled outside their neighbor's garage spurred more suspicions than Leonard wanted to confront in the wake of a diverted tragedy. Distant sirens wailed, and with actions more protective than prudent, he shoved aside the troubling particulars, plucked Desiree from the ground, and spirited her into the house. Following, Maggie slid the vertical blinds closed behind them, as he placed his daughter on the couch.

With chilling seriousness, he turned to Maggie. "Watch her. I'll be back."

Taking the phone from the woman's hand, he kissed her, and stepped into the kitchen. She heard him tell Gus that they had smelled smoke, that he had checked it out, and that the fire department was en route. She couldn't help but notice however, that he kept his daughter's name absent from the details. Maggie drew a hassock next to the couch and took Desiree by the hand.

"I used to be a medic. I'm qualified. May I at least check you? Smoke exposure can be very dangerous."

The younger woman started to pull away, but stopped when Maggie clutched her hand a bit tighter and said more softly, but with greater authority, "We can still call an ambulance, if you prefer."

Secrets required cooperation amongst their keepers, something that gave Maggie a new degree of power, a new degree of respect. But as she examined the pallor of Desiree's fingers and toes, peered into her nostrils and throat for signs of soot, and placed an ear to the girl's chest to listen to her breathing, the woman's conscience whispered of ill-gotten gain and of secrecy's ugly relative, dishonesty.

Leonard returned and sat on the floor, brushing his daughter's hair with a large callused palm, and then looked to Maggie for some reassurance. She placed an arm around his broad, sagging shoulders, and said, "She looks surprisingly good. We'll keep an eye on her for a couple of days, to watch for symptoms. So far, Desiree, it appears that you're a very lucky young woman."

He could have lost her. Suddenly, the thought toppled the huge man, and he took his oldest child into his arms. Both father and daughter sobbed, as if coming so close to loss had allowed them to find something, and through the tears, Desiree spoke words that, in recent years, Leonard Stark had rarely heard her use.

"I'm so sorry! I love you, Dad. Thank you. I love you."

Quietly, Maggie rose and went to the kitchen. She understood loss; five miscarriages and a divorce had taught her well. But her Presbyterian upbringing had taught her about "closed doors" and "opened windows," and, as she finished topping tortilla chips with pepperjack cheese, she reminded herself that her move to the city, the job at the plant, and her dear, sweet Leonard would never have been parts of her story, had she not lost. Sometimes, beauty grew from beneath ashes.

From the alley, the low rumble of a fire truck's engine extinguished the lovely thought. Too many questions. Not enough answers. Love could cover up imperfections, but could it cover up a crime? Maggie felt her jaw habitually tighten, and a phrase drifted into her thoughts. Ashes to ashes. As gray and ominous as fallout, the sentiment blanketed the mood, shifting it from serious to somber. She could see the lights of police cars throwing splashes of color across the dark lawn where she, Leonard, and Desiree had made their silent pact. Fearful, Maggie drew the kitchen curtains closed and slowly backed away from the window, and, with trembling hands, placed the nachos in the microwave. She watched the plate rotate, the cheese melting, bubbling, turning brown, as, under her breath, she uttered a prayer.

When she had delivered the snack to the oblivious boys, who were, as they had been since they came indoors, engrossed in some online medieval fantasy game, Maggie found Leonard with the cell phone at his ear, nodding and pacing. Desiree drew her knees up and offered her a seat on the couch. Maggie sat, noticing that the girl still smelled accusingly of smoke. The brief phone conversation concluded, and Leonard turned. The two women, beautiful polar opposites of one another, the feminine powers that seemed to keep his whole world balanced, both looked at him, full of tortured expectation.

"The fire is out. No one was hurt."

Some of the tension drained from Maggie's face, but Desiree remained edgy

As she asked, "What about the apartment?"

"Some minor smoke damage to the garage. The upstairs will need to be aired out, but it's fine."

Desiree's mouth tightened, she nodded, and tears ran down her cheeks, leaving their wet marks upon the red, yellow, black, and white quilt wedges. She pulled the blanket closer. This quilt, like the table and chairs, had their stories forever woven into its fabric. It was where she had hosted tea parties, Leonard and her stuffed animals as guests, where the big man had awkwardly sat cross-legged, a tiny plastic saucer between thumb and index finger, as he raved about the contents of each empty cup she poured. It had served as the roof of many a couch cushion fort he had built for her, despite Anita's protestations. On cold winter nights, she had cuddled beneath it, on his lap, as he read her books about a velveteen rabbit, about wild things, and about a tree that gave and gave. When he had finished the picture books, he told her about how his grandfather had taught him to harvest wild rice and how to tap the maples for making syrup. He told her about their people's language and how some Ojibwe words had become part of the English dictionary. For a long time after, they had given each other a satisfied wink, every time they heard someone say "raccoon," "moccasin," or "moose." Tonight, once again, he had, with the star quilt, with his arms, with love beyond conditions, protectively sheltered her. She must, for him, do the same.

Clearing her throat, she started, "Dad, I want to explain," she paused, knowing that the words must be chosen carefully, and the truth avoided at any cost; not for her sake, but for his sake, the sake of her father. "I didn't mean for—"

Leonard raised his hands, shook his head, and said, "No, Desiree. I think the three of us know what happened, if we're ever asked."

As the women, who held separate, yet equal, parts of his heart, listened, he took command as story teller, protector, father. When he had finished, he said, "I believe that's the sequence of events, don't you?"

Maggie agreed. Shocked at this previously hidden, darker aspect of Leonard's personality, Desiree slowly nodded, too.

"In the case, that no one witnessed your attempts to help our neighbors," he said, his glance resting upon his daughter's face, "we won't speak of this, again."

And as the three concurred, a spider crawled through a hole in the kitchen screen and began to weave a web.

21

Afterglow

Barb awoke to the scents of minty fresh breath and aloe vera shaving cream, and the sensation of Gus IronHorse whispering sweet nothings into her ticklish ears.

"Good morning, Miss StandingBull. I'm here to finish your massage. We were so rudely interrupted last night, and I never like to leave my favorite clients dissatisfied."

"Favorite clients plural?" Barb teased, as she rolled into his arms. "I'd better be your only client, favorite or otherwise."

Gus ran a hand down her back until he reached a bare cheek, where he stopped and cupped its lovely roundness.

"Oh, you're a favorite, baby."

"I must be," Barb said, running a finger lightly across his cheek. "You shaved."

"I aim to please. Now, what position would you like to assume for your massage's happy ending?"

Throwing a supple thigh over his hip, she pushed him onto his back, and straddled him. She learned early on that IronHorse's massage offers always started as such, but never ended with just her back, and simply having a knot rubbed from her shoulder upon request was almost unheard of, but last night, she had wanted Gus' version. The morning had only strengthened her desire.

Though Jack and Seattle were exemplary guests, Gus and Barb had looked forward to the ultimate privacy of an empty house. As Isaac and Jack pulled out of the driveway and Leonard returned home with the three boys, Gus had grinned salaciously as he pressed against her and said, "Now you're free to cry out my name, as loud as you like."

Gus had always joked that StandingBull's boisterous bedroom tendencies would have made her ill-equipped for traditional Lakota teepee living. Smoking a buffalo hide could make it waterproof, but, he was pretty sure, it didn't make it soundproof.

"Oh, Mr. IronHorse, you have to earn that honor. Up to the challenge?" she had retorted, as she leaned into him, making sure her rear end connected with just the right spot, before nimbly side-stepping him, and flitting away.

After a late dinner of citrus marinated shrimp and angel hair pasta, Gus had encouraged her to go relax while he washed the dishes, saying, "When I'm done, I'll treat you to one of my world-class massages."

But the fire, the questions and authorities that accompanied it, and nervous tension, had squelched the passion, and when they hit the sheets for the second time, their need for sex lost to a crushing need for sleep.

Now, well rested, neither mind lingered on that fire.

He slid inside of her, and, as she moved, the tips of her long soft hair brushed his chest, sending chills across his skin. Dawn light spilled into the room and painted their nakedness as they found their familiar rhythm. They lost themselves in the long sumptuous dance, savoring the prolonged pleasure of each other's flesh. When at last she neared climax, StandingBull tossed back her head, arched her spine, and he felt the caress of her swaying hair against his inner thigh. No longer able to refrain, IronHorse thrust upwards in release, as he cried out her name.

***

Jack Bordeaux awoke to the faint scent of eucalyptus and the happy sound of Isaac TwoBears singing in the shower of the master bath. He tried to judge the time by the light streaming through the bedroom window; it seemed early. Rolling onto his back, he stretched, yawned, thought about getting up to try his hand at Isaac's complicated-looking coffee machine, but the bed's crazy comfort kept him there. He had never slept in one so luxurious. Then the thought hit him, diminishing some of the serene softness. He had slept here, in Isaac's bed ... all night. Something in his chest began to jog, then sprint, and he scrambled to find shorts, suddenly thinking that he'd rather face the espresso machine at that moment than TwoBears. Yanking on the first thing he found, he hurried to the kitchen before the singing and the shower ended.

Jack fumbled through the cupboard above the machine. Finding a bag of whole beans, he opened them, spilling several, which he then knocked on the floor as he tried to sweep them back into the bag. What did it mean? He had never slept at a guy's house, not all night. He scanned the kitchen. Where the hell was the grinder? You didn't put the beans in the damn thing whole, did you? What was he going to say to Isaac? How many beans did you use? Had he ever wanted to leave Isaac's bed last night, or had the best sex he'd ever had just put him into a coma afterwards?

"Shit!" he said, tipping and spilling the beans again as he tried to locate where they went into the coffee maker.

"Not a morning person?"

Jack whirled, sending a few beans to the floor, to find Isaac leaning against the door jamb, smiling. He had a burgundy towel tucked around his hips, and a few drops of water still ran down his torso, as if he had hastened to the scene of a potential espresso machine murder. He looked so damn sexy Jack couldn't do anything but stare while a few more beans plinked against the tiles. Casually, Isaac walked around them, kissed Jack, and invited him to take a stool at the island. He went to the freezer and took out another bag of coffee beans, saying, "This is where I keep the good stuff."

Extracting a grinder from the corner cabinet, he placed it on the counter, pushing aside the spilled beans.

"My sister gifted me those," he said, pushing some more aside with a bare foot. "Nice thought, but they're flavored with something coffee just should not be flavored with. Mango strawberry, I think. I keep it for when she comes for a visit. I brew her a really strong pot. She hates it. It's subtle encouragement to not buy it for me ever again."

When the coffee was underway, he sat on a stool across from Jack. The scent of eucalyptus rose from his bare skin, and Jack flashed upon the previous night's most erotic moments. His attraction for this man was so strong, Jack hoped it wouldn't find him acting a careless, or, perhaps worse yet, an overly cautious, fool.

"I bake some mean blueberry muffins, if you're interested," Isaac said, and then, noticing Jack's nervous little twitch, added, "Unless you need to get back. I know this was Seattle's first sleepover."

TwoBears saw Jack's archetypal deer in the headlights response to the comment, and hazarded a guess.

"Your first sleepover, too, Jack?"

Bordeaux's expression softened from scared shitless to sheepish, which touched all Isaac's sensitive and sexual places. Slow down, TwoBears told himself. *You're falling too fast.*

"It's true," Jack said. "This is out of my comfort zone."

"Is that a bad thing?"

"No, just unfamiliar territory."

After Madesio, Jack had eventually convinced himself that sex detached from emotional trappings could cure his physical needs. With a poorly-rendered fake ID, he spent weekends prowling the clubs, where he found what he had been looking for in men's room stalls and after-hours parties. With acceptance to the university, a time shortage took him away from the downtown scene. Once, with no intention of attending, he had sat at a study cubical and watched the GLBT student group participants as they filed into the assigned meeting room. At the gathering's conclusion, he spotted a young man leaving alone. Jack made eye contact and smiled. A couple of hours later, he exited the guy's dorm room, hopped a bus to work, and washed away the guilt of having introduced himself as "Madesio" with a mental plunge into the pages of a geology text. Jack couldn't even categorize the encounter with the freshman, eight months earlier, within the same universe as last night with Isaac TwoBears. After surviving on something sexually akin to fast food, Isaac seemed like five-star cuisine, satisfying and complete, and, in its perfection, damned unnerving.

"Don't fear what you want," Isaac said. "There's no rules to break here. I respect the pace you want to set. The last thing I want to do is to complicate your life."

Jack nodded, feeling the man's sincerity catching him like a safety net. *I could love him*, Jack thought, before he could barricade the inspiration behind past experience's cynicism.

"Now, since I'm starving, and, in my honest opinion, home-made muffins do *not* symbolize an impending marriage proposal, can I please pour us some java and make some breakfast?"

"I'd like that. Thanks," Jack replied, ignoring the tug of war between what he truly wanted and his fear of losing it.

With nothing less than impish joy, Isaac leaned across the counter, stole a kiss, and said, "By the way, you look really good in *my* underwear!"

Jack looked down at the black boxer briefs, blushed, and then grinned. He loved this man.

22

Aftermath

Leonard Stark awoke late morning to the sound of gunfire and detonating explosives, and the delectable aroma of waffles. He groaned, rolled out of bed, and tugged on jeans and a T-shirt. In front of the bathroom mirror he surveyed the damage. A few more gray hairs, check. Deeper lines across the forehead, check. Dark, baggy circles under the eyes, check. Sighing, he grabbed a toothbrush and turned on the water as he cast his gaze away from the sleep-deprived image and tried not to think of the reason for its lack of rest. Though Maggie had encouraged him and promised that she would regularly check on Desiree, Leonard had tossed about, grappling with his conscience, until the early morning hours, when sleep finally overtook him. He rinsed his mouth, threw some cold water on his face, and ran his wet hands over his short, unruly hair. From the kitchen, he heard Maggie sweetly warning Oscar that she thought he had enough butter for two waffles, whereupon the boy insisted that every square had to contain butter and syrup or he couldn't eat it. Time to send in some parental reinforcement.

Leonard found the boys in the living room, trays in front of them, gorging themselves as they bounced and slammed against the back of the couch with every loud blast coming from the television.

"What are you guys watching?" he asked, as more sirens, gunfire, and burning rubber sent Owen into a hyper frenzy.

"*Die Hard,*" Oscar shouted, sending a huge glob of chewed waffle onto his plate.

"Super gross!" Owen said to his brother with obvious admiration, and then stuffing half a sausage patty in his mouth, said, "Seattle's never seen it, Dad."

Leonard frowned, and said, "Oscar! Owen! Show a little couth. If you're talking, no chewing. If your chewing, no talking. Got it?"

"Did you say show a little tooth?" Oscar chimed in, a hunk of waffle hanging from his shit-eating grin.

"You're poking a grizzly bear with a stick this morning, kid. Better shape up"

Oscar caught the tone, closed his mouth, and chewed up the waffle. Leonard stalked off to the kitchen, and Seattle said in a quiet voice, "Your dad looks kind of pissed off today."

"Yeah," Oscar said. "He probably didn't get any last night."

The three boys cracked up, snorting at Oscar's obscene hand gestures.

"How did you manage not to kill them yet?" Leonard asked as he wrapped his arms around Maggie's waist and kissed her.

"I grew up with younger brothers, so I've seen most of the plays out of the pubescent boy handbook. Fart competitions, belching wars, and all their other wretched forms of entertainment, including obnoxious pranks, are nothing new to me. Did I ever tell you what my brothers did on prom night?"

She offered him a plate full of waffles and sausage.

"No," Leonard said, seating himself at the table. "Whatever it was, you'd better whisper. Those hellions don't need any more ideas."

She poured a cup of coffee and sat down, leaning closer, as she looked over her shoulder, where the boys seemed fully engrossed in gratuitous violence.

"I was getting ready for junior prom, and, my brother Jason, I think he was twelve, ran into my room and swiped my dress off the closet door. Dad was out in the fields, planting, and Mom had run to town to buy film for the camera, so I thought we were alone. I chased the little shit down stairs, outside onto the front porch, and into the yard, before I realized the two neighbor boys were parked there on their dirt bikes."

"What did they do, take your dress and ride off with it?"

"No, they were too busy gawking at the seventeen-year-old girl who was standing there in a red lace push-up bra and thong panties."

Leonard knew that he shouldn't, but simply couldn't stop himself, as he burst into laughter.

"Oh, wait. It gets worse. I turned to run back into the house, but Paul, the eleven-year-old, had locked the front door. About that time, Mom arrives home. The boys, of course, were in serious trouble, but so was I."

"Really? Why?"

Shifting into a haughty, righteous voice, Maggie imitated, "Maggie Elizabeth Gustafson! You go upstairs and put on some proper undergarments. No daughter of mine is attending prom looking like a prostitute!"

She had tried to salvage her intimates with the argument that no one would know she had them on under her dress, a point that backfired when her mother raised a suspicious brow and asked, "Then your white cotton panties will be just fine, won't they?"

Grinning, Leonard said, "What a bad girl! Do you still have that thong?"

Her cheeks turned pink at the thought, out of fear of Leonard actually viewing her body at this age in such apparel, but also out of pleasure in the notion that he wanted it. She asked how he liked the waffles.

"Awesome," he said, heartily cutting into the stack.

"I put some aside for Desiree. She's still sleeping. I checked on her a half hour ago. Everything looks good, Leonard."

Some of the light faded from the man's eyes, and he slowly shook his head, saying, "Where did I go wrong?"

He turned toward the living room, and then looked back with a pained expression. The boys needed more discipline, less indulgence; Desiree, the same. Suddenly, he wondered if the kids had received enough counseling after their mother's death. When it came to the children, was his new relationship with Maggie beneficial or detrimental? He had rolled through fatherhood for years, thinking, for the most part, that the track seemed functional, but now it felt as if his parenting skills drastically needed reassessment.

Maggie laid a gentle hand on his arm. "You're a good dad, Leonard. Don't make yourself crazy trying to unravel all the questions and find reasonable answers. I doubt you'll ever find them. Just start from today. This is Day One."

The loving support of a woman still felt foreign after decades of his mother's and Anita's destructive criticism, but Leonard Stark decided he could certainly get used to it. He took the dishes, rinsed them, and placed them in the washer. Laying his strong hands on Maggie's shoulders, he kneaded, the touch releasing all her tension, and then he turned her chair, knelt, taking her hands in his.

"I love you," he said, his look so earnest and pleading Maggie felt tears welling.

It was the first time he had said those words, and although the din of whooping boys and fast-paced action movie music seemed like an out of sync soundtrack for a moment like this, it felt perfect, and she kissed him full on the mouth.

"I love you, too."

"Day One"

"Yes," she said, hazel eyes alive with adoration. "Day One."

***

That afternoon, Leonard ventured out the back door, through the gate, and down the alley. The garage's two big doors stood open, as well as all the apartment windows, and Leonard heard several fans running. He stepped into the vacant garage and looked around; no signs of fire remained, only a very faint smoky odor. Exiting, he circled to the back yard, where he found Gus and Barb sharing a late lunch on the patio.

Hey, there's the man," Gus shouted, when he spotted him. "And check out that shirt!"

A bit befuddled, Leonard shrugged, saying, "I think it's a clear cut case of false advertising, but Maggie gave it to me, and as long as she thinks so, well …."

Barb squinted at the blindingly white shirt and said, "What does the writing say?"

"Tell her, buddy. That way, when she gets me mine, she'll know what to ask for."

Clearly embarrassed, Leonard mumbled, "It says, Here Comes One Good-Looking Indian!"

"That's a righteous shirt, Brother. I'm serious. I need one of those, baby," Gus pulled up a chair for Leonard.

Barb smiled and said, "Sure, honey. I'll talk to Maggie. Would you like some lunch, Leonard? I have some tuna salad and honeydew melon."

Leonard graciously declined. "I went overboard on Maggie's waffles this morning. I'm still full." Then, feeling the moisture leave his mouth as the distant hum of fans reminded him of why he had come, he added, "A glass of water would be great, though."

Barb rose and went inside, saying, "It's the least we can do for our hero."

Leonard winced at the praise of which he felt unworthy. A stifling guilt, as suffocating as if he himself had lit the blaze, tossed acid into his gut. Pressing a fist to the spot below the sternum, he accepted the burn as reparation, and said, "Do you need help cleaning up?"

Gus shook his head, "Thanks, man, but it wasn't too big of a deal when it was all said and done. A little smoke is all. Fan's are taking care of that."

"Really?" Leonard said, his parched tongue impeding him from saying more.

Barb returned and offered him a large tumbler of ice water. He took it and, with two huge swallows, drank half.

"We lucked out," Barb said with a smile, as she laid the white cane under the table and patted IronHorse's back. "Gus left the garage window open when it rained a couple of nights back. It kept the fire small and smoky. A happy accident."

Gus tossed a chunk of melon in his mouth and shrugged. "I told Barb she has to quit sneaking out to the barn to smoke pot. We got impressionable young men living here now."

Barb rolled her eyes, playfully slugged Gus in the arm, and said, "Come on, Gus. We all know you're the midnight toker in this family."

Their levity plucked at his knotted conscience, and Leonard felt a hint of a smile, as he remembered several mellow evenings he had spent on this very patio, he and Gus passing a joint and swapping dude stories.

"Actually," Barb said, "the fire fighters think some underage kids might have been using the stairs beside that window as a place to hide out and smoke Marlboros. They found a few cigarette butts in the alley not far from the steps."

Although random trash strewn in the narrow lane that divided the block wasn't unusual, or, in Leonard's opinion, a valid connection to an accidental fire, he nodded, looked at a ragged hangnail he had inadvertently been digging at, wiped the bloody finger on his jeans, and asked, "Any idea about the kids involved?"

As soon as the words reached his ears, Leonard wished that he could reel them back. Gus grew serious, leaning back, folding his arms, pushing out his chest a bit, and in a voice tainted with exaggerated authoritarianism, said, "Where were *your* boys last night, Mr. Stark?"

For one horrifying moment, Leonard froze, his mind blanking, as if it had curled into a fetal position, as if it were in stubborn refusal of the lies it might have to concoct.

Digging his nails into the palm, the sting prodded the mind alert, and Leonard realized that Gus had said "boys," not "kids." Desiree's exclusion allowed him to take a tentative breath, so that he could proceed with the conversation, casual and cool.

"Those boys were glued to the computer all night, lopping off the heads of trolls, or blowing up zombies, or something like that. They love that crap."

Gus chuckled and shoved a hand in the potato chip bag. Crunching, he said, "I'm guessing Oscar is more of a cigar man anyway. Am I right?"

Leonard managed a small smile, and nodded at the joke that, for him, had all the humor of a rabies shot. In truth, Stark had been exposed to something dangerous, sick, and possibly lethal; he must take the antidote, one tension-filled phrase at a time, until he knew he and his family were cleared of any suspicions. Working the torn cuticle again, he asked, "Cops going to follow up on it?"

Gus shook his head, saying, "No, it didn't look like the fire was set intentionally. It's not an arson case. It's a done deal."

Barb nodded, and said, "The best part is that the apartment is in great shape. It doesn't smell any worse than if someone burned a piece of toast. Jack and Seattle will be able to move in soon."

That's great news," Leonard said, as a building sense of relief and normalcy, allowed him to believe that maybe, just maybe, soon the smoke, the fire, the vast bottomless gaps in truth, would become like free radicals, contained within the body of the family, carefully managed, and rendered unable to manifest malignancy.

Finishing the water, he set the glass on the table and got up to leave.

"If you change your minds and need some help, give me a call," Leonard said. "Maggie's got her hands full over there with the boys. I'd better head home."

As he turned to go, Gus stopped him. "Wait! I got to read the back."

He halted and shifted his broad shoulders so that IronHorse could get a full view.

"There Goes One Good-Looking Indian!" Gus read, and then clapped. "I love that shirt. Man, I need one. Have your lady call my lady."

He offered Gus an amiable thumbs-up, turned out of sight behind the barn, and went home.

***

Desiree awoke to the smell of smoky hair pressed under her cheek and the silence of an empty house. Throughout the night, her dad and Maggie had quietly crept into the room, standing over her, listening to her breathing, trying not to wake her, though she lay awake with her eyes closed. The soft sounds of their safekeeping had finally eased her into a sleep of sorts, where spiders made of matchsticks crawled across her dreams.

Rising slowly, she saw the bowl of ice on the bed stand, bottles of water and orange juice arranged among the melting cubes, a note scripted in Maggie's neat hand beside it, and the sudden sadness of her solitude diminished slightly with these deliberate acts of kindness. Desiree opened a bottle of water and read the note. They had taken the boys to the Science Museum of Minnesota. Breakfast was in the refrigerator on a blue plastic-wrapped plate. Dad had his cell. They loved her.

Yesterday, she would have contemptuously crumpled it and tossed it aside, but today the simple note felt like a fragile lifeline. She carefully folded the paper and carried it with her into the bathroom. She tucked it into the mirror frame like a favorite photograph and stepped into the shower. She shampooed and soaped, soaped and shampooed, until the scalding water grew tepid, and still she thought she smelled smoke when she held an arm to her nose and breathed in the scent of her skin. Perhaps it would cling to her forever, like a layer of sick cells that she would never shed.

She turned off the shower, dried, wrapped the towel around her, and looked down at her charred nails. The sight of the blackened, bubbled enamel nauseated her, and she stole a glance at the slip of paper, questioning the sanity behind the commitment the message imparted. She was a monster on a level of which both her father and Maggie had experienced, and on a level of which they must now suspect, and, on the worst level of all, a level to which most people's imaginations could not venture.

Taking a pair of manicure scissors from the vanity, she cut away the burnt nails and let them fall into the toilet bowl, discarding little pieces of herself, as she feared they would do. When all the conditions came to light, their unconditional love, challenged by common sense, would become obsolete. After the last cut, she wiped the nail beds with a remover-soaked cotton ball, closed the lid, and sat down to stare at hands she no longer recognized as her own. Her mother had taught her how to manicure, moisturize, shape and polish, and from adolescence on, Desiree's hands had always resembled Anita's perfect satiny smooth, acrylic-tipped versions, which drew the admiring comments of strangers, and made Anita simper with pride. When it suited her, Anita acknowledged the girl as one of her beautifying extensions, valueless until the woman's vanity glued them together.

Gone was the shiny, blood-colored lacquer. Gone were the long bird-like talons. The connection had been broken, and Desiree Stark's hands now rested upon her knees, plain, blunt-nailed, and bare. They looked like the tools of honest hard work, and clean sparse practicality. They looked like the hands of Maggie Gustafson. They looked like her father's hands.

23

Concrete Moccasins

The warmer than normal spring melted into a brutally hot summer, and time moved through the city like gridlock. Blistering days that left pedestrians wandering between skyscraper valleys, plodding doggedly over the sticky asphalt and huffing a barely breathable soup of pollution, humidity, and sweat rolled slowly into nights, where darkness brought no relief, and it seemed as if the sun and moon were only doing the same white, hot job on different shifts. By August, the general mood of the metropolis hovered near weather-related road rage, and those who could escaped the urban hell. The more fortunate headed north, for someplace with deep pines, cool lakes, rustic cabins, and nearby sources of good bait and Canadian beer. Everyone else improvised.

On one of his rare August days off, Jack pitched a plan for a picnic, so Isaac and Seattle loaded a cooler into the truck, and Jack slid some lounge chairs in behind it. Lake Calhoun, the lower middle class urbanites' version of a day trip, beckoned them out of their shared sullenness as they set out for Thomas Beach. Jack had often taken Seattle there; it was a place they could reach by public transportation, and they both had learned to swim in the choppy, algae-flecked water. Not all of the citizenry appreciated the fact that a bus line dropped its inner city riders only a couple of blocks from the park, a complaint that grew as more non-Caucasian beachcombers arrived. As Isaac pulled into a parking place, he perused the area, and, noticing a mostly white crowd, jovially announced, "Better circle your picnic tables, my wasicun friends … the Indians are here!"

As they prepared to dive in and cool off, they trekked down to the water and dropped their gear in the sand, receiving only a couple of looks from the other beach occupants. A pretty girl in a blue bikini, with small, but noticeable breasts, smiled at Seattle and said that she liked his long hair, flustering him a bit, but making him wonder about their proximity in age. A toddler in a saggy swim diaper noticed them, too, excitedly darting over as if he knew them, until, in exaggerated panic, the mother cautioned that he return to her. Either her stern tone or the realization that he didn't actually know them, caused the boy's glee to dissolve into bawling terror, and he turned and scampered away. For the most part however, their arrival only seemed to elicit people's lethargic, over-heated indifference.

That was about to change.

Jack and Seattle wore board shorts, and stripped off their T-shirts, but Isaac had on a pair of long safari shorts, which he now slipped off to reveal what dozens of sunglass-clad stares stuck to all at once. TwoBears wore a black, barely-there Speedo.

For the most part, Seattle's acceptance of his uncle's relationship with Isaac came quite naturally. He had never liked the nasty secretive way Paulette, Dave, and Angie had whispered about Jack's "preferences." This new openness made him comfortable—and happy with the idea of his uncle's contentment. He really liked Isaac; he included Seattle in conversations, asked his opinion, and didn't treat him like a stupid kid or an inconvenient add-on. When he asked if he could call Isaac "Uncle," the man had said that it would honor him if the boy did so.

"Wow, Uncle Isaac, that's, uh … some bathing suit."

Isaac preened, saying "I do look good, don't I?"

Seattle shrugged.

"I guess, but I wouldn't want all *my* junk showing like that."

"Yeah," Jack teased, as they walked into the shallows. "Don't swim out too deep. A walleye might mistake you for a fishing lure."

Unabashed, Isaac waved off their laughter, and dove, surfaced, and swam to the floating platform. Jack swam out to join him, but Seattle glimpsed the blue bikini girl walking toward the water and stayed behind. Suddenly wanting the chance to get closer to her, and further away from Isaac's attention-grabbing black banana hammock, he decided to wade in up to his waist and see if she might talk to him again, a thought that both terrified and titillated him. As she got closer and stepped gingerly into the lake a couple of yards from him, Seattle stole a look at her short strawberry-blonde curls, lightly freckled nose, and sapphire-blue eyes. Catching him, she smiled again, and said, "Hi, I'm Megan."

She moved in a few feet closer and splashed water over her arms.

"Seattle," he said, suddenly wishing he had a popular moniker, such as Justin or Zack.

"Very cool name," she said, and then nodded towards the raft. "Are those your dads?"

"No," he said, silently cursing Isaac's uninhibited nature. "Uncles."

Bending her knees, she dipped down, and swayed her arms to keep balance against the lap of the lake.

"Mom saw the lambda sticker on your cooler, so we thought …."

A wave of unexpected protectiveness rolled through Seattle, shifting his tone from shy, but friendly, to wary and defensive, as he said, "You and your mom thought what?"

"We thought your family was like ours. Mom's a lesbian."

As much as he wanted to dive beneath the green surface and swim until he couldn't hold his breath any longer, he instead worked at a stone with his big toe until he could muster some kind of recovery.

"Sorry, I just thought—"

"That we're homophobic jerkwads?" she interrupted, still smiling with complete guilelessness.

He noticed that her upper front tooth was a little crooked, like his own, and offered her an apologetic, similar asymmetrical grin.

The guy in the board shorts, that's my Uncle Jack. I live with him. He and Isaac are dating."

"That's Trish," Megan said, waving at a woman sprawled across a beach towel, reading a paperback, "my birth mom. My other mom, LaDonna, is at work. She designs wedding cakes, which is ironic, because Minnesota doesn't recognize gay marriage. My parents consider themselves married, though. It's only the stupid laws and the haters that say they're not. "

With animated gestures that release the pleasant aroma of coconut-scented sunscreen, Megan elaborated on California's Prop 8, how delicious LaDonna's, or, as she called her, "Mama's" cakes tasted, and some British boy band she loved that Seattle didn't recognize until she hummed their catchy hit song. He hadn't had many real conversations with girls, but if nodding and smiling and paying some attention to what they said while grabbing little looks at their chests as they told you their entire life story summed up a boy/girl face-to-face, Seattle thought he had the hang of it. Megan's conviviality made it seem easy, directing only a few simple questions his way every now and then.

"What grade will you be in this fall?"

"Seventh."

On hearing this, she launched into a whole new set of topics, saying that seventh grade sucked, she couldn't wait for eighth, and that some of the girls at her private school had gotten busted for ripping off prescription pain killers out of the field hockey coach's glove compartment.

Seattle just kept listening and nodding, checked out the lovely little crevice of creamy flesh that formed between the triangles of bathing suit top when she crossed her arms, which she seemed to do quite often, and prayed that the cloudy water and loose board shorts would conceal his untimely physical response.

"My friend dates a sophomore. He's got a car," Megan said, shifting subjects yet again, as she lifted a leg and let her bright blue painted toes peer above the water line, closely examining the silver ring shaped like a Celtic knot that she wore on her second toe.

Seattle felt several parts of himself deflate, sure that she had just demoted him to her "too immature for me" list.

"He's a total asshole, though. I think most high school guys are," she said with an air of contempt, and then, sweetening again, asked, "Do you have a girlfriend?"

The directness threw him off kilter and blasted a little firecracker of panic off in his belly. She required an answer, but the question had implied something that raced Seattle's thoughts forward and caused him to imagine what one of Megan's perky fourteen-year-old breasts would feel like if she allowed him to touch it. When his spontaneous fantasy fondle finally relinquished enough of his brain so that he could form a coherent sentence, he said, "No, I don't have a girlfriend."

"A boyfriend?" she said with a wink.

"No," Seattle said, as he glanced at the raft, and was briefly struck with thoughts of his uncle and Madesio DeMarco.

"Interesting," she said in a way that drew all his attention right back to her lithe body.

On the shore, Trish closed her book, motioned to Megan, and tapped on her watchless wrist.

"Guess I got to go," Megan said, rising from the water, and brushing a soft, pale hand across Seattle's shoulder as she passed. "I'll leave my number by your cooler. Text me, okay?"

"Sure," he answered.

She quickly ran a finger beneath the hem of her bathing suit bottom, releasing the wet nylon from where it had wedged itself, and leaving Seattle with the epiphany that, in a string bikini, some girls look painfully good, front *and* back.

Isaac and Jack watched as the bubbly blond girl reached the sand, tied a sarong around her waist, scratched something on a piece of paper, and walked towards their blanket. Lifting a corner of the lambda sticker, she attached the note, and blew a kiss to Seattle. Isaac elbowed Jack and grinned.

"What a player! We've only been here fifteen minutes, and the kid's already scored some little freckled-face cutie's number. Time to have the talk with him, Uncle Jack."

Bordeaux dangled his feet in the cool lake water, and said, "He's got the basics: man plus woman plus sex minus condom equals baby."

Or just an S.T.D., if they're lucky," Isaac interjected facetiously, and then added, "Has he asked you any specifics?"

Jack gave him a funny look, saying, "Like what?"

Isaac shrugged and said, "I don't know ... like how do you unfasten a bra with one hand, or what if a girl gets lipstick stains on your underwear?"

"Are you serious, Isaac? What kid ever asks parents questions like that?"

Okay, so maybe not those particular questions, but what if he wants to know," TwoBears voice turned theatrical, " how to make love to a woman?"

Jack grew quiet as he watched Seattle swim into the deeper part of the roped area, submerge, and resurface beyond it.

"Honestly, I don't know what I'd tell him. I've never been with a woman."

"You didn't even experiment while away at summer camp?"

Jack chuckled and said, "No summer camp. No experiments. What about you?"

Isaac sighed, leaned down, and splashed some water on himself.

"I was fifteen, at one of those my parents are at work, we're all bored, let's go to the garage and raid my dad's beer stash parties. At some point, everybody started pairing off, and I ended up with this really introverted chubby girl, who started to cry when I said that I didn't want to make out. I felt sorry for her, and I felt sorry for myself because the captain of the hockey team didn't want to get naked with either one of us. I kissed her—no tongue—for what seemed like a fricking eternity, and then she shoved my hand under her shirt. She was a big girl. She should have been wearing a bra. She wasn't. I bet those babies are riding around her knees these days. But I digress. Not long after that unpleasant experience, the parents arrived home, and we all scattered."

"So sorry, sweetie," Jack said sarcastically. "That sounds rough. Peer pressured, pity-provoked heterosexuality is destroying our country's gay youth."

Isaac feigned distress, saying, "I suppose now I'll be denied enrollment since I'm not a pureblood gay like you."

"We'll make an exception for you," Jack said, casually letting his knuckles slide down the outside of Isaac's thigh. "Of course, you *will* have to work extra hard to prove that you really want to be a member of the tribe."

"Not with all the nice straight wasicuns watching, dear," TwoBears whispered in his ear, as he rose and dove from the platform.

All joking aside, Bordeaux sometimes worried how he would handle all the milestones of raising an adolescent boy. With no father, and only Paulette as an example, he knew most everything was going to have to come from the gut. Although childless themselves, Gus and Barb praised his efforts, and offered support and suggestions when Jack requested them.

But despite the votes of confidence, the contentment of companionship, and the current calm that seemed to prevail upon the surface, Jack never felt quite free of the fear that, just below, treacherous whirlpools awaited his inevitable inability to stay afloat. All his life, Jack

Bordeaux had watched people flail, fight to keep their heads above the cold numbing waves, and, finally, with so many ghosts knowing them by name, sink to the deepest depths. Those who tried to save them more often than not were dragged down and drowned, too. Old stories spoke of the great frigid lake, the one now known as Superior, and how it had swallowed up many an Ojibwe who paddled forth seeking honor, or redemption, or love. The city had its way of swallowing you up, too, and Bordeaux often wondered if, in his pursuit of happiness, he would someday become just another tragic figure in an urban Indian legend.

Jack heard Seattle laugh out loud as Isaac surfaced and the boy flung a clump of algae that landed, dead center, on TwoBears' forehead. Good-naturedly, Isaac wiped the muck off, and, as the boy quickly swam for shore, promised future retaliation.

For today, Jack would compartmentalize some earlier unaddressed misgivings, try his damnedest to let himself breathe, and enjoy the momentary buoyancy. After all, he had been the one who had suggested the beach. He shouldn't waste the temporary escape he had given himself.

On the shore, Isaac and Seattle returned to their spot, where the boy frantically shook TwoBears' safari shorts at him, with the obvious non-verbal suggestion that he put them back on. Jack wished that he would, too, but for very different reasons. Isaac did look really good in the Speedo, and an unexpected and most unwanted streak of jealousy had hit Bordeaux when he noticed several women, as well as the twenty-something male lifeguard, watching Isaac appreciatively.

Choosing a less conspicuous dismount than his poised partner, Jack went to the platform's side and lowered himself into the water's welcome chill by way of the ladder. He swam a few leisurely laps, and then returned to the beach to find that Isaac had slipped the more modest shorts back on. He offered Jack a bottle of green tea. Bordeaux took the drink, grabbed a towel, dried off, and flopped down on the blanket beside TwoBears. Taking a sandwich from the cooler, Seattle wolfed the turkey and provolone, and carefully wiped the bag clean of mustard. He then placed the slip of paper that contained the girl's number inside like a rare biological specimen.

Isaac laughed. "That's right, kid. Keep that little chick's note safe. A gust of wind and a soggy hunk of smeared numbers would be a truly shitty ending to a summer teen romance."

"It's not romance," Seattle said, the word assaulting all pre-teen male codes of coolness. "She just wants me to text her."

Not particularly at ease that day with the idea of romanticism, either, Jack gave him a knowing look, and said, "So you wouldn't want to get too serious, right?"

The boy took a sudden interest in an old bottle cap half buried in the course sand, and didn't answer. Isaac chuckled.

"Okay, we get it. No romance. No kissing. Girls are icky."

Seattle's upper lip rose over the slightly crooked front tooth in an inescapable grin. "I never said that. Megan's kind of cool."

Isaac winked at Jack, saying, "And so it begins"

***

Late afternoon, southern storm clouds, full of heat lightning and the promise of rain, banked on the horizon. The wind gathered strength and churned foamy whitecaps against Calhoun's shore. By the time they reached Isaac's truck, the sky had opened, and the clouds moved with a sinister swirl. In the calm manner that Isaac approached most everything, he started the truck, patiently waited while the more frantic gunned their vehicles out of the lot and the pile-up at the exit cleared, and then he casually switched the wipers to high, put the truck in gear, and slowly drove home, maneuvering flooded side streets like a seasoned barge captain. As they pulled into TwoBears' driveway, Isaac caught Jack's serious expression, and said, "Got the concrete moccasins on again?"

They had coined the phrase while looking through some of Isaac's old pictures.

"Is this a relative of yours?" Jack had asked offhandedly, when he turned a page in the battered album, and spotted a picture of the gigantic figure looming before the washed-out gray backdrop of a Midwestern winter.

"That beauty," Isaac said, "is none other than Pocahontas, memorialized in twenty-five feet of glorious concrete."

"Damn," Jack had replied. "Where is this at?"

"I think this picture was shot on a trip to Sioux City. My cousins live there, and, when I was a kid, we used to go for Christmas sometimes. She's along the highway, next to a little rural Iowa town of the same name."

The image was a grotesque rendition of stereotypical Indian stoicism, and scaled to such monstrous proportions it seemed as if its design had been inspired from a 1950's Japanese horror flick. Jack had commented that it looked like that at any moment she could attack and crush the puny white villagers.

Shrugging, Isaac had said, "Sure, but it's a real bitch walking around in concrete moccasins."

"Even harder to dance in them," Jack added.

They had fallen silent for a moment, as they failed to feel the humor of their own jokes. Finally, Jack had closed the album and handed it to

Isaac, saying, "It's heavy sometimes …"

" …being an Indian," TwoBears had finished.

They sat in the truck, while the rain pounded the world outside. Completely absorbed, oblivious to anything but the cell phone in his hand, Seattle took no notice of the fact that they had arrived as his thumbs flew and another line of text sailed through the storm and, somewhere in St. Louis Park, the strawberry blond girl giggled.

Isaac began to say that whatever was bothering Jack, they would handle it, to which Bordeaux gave no response. The carpenter, the builder, the man who reconstructed, improved upon, and refurbished things for a living, had, of late, caused Jack to feel as if he himself was some kind of fixer-upper. Though well-intentioned, TwoBears' proactive approach to solving all Jack's problems seemed to have turned the relationship's direction to his advantage. Isaac had repeatedly assured Jack that they could go at Bordeaux's pace, but, despite that, a few incidences had left Jack believing otherwise.

When Gus said that the garage apartment needed electrical work done, Isaac said that he knew a guy who would give IronHorse a fair deal, but three months later, the electrician, according to Isaac, was still swamped. With sweltering heat, and no air conditioner in Gus and Barb's second floor, TwoBears offered Jack and Seattle an invitation to his place. After much cajoling, and Jack's unequivocal stipulation that it would not be every night, nor would it be permanent, he finally accepted Isaac's proposition.

Now, as they sat in TwoBears' truck, in TwoBears' driveway, in front of TwoBears' house, the torrents of rain confining them there behind fogged windows, Jack Bordeaux suddenly felt claustrophobic. Isaac tilted his head towards the back seat, indicating Seattle, and said, "Is it that?"

The cell phone beeped as another incoming text arrived, and Jack shook his head. The rain came down harder, mixed with pea-sized pellets of hail. Admitting to the reason for his sober mood would open a lengthier, more complicated conversation that Jack did not want to have, a conversation about commitment, about considerations, about expectations. How could he confess that, regardless of Isaac's help, his kindness, his love, Jack did not fully trust him. How could he tell TwoBears that the more he did, the more Jack distrusted? He knew it sounded ridiculous, that it made him seem broken, that it proved him a coward, but he could not force his doubt aside. He had learned a long time ago that nothing good ever lasted. Those who defended you died. Those who loved you left. Those who hugged you one day hit you the next.

The sky lightened, the hail stopped, and the rain subsided, but Isaac watched Jack's face darken further, and he sensed that the storm was not over. Jack's mood had so drastically shifted since they had left the beach, and his silence felt dangerous to TwoBears, but despite this, he didn't try to shield himself. He had never been good at it. Why love, if you didn't assume the risk? Holding a hand out to Jack, he said, "Let's talk. Whatever bothers you bothers me."

Jack dropped his gaze from the window to the dash, but didn't reach back . He had been fighting it since this morning, when he'd caught a brief exchange between Isaac and Seattle. Isaac had asked the boy if he would like him to cook shrimp pesto next week. Seattle eagerly said that he loved Isaac's pesto. After jotting the needed ingredients on a grocery list, he added that he would pick up more orange marmalade because he knew that the boy liked it on toast. As innocent as it all sounded, Jack bristled at the words "next week" and he knew for a fact that the jar of marmalade was still more than half full, which implied something disquieting: Isaac was becoming too comfortable and secure with the living arrangement, and, worse yet, he was drawing Seattle in, too. These small details had plagued Jack, until, in a valiant attempt to shake his misgivings and enjoy at least some of his time off, he had suggested their trip to Calhoun. As if the lightning had disrupted all his positive circuitry, Bordeaux felt the weight of "next week" pressing with intense irritation against his nerves; a sensation that was slowly mutating into anger.

"I need you to take us—" He had almost said "home," but then realizing that they were still in residential limbo, conceded its inaccuracy and started over.

"Seattle and I need to go back to Saint Paul."

Isaac brightened, saying, "Is that all? No big deal. We can swing over there, you guys can grab what you need, and we can be back before dinner."

Jack shook his head.

"No, I mean we need to go back … for good."

"Oh," said Isaac, soberly accepting a pair of his own concrete moccasins. "I see."

No argument would keep them here, not that he would try, because Isaac saw Jack's spooked animal look. Pursuit would only cause him to run faster and farther. Isaac turned the ignition key and started the truck's engine.

Jack pulled the boy's attention away from the cell, and they went in the house to retrieve their belongings while Isaac sat in the truck and stared blankly at the bungalow, as if it was suddenly less familiar to him. For a moment, wistful thoughts of Bordeaux's warm body beside him in bed, the hidden bag of Gummi Bears he'd bought to surprise Seattle, Jack's hair brush on the vanity, last night's bowl of buttered popcorn the three of them had shared while watching *Powwow Highway* flashed as teasing slices of the life TwoBears wanted more of, but, for now, could not have. Once again, he had let himself become too confident, too happy, too hopeful. Vaguely, Isaac rubbed a thumb over the once-broken bridge of his nose, remembering. You're a slow learner, TwoBears, he thought. A damn slow learner.

24

A House That Jack Built

"May I come in?"

Jack turned from the cupboard where he was arranging plates and drinking glasses to find Barb's pleasant face at the garage apartment's side entrance. Over her shoulder, she carried a cloth shopping bag.

"I have house warming gifts," she said brightly.

"Welcome," said Jack, pulling a chair for her at the kitchen table. "I'm setting up our kitchen—not that Seattle and I will be doing much more than microwaving frozen dinners. I'm afraid cooking isn't our strong suit."

Barb sat down and placed the bag at her feet.

"Well, it's a good thing you have a neighbor lady who plans on making sure neither of you boys starve. My kitchen is only a few yards away and, because I've never managed to scale down my army size recipes, we tend to always have more than enough. I'm willing to provide back door carry-out."

Seattle emerged from one of the small bedrooms and went to the fridge, saying, "Would you like some sun tea, Barb? I brewed it like you showed me. It's really good."

Barb accepted, and Seattle poured a glass from the big jar, added a lemon wedge, and placed it on the table in front of her.

"Thank you. Very classy!"

Between Leonard, Gus, Barb, and Goodwill, they had managed to acquire most of what they needed to set up house. Jack had purchased a scratch and dent return television from the store where he worked, along with a laptop that he and Seattle would share when the school year began in a few days. Barb and Gus had provided window blinds and an old desk that had collected years of basement dust before Jack cleaned it up and painted it a funky purple. The color matched a tiny petal pattern in the second-hand floral couch. Working from the same creative decorating vibe, Seattle had structured a set of board and glass block shelves, also purple, where they arranged their many books. The slightly scratched new Samsung set atop with the illegal cable hook-up Gus had rigged for them, despite Barb's reproach.

"They delivered my bed this morning," Seattle told Barb. "It's brand new. No one has ever slept in it. There's still plastic on it."

Jack's funds had barely covered the twin mattress and box spring. With the money he had left, he had purchased an inflatable for himself.

Gus had offered to move one of the beds from upstairs for him, but Jack declined, saying that the blow-up would suit him fine until his next payday.

Barb set the ice tea aside and reached into the bag.

"Here's something in case plastic isn't your thing," she said, handing Seattle a bulky plastic zipper bag.

"This is so cool," the boy said, flipping the package around so that Jack could see the label.

"Bed in a bag. That is *very* cool," Jack said, sliding a cookie sheet and a pizza pan into the drawer below the oven.

I took the liberty of opening it so that I could wash the sheets. Fabric softener always makes the new ones feel nicer. Can I help you make up your bed?" Barb asked.

"Sure," Seattle said and bolted into his room.

Jack clutched Barb's hand, and said, "Thanks. You do way too much for us."

Seattle had the sheets and pillow case out of the bag, and was looking at the dust ruffle quizzically when Barb entered.

"What's this thing?" he said, laying the light blue bed skirt in Barb's hands.

"It's a dust ruffle. It goes between the mattress and box spring so that you can't see the metal legs of the bed frame. It's just for appearance sake."

"A ruffle? I bet Oscar and Owen would really razz me if they see a ruffle on my bed."

Chuckling, Barb assured him that the Stark twins probably had them on their beds and didn't even know what they were, so he shouldn't sweat it. Seattle shrugged, seeing the point of it, and lifted the twin mattress while Barb slid the fabric under it. The sheets and pillow case had longitudinal stripes of navy, light blue and white, and the solid navy comforter and sham had light blue piping around their edges. When the bed was made up, Seattle stood back and whistled.

"Wow! It looks awesome!"

"Good enough to sleep in?" Barb asked, affectionately patting the grateful boy's back.

Seattle threw his arms around her neck and told her that he loved it and that he loved her, too.

"Love you, too, sweet boy."

Returning to the kitchen/living room, she lifted the shopping bag onto a chair and took out something else.

"This is for you both," she said, offering Jack the bundle of red fabric tied up with a brain tanned leather thong.

Carefully placing the gift on the table, Bordeaux untied it to find a large shiny abalone shell, sweet grass, white sage, pieces of cedar, and the wing feather of an eagle.

"For the purification of your home, your minds, and your hearts."

Though Barb StandingBull had kept a safe distance from the subject of Isaac, Jack caught the overtone. His heart did need a thorough spiritual cleansing, he was certain of it, but for now, the act of establishing a home for himself and for Seattle, a secure place that they could call their own, seemed like the medicine he most required. He kissed Barb's cheek and thanked her for such a thoughtful and sacred bequest.

"I must get back to my kitchen," she said, rising from the chair and heading towards the door. "Isaac's coming over tonight after work to help Gus put a ramp at the back door for Finnegan. I promised a roasted chicken and peach cobbler. Do you guys have plans for dinner?"

At the mention of TwoBears' name, Jack felt his stomach turn to lead. At the mention of peach cobbler, Seattle felt his stomach growl.

"My brother Clayton is coming tonight. He has a dresser for us, and something else that he said was a surprise, so we need to stick around home. Thanks for the invite. We'll take a raincheck."

For a moment, disappointment registered on Seattle's face, until Jack reminded him that they would try their hand at spaghetti and meatballs later.

"Garlic bread, too. Right?" the boy said hopefully.

"Of course," Jack said. "We have to have something to eat if the main course is a total flop."

Barb laughed, saying, "If you need any pointers, I'm just a phone call away. Also, you're still welcome to stop by after dinner for some cobbler."

As much as Jack enjoyed Barb's desserts, he decided as he heard her descend the stairs that Seattle could go alone. Though Isaac and he had spoken briefly and exchanged a few text messages, Jack still needed time and space before they faced each other again.

Grabbing the laptop from the desk, Seattle told Jack that Megan would want to see his new room.

"You can only Skype for a half hour. I need to review my university schedule, your middle school address, and the bus routes," Jack said, a hint of pride in the idea that Seattle wanted to show Megan his home, causing a little rush of happiness.

"Owen said that his dad'll give us a ride tomorrow, so we don't need to worry about all that."

Jack frowned and said, "Are you sure you don't want me along on your first day?"

"It's not Kindergarten, Uncle. I'll be fine."

The fond memory of Seattle's first day of school, and how nervous the little boy had looked as he turned around on the last bus step, and, with sad eyes, offered a half-hearted wave to his teenaged uncle, gripped Jack. He had been there since the beginning, but Jack knew the importance of rites of passage. The kid was really growing up.

"Okay, little man. Go Skype your girlfriend."

When Clayton Bordeaux pulled up and honked the horn of a white minivan, Seattle and Jack had just finished their inaugural dinner in the new apartment, a meal that both deemed a smashing success, and they tromped downstairs to help with the second-hand dresser and whatever Clayton's mysterious surprise happened to be. The van's back doors stood open, and Clayton had slid the empty dresser drawers partially out.

"Hey, guys. Nice neighborhood. You did good here, Jack!"

"Thanks, man, but I can't take too much credit. The neighborhood more picked me than I did it. We lucked out."

Clayton ruffled Seattle's hair, saying, "Hey, kid. Great to see you. You be in charge of the drawers and Jack and I'll lug the dresser."

When they had the piece of furniture maneuvered up the narrow staircase and inside the apartment, Clayton gazed around and said, "Nice bachelor pad. It looks great, and smells like home cooking, too. Who's the Italian chef? Is that garlic bread?"

"It was a combined effort," Jack said, offering his brother a seat on the couch. "We're learning as we go. I can heat you up some spaghetti. Are you hungry?"

Clayton nodded, saying, "That would be awesome. I took off before Jenny had dinner ready. She was going to put a plate aside for me, but, quite honestly, she was whipping up some kind of super healthy thing with kale and lima beans, and a bunch of other stuff that doesn't exactly trip my trigger, so some red meat and noodles would make my night."

Excited that they had a willing third party to sample their culinary efforts, Seattle went to the kitchen to reheat dinner.

"Have you talked to Ma lately?" Clayton said, as he accepted a glass of ice tea from Seattle.

"I called last week and talked to Renee. She's living there now, helping out, or getting helped out. Either way, it's all right."

Clayton took a sip of tea, and then said, "Yeah, I know. They need each other. I stopped there before I came over here."

Since the heart attack, Clayton had, in small doses, reinitiated contact with their mother, which, at first, had consisted of a weekly phone call.

"I didn't feel right in heading this direction to see you without at least checking in. I have to say not much has changed, except for the fact that my ability to handle it has gotten better as I've gotten older. I think the

Buddhists have a name for it."

"Detached compassion," Seattle broke in, as he set down a plate piled high with pasta, meatballs, and red sauce.

"Exactly," Clayton said, twirling the fork in the center of the heap. "Damn, kid, you're one smart cookie."

Jack waved at the many titles lining the shelves.

"He's read them all, and countless more. Seattle loves books."

Clayton swallowed, wiped his mouth, and said, "My girls like to read, but Clay, well, if it's not a puck, basket, foot, or baseball, he's oblivious to it."

Lighting up, Seattle went to the shelves and slid a hardcover out. The boy laid it on the table for his uncle.

"Take this to Clay. It's about Jim Thorp. He was an incredible American Indian athlete. He was known best for his football career, but he also played baseball."

In that moment, Jack felt a triumphant, shining pride sweep over him. Seattle, who had always managed with so few material possessions, had learned one of their people's most important cultural lessons: let go, give away, share. Both the act and the knowledge being passed along through it gave Jack Bordeaux a gift, as well. It gave him hope.

Touched by the simple, kind gesture, Clayton thanked Seattle. For a moment, perhaps by a trick of the indigo twilight that spilled through the blinds, or the way the boy's thoughtful behavior had acted as a rusty key in a lock long sealed, he saw his little sister, dear blue-eyed Lily, standing, sad and innocent, before him. He cleared his throat, reality returned the departed girl's brown-eyed son into view, and, heavy-hearted, Clayton said, "Dave's girlfriend took the baby and moved out of Ma's last weekend."

Jack frowned.

"What the hell did Dave do this time?"

"Apparently, he disappeared for about a week, and, when she tracked him down, he had been shacking up with some barfly. Renee said it got pretty ugly. The usual: cops, broken glass, Dave threatening not to let her leave with their kid. I guess after she left, Dave gathered up his stuff, and went back to the barfly's place because Renee hasn't seen him since. The girl and the baby are in North Dakota with her parents."

Shaking his head, Jack thought of the little girl who would now probably grow up without knowledge of her Ojibwe heritage, another tragic result of a truly fractured family. The sacrifice of culture for physical survival wasn't a new concept, just a miserable one.

"Can't say I didn't see that coming. Angie needed to get out of there. The hard truth is that she and the baby stand a hell of a better chance away from Dave and the family."

Clayton took another drink, then nodded agreement. "We all know from firsthand experience that's true. Sometimes the detachment has to be literal."

He set the glass down, took his empty plate to the sink, washed it, and placed it in the drainer. "Great grub. I'll hit you guys up for a meal anytime."

Rifling into the pocket of his jeans, he fished out some papers and unfolded them.

"Now, before I have to run, I've got something else for you. It's downstairs. Come on."

They headed to the van and Clayton unlocked the driver's door. With a grin like half of a wide white Wisconsin cheese wheel, he handed the papers and the ring of keys to Jack.

"It's all yours, Bro."

Jack stood frozen, not quite fully unraveling what he had just heard, until Clayton laughed and said, "I'm not shitting you, man. I know it's not the coolest ride, but I thought with winter coming, some wheels would come in handy."

"Clayton, this blows my mind!" Jack said. "I don't want to offend you, but can you and Jenny afford this? I can't accept it if I think I'm taking food out of your kids mouths."

Clayton shook his head, and pointed to the logo on the van's side that Jack hadn't yet noticed. "Jenny's dad is a minister of our Unitarian church, right?"

Jack nodded.

"This van was donated a few years back for our youth group, but our congregation has grown, and the van doesn't fit the numbers anymore, so they decided to raffle it as a fund raiser. It's got high mileage and wouldn't bring diddly-squat as a trade-in. Well, Jenny and I talked it over, bought a wad of tickets, and we won."

"Don't you and Jenny have use for it?"

"The whole idea was to win it for you, and Seattle, and," Clayton's voice cracked, and he mouthed, "Lily."

Clayton's estrangement from the family had happened shortly after his little sister's death, when, despite countless counseling sessions with his father-in-law, Clayton couldn't make room in his heart for both anger and forgiveness. Time had worked the power of its magic, and he found himself struggling to catch up with all the things he wished he had done to help his younger siblings, and their children, especially Seattle.

Circling the van, Jack observed the small patches of rust intruding on the white paint, the worn carpeting and upholstery, and, much to his amusement, the words, "God Is Good...All The Time" which were featured in bold red and gold block letters across the two rear doors. Jack had scoffed at the idea of a driver's license when Angie had suggested it to him a couple of years earlier, but she had offered him a few lessons and taken him to the DMV, and now, as he held the keys, he thought fondly of the ne'er-do-well girl who had finally left his brother in her taillights.

A set of headlights swung into the alley, and Clayton slapped his brother's back, and grabbed Seattle into a group hug as he said, "I love you guys. My ride's here. My trucking buddy's giving me a lift back to Stillwater. Give me a call … anytime."

Clayton Bordeaux tucked the Jim Thorp book under his arm, jogged to the end of the alley, climbed the diesel tractor's side, and hoisted himself into the cab. As the huge machine reversed, Jack and Seattle both made the same universal arm signal, and the truck horn gave a couple loud, short bursts.

***

Close to midnight, a soft knock awoke Jack from where he had fallen asleep on the couch. Foggy-headed, he rose to check on Seattle. The boy slept peacefully beneath all the soothing shades of blue bedding, so Jack closed the bedroom door and went to see who could be dropping by so late. He found Isaac on the landing, with an apologetic smile and a pan of peach cobbler.

"Sorry about the late hour. I saw the lights on and hoped you were still up. Barb insisted that I bring this to you. You know there's no arguing with that woman."

"Would you like to come in?" Jack said, taking the dessert, hoping that his voice wasn't reflecting the eagerness he truly felt.

For weeks, TwoBears had suffered the distance Jack had chosen to place between them, and it was all he could do not to rush inside the apartment and throw himself on Bordeaux, but he resisted, instead, strategizing the end game.

"I'd love to, but," Isaac hesitated, the sight of Jack's long, unbound hair almost throwing him off.

"But?" Bordeaux said, mentally kicking himself for sounding needy.

"I have to be at a new building site at the crack of dawn. Another time?"

I'm giving you what you want, Jack. Distance, time, control, TwoBears thought, as he watched confused torment briefly roll across the younger man's handsome face.

"Absolutely. Maybe I could pick you up and take you out for dinner this weekend."

Isaac glanced back down the stairs, and said, "So that van belongs to you?"

Jack nodded.

"Wow," Isaac mused. "Much has happened since the last time we spoke. You've obtained transportation and apparently, by the looks of your signage … salvation."

"I'm full of surprises, aren't I?" Jack said, leaning against the door jamb and balancing the cobbler on his hip. "A paint job is in its future, but until then, God Is Good …"

"… All The Time," TwoBears said, the warmth of his words caressing Jack's soul, heating his flesh. "Call me."

TwoBears descended the stairs with slow deliberate steps, letting the departure press against Bordeaux with its full, lingering weight, allowing him time for actions, words—or nothing. As Isaac's boot touched gravel, he heard the apartment door close. Behind it, Jack laid his forehead to the frame, his fingers sensing the warm places Isaac's hands had left along the cool metal pan.

I love you, Jack thought, as he heard Isaac TwoBears rev the '96 Mustang's rebuilt engine and roar off into the night.

25

Unktomi

Desiree Stark tugged the pea coat's collar around her neck and squeezed chin closer to chest as a blast of wind, carrying dead maple leaves and flecks of late October snow, blew across the Inver Hills Community College student parking lot. Eager to reach the shelter of her car, she hurried on, and pretended that she couldn't hear the shrill voice of Bonnie KillsTwice, but as Desiree fumbled with numb fingers to unlock the door, her friend caught up, saying, "Damn, girl! Good thing it's not after dark and I wasn't getting dragged off into the bushes by some pervert. Are you deaf? I've been yelling your name since you came out of the admissions office. What's up?"

"Just get in," Desiree demanded impatiently, as she finally got the doors to unlock on her third attempt. "It's too fricking cold!"

"Cold?" Bonnie laughed, as she climbed in beside her shivering friend. "I thought you were Ojibwe. Are you really secretly a Seminole?"

Desiree fired up the car's reluctant engine and cranked the heater to high. She had been chilled ever since she rolled from under the warmth of her comforter and pulled a dresser drawer open to find a small spider skittering across the folded sweaters. No longer sure that a spider was simply a spider, she had reared back in revulsion and held her breath for several long moments, but nothing earth-shattering followed the spider's appearance, so she dug a nondescript beige cable knit from the dresser, along with a pair of baggy jeans, and closed the drawer. Desiree had told herself that, with the weather turning colder, creatures of all varieties sought refuge indoors.

Ten minutes later, when Desiree untwisted the bag of wheat bread, and slid a piece into the toaster, she spotted another tiny spider crawling along the length of the cord. Again, she had eased her mind with the notion that seeing two spiders in one morning wasn't that unusual, even for her.

But as the day progressed, her silent assurances became less and less effective with each additional sighting. A tiny spider scurried from the interior of her boot. One clung to her car antenna. When she arrived at composition class, another rode out of her satchel on the end of a pen. Later, in a restroom stall, Desiree glimpsed an eight-legged speck of black on the white tile before it disappeared between the slots of a floor drain. All day they had crossed her path, until she wondered if she were the only one able to see them, but had felt too nervous to inquire, in fear that someone might think her crazy. Whether or not the parade of spiders existed only as figments of her imagination, they certainly could not be written off as coincidence. Their arrival meant something, predicted something, were a prelude to something.

Bonnie reached for the closest vent with the intention of shutting off the hot air that was hitting her round, full face. Women of her size waited with great anticipation for lovely cool temperatures like today, and her friend's strange behavior threatened to roast her like a wild turkey.

"Hey, look at that," she said leaning closer to the dash and squinting. "There's a little Unktomi in your car."

Desiree focused on the corner of windshield where Bonnie pointed. A small, but intricate web held its minute black builder. A mixture of relief that Bonnie could actually see it, and dread that this equaled spider number thirteen, trickled icily through Desiree, as she reached towards the window glass.

"Don't kill it," Bonnie shrieked.

Startled, Desiree yanked her hand away and scowled at her overly excited girlfriend as the frosty sensation pierced her bones.

"Untomi is a trickster," Bonnie said with stern foreboding, as if speaking to an unknowing child. "We don't want to piss him off."

If only she knew how familiar Desiree had become with the wrath of a trickster. But rather than open herself to scrutiny, for she couldn't know how far Bonnie KillsTwice's belief in her Lakota cultural stories ran, Desiree reluctantly nodded, and carefully reversed from the parking space as her friend continued.

"Some think that Unktomi, like the other trickster characters, only makes mischief and causes all kinds of trouble for people, but that's not always true. Sure, he loves his pranks and can really pull some shit, but there's the other side. Sometimes, he plays the good guy and helps the people out. My grandma used to tell us kids stories. Sometimes, Unktomi would really fuck things up; other times, he would save the day."

Suddenly taking Desiree's silence to mean disinterest, she shrugged, saying, "Anyway, that's why I don't kill spiders. So, want to give me a lift to the mall? Teddy and I are going to a costume party as really sexy vampires."

Although Desiree thought that Bonnie and her portly boyfriend might more easily pull off roles as Halloween pumpkins, and, in the recent past, would have verbalized the opinion, whereupon Bonnie would have called her a "skinny bitch," while seemingly unbothered, Desiree Stark had changed her ways. She had reined in the overt sexuality, toned down the haughtiness, and squelched the habit of turning to cruelty for her own amusement.

KillsTwice paused, expecting a snide comment that, to her shock, did not come. Lately, she couldn't read the girl that she had known since elementary school, having, over the many years of their relationship, gotten used to a certain dynamic: Desiree, the head-turning, selfish "it" girl, she, the masochistic hanger-on who expected little and received even less. Since summer, Desiree seemed to have transformed from the predictable "frienemy" that Bonnie had loved and hated, into someone more … human.

"Which store?" Desiree asked. "We could hit Mall of America."

Bonnie wrestled out of the flannel shirt she had worn as a jacket over her thermal, shoved it in the backpack situated between her feet, and retrieved a bottle of Diet Mountain Dew. For a moment, as she watched Desiree huddling inside her wool coat, hands still clad in a pair of rabbit fur-lined Ojibwe style leather mittens, she was struck with a horrible thought. Was Desiree sick? Was she suffering from some incurable illness? In a few short months, Desiree Stark had shed her skintight, undersized, plunged to the navel numbers for drab sweatshirts and plaids that looked as if she had stolen them from her father's closet. She had traded her signature stiletto heels for flat-soled boot moccasins, and the long dark mane she had always worn swinging seductively above an exposed thong and low-rise skinny jeans now often appeared unwashed and piled in a plastic clip or bound in an unkempt ponytail. No more lipstick, no more dragon lady nails, no more flashy bobbles or bangles; Desiree had shifted from siren to simple. Of course, she was still strikingly beautiful, perhaps more so, but there existed an odd sadness, a loss of self-possession, and an uncharacteristic nervousness that made the outer changes seem more worrisome.

"Are you feeling all right? You're shaking, and, quite honestly, you look really pale," Bonnie blurted.

"I'm fine. Just cold and stressed out."

"School shit?" Bonnie asked expectantly, hoping that it was something as easy and relatable as multiple term papers or a low test score.

"Sure," Desiree said, with a sense of Bonnie's need for the least complicated response. "Isn't it always?"

KillsTwice agreed, took a slug of soda, and said, "Maybe you're coming down with a cold."

"Probably," Desiree said noncommittally, and stole a glance at the web.

The spider was gone.

Despite the constant media reminders that the economy currently existed in the crapper, at America's largest mall, the consumers were still insatiably consuming, and Desiree ascended several levels before Bonnie pointed to a parking place. When she had unfolded herself from the driver's seat and hit the lock button, Desiree turned to find another spider perched on the side mirror of the adjacent vehicle. It was almost as if it waited there, watching for her reaction, and when she shuddered, her perfectly white teeth audibly chattering, the creature, seemingly satisfied, darted through a narrow space between the glass and metal.

"Let's go grab a hot drink," Bonnie suggested when she rounded the car and glimpsed her friend's miserable state. "All your shaking and shivering is starting to make me think that *I'm* cold, too. Come on."

Grasping Desiree's arm, Bonnie directed her towards the elevator, the door slid open, and they stepped into the inner warmth. As they descended alone, Desiree unexpectedly heard herself say, "Bonnie, what would you do if Unktomi appeared to you over a dozen times in one day?"

KillsTwice raised an eyebrow. "Seriously?"

Desiree nodded.

Bonnie grinned, her brown eyes filled with dark amusement. "I'd shit."

The elevator stopped, the doors slid open, and a frazzled-looking woman with piles of shopping bags and a stroller containing a pair of fussy twin toddlers got in.

Bonnie leaned close and whispered into Desiree's ear. "Something crazy bad or something crazy good is going to happen to you, but either way, girlfriend, I think you're about to get your world rocked."

On the next floor, they exited and headed for the nearest Caribou Coffee, where Bonnie bought two large mocha lattés, thinking that the caffeine and sugar would do both of them some good. She felt relieved when she noticed that Desiree had slipped her hands from the thick mittens and had unbuttoned her coat, though she still seemed a bit ill at ease.

"Listen, Dezy," she said, as she sat down across from her friend at the small bistro table. "About all that Unktomi stuff, don't take it too seriously. They're old stories meant to scare little kids into doing the right thing. I didn't mean to freak you out."

Desiree stared at Bonnie, both of them knowing that the conciliatory retraction wasn't based in her true feelings, but KillsTwice went on in the futile attempt to assure her friend anyway.

"Besides," she said, as she gestured at the mall's materialistic world of make-believe, "Trickster has no power in a modern marvel like this."

"Are you sure he's not the one who built it?" Desiree countered, sipping the scalding coffee with a painful grimace.

"It *is* pretty hard to escape this crazy web without the cash getting sucked out of your pockets. Maybe you're right."

Desiree listened to the far off mechanical clatter and adrenalin soaked screams produced by the indoor roller coaster. She detected the faint scent of salt water coming from the massive aquarium that imprisoned the multitudes of sea creatures, damned to an existence a thousand miles from any ocean. Sullen teenagers, pinched-faced women, and elderly shufflers moved in all directions, in search of something to fill the empty spaces in their closets, in their homes, in their hearts, in their minds, and although they sometimes thought they had found the thing they had been looking for, time only served to prove them wrong, and they returned, forever caught up in a vicious circle of desire and acquisition.

Suddenly struck with how bizarre this fluorescent world of potted forests and fake rivers really was, Desiree Stark felt, by comparison, oddly normal, or, at the very least, natural.

She finished her coffee, and said, "Come on, KillsTwice, let's go find some sexy vampire gear."

As they stood to leave, a young boy dangling an elastic band with a huge rubber spider at the end chased a squealing little brother past their table, while their mother glanced up from her smart phone and gave them an apathetic reprimand.

"Fake ones don't count, do they?" Desiree said to Bonnie with a half-hearted smile.

"Hell, no," she said, noting the slight improvement in Desiree's mood. "Only the real ones can bite you."

After spotting the perfect gothic attire at Hot Topics, but quickly realizing that the sizes weren't large enough and the prices weren't small enough, Bonnie decided that vampires were out, zombies were in, and they headed for a store devoted exclusively to everything Halloween.

"I'm going to look for some really ghoulish make-up," Bonnie said, gesturing towards an aisle full of masks and wigs.

In an unusual moment of sibling fondness, Desiree decided that she would find something for Oscar and Owen, and told Bonnie that she would meet her at the counter. She wandered through rows of little ballerina tutus, plastic Ninja swords, and glow-in-the-dark candy buckets until she reached the kind of grotesque paraphernalia that her brothers loved: jars of fake vomit, rubber dog turds, aerosol cans full of something that smelled like farts, blood-shot rubber eyeballs, severed fingers, and very realistic-looking dead rats. Ruling out the fake flatulence, as the boys never seemed short on their own supply, Desiree thought some detached body parts and a pair of creepy rodents might brighten their day. As she pawed through the bin of eyeballs, she suddenly found herself facing an entire row of spiders. Having allowed herself to relax a little, she thought at first that the line of arachnids were just more plastic Halloween props, until, in unison, they began to crawl along the edge of the display shelf.

"Wow! That's amazing!" a voice behind Desiree mused.

Startled, she whirled, and bumped into a young man with dark brown curls, a five o'clock shadow, and penetrating green eyes that were fixed upon the single file parade of eight-legged marchers.

"Arachnophobia?" he said, as he gently grasped Desiree's arm to steady her.

"What?" she said, dropping one of the gruesome eyeballs, which bounced several times before rolling down the aisle.

"Are you afraid of spiders?" he said, realizing that not everyone took as great an interest in them as he did.

The answer to that particular question was far too complex for any kind of honest response, so she just shook her head, and said, "Not really ... though I usually like to keep my distance."

"I wish I had a decent camera on me," he said, as he watched the odd scene unfold.

One by one, the spiders rounded a corner on the shelf and vanished behind a pyramid of plastic wind-up skulls, mysteriously causing two of the jaws to clatter as if they were maniacally laughing. When the last spider had gone, the young man reached up and moved the skulls aside, only to find an empty metal shelf. Raising a brow, he turned to Desiree.

"Quick, aren't they?"

Bending down, he retrieved the items that she had dropped and handed them to her, their hands briefly brushing against one another. Desiree felt a quickening of her breath as she glimpsed the design tattooed on the top of his right wrist.

He smiled pulling his cuff up so that she could get a better look as he said, "Funny coincidence, I guess."

Without thinking of consequences, Desiree ran a finger over the spider resting upon the fallen red rose petal that adorned his arm. He shivered, and she pulled her hand away, apologizing.

"It's all right," he said, the kindness in his green eyes so apparent she didn't turn and run, although it was her first instinct at having been so tactless. "It looks quite real, doesn't it?"

"It does, but I shouldn't have invaded your personal space like that."

He laughed. Any man would jump at the chance to have this beautiful girl even speak to him, let alone touch him. He recognized her then, and said, "I'm a student out at Inver Hills. Haven't I seen you there?"

Although the first time he had spotted her she'd had a very different look than she had now, he wouldn't forget such a striking face. As an artist, he had found her beauty intriguing, but as a borderline introvert, straight male, he had found her somewhat trashy attire intimidating. Her dialed-down version had a much more powerful effect, and suddenly he didn't want her to walk away without at least knowing her name.

"Yes," she said. "I'm working on an Associate's degree."

She stole another glimpse at the tattoo, and then at his incredible eyes, and the strong lines of his handsome face. Having always before played the role of pursuer, she now hesitated, confused by a wave of shyness that tangled her thoughts, along with her tongue.

"I'm Evan," he said. "Evan Rubinfeld."

"Desiree Stark."

"So, Desiree, I'm going to make a leap and guess that you have younger brothers," he said, pointing to the articles that she held.

"Yes, twins. They're twelve and love anything on the gross side."

"As a former adolescent boy, I guarantee that stuff is going to be a hit."

"Nothing says 'I love you, little brother' like a dead rat, right?"

Evan grinned and said, "Absolutely."

An awkward pause fell, as neither one knew where to take the conversation next, although both wanted their interaction to continue. Just then, Bonnie strolled around the corner with an arm full of zombie equipment. When she saw Evan, she said, "Hey, you."

"Bonnie," Evan said, flashing her a smile that sent a tinge of jealousy through Desiree. "How's it going?"

"This guy is the bomb," Bonnie said to Desiree. "He totally had my back in our ethics class today. We got on the subject of Indian mascots, and you know I can't keep my mouth shut about how racist that shit is, and the instructor took a real self-righteous douchebag approach. All the little sheep were just nodding their heads at him, and I thought I was going to have to start bitch slapping some people when Evan spoke up and agreed with me. His grandmother survived a Nazi concentration camp, so he's not cool with—what did you call it?"

Last semester, Evan had researched the caricatures that the Third Reich had manufactured as their propaganda to degrade Jews, and run across a comparative study that revealed how disturbingly similar they were to some of the representations of Native Americans currently being flaunted by American sports teams.

"Dehumanizing imagery," Evan said.

"Yeah, dehumanizing imagery," Bonnie said, giving him a fist pump of camaraderie before turning back to Desiree. "Evan's the smartest dude in the class. I think he should be teaching it, rather than taking it. He knows a hell of a lot more than that jack-off they have now."

He shook his head, saying, "Not my thing, but thanks for the compliment."

"So what is your thing?" Desiree asked, desiring the return of the attractive, intelligent man's attention before her gregarious friend stole the show.

"Painting," he said, turning his hypnotic grassy gaze back to her, the intensity of it making her insides somersault. "Water color and acrylic, mostly. I dabble a little in photography, too. I would have loved to have caught a shot of those spiders."

Bonnie gave Desiree a look. Desiree offered a "not now" glare. Shifting the cuff aside again, Evan said, "It's an appreciation for their creativity that compelled me to choose her image."

"Her?" Desiree asked, admiring the intricate detail of the tattoo.

"Yes, female creative energy is the most powerful, is it not?"

"Damn straight, brother," Bonnie interjected.

He smiled, never taking his attention off of Desiree, who still seemed transfixed by the lovely creature painted on the pale skin. Catching the vibe between them, Bonnie KillsTwice suddenly knew that her exit would be much welcomed, said good-bye, and started for the cash register.

Evan soaked in as much of Desiree's image as he could, and hoped that, later, when he had brush and pallet in hand, his memory would serve him well. Imagination began to weave her visage into an intricate spider's web, her shiny black hair fused with the silken strands, and, before he could halt the process, he had formulated the contents of his next canvas.

"I really should get going," she said, anxiety tickling her as if all the spiders of the day had found their way beneath her skin. "But I would love to see some of your work. Do you have a gallery?"

"I don't have any gallery shows scheduled right now," he said, a bruise darkening his ego before he quickly recovered and added, "But I have a few paintings displayed at a café downtown."

Brightening, Desiree asked the address.

"Are you free this weekend? We could have dinner and I could show them to you."

Something clicked suddenly, and Evan panicked. What had he just done? He had never approached a girl this gorgeous, let alone asked one out. She was clearly out of his league.

"I'd love that," she said, the light in her pupils warming like fire, chilling him like ice.

Then Desiree Stark gave the man with Unktomi on his wrist her number, and felt her world rocking with a most delicious sway.

26

Bone Chokers

"So when can I sample that?" Gus IronHorse asked, as he peered over Barb StandingBull's shoulder and inspected the progress as she basted the turkey cranberry pecan sage stuffing.

"Not yet," she said, exercising the patience she had to exhibit every year when Gus began salivating for a morsel hours too soon.

"When will Marie and her friend get here?"

"The flight arrives at noon, so … around two."

"Will we eat then?"

Barb closed the oven, laid the hot pads aside, and wiped her hands on a faded gingham apron that had once belonged to her grandmother, then her mother, and now, her.

"I suggested to Marie that we could schedule dinner for then."

Gus took on a temperamental tone, crossing his arms over his chest and striking a pose as if he might start stomping a foot any moment.

"I'm hungry *now*! I can't wait until two o'clock. I'll starve."

"Really?" Barb grinned as she found the bit of belly hanging over his belt and gave it a soft poke. "There's a nice tray of raw vegetables and some spinach artichoke dip in the refrigerator. If you become weak with hunger, drag yourself on over and enjoy."

Pouting, he said, "I ain't that hungry—yet. But if I *get* that hungry, I'm coming for the bird, woman! You can't stop me."

Barb put her hands on her hips, stared him down, and replied, "Old man,-don't take on a blind woman with a carving knife. You could lose something important."

"Idle threat." Gus grinned as he grabbed her around the waist, nuzzling her neck. "Now kiss me and apologize for calling me old."

She kissed him, then pushed him out of the kitchen, saying, "Relax. We're eating at noon. Marie didn't want us to wait in case their flight isn't on time. They'll be here for dessert. Now get out. There's not enough room for the cook. Go watch some football, Okanna."

IronHorse stuck his head around the corner a few seconds later. "Hey! Doesn't Okanna mean Grandpa?"

StandingBull smiled, shoved the beaters into a pan of hot sweet potatoes, and turned the mixer on high.

***

Marie Barfield boarded the plane at the Ashville Regional Airport with a healthy mix of anticipation and in trepidation. She hadn't seen Gus, her nephew through affection rather than blood, since he and Barb had visited North Carolina three years earlier. They talked on the phone regularly, but it sure would feel good to wrap her arms around him, see the familiar lines of Billy IronHorse that made up Gus' face, and reminisce with someone who missed the old man as much as she did.

Barfield had met the teenage IronHorse and his grandfather shortly after Gus had taken flight from California, his mother, Randall Trigg, and the half-siblings, and landed back in Cherokee, North Carolina. The boy had enough anger and disturbing stories of his cross-country journey for any man thrice his age, and, initially, Gus had stormed out each time Marie, or as he hissed under his breath, "that white woman," came to visit Billy. It took several months before she could even expect a grunt of greeting from him.

When they reached the stage of full sentences, Gus informed her that anthropologists and ethnographers like her gave him a pain in his red ass. Barfield could still hear the calm force that Billy IronHorse exacted upon his grandson that day. He had taken Gus firmly by the arm and sat him in the kitchen chair across the table from Barfield, saying, "You're entitled to your opinion, boy. What you're not entitled to is the right to disrespect a guest in my home. Are we clear, Augustus?"

The boy had nodded, shame washing over his young troubled face.

"First, apologize to Miss Barfield, then get out back, grab an axe, and work off some of that self-pity and hatred. Those logs need to be cut down; our friend here doesn't."

Randall Trigg had left his Cherokee wife's son with a deep-seated distrust of white people, and Barfield soon realized that, in order to have a relationship, she would have to use the same principles as she had with the abused dogs she had rescued: do nothing that could be misconstrued as aggression, speak with kind softness, and let him be the one to approach.

With time, Gus lost some of the animosity that saddled him, and grew fond of the UNC faculty professor who had the trust, friendship, and admiring randy eye of his grandfather. Though decades existed between her and Billy IronHorse, they became lovers, and, despite the fact that they kept separate residences, they, along with Gus, formed a family.

Marie Barfield's patience had prevailed, and had opened an academic opportunity for Augustus IronHorse, as she saw a level of intelligence that deserved a nurturing environment, and, when he finished high school, Barfield proactively assisted in getting him enrolled at UNC's Ashville campus. Their kinship had stretched beyond Billy IronHorse's death, and now, as Marie Barfield took her seat in coach, slid the window shade down against the rising sun, she worried that the plans she had set into motion would jeopardize everything.

***

"So Marie's got herself a new boyfriend," Gus said as Barb sat beside him on the couch, and he flipped channels, stopping on an NFL game before seeing the helmets with the stoic Indian head, muttering about sanctioned racism, and clicking onward.

"Apparently," Barb said. "I assume that's why she made hotel reservations rather than stay here. They probably want privacy."

IronHorse shook his head and grinned. "Marie's quite the live wire. Her boyfriends are always interesting. Bet this one won't disappoint."

On their last visit with Barfield, they had met Tim, an environmental rights activist with whom she had been chained to the same redwood while on an anti-deforestation mission. The romance hadn't lasted long; their shared passion for trees had not translated well in the bedroom.

"Between you and me," Barfield had confided to Barb. "Tim needed the little blue pill, if you know what I mean, but because he's very against the big pharmaceutical companies, well, it's better that we're just friends."

So Tim, who literally, and admirably, hugged trees, went into Marie's ex files along with the ACLU lawyer, a visiting French philosophy professor, a New Age minister, the hydroponics gardener who claimed to specialize in tomatoes, and the yoga instructor who had helped Marie rediscover her G-spot while simultaneously throwing out her back. The string of short-lived affairs had begun a year after his grandfather's death, leaving Gus to wonder if the twenty-year relationship with Billy IronHorse sealed the older man as Barfield's soul mate. Some believed that a person has more than one in a lifetime. For Marie's sake, Gus hoped that it was true.

"What's the new dude's name?"

"She didn't say," Barb said, suddenly struck with a discomforting pang of anxiety as she thought of how little Marie had told her about the man Barb had so readily invited into their home.

StandingBull had taken an immediate liking to Marie when they met over a decade ago, and, although sometimes Barfield's brash personality stood in harsh opposition to the harmonious quiet that Barb liked to maintain, she had accepted the older woman's quirkiness, always reminding herself that Marie was Gus' only family—at least the only family with whom he had any contact.

Touching the haphazard ponytail at the nape of IronHorse's neck, she asked, "Would you like me to braid your hair?"

Wordlessly, he turned, closing his eyes like a contented cat as her gentle fingers separated the strands of black and gray into thirds and wove them into a long neat plait. No woman had ever loved him quite like Barb, and on this day, like all their days together, a deep sense of gratitude shone its way into his darker corners, disallowing thoughts of who he did not have to overshadow those for whom he was so thankful. Holidays could bring melancholy that, on other days, the routine grind of life, kept at bay, but holidays meant family, and family, well, that for some had its own set of complications.

Soft instrumental Christmas music drifted from the television as a masculine voice proclaimed undying love for his wife and the mother of his children, before another male voice, less fraught with emotion, asked the question, "Doesn't she deserve a diamond this year?" Barb wrapped the end of the braid and let it fall between Gus' shoulder blades, as, for a moment, her thoughts turned to the annual card that arrived in their box, postmarked from California. It had held an address label that had, up until three years ago, read "Lt. and Mrs. Randall Trigg". After that, the cards had no longer arrived. Barb would leave them propped and unopened on the desk in Gus' home office, and later would find them, still unopened, in the metal bin where he threw mail for the shredder.

The first year, StandingBull had made the mistake of asking him about the sealed card. Are you sure that you don't want to open this, Gus?" she had asked, timidly holding the bent envelope like a pinless white paper hand grenade.

"Very sure," he had replied, the hatred in his tone spilling over and burning its way towards her before she had a chance to escape. I suppose that makes me a real asshole."

"She's your mother," Barb had ventured, and then immediately wished she had thrown the card in the shredder and run, as IronHorse's face turned stony.

"That woman and that word lost a connection for me a long fucking time ago. For once, Barb, back off, put the do-gooder shit aside, and leave it alone!"

Later, he had found her in the upstairs bedroom, where she had chosen to sleep, and crawled into the single bed beside her, curled into her arms, and cried. She had held him, stroked his hair, and silently accepted the apology of the wounded boy that lived inside her man.

As another retail chain solicited its secular brand of the approaching religious holidays, instilling in every child, as well as every adult, more items for their never-ending must-have lists, Finnegan lumbered over. He tried to hoist himself between them, without much luck, until Gus grabbed the old dog's haunches and gave him a boost. Joyously, the Lab slobbered all over Barb's freshly laundered skirt, which she had just changed into for their visitor's arrival. Sighing, she lovingly rubbed Finnegan's neck, and leaned down, kissing him on the top of the head.

"I love you guys," she said, as thoughts of how short life really is reached deep into her chest with a torturous tug, and maternal tears fell upon the dog's velvety ears.

***

The plane began its descent, and Marie Barfield grew quiet, no longer making conversation with the man who sat next to her. He didn't mind her silence; it offered him time to untangle all the possible scenarios of this trip. Whereas his plan to come to the Twin Cities had seemed rooted in the most honorable intentions, and Marie had initially sensed this, hesitantly agreeing to accompany him, he now began to feel the chill of premonition, followed by a gut-tightening apprehension. They looked at each other when the engine stopped and the aircraft stood still, Marie offering him a small pat on the hand, and a slight nod, a meager consolation that told him that she had her doubts, too.

She had warned him of the Minnesota November cold, and he had worn the warmest coat he owned, but as they walked to the rental car, the wind ripped at his face with icy claws, as if to say, "You are not welcome here." Their exchanged words stayed perfunctory as he drove, his hands two frozen spheres of granite upon the wheel, she giving directions, he mechanically executing them. At the hotel, they checked into their adjoining rooms, entered their lodgings, and both fell with great sighs, onto the unyielding hardness of the rented beds. When she had collected herself, Marie Barfield dug her cell from inside her purse, called the number, and said that they had arrived.

"By the way, Marie," Barb StandingBull asked. "I'm curious. What is your friend's name?"

Barfield saw a flock of agitated starlings take flight from the bare branches of a tree outside the window, their wings moving in sync with the flutter in her own breast, as she said, "His name is Alistair."

***

The less-than-common name bounced around Barb's head like ricocheting gun shot, her memory filing through faces, social situations, old schoolmates, characters from recently read novels, and nightly news headlines as she tried to locate the source of the unsettling familiarity she felt at having heard it.

They sat around the rarely used dining room table, their empty plates still in front of them, as they talked, laughed, and sipped wine. Leonard and Maggie shared the details of Desiree's new boyfriend, and how he was the first young man she had ever brought home to meet the family. Leonard said that he liked Evan, and didn't mind that Desiree had chosen to spend the day with him and his parents in Woodbury.

Jack lamented the approach of Black Friday, and what it would mean for him at the electronics store, recounting a darkly humorous story about last year's fist fight between two elderly women vying for the last super sale laptop.

Isaac and Gus began their expert predictions about the ill-fated Vikings and their upcoming match-up with Green Bay. From the "boy table," relegated to the kitchen, which suited the three exiles just fine, Owen, Oscar, and Seattle had put their dirty young minds together and were creating an impromptu rap that involved pilgrims, turkeys, and some extremely revolting, yet hilarious, circumstances.

Despite all the levity, Barb felt the yoke of the elusive name, pressing down her mood, as she excused herself, and began to clear the serving bowls of gravy, green bean casserole, and scalloped corn. Maggie rose to help, and, as Barb was about to walk away, Leonard nodded towards Gus, and said, "By the way, I really like that bone choker you're wearing, Brother."

With that, the name and the distant memory crashed together in StandingBull's brain, the gravy bowl smashed against the hard wood floor, and the doorbell began ringing.

***

Alistair had knocked on the door of their adjoining rooms, and Barfield had found the young man nervously holding the bone choker. She had given it to him a week earlier, on his birthday.

"Can you help me tie this?" he asked, as if the question were something of which he should feel ashamed, something that disenfranchised, disqualified, and peeled away the thin fragile layer of fresh identity for which he had fought. "I don't know how tight it should be."

For an instant, she had wanted to offer up a joke, wanted to tell him it should be tight enough so that the enemy couldn't get his knife between it and his throat, but, seeing his vulnerability, she thought better of it.

He came into her room, sat on the desk chair, while she placed the choker around his neck and tied the leather straps. As she did so, he looked at her reflection in the mirror in front of them. Her short plum-colored hair stood in crazy spikes; her latest "do," or, as she had shrugged and said, "Maybe a "don't." She wore a flowing denim skirt with embroidered flowers, moons, and stars around the hem, a pair of bright red cowboy boots, a purple turtleneck sweater, a tangle of silver and bead necklaces, huge hoop ear rings, and the kindest smile he had ever witnessed upon the face of a woman. Placing her ringed fingers on his shoulders, she had met his gaze in the mirror, and said, "Real family doesn't come easy. No matter what happens, I consider you mine."

Now they waited; Marie with her long purple finger nail pressed to the doorbell button, Alistair standing behind her at the bottom of the porch steps, his pulse beating behind the bone choker, a store-bought pumpkin pie awkwardly balanced in his gloveless, shaking hands.

***

Isaac stooped and helped Barb pick up the shards of broken bowl.

"I have to answer the door!" she said, frantically trying to sop up the congealed gravy that dripped from her skirt.

"Gus has it, sweetie," Isaac said. "Relax, go change your clothes, and I'll clean this up."

The massive antique walnut dining table lay between her and the entrance to the living room, so she darted into the kitchen, ripped a large clean tea towel from the drawer, tucked it into the waist of the skirt, covering some of the greasy stains, and hurried to prove herself wrong. She couldn't be right. Marie wouldn't do that, would she? A bizarre coincidence, that's all it was … an odd happenstance. She clung to the notion as she hastened on, a deeper instinct for truth telling her that coincidence as explanation was as tangible as wind collected in one's pocket.

In the muted sunlight of the doorway, Marie and Gus embraced, their voices airy delighted, and full of love, but, behind them, Barb could make out the blurry shape, standing tall and silent, awaiting his introduction, and she froze. Marie Barfield let go of Gus, and motioned for the shadowy, silhouetted figure to come into the house. Barb moved closer, positioning herself at IronHorse's back, her hand resting against his spine.

The men's eyes met, Alistair's with eager openness, Gus' with a friendly lack of recognition. Marie placed a hand on each man's arm, her voice calm and low, as she said, "Gus, this is Alistair."

At the sound of the name, Barb felt the muscles of his neck harden beneath her touch, as he backed closer to her, and away from them.

"Alistair Trigg," said the young man who wore a choker, identical to the bone, bead, sinew, and leather that encircled IronHorse's throat. "It's been a long time, Brother."

27

American Apple Pie

Helen Trigg shuffled through the mottled sunlight, beneath the fig palms that lined the courtyard, clutching the forearm of the woman that earlier in the day she had recognized as her daughter. With gentle coaxing, Helen had also recalled that her name was Amanda. The recollection had bloomed a beautiful, broad smile upon the younger woman's face, and had compelled her to reach affectionately towards Helen, a physical gesture which sent the older woman into a fit of fearful screams. Apologizing profusely, Amanda had backed slowly away from her mother, hands held up in a kind of surrender to the frail woman's unfounded fright and to her own longing ache, as the merciless disease that swallowed more of her mother's mind each day ripped away another fragment of Amanda Trigg Garcia's hope. When the distressed woman had calmed, Amanda tried again, but her mother could no longer place where she had once met the vaguely familiar woman, who claimed to be one of her offspring.

"Would you like to go outside for some fresh air, Mrs. Trigg?" Amanda finally said, when she resigned to the fact that her mother's precious moment of lucidity had slipped away and that pleading the truth of their blood connection would more likely than not end with fruitless frustration.

Helen had allowed the kind woman with a bent little finger that closely resembled her own curved digit to remove the slippers from her swollen feet, tenderly slip on the black lace-ups, tying them, as Helen observed, with the same odd technique she had herself once used, and lead her out into the balmy sweetness of the San Diego afternoon.

As they made their slow rotations along the neatly manicured hedges of the nursing home's garden path, Amanda commented on the beauty of the groomed roses, and the sound of a songbird that she could not name, as it revealed itself only as flashes of brief yellow gold between the deeper darker shades of green. Occasionally, Helen nodded, her apathetic gaze never landing upon the spots where the younger woman pointed. Suddenly, as if pulled from the lethargy by a quick jerk of urgency from some invisible string, she stopped short, tugging fiercely at the sleeve of Amanda's blouse.

"What is it?" she said, concerned that her mother's medications had caused dizziness, as they sometimes did. "Are you all right? Would you like to sit down?"

"Do you know my son?" the old woman asked, a note of suspicion tingeing the question as if it was a test that Amanda must pass if their tedious trek was to continue.

Yes, I know Alistair."

These kinds of inquiries had become more common as bits of long and short term memory fluttered around her mother's head like moths, sometimes landing briefly before taking flight beyond the range of her clarity, leaving only hazy clouds of wing dust behind. Last week, she had asked about a visit from her husband Randall, three years after his fleeting pancreatic cancer battle concluded with a formal military burial. The week before, Helen had offered Amanda a picture of a full-faced girl with pigtails and a missing front tooth among the white of her shy grin. She held the small frame, shaped like a golden apple, that she had given to her mother last year, and listened patiently, as Helen introduced details—some fact, some fiction—about the child, as if Amanda were a stranger to her own daughter. Sometimes, her mother spoke of names that Amanda Trigg Garcia knew only from the inconspicuous wicker sewing basket that she and her brother had found hidden behind stacks of linen, precisely placed pairs of low-heel pumps, and plain cotton dresses within the depths of their mother's closet.

"Who is this Alistair?" she said, a blank expression falling like an impenetrable veil over Helen Trigg's face. "My son's name is Augustus."

***

Augustus IronHorse and Alistair Trigg looked at one another, each man trying to find traces of himself in the other, and during the painfully uncomfortable moment of assessment they found their mother's genetic marks. Alistair had her long forehead, Gus, her slightly pouty bottom lip, and both had a natural part in their hair that fell left of center. For Alistair, the similarities took shape as symbolic signs that solidified the fraternal relationship they both had been denied all these years. These small physical features that biologically connected them to one source seemed to validate his wish to know the brother he only recently had discovered at the bottom of an antique sewing basket, beneath spools of thread, bent needles, and scraps of fabric.

Neither Alistair nor Amanda had any recollection of Helen ever sewing, and, from the moment they unearthed the old wicker case, a disquieting aura had hung around it, and they had circled cautiously, as if some precarious organism lived within it. Perhaps they had sensed the secrecy, the shame, and the sorrow that it held, somehow knowing on a visceral level that its contents would only deepen, only widen already existent rifts that lay between them and their parents. Amanda had chosen to remain absent from their father's bedside as Randall Trigg's soul made its exit, freeing him from the thorough disappointment, theft of his God-given masculine right of familial control, and lack of respect, his children had inflicted upon him.

"The girl" as he always had liked to refer to Amanda when railing about his daughter's perceived shortcomings, had run off and married a Mexican. Although she claimed that the man had been born in Los Angeles, it mattered not to Randall, who saw the brown-skinned young man without any military service as a complete affront upon his own image as father figure.

With an expulsion from Hill Crest Military Academy, followed up a few years later with enrollment at UC Berkley, Alistair had by no means escaped the lieutenant's scorn. His father claimed that it was "that damn liberal hippy college's" responsibility for drawing out Alistair's desire to know more about Helen's Cherokee lineage.

"Native American, American Indian, or whatever it is they're calling themselves these days," his father had said, as he slammed a fork through a slice of apple pie with enough force to send flakes of crust sailing onto the lace table cloth. "The important word in all that politically correct garbage is American. We're *all* Americans, Alistair, your mother, you, your sister, and, of course, me."

Then he had slammed a fist to his heart with a zeal that dared anyone to challenge his indisputable patriotism, and, as Alistair felt himself being incrementally thrown under a bus, his mother watched the vanilla ice cream melt its whiteness over her slice of warm pie and absently nodded the approval that her husband never sought. Her mind drifted to the careful hour she had spent cutting away the bright red peel from the apples' tart, crisp fruit, her fork probing for any mistakes she might have left behind, but finding none.

"I went to Korea," Trigg announced, as if it were breaking news. "I served my country. There isn't anything more American than that!"

Helen never met the gaze of the son whose honey skin resembled her own, more closely than his fathers. She never looked up from that damn apple pie—Lieutenant Randall Trigg's favorite dessert—but simply sat in her silence and allowed Alistair to believe that, to her, their shared ancestral connection was less relevant than a slice of flour, lard, and sugar syrup-drowned fruit.

Even when Alistair had managed to catch his mother alone while Randall golfed nine holes with a retired captain, Helen fluttered a hand like an overwrought, amateur magician praying that the concealed would vanish, as she said, "Leave well enough alone, Alistair. I have nothing to tell you. I grew up in foster homes, with nice white families. I know nothing about the Cherokee or what it means to be one. Just thank God that you had the privilege of being raised as a normal American boy. Don't search for trouble, son. Be content with who you are."

"Who exactly is that, Mother?"

She checked him with her stare, not about to free him from the cold, hard point that she hoped would save them both from his disturbing curiosity.

"As your birth certificate indicates, you are Alistair Martin Trigg, Caucasian male, born in the United States of America. Nothing more, nothing less."

So when the last piece of furniture, the last box of dishes, pans, and utensils, the last crate of toys played with in their youths, and the last rugs had been rolled up and loaded onto the truck, bound for the estate auction, Alistair and Amanda had sat cross-legged on the bare floor of their childhood home with the ominous sewing basket between them. After long dusty, unbreathable moments, Alistair unhooked the latch, lifted the bone-dry wicker lid, and began to remove the contents. The pictures, the birth certificate, the divorce papers, and a cracked leather address book were hidden beneath the torn fabric liner. Gasping, Amanda had plucked the first photo from the pile, saying, "This is the boy in my dream—or what I told myself was a dream."

As a toddler, Amanda had remembered a kind-faced older boy who played the "toss a toy" game with her, she hurling a rag doll, a rattle, or a teething ring from her crib, and then wailing piteously until the boy retrieved what she desired, handed it back, and made funny faces at her until she laughed, smiled, and flung the object away again. Around age two, Amanda no longer saw the boy, and, because no one ever spoke of him, she began to believe that he was nothing more than a remnant of a pleasant dream. But the boy had not been a dream. He had been real, and was looking back at her from the old snapshot. Turning it over, she saw her mother's flowery penmanship.

"Augustus IronHorse, age thirteen," she read aloud, and then handed it to Alistair, who wrinkled his brow and admitted that he hadn't a clue.

The birth certificate and the divorce papers clearly told the stories that Helen Trigg chose not to tell, and as if the opening of the Pandora-like basket had released all the memories that Helen had been trying to forget for so long back into her failing mind, she began to feel herself randomly tethered to the regrettable past more often than to the preferred present. But like so much of what entered and exited her jumble of thoughts, Helen could not fit the additional puzzle pieces into the larger picture of her life. When Alistair and Amanda showed her the documents, photos, and address book, their mother's expression glazed over with the befuddled disconnect to which they had grown accustomed, leaving them with only a paper trail and differing opinions on whether to follow it.

Now, as Alistair balanced the pie in his left hand and offered the right one to his half-brother, Augustus IronHorse stared at it for a moment before quietly excusing himself, turning with a slow deliberateness, and leaving the room, Alistair thought of Amanda's parting words as she drove him to the airport.

"Mom has already dumped enough on us," she had said, her weary resentment hanging like dank fog. "She burned your damn house down, for Christ's sake."

Helen had simply forgotten the scrambled eggs on the stove and walked out the back door to follow a stray dog that reminded her of a Springer spaniel that one of her foster families had owned when she was a girl. By the time Alistair had received the call at work, the house was a complete loss. The event marked the beginning of the end for his already-strained marriage, and convinced both Trigg children that their mother's condition required more supervision than either of them could provide.

"It wasn't her fault. I know that," Amanda relinquished, and then, softening her sharpness, said, "I understand what you're looking for, but I feel saturated, and I won't go hunting for more family, more problems, more responsibilities. I think we already have enough. Besides, Alistair, did you ever think that this long-lost brother of ours, may want to stay lost?"

***

Gus walked into the kitchen, through the laundry room, and down the stairs to the basement, all the while clutching at the bits and pieces of earlier calm he had attained over dinner, in a wine glass, with those he deemed family. Beside the furnace, he dusted off a rickety wooden stool and sank upon it, a man seeking refuge from the world above. Torn between the overwhelming need to sob and an urge to scream away the percolating rage, he remained silent, hoping that all feeling would just burn away. Closing his eyes, pressing his palms against the sockets, he could see the past fused into Alistair's features: Randall's thin lips, Helen's cheekbones, Randall's prominent ears, Helen's meek voice. There they both were, in his house, in his living room, in this stranger who called him "brother." They had come for him after thirty years of wondering why they hadn't, after Helen Trigg telling Billy IronHorse that it would be better for everyone if he just kept the boy, after Gus had, in a moment of redemption, called California to share the joy of having graduated from college and heard the automated message that their number was no longer in service. Sure, they had sent out scouts in the form of those fucking Christmas cards, but he hadn't let the poison out of the envelopes, hadn't responded, hadn't divulged the whereabouts of his encampment. And yet, despite his long-since discarded desire for contact with the woman who had borne him, they had come.

The sound of the boy's laughter echoed down the stairs, and Gus could hear footsteps moving across the creaking boards of the living room, moving towards the dining room. He heard Leonard's baritone voice asking where they kept the filters, and a few minutes later Gus smelled the aroma of dark roast coffee. He knew that Barb wouldn't come looking for him. Lakota traditional etiquette would never allow her to abandon guests, and, for a moment, he felt embarrassed at having left her alone to sort out the situation. What kind of man was he? Maybe as predicted, he had become much like his father, Jimmy IronHorse. Helen hadn't been all wrong in her assessments of her ex-husband; Gus' grandfather had supported many of them.

"Your dad was full of anger," Billy IronHorse had told the boy upon his return to North Carolina. "He tried to douse it in alcohol, but, as it usually does, it just made him a hell of a lot meaner. He was crazy drunk the night he stabbed that man. The guy called your mom a squaw. Jimmy snapped, and stuck a knife in that man's shoulder. Only missed the heart by an inch. He was fueled by booze the night he got out of prison, too. That's when he heard that Helen had remarried and taken you out west. That's the night he roared off in my truck, robbed a liquor store, and flew that old Ford right off the mountainside. My son lived an angry life … and he died an angry death."

As the furnace kicked on and the stink of burnt dust crept into Gus' nostrils, he wondered where his own anger would land. He thought of Marie, the obvious facilitator of this forced family reunion, but couldn't fully dredge up enough ire to snuff out what, if he were to be truly honest with himself, was well-intentioned. Short-sightedness had often plagued Marie, but her goodness had prevailed, time and again, making animosity towards her seem like an unwarranted attack upon an innocent animal.

Alistair Trigg, on the other hand, seemed a more likely candidate for IronHorse's wrath. What agenda did he have, showing up on Thanksgiving, ruining a perfectly good Indian feast?

"God damn Pilgrim," muttered Gus, dislodging a piece of turkey from between his molars and spitting it into the floor's sump pump hole.

What did this guy want from him? Handshakes, hugs, slaps on the back, a brotherly game of basketball out on the driveway to make up for lost time? Did Alistair have an inkling of accurate information about how their illustrious mother had, when Augustus no longer fit into her automatic dishwasher, picket fence-lined subdivision, respectable white husband, cream-colored children life, tossed her oldest son aside like a worn out pair of moccasins? Sardonically, Gus smiled, examining the flesh of his forearm, and thinking that time had skimmed much of Alistair's cream away, leaving a man with a complexion not much lighter than his own. He hoped that Helen and the lieutenant were doing back flips over their tan, bone choker-wearing offspring, and that the older one, Amanda, had moved to Arizona, married a Navajo sheep herder, and taken up hoop dancing.

When the petty reel of retribution had run out, other, more empathetic questions came in its place. Had Helen inflicted a similar reception upon Alistair's outward identity? Like Gus, had he broken away from their mother and Trigg? Why had Amanda chosen not to accompany her younger brother?

Like blue jays diving at a cat on a tree limb, with each additional question that flew at IronHorse's conscience, his anger retreated, and, knowing that he would find no answers in the dark, damp basement, he sighed, rose from the stool and lifted a foot onto the first step.

At the encouragement of their hostess, they had begun dessert during Gus' absence, and he found the group around the dining room table, engaged in subdued polite conversation, cups of coffee, and slices of pecan and pumpkin pie. As he passed her, he touched Barb's shoulder, and she caught his hand with hers, holding tightly so that he had no choice but to pause.

"Did the fresh air help?" she asked, as she squeezed his fingers in a familiar way that said, "just go with it."

"Yes, feasting can be brutal on a health-conscious man like me."

Most at the table chuckled. Marie and Alistair simply nodded and sipped from the china cups, which looked awkward in his large fingers, and out of place against her garish purple nails. Barb released his hand, and as he took his chair at the head of the table, said, "I introduced everyone, but not properly."

Marie cast her gaze briefly towards Gus before concentrating again on her coffee. Gus stole a glance at Alistair, who looked back with such a rueful, hangdog expression, that Augustus IronHorse actually felt something akin to pity. The younger man's hair, which was in the impossible stage between short and not long enough to manage, fell across one side of his face, and he hid behind it, giving Gus a slight shake of his head. IronHorse took it to mean that the guests had not been informed of their connection, but Gus still couldn't help but wonder if Leonard had asked about Alistair's bone choker, if Maggie had noticed the family resemblance, or if Barb had ever told Isaac anything about his childhood.

He scanned the faces around the table. Leonard, Isaac, and Jack, each man he considered a brother and a friend. The three part-time miscreants in the kitchen, well, they had become nephews. What a family, what a circle, what a tribe they had formed together. Augustus IronHorse sat up straight in the antique oak host chair, and placed his palms on the table, saying, "If I may then, I would like to offer proper introductions."

From the opposite end of the table, Barb StandingBull offered a single, almost imperceptible nod of approval, and Augustus began, moving counter clockwise, sharing good memories he had collected with each person along the way, until, at last he reached the man with the matching bone choker.

"I don't have many stories to tell," said Augustus, the collective mood simultaneously downshifting as they all sensed something patchy ahead. "It's been a very long time."

He blinked, for a moment catching sight of the quiet, cool pines where Billy IronHorse had sprinkled his son's ashes, a place he had hoped Augustus' father's spirit would finally find peace, and then, without knowing what compelled him, he unfastened the choker from around his own neck and laid it in front of Alistair. With sincere solemnity, the younger man offered his own protective throat covering. The older man took it.

"This is Alistair Trigg. My mother's son. My brother."

***

In a dining hall, decorated with fat accordion-style paper turkeys, happy-faced pilgrims, and not an Indian in sight, an old woman sat with her daughter and a slice of apple pie, and, as the vanilla ice cream melted away into ruined white pools, Helen Trigg began to cry.

28

The Hardest Moon

In the mother tongue of Isaac TwoBears' people, the month of January translates into English most literally as "hard moon," and as he chiseled away at a thick layer of ice on the truck's windshield with a plastic scraper, his fingers numbing beneath the leather gloves, Isaac's breath hung like frosty clouds in the late afternoon darkness, and the connotations pricked a place of dull sadness within him as discomforting as the needles of cold that pierced the bare flesh of his face. New Year had delivered him and Jack from some of the difficulties brought about by Bordeaux's relationship stalemate, and they now spent more nights together than apart; weeknights at Jack's apartment to accommodate Seattle's middle school schedule, weekends in Minneapolis at Isaac's place. Although, during a holiday visit from Clayton, Jack had introduced TwoBears as "a special friend," Jack hadn't balked when, a few days later, Isaac had taken him to meet his parents and called Bordeaux "my partner." Slow steady progress towards the permanence he sought had given Isaac a sense of solidity, a feeling that the odds of their survival as a couple, as a family, were growing better all the time.

But now, beneath a starless sky that seemed to hold only promises of winter's forbidding force, deep deprivation, and utter wreckage of all that is weak, Isaac chilled at bitter black-iced deliberations of moments when his world had, without warning, slid from under him. In those out-of-control times, he had fallen so hard that his spirit fractured, the shards left behind as jagged cutting tools that had slashed at his sanity. Time had fused Isaac's pieces back together, but, for whatever reason, this frigid moon seemed to be shining its cold, heartless light upon Isaac TwoBears' like an emotional X-ray, exposing all the mended little cracks.

He shook the ice shavings off his hands and climbed behind the wheel with the haggard movements of a man only wishing for the day to end so that the next might bring something less burdensome. Isaac did not like to do jobs during the winter, and tried to squirrel away earnings so that, like his ancestors, he could spend time beneath his blankets, in front of the fire, stories told to him in the form of good books. But modernity dictated other plans, and when his stores ran low, he forced himself out of the lodge, hunted down small remodeling jobs, and spent an afternoon or two laying bathroom tile, hanging dry wall, or refurbishing a walk-in closet so that Mrs. So-and -So could cram another hundred pairs of shoes into her collection. He had spent this afternoon installing some shelving units in an Eden Prairie kitchen pantry, a task that did not warrant the fatigue he now felt, and, for one tired breath, he wondered if it was related to the fact that he was bulleting towards middle-age, but then deflected that thought with thoughts of Jack, the pleasant fact that his younger lover would arrive home for a late dinner that night, and that they had the whole weekend ahead of them.

As Isaac maneuvered into north-bound rush hour traffic, he yawned, and a strange, sickening scene crashed into his brain, a scene he had barred from his conscious thoughts years ago, but it had somehow broken through the guardrails and impacted with a horrible explosion. Like the ghost limb of an amputee, the once-broken bridge of Isaac's nose began to ache. He slid a glove off and applied pressure to the phantom pain, while driving the dangerous memory from his mind, until both died away and he was left to consider their catalyst.

Traffic unknotted as he got closer to home, and Isaac's foot grew leaden on the truck's gas pedal, the sheltering safety of his house calling to a persistent uneasiness that he couldn't shake. The wild, starving dog feeling chased Isaac until the truck tires crunched through the insignificant little drifts of dry snow that he had not bothered to scoop from the driveway. But before he could even turn the motor off and slip the earlier discarded glove back on, his phone rang. Had it not been Seattle, he would have ignored it, and escaped inside, locked the door, and wrapped himself in the relief of a hot buttered rum.

"Hey, kid. What's up?"

"Could you come pick me up? I'm ready to go."

TwoBears hadn't expected the call until much later, and he asked, "Everything alright?"

After a pause, the boy cleared his throat, lowered his voice, and said, "Megan just broke up with me. I really would like to get out of here … you know what I mean?"

Cringing, Isaac imagined poor Seattle uncomfortably stranded in the living room with one or both of Megan's mothers, the teenage girl probably having abandoned him for the security of her bedroom.

"Oh, shit! That's awkward. I'm on my way, kid."

Tossing the phone back into a cup holder, TwoBears reversed course, on the road to rescue a young man from his first bruised ego and broken heart. When he reached the end of the block, he yielded to a taxi turning from a side avenue, and as the car passed beneath a light pole onto his street, a strange stab of fear hit him in the chest, and a searing jolt assaulted the unnatural hump on his nose, causing water to leak from his eyes. He leaned across the center console and retrieved a box of tissues that had fallen onto the floor mat, just missing a glimpse of the cab's passenger. Had he taken a look in the truck's rear view mirror, Isaac would have noticed that the taxi had stopped in front of his house. He might have recognized the figure that climbed out, walked to TwoBears' front door, and rang the bell. Had the irrational apprehension that had stalked him all day not prevented him from observing what was behind him, he would have anticipated the fissure and held onto Jack so that he did not fall through, but Isaac drove on, deaf to thunderous peals of everything cracking, splitting, and grinding apart.

When Isaac reached the St. Louis Park home of Seattle's now ex-girlfriend, LaDonna accompanied her daughter's now ex-boyfriend into the foyer, and with a gesture of genuine conciliatory affection, placed an arm around his shoulder.

"Girls are fickle. I speak from every level of experience. I'm truly sorry. You're such a nice kid."

She then handed Seattle off to Isaac, offered TwoBears an apologetic nod for having any part in the teenage angst he and Jack had ahead of them, and closed the front door that still held a festive lit wreath. As they drove away, Seattle did not look back.

"Do you want to talk about it?" Isaac asked.

The boy shrugged, paused for a few minutes as if he preferred silence, but then spoke in the flat tones of the recently defeated. "She likes another guy."

"She told you that?"

"Not exactly. I kind of tripped on it."

"That's a rotten thing to trip on," TwoBears said, a long-buried anger beginning to tremor within him as the bridge of his nose tingled back awake. "Deception hurts like hell."

"We were downstairs in what they call the media room, which basically is just a big living room with a sixty-two inch flat screen and a laptop they stream movies with. Megan hadn't logged off of her Facebook page, and when she ran upstairs to grab sodas, I saw these pictures a friend of hers had posted. They were all of Megan and some guy named Tyler, shots of them on the hood of a Prius, which I guess belongs to him. He had his hands all over her, and she was smiling and pointing at this huge fricking hickey on his neck like she's really proud of it. So when Megan came back, I ask her who the hybrid d-bag is, and she starts yelling at me because I invaded her privacy. She left the damn computer right on the coffee table, open, on her page, with the photos in plain sight … what the fuck?"

"It sounds to me, like Megan wanted you to accidentally see those pictures. That way, she could feign some indignation, and feel that her little make-out session with Mr. Prius was justifiable. I'm sorry, Seattle. I know that you really liked her, but her mom is right, girls can be really all over the place with their choices at your age. Boys can be, too. Trust me, there will be better little ladies in your future."

Seattle nodded sullenly as he tugged his cell from a coat pocket.

"You're not going to call her, are you?" Isaac said, the idea of Seattle throwing himself back into the relationship ring with such an unfair opponent causing TwoBears to stomp down on the accelerator, as if he could somehow rocket them out of cell tower range.

"No," he said, with a kind of certainty that brought Isaac's foot off of the gas. "I'm erasing her from my contacts."

Because Isaac had not expected Seattle for dinner, he had planned a special Ojibwe feast to surprise Jack. The walleye fillets and wild rice would only cover two appetites, so TwoBears made a stop at a Rainbow Foods.

"Pick out anything that will make you feel better—as long as it's legal," he told the boy. "Break-ups need comfort food."

With a cart of soda pop, chipotle-style corn chips, hot wings, pizza rolls, a jumbo box of Captain Crunch, and a package of Skittles so large it demanded its own grocery sack, they checked out, loaded the truck with the contraband, and headed home. Isaac would have some explaining to do to Jack, who had recently been making valiant efforts to feed his nephew nutritionally balanced meals, but perhaps Bordeaux would forgive Isaac's wish to soothe Seattle with a brief junk food detour, something that might bring smiles to the face, but screams to the digestive tract. As they turned onto TwoBears' street, Seattle spotted the retired church van, which they had affectionately named "GodZilla," parked in the space Isaac had scooped beside the garage.

"Jack's home early."

"Yes," Isaac said, an odd uneasiness forming a chunk of ice in his gut, as questions fell into his head with arctic sharpness. Hadn't Jack wondered where he was? Why hadn't he called? Why did the house seem so dark? Eager to begin his frenzy of carbohydrate chaos, Seattle was already slinging plastic bags onto each arm and disembarking from the truck, before Isaac had an opportunity to collect courage against the random worry that he had something to fear, something to confront. He breathed heavily and tried to absorb warmth from the fact that the man he loved was just beyond the door, in the sanctuary of his home, but the bizarre, bleak chill that had pursued him through the bitterly cold afternoon and into the deadly cold night, kept following him.

Isaac found Jack seated on the couch, half-lit by weak lamp light. On the black lacquer table beside him, a folded piece of robin's egg blue paper stood propped against an empty beer bottle.

"Hello," Jack said.

Isaac stepped into the living room, but Bordeaux didn't rise to kiss him. Instead, he picked up the blue rectangle by a corner, as if it were fragile or perhaps, contaminated.

"Your favorite color," he said as he leaned an elbow on the arm rest and turned the paper to one side and then the other. "It was tucked in the door when I arrived. I thought it was from you ... for me. I was wrong."

Jack rose, handed Isaac the paper, and walked away. The refrigerator door opened, glass bottles clinked, and metal pried away metal with a soft liquid hiss. A sudden blinding pressure brought the back of a hand to Isaac's upper lip, sure that he tasted blood, but when he examined his knuckles, they were clean. Dropping onto the couch, he unfolded the note, a shade symbolic of innocence and rebirth. How incongruous it was with a hard moon. How absurd it was beneath the weight of the words that rushed at Isaac TwoBears like a fist.

Isaac,
I've missed you. I want to see you. Please call.
Ken Kumagi

29

A Place for Bears

The story of Ken Kumagi was one that Isaac TwoBears hadn't told since its ending over five years earlier, but now, as Jack sat calmly down beside him and offered him the mug of hot buttered rum for which he had silently wished all day, Isaac knew that he must pull those crumpled pages from the deep, dark place where he had once discarded them. Though he had expected the pale blue note to send Bordeaux slamming out the door, roaring down the street, and out of his life forever, Jack had remained in the unquavering, vaguely emotionless state of the wronged party, his quiet placidity screaming accusations louder than any melodrama ever could, leaving TwoBears no choice but to respond with a similar level of maturity. Only frankness, only full disclosure could move them beyond this moment.

Isaac sipped the warm spiced liquor, set the mug down, the blue square of paper beneath it, and began.

Their first meeting had been bound by the hard lines of business, Isaac, one of a dozen contractors pitching a bid on a corporate project, Kumagi, a company architect serving on the team that would hire one lucky outside independent builder. Immediately, TwoBears' surname intrigued the third generation Japanese-American, whose own family title meant "Bear Valley," and, later, when Ken Kumagi just happened upon Isaac in a downtown Minneapolis drinking and eating establishment that the architect had come to know drew a large gay clientele, Ken Kumagi skillfully included the serendipitous similarity as a pick-up line.

With little regard for the company's conflict of interest clauses, Ken accepted Isaac's invitation to join him, and after dinner, several drinks, and an obvious mutual attraction, Kumagi slid the waiter his corporate credit card and asked TwoBears if he was free the following night. Isaac liked the comfortable way they were able to converse about their shared knowledge of building and design. He liked the smooth way Kumagi carried himself, the expensive silk tie casually loosened, the Armani jacket flung carelessly over a chair, the hint of gray at each temple, and the faint smile lines that indicated he had a few years on Isaac. Most of all, he like the hungry looks that betrayed the cool exterior every time he caught the scrupulous man's subtle glance.

"A business dinner?" Isaac asked.

Ken Kumagi shook his head.

"Then I am free," Isaac had responded.

The next evening, they met at a quiet Italian restaurant just outside the city. Ken was already seated in a back booth when Isaac arrived.

"I got some good news today," TwoBears said, as he seated himself across from Kumagi.

Yes, I know," he said, looking at Isaac from behind the wine list. "Congratulations. Welcome to our company."

For that instant, TwoBears had thought he had detected an undertone of paternalistic superiority. It restrainedly plucked at his self-confidence, as well as at his notion that he had won the bid based solely upon his impeccable references and a long list of clear-cut examples that showcased his capabilities. But Kumagi's hungry stare and shadow of a smile brushed away his misgivings, and when the waiter brought the two-hundred-dollar bottle of champagne that Ken had ordered, Isaac drank, though he did not care for the taste.

As they were finishing the last bites of tiramisu, Ken again mentioned the meaning of his name.

"A valley is a nice place for a bear, don't you think?"

Isaac had agreed, willingly following where he knew Kumagi was leading.

"Even better when there are two bears," the older man added, and slid a key card under Isaac's palm. "Wait twenty minutes. I've ordered you another coffee. I'll see you at the hotel."

Isaac watched through a narrow, heavily tinted window as Kumagi climbed into the shiny black Escalade, and the inner voice of some self-savior whispered that he should not follow. But when he had drained the pedestal cup, leaving the biscotti on the saucer, untouched, he checked his cell, saw that the designated time had passed, and took his leave.

On the freeway, traffic clogged, the result of a fatal crash involving multiple vehicles including an over-turned semi that had been transporting cattle. TwoBears slowed as he approached the exit that would have taken him safely home, the flashing strobes farther ahead filling the night like a migraine aura's ominous dreamy light, and he considered avoiding the certain carnage of the next miles. At the last second, he saw himself as the sexual star of a blue collar fantasy that he was almost sure that the neatly packaged professional awaiting him, possessed, and his hands refused to turn the wheel, as ego and libido kept the original course. The accident scene was unlike anything TwoBears had ever seen. Dying and injured animals bellowed their terror from their entrapment inside the wrecked trailer, the ill-fated beasts meeting their fates earlier than planned. The rig lay on its side, propped atop a Volkswagen's crushed remains. Blood diamond shards of glass twinkled with every beam that passed over them, their deadly implications sobering each driver in the slow, single lane procession. Isaac's stomach knotted, the gourmet coffee turned to acid, the apocalyptic images suddenly seeming like signs of all that was wrong with this route, but, again, TwoBears resisted better judgment, and allowed craving to take him captive.

Isaac found Kumagi stretched out on the hotel suite's damask couch, a half bottle of Gray Goose, a cut crystal tumbler of melting ice, and suspicious white, powdery residue on the glass top table. The hungry eyes seized Isaac, their dilated pupils black holes, and he felt himself coming apart the moment Kumagi rose naked and silent, his savage embrace, the inescapable event horizon. Absorbed into the frenzy of the older man's crazed need, Isaac's grasp loosened from what he wanted, what he didn't want, knowing that any objection was futile. Kumagi's stone-cold touch hurled them both towards satiation, and Isaac crawled the thin, thrilling line between pleasure and pain, all the while hearing Kumagi's callous, hostile sounding assertion that he liked it, until, at last, TwoBears knew that he did.

Only afterward, when Ken had risen from the carpet, slumped onto the couch and, in a detached, dismissive tone, asked him to leave, did something like shame shove Isaac into the razor sharp reality of the degradation he had accepted. Swearing that it would not happen again, he left the hotel by side entrances, and tossed the key card down a storm drain. But Ken Kumagi was not finished.

A note of apology, blaming vodka and jet lag for his rude behavior arrived a day later, along with a gold watch with diamonds set at the quarter hours, and another dinner invitation. Shortly after the obscenely excessive placating gesture, Kumagi had called.

"I am an extremely busy man. Time is always in short supply. I rarely see my permanent address in San Francisco. I do not offer my time to anyone I deem unworthy of the gift. You are young, good-looking, and I find you interesting and intelligent. If you can accept the limited time that I have to give, then it is yours."

Perhaps it was the compliments from someone whom he sensed rarely extended them, perhaps it was fear of potentially losing the lucrative contract with Kumagi's company, perhaps it was the flattered way the expensive gift made him feel, or perhaps, if he stared in the raw face of his own truth, he would have to admit that he had enjoyed the rough, deprecation of the sex, but, whatever the catalyst, Isaac TwoBears took the time. For three years, they met, dined, and fucked. Ken Kumagi would depart back to California, or to whichever city his company sent him. Isaac never introduced Ken to his family. Kumagi never invited him to San Francisco. They never kissed on the mouth. Frequently, packages with international postage came to Isaac's door containing designer silk shirts, rare colognes, an iPhone, bottles of fine wine, top of the line sets of tools, a Hugo Boss tuxedo, more silk shirts, ties, underwear, bed sheets, most in TwoBears' beloved robin's egg blue. The present that Isaac loved the most, the black lacquer table with the graceful white cranes, came a day before their last meeting

Kumagi's Minneapolis layover didn't give him much time, but he scheduled a meeting with Isaac nonetheless. With his habitual, perilous landslide approach, he attacked the younger man the moment that he entered TwoBears' living room, ripping fabric the only prelude to the hurried, ragged, violent sounds of their animalistic physical encounter. When done, Ken wordlessly went to shower. As Isaac retrieved clothing and started to dress, beneath the edge of the beautiful shiny table, a cell phone rang. Isaac answered it on the third ring.

"Daddy, it's Lisa. Where are you? Will you be home tonight?"

Momentarily confused by the child's voice at the other end of the iPhone, Isaac cleared his throat. "I think you have the wrong number, honey. I'm sorry."

"I don't have the wrong number," the girl said, a familiar indignant contempt making the hairs on TwoBears' neck prickle. "This is my dad, Ken Kumagi's, number. Who are you? Did you steal his phone? I'm going to—"

But Isaac had disconnected before Lisa Kumagi could issue her threat. He shivered, turned the cell that looked identical to his own over and over, listening for sounds that might indicate the man had finished showering. Then, with bile rising, he accessed the contacts menu. Running an icy finger along the flat screen, he found his number, listed impersonally as "TwoBears Construction," and just as the night of their first encounter, an inner voice pleaded for him not to move forward, and just as that night, he continued on. The contact "home" had a tiny digital image of a family, and though Isaac had to squint to make out the faces, its meaning loomed larger than life. Five people posed on some rocky shoreline, wind whipping at their high-end outdoor wear: a slender woman whose lips bore a forced smile and whose ears carried a carat worth of diamonds; a supercilious-looking teenage boy in designer sunglasses; the girl, presumably Lisa, kneeling in the sand, her arm around a plump boy, whose small sausage-like fingers clutched Kumagi's khaki pant leg; and Ken, hand possessively locked onto the shoulder of the attractive woman, staring at the camera with an implacable defiance that offset his whitened smile.

"What are you doing?"

Isaac spun to meet the same look on the older man's granite face. He ripped the device from TwoBears' grasp, glanced the image that Isaac had been gawking at, and hurled the digital declaration of his matrimonial and parental status towards his briefcase.

"How dare you," Kumagi snarled at him from behind clenched teeth. "You have no right."

A single tick too late, Isaac TwoBears had read the profound threat in his accuser's body language and stepped back, but not before Kumagi's fist smashed into his solar plexus, knocking the wind from him and causing him to stagger forward into another blow. Explosions of hot sparks filled his vision, blood filled his nose and mouth, the nauseating sound of crushing cartilage and breaking bone filled his ears, while a dark, velvety fog began to descend upon, and fill, Isaac's mind. Viciously, Kumagi punched and kicked the object of all his secret desires, the object of all internal and external loathing, the objectified person whom he had wanted to, but could never, possess, all the while spitting the acidic slurs of the haters and the homophobic.

Towards the end of Kumagi's rampage, as Isaac began to believe that the man might kill him, and the ranting seemed to take on more victims, TwoBears thought of Mrs. Kumagi's sparkling ears. From somewhere down a long corridor of melting sound, Ken Kumagi's final words, "fucking bitch," punctuated his final blows, and Isaac TwoBears fell into a most unnatural sort of hibernation.

When the world broke its way through the membrane precluding his senses, he was alone, late twilight spilling bruise blue into the silence, while shock, shame, guilt, and pain battled within him for ultimate control. He stumbled to the bathroom, the steam of Kumagi's shower still coating the mirror, and, as he wiped it away, he assessed the damage. Though the nose might have healed straighter had he tamped down the humiliation he felt and sought medical attention, the remnants of his pride had instead caused him to rummage through the medicine cabinet until he found the leftover painkillers from a wisdom tooth extraction. Throwing down a pair of tablets with a palmful of water, he had cleaned the blood from his face, made an ice pack, and crawled to bed, where he stayed for several days, cut off and shut down.

When necessities finally drove him from his goose down den, he returned to the construction site, unshaven, without a shower, and with a story for his crew that included a drunk Injun-hating' cowboy type and a parking lot showdown of which every man was easily convinced. When, after avoiding his parents for a few weeks, Isaac's mother appeared unannounced on his doorstep, while lovingly accepting the crock pot of venison stew, he tried to fabricate an account of an on-the-job accident, Victoria TwoBears only eyed him as if the tale was as shifty as the pile of two by six boards that had allegedly toppled from some scaffolding and into her son's face. She knew him too well, and she tried to question him further, but he cut her off with a dismissive, "Shit happens, Mom. Let it ride."

"True enough, Koska, shit does happen," Victoria said knowingly, her shrewd observation registering every twitch of her son's battered face. "Let's hope whatever shit did that to you has had the good sense to move out of my range."

Victoria Marshall TwoBears had spent her late teens and early twenties immersed in the 1970's activism of the American Indian Movement and the violent response the organization had often drawn from Minneapolis cops, state troopers, and the feds. She was no stranger to what the bad end of a beating looked like, and she wondered the reasoning behind Isaac's incident. Was it because he was Indian? Was it because he was two-spirited, what non-Native society called gay? Something else less obvious? Whatever happened, she knew one thing: her son had not been the first to throw a punch, if he'd thrown any at all. Unlike herself, Isaac preferred diplomacy over a good old fashioned ass kicking, and had spent most of his childhood trying to bust up fist fights between his sisters, who were all natured, sometimes fortunately and other times unfortunately, like their mother.

"My boy's a lover, not a fighter," Chick TwoBears had proclaimed loudly throughout his only son's youth, until Isaac came out, and the reluctantly accepting father went with the more comfortable, "He's just a good kid, that's all."

Victoria didn't press, and Isaac never confessed the truth, but they both knew the other's suspicions and left it alone.

***

"You must have felt really alone," Jack said when Isaac was done with his story. "I'm sorry."

TwoBears looked down at his hands and shook his head, saying, "No, it's okay. Don't feel sorry. I'm just pissed that he's floated back to the surface after all this time. I need to make it clear that he no longer has a place in my world, which means contact, and, quite honestly, that's something I do not want."

Jack leaned forward, rested his elbows on his knees and looked at TwoBears with solid intensity. "I'll deal with Ken Kumagi."

"Define deal," Isaac said.

"Speak to him in a way that he *will* understand."

"I should clean up my own messes, Jack. I don't want any trouble for you. There's Seattle to think about, and—"

Bordeaux cut him off. "No worry. No rough stuff. Just thought-provoking rhetoric."

Still reluctant, Isaac shook his head, as the aspect of himself that believed he should fight his own battles tried to convince the part that never wanted to see the face of his attacker again that he should turn down Jack's offer. But his young partner became more adamant, until Isaac began to see the logic hidden behind it. Perhaps this was something that Jack needed to do, something that would prove his willingness to defend and protect what he deemed as his own. Something that would balance their relationship back from this latest tilt.

Finally, with more relief than he wanted to admit, TwoBears sighed, and said, "All right. I turn it over to you because, and only because, I trust you have the wisdom to finish this with decency that Kumagi does not have."

That night, they held each other, and, although they did not make love, their profound closeness comforted them both as Jack wrapped his long, muscled arms protectively around him and Isaac melted into sleep.

They rose early. Jack left to take care of some necessary business, and, as agreed upon, Isaac sent Kumagi a text inviting him to the house that evening. When the message was sent, he crumpled the paper into a tight ball, opened the door, and pitched the blue egg-shaped lump out into the unforgiving frozen snowscape. He then removed everything from the surface of the black lacquer table. The purification had to be complete. The exorcism of even that which might work its dark magic upon him on some subconscious level had to take place. Over the years, he had loved the eighteenth-century Taiwanese article of furniture, caring for it as delicately as if it were a fragile hatchling, without a single thought of the man who had sent it. He polished, dusted, and frequently checked for scratches, never once layering the horrid with the beautiful. Even now, as he ran a finger along the carved edge, he could not bring himself to transfer any negativity towards the innocent object. It was as if the little table had always had a life separate and sacred.

As Isaac began to lift it from where it had set for half a decade, a sadness swept over him. Suddenly unable to go through with it, he stopped, and set the table down. As he did so, his finger depressed something along the carved ledge, just beneath the table's top. Alarmed, he dropped to his knees, sure that he had broken a fragment of wood from the antique, but, to his astonishment, a small hidden drawer slid open a crack. He stared at it quizzically, wondering how he had missed it before, then decided that it was because that side had always faced the wall, and Isaac had cleaned the edge by blindly running a narrow feather duster over it. Someone's, maybe many someones', secrets were in that tiny drawer, and Isaac TwoBears slowly slid it the rest of the way open.

Morning brightness poured into its corners. The little drawer, though empty, revealed its clandestine purpose. Intricately hand-painted poppy flowers, in an array of colors ranging from milky white to brilliant magenta, covered the interior surface, and along one side several of the fragile-looking petals had bubbled and cracked, as if something too hot had once been lain there. Like poison pollen, the scorched blossoms blew hideous hollow-eyed addicts, their blackened little metal opium pipes braced between bone fingers, moaning into Isaac's imagination, bringing with them thoughts of Jack's sister and her untimely death by the substance's dangerous derivative. Vice and victim and all the viciousness and sickness that lay within secrecy, the merciless pain and punishment that came bound to imperfect pleasures, shameful little drawers, cruel little compartments, hidden away, ready to spring open and spill forth their ugliness and unacceptability, it all compelled Isaac TwoBears to quickly close the disturbing discovery.

He left the bare table in its place, like an open grave, and waited for Jack. When Bordeaux returned, Isaac exposed the table's surreptitious spring latch, and said that he would get rid of it. After a long moment of staring into the empty rectangle of space, Jack asked what Isaac thought he might do with it.

"I'll give it away," Isaac said. "I just want it gone."

It *is* beautiful, despite its secret," Jack said frankly, and then added, "Or its origin. I'm sure it's quite valuable."

TwoBears nodded. He had once searched Asian antique sites and knew the unique piece's approximate worth. The enigmatic opium compartment probably only added to the price. Bordeaux was peering into the strange little drawer again, and, musingly said, "It's humbling to know that all medicine has two sides, one that cures, and one that kills."

The words released a sudden lucidity that set Isaac to the task of arranging the objects he had removed back atop the shiny black lacquer surface. Watching with slight perplexity, Jack stated that he thought TwoBears wise for having changed his mind.

"It is beautiful," Isaac said, running a soft cloth over the white water birds, "and very valuable, which I'm sure will only accrue."

Bordeaux nodded.

"In fact," Isaac said, straightening the rice paper lamp shade. "I bet, in a few years, it will make a nice big dent in Lily Bordeaux's son's college tuition."

Later, Leonard Stark picked Seattle up for bowling and pizza, Isaac and Jack ate a light dinner in nervous quiet, and finally, at the indicated hour, the doorbell rang. Isaac looked at Bordeaux, who nodded reassuringly, and TwoBears left the room. Despite the below zero night, Jack pulled his shirt off and adjusted what lay fastened to his belt before he answered the door.

In the frigid shadows stood Ken Kumagi. He was tightening a cashmere scarf and visibly shook beneath the thin wool of his inadequate designer topcoat. Upon seeing Bordeaux, he took a step back, almost losing his footing on the icy walkway. A head and a half above Kumagi's diminutive stature, Jack stood in the lit vestibule, bare-chested, thumbs casually stuck in the belt loops of faded jeans, a beaded knife sheath firmly fastened against his left hip. He straightened, resting a forearm against the jamb, a pose which eclipsed any view the other man might have of the home's warm interior. Slowly, Jack looked him up and down, and then said, "You must be Kenny."

Kumagi began to correct him, began to say that he did not allow anyone to call him that, but the striking yet formidable young man had shifted, the light hitting a place on his smooth, brown chest, a place just above the heart. As Jack had hoped, the man's line of sight attached to it like a swinging crystal pendulum, time freezing him to the moment.

Smiling wickedly, Bordeaux looked down at the fresh tribal tattoo of two black bears peacefully facing one another, medicine bundles adorning their backs.

"Like it, Kenny?"

Kumagi offered something between a nod and a full body tremor, as a north wind hit him in the shoulders. Jack laughed, slapped his hands together, rubbing them ferociously, and said, "Brisk, isn't it?"

Kumagi pointed a black leather gloved finger at Jack's chest, and asked, "May I see him?"

Bordeaux sighed, caressed the bone handle of the skinning knife that he had borrowed from Barb, the one that had once belonged to her Aunt Victoria, who, rumor had it, once used it to shave every hair from a man's head after he cheated her husband at a game of Sonny Six Killer, and said, "No, Kenny, you may not."

For clarity's sake, he slid the blade a few inches out of the sheath, paused to enjoy the additional pale the action splashed into the man's complexion, and then let it drop back into the rawhide cover.

"Another time then," Kumagi said hurriedly, as he turned to leave.

Jack swiped a hand out like an aggressive paw, grabbed a wad of cashmere and gave it an explosive yank, until the smaller man was close enough to feel the heat waving off of Bordeaux's bare chest.

"No, Mr. Kumagi. Not another time. Not ever," he growled. "Time is precious. You are unworthy of it."

He then discarded the flimsy fabric from his fist like a filthy rag, watched the man quickly retreat, and slammed the door.

A bit shaken by how far he knew he might have gone had it been necessary, yet still pleased with himself, Jack Bordeaux hid the skinning knife back in his book bag. He had told Barb StandingBull that he was going to include it as part of a history lesson, which seemed true enough, as he was fairly sure Ken Kumagi had learned something, and would not repeat it. As he tugged his shirt back on, he called for Isaac.

TwoBears joined him in the living room, saying, "I saw the taillights headed down the street. That was quick. With rhetorical skills that good, perhaps you should reconsider law school."

"When necessary, I get my point across. Besides, look at these guns," Jack grinned as he flexed his biceps. "That little dude couldn't take *this* show."

TwoBears raised a brow, but didn't laugh. With a couple days of chin stubble, a disheveled ponytail, and a take-no-prisoners stare, Jack did have the capability of looking a bit intimidating—and a whole lot sexy. Isaac moved closer.

"So, my knight in buckskin armor, with the dragon slain, and the kid out for the evening, how can I show you my eternal gratitude?"

Bordeaux smiled. "Take my shirt off."

"That's a good start," Isaac said, as he ran his hands along the hem, clutched the thick thermal, and peeled it over Jack's head.

Then Isaac froze, a euphoric flutter freeing itself, a thousand electrified wings flying through him, as he searched for the meaning of the beautiful animals drawn upon Jack's skin.

"What do you think?" Bordeaux asked, as a tear traveled the ridge of Isaac's cheek. "Do you like them?"

TwoBears slowly slid his gaze away from the symbol of his family name, until his eyes met Jack's dark, liquid stare. A century and a half ago, while hunting rabbits one hungry spring, in the blind desperation of a man whose woman's and children's bellies had gone empty too long, TwoBears' great-great grandfather had come across the pair of grizzlies. Recently revived from their winter slumber, the huge males stood equal distance from the steaming carcass of a slain mule deer, but neither bears' muzzle was bloodied, nor did they growl the fierce warnings one would expect from famished predators competing for fresh meat. They stood on all fours, looking at one another, the breath from their nostrils visibly rising in the chilled air.

Frozen from the holes in his moccasins and the fear that one of the great furry beasts might realize that another meal lay so close within reach of razor-sharp claws, Isaac's grandfather crouched in the icy mud of a creek bed, watched, and waited to die. As he softly sang his death song, the somewhat smaller of the gigantic creatures turned towards the deer without protest from his larger, presumably older, counterpart. Grabbing hold the left rear leg, the younger animal tore loose the limb with a generous section of haunch still attached and lumbered into a dense stand of scrub pines. The man, then known as Bent Arrow, a name given to him because of the unique, slightly off-set way he had adapted to secure flint to shaft, making the weapon's shot accurate in his hands alone, sang his death song louder. He was sure that the older grizzly, not replete from the remains of the kill, would soon turn his hunger upon him, but the bear did not behave in the expected manner. Rather, he glanced in the direction of the mournful chanting, snorted the blood scent in the early morning air, and, without making meal of man or deer, departed.

When Bent Arrow was sure that the bears had gone for good, he stumbled towards the carcass, fell to his knees, and stuffed bits of raw meat into his mouth, until it delivered the strength to him that he would need to haul the lifesaving gift back to his people.

From that place, he also carried the lesson that no man, no bear, no living being's actions are unbreakably bound by others' expectations. He carried away a sense of renewed awe for the ever-mysterious, always shifting powers of the universe. He carried with him a new name. Behind him, the man once known as Bent Arrow left an offering. He took from his quiver a solitary symbol of who he had been, thrust its point into the ground and strung three tobacco ties to the shaft in recognition of his gratitude: one for the sacrifice of the deer, and two for the wisdom of the bears.

Bordeaux, the great great grandson of a French fur trader, was the first person with whom Isaac had ever shared the story, and, for the first time, TwoBears had felt the guiding force of a title not earned, but delegated as a family surname under the quill and ink of a government agent. The older bear had relinquished some power. The younger bear had gained some power. Both were stronger for it.

"I love them," Isaac said.

"I'm glad," Bordeaux replied. "Because I love you."

He pressed two fingers gently against the new ink just above his own heart.

"This is a good place for bears."

30

Four Questions

Hand in hand, Evan Rubinfeld and Desiree Stark strolled down the Minneapolis avenue, the March sunshine quickly melting away the last dingy patches of snow, and elevating the couple's mood to the contagious kind of jubilation. They laughed easily and often as they pointed out all the little idiosyncrasies that the city had to offer that day, and Evan captured a few of the best on a digital camera.

"Wait, wait, wait," Desiree said, afflicted with another surge of spontaneous giggles, as she tugged Evan to a halt. "Over there, across the street, at the table in front of that diner.

"That's a sick shot. Awesome!" he said, as he zoomed in on a man wearing a parka, Bermuda shorts, and flip-flops, one foot propped on a hump of snow that a week ago had probably rivaled him in height. "Let's sell it to the Minnesota tourism board."

"Hell, yeah! Who needs Daytona Beach?" Desiree said. "Minneapolis is the new spring break hot spot."

Evan clicked the picture, pocketed the camera, and they strolled on. Since the conception of their relationship, both had roused a levity in one another previously rare to the brooding artist and the cynical beauty, and everyone agreed, the couple's lighter versions were a welcome change. At first, the new feeling of lightness felt strange to them, and each one worried about what they thought would be an inevitable crash, a return to the cobweb corners of their former selves, and did not fully trust the natural high they had found in one another for some time, until the feeling lasted beyond something fleeting, and they came to accept and embrace it.

On the corner, at a yellow light, Desiree impulsively rose on tip-toes, and kissed him.

"What was that for?" he said, a silly, surprised grin marking his pleasure and shock at her out of the ordinary public display of affection.

"For this wonderful day, for being you, for luck."

The light turned green, they crossed, and Evan said, "You make me feel as if I'm already luckier than I deserve."

"You deserve way more and today's the day. I just feel it."

Midway down the next block they stopped in front of a gallery. He took the portfolio Desiree had been carrying since the impromptu photo shoot, and said, "Let's hope that this studio's owner feels the same. I would *love* to have a show here."

Again, she kissed him. this time on the lips, her soft fingers framing his cheek. For several weeks, she had been experiencing a kind of increasing vibration beneath her skin every time he spoke of his work. Tingly little flecks of excitement rushed through her veins when she awoke in his bed to find him half hidden behind a large canvas, the earthy, oily smell of paint hanging like a rapturous cologne that she had come to associate with the depths of Evan Rubinfeld's pure passion. Her mind hummed electric whenever he snatched up a pad of paper and began to sketch another image that he would gestate into strokes of color and light and life itself. Yes, she had felt him swiftly moving towards something colossal this time, an elevation from which, rather than fall, he would take flight, and she, moving towards it beside him, would fly, too.

"You will have your show."

The power of her certainty braced him, and, as Bonnie KillsTwice, her boyfriend Teddy behind the wheel, pulled to the curb and Desiree got in the car bound for Birchbark Books, Evan entered through the gallery's front door with a kind of smooth fluidity that mimicked levitation. The girl loved him, she believed in him, and, with his complete acknowledgement, and his utter, blissful acceptance, Desiree Stark possessed him.

After the interview, Evan went to the nearby coffee house where he and Desiree had agreed to meet. The sun had begun to dip behind some of the taller buildings, only a few shafts of warmth still touching the sidewalks, and the air had taken on a biting chill. After waiting at an outside table for fifteen minutes, the cold sent Evan inside with a half full paper cup of lukewarm Columbian. Everything was shifting, and he could not decide if the changes were for the better or for the worse, he only knew that his indecision felt far more like delirium than delight.

When Desiree finally arrived, her happy glow dimmed when she saw the subtle torment of his expression, and she sat down beside him, leaving the book of love poems, and the new sparkling cut glass bead and quill earrings that she had intended to wear to his gallery exhibition, in the bag. He slid the covered cup of coffee towards her, and said, "It's probably cold."

"I'm sorry. Teddy and Bonnie don't have a good working relationship with the clock, and I can really lose all track of time in that store."

Evan nodded. "Indian time, right?"

"That's what we call it," she said, taking a sip, and suddenly feeling oddly protective. "I suppose you would just call it late."

He didn't answer. His silence caused her to shift ever so slightly in her chair so that her knee no longer touched his, but he moved, gently pressing his leg back against hers.

"They offered me a show," he said, the tone so flat that she thought at first that he had just delivered the disappointing contrary.

"You got it?"

"Yes. The opening's scheduled for next month."

She threw her arms around him, almost toppling his cold coffee.

"That's incredible! I knew they'd want you. You're amazing!"

He couldn't help but get swept upward in Desiree's happiness, if only for a moment, before the weight of what he must ask her, pulled him towards earth once more.

As she released her embrace, she looked at him, confused by his seriousness. "Is something wrong? Aren't you happy? I thought that you wanted this. Now that you've got it, shouldn't we be celebrating?"

He ran a nervous hand over his thick brown hair, sighed, and mustered a half-smile, saying, "Sure, it's what I want. It could really launch my career, get me noticed by the art critics, the media. all that. It's just …."

"It's just what?"

Evan reached for Desiree's hand, held it, and, for a moment, allowed himself the pleasant distraction of her lovely long fingers, satin skin, the fragile bird-like bone structure, before he forced the phrases that could be the beginning of an end and the end of a beginning. Outside, in the deepening shadow and chill, black wings came to land upon the iron chair where the artist had earlier sat, and intelligent black eyes followed the unaware young lovers' every motion, every emotion, their every silent word.

"Desiree," Evan Rubinfeld said. "There is something I must ask you."

***

Barb StandingBull, as she always did when she and Gus IronHorse hiked the trails, asked him if he remembered what the park's name meant, and, as he usually did, he messed with her.

"Kaposia," he said, scratching his head as if locked in deep concentration. "Let's see. Isn't it Dakota for 'place where the know-it-all woman walks'?"

She had knelt to retie her boot lace, and when she rose, she whacked him on the seat of the pants with the folded white cane before extending it and heading down the path without her tormenter.

"Wait up!" He laughed, trotting after her. "You might wander off into the woods and be eaten by a fox or a coyote or a pack of carnivorous squirrels!"

Laughing, she slowed and let him catch up.

"The meat-eating squirrels got you, didn't it? Don't laugh. They're real. I saw it on the internet."

"Seriously?" Barb said, and then chastised him for believing everything he saw on the web.

"Oh, yes!" Gus pontificated as if behind a college lectern. "The sub-species is very prevalent here because of the name."

Really. Do go on, Professor."

"The translation, of course, means 'travel lightly', which refers to archaeological and anthropological evidence that the Dakota Sioux Indians utilized the area as a temporary hunting camp."

"Fascinating," she gushed as if impressed. "But how does this relate to squirrels, meat-eating or otherwise?"

IronHorse linked his arm through hers, and gave her hand a solicitous little pat. "Inquisitive. That's very good, Miss StandingBull. You will go far in my class."

Losing patience, she snatched her hand away, and snapped, "The squirrels, tell me about your damn squirrels already!"

"Feisty as a Kaposia Meat squirrel, you are, young lady," Gus teased, and dodged a swat. "See, the squirrels, after years and years of eating vegetarian at the demands of their squirrel wives, saw your ancestors chowing down on some tasty venison and the like, and decided nuts and seeds were for the birds."

Barb reached up and tapped a finger against IronHorse's forehead. "Very clever, but does it ever get scary living in there?"

They trekked on through the unseasonable warm March day, breathing the deep rich scent of newly thawed earth and fresh, crisp air not yet assaulted by the ever-circling city. They fondly remembered the times they had brought Finnegan to the nearby dog park, and the love-struck toy poodle that had followed the slow-moving Lab around the fence line, but as the realization of the elderly dog's progressing arthritis hit them both, they grew quiet and reflective. Time, the benefactor and the thief, rolled on, until the trees' shadows fell long, and their own legs felt the accumulation of their years, and they retreated to where the Mustang was parked.

"Let's go home and hug our four-legged children," StandingBull said, fastening the seat belt.

Gus sat holding the car key, but didn't place it into the ignition. For more than a month, as spring break approached, IronHorse had tumbled around with troublesome thoughts. Barb had been right, his mind had for some time, on again and off again, existed like a haunted dwelling, a place full of the restless past, present, and future, and now, with no warning, Barb's words had shoved him through the front door where a spectral chorus begged for an answer. Augustus IronHorse sat back, leaned his head against the rest, and closed his eyes.

"Barb … there's something I have to ask you."

***

Isaac TwoBears decided that a day so beautiful was wasted upon work, and early that afternoon phoned Jack. "Skip your next lecture. I'm coming to pick you up. We're going to the falls," he said, as he rolled down the truck windows, turned on the CD player, and cranked a John Trudell tune.

An hour later, they had a bag of sub sandwiches, some white chocolate and macadamia nut cookies, a thermos full of coffee, and were headed towards Minihaha Park. The first recognizable day that might indicate winter was on the run had brought droves of joyous vitamin D-starved Minnesotans out of their caves, so rather than search for a spot suitable for their impromptu picnic, Isaac backed the truck into a slot that faced what would, if the balmy temperatures continued, soon restore itself back from brown to green space, and they tailgated.

"So what did you tell your crew?" Bordeaux asked, as he poured Isaac a cup of coffee to wash down a third cookie. "Family emergency?"

"No. Right now, I'm doing a measurement and estimate on a deck in Shakopee, as you can see."

The advantage of self-employment."

"Being my own boss *does* rock," TwoBears grinned. "What about you? Did I steal you away from a pile of IronHorse's term papers?"

Jack shook his head, and unwrapped another sandwich. "Actually, Gus bugged out early, too. He left me a note, something about traveling lightly."

The sun shone wonderfully warm through the still bare branched oaks and silver maples, bringing with the heat a sense of hope, and health, and an irrefutable promise of future contentment. Both men leaned back and let the glorious feeling hold them, until Isaac yawned and admitted that he needed to walk off the cookies. Jack agreed, and they strode towards the falls. As they walked, Isaac casually grabbed Jack's hand; Bordeaux responded by closing his fingers tightly over TwoBears'. They exchanged smiles with some as they passed, and kept smiling when others frowned, but they didn't let go. As they approached the statue of the chivalrous Hiawatha carrying the maiden Minnehaha so that her moccasins remained dry, Isaac stopped and pointed his chin at Longfellow's immortalized fictional characters.

"Would I carry you over the creek, or would you carry me?"

Bordeaux thought about it, grinned, and then said, "I'm taller, and weigh more, but I have to admit, I think your upper body strength is superior, so … you carry me!"

TwoBears raised his brows as if stunned. "Baby, I'm ten years older than you. Do you want me to drop dead halfway across?"

"No, nobody's dying in this scenario," Jack laughed. "I'm sick of gay love stories where one guy has to croak at the end. I have a better idea. How about we both roll our deerskin leggings up, throw our moccasins to the other side, and wade across together?"

In that moment, in that instant, as the beauty of the day and the simple sweet notion of his partner's words cradled his heart in a splendorous way that he had never known, Isaac TwoBears dropped to the muddy ground, upon one knee, and grasped the younger man's hand.

"Jack, my love ... there's something I'd like to ask you."

***

As a spectacular sunset lit the windows of her townhouse, Maggie Gustafson lit the tall white tapers that adorned the table set for two. From the kitchen, the rich aroma of beef burgundy, roasting vegetables, and a warming French loaf seductively floated, mingling with the faint floral of Leonard's favorite perfume upon her neck and wrists and the secret places where she hoped to later lead him. That afternoon, she had turned her hair, her skin, her nails, all over to an eager band of salon professionals. After they had transformed the plain, wholesome-looking former farm girl into what her mother would call a siren, Maggie shopped for a dress, and, for the first time in her life, selected one based on its luxurious fit and the favorable way it drew the eye to her best assets, rather than the cost. In fact, even as she cut the tag from the garment, she had not given the numbers so much as a glance. She bought fresh flowers, expensive wine, the best cuts of meat, organic produce, imported chocolate, and real silk stockings, complete with garter. Tonight, everything must be perfect, must be worthy, must be magic.

Precisely at eight, she heard Leonard Stark's soft knock. Unprepared for the vision of loveliness that answered, he stood frozen to the step, like a wall flower asked to dance, until, with a shy giggle, she took his hand and led him inside.

"You're beautiful," he said, mesmerized with the mystical way the blue silk dress seemed to enhance the sparkle in Maggie's eyes.

"Happy birthday," she said, kissing him tenderly.

"This is for you," he said, offering her a gift wrapped with an endearing lack of expertise.

She accepted it, saying, "Shouldn't you be the one receiving presents today?"

"It's my giveaway ... to show my gratitude for having been granted another year of life."

Leonard grew pensive as Maggie slid the ribbon and paper from the book of love poems that Desiree had helped him procure. He had never been a man of eloquence or one who could easily define the depths of his emotions in words, and, for most of his life, Leonard Stark had felt, that even if he had these qualities, there had been no one who would have wanted to listen, to hear, to know the contents of his heart.

"I can't make the words to say all of the things that I would like to say to you, but those are words, both old and new, of my people, and I feel them very strongly ... I feel them for you."

Maggie held the book gently, tears falling, and said, "Your words are perfect."

The big man smiled a boy's smile and looked at the toes of his scuffed dress shoes. She was the first: the first with whom he had ever wanted to share the cherished book of poetry, the first who had ever thought anything about him perfect, the first woman who had ever truly loved him.

"Thank you, Maggie."

All the plans of the evening, the sumptuous meal, the fine wine, the chocolate fondue, the strawberries, the red velvet birthday cake, suddenly seemed silly, needless accoutrements and phases to lead her to a moment, a moment for which, as she opened the book and saw what Leonard had written in his own unsure hand, she no longer wanted to wait.

"For Maggie," it read. "I am yours."

Maggie Gustafson placed the sacred pages beside the vase of roses, and, trembling, took Leonard Stark's large rough hands in hers.

"Leonard, my darling ... there's something I'd like to ask you."

31

Memoirs of the Forgetful

The red envelope finally convinced Augustus IronHorse. Alistair Trigg's reports and an olive branch email sent from Amanda Trigg Garcia had only slightly budged him, and Barb's gentle prodding had begun to feel like a sharp stick that he quickly learned to dodge, but the small crimson envelope, sealed with a pink heart-shaped sticker, had, in all its hopeful innocence, sweetly coaxed him across the emotional line that he had drawn. It arrived a day or so before Valentine's. When he saw the California postmark, old feelings of fear left fingerprints of perspiration along the paper edge, and, for many minutes, he stood planted in the entryway, neither forward nor backward motion seeming possible. When at last he remembered that Helen's holiday correspondence had stopped coming years earlier and the reason why, he opened it, a mix of relief and remorse churning his thoughts, as he slid out a homemade card. Flecks of silver glitter rained onto IronHorse's shirt as he opened the Valentine and saw the picture glued inside, tiny soft pink plastic jewels and feathers carefully attached around it like a fancy frame. The girl in the photo wore white lace and satin; a first communion gown, an old-fashioned mantilla affixed over her dark brown curls. The child's long lashes, dimples, and beguiling smile would have been enough, but it was Isadora Garcia's block print letters, white crayon upon red construction paper, that wrapped their way around IronHorse's heart.

FOR UNCLE AUGUSTUS
AND AUNT BARBARA,

WE HAVEN'T MET
YET, I AM YOUR
NIECE, ISADORA,
BUT EVERYONE
CALLS ME DORA.
HAPPY
VALENTINES
DAY!!,
XOXOXO

He shared it with Barb, and although she could have voiced her opinion, she kept the sharp stick hidden away and let a little girl's simple gift work its magic.

So, as they sat in the deepening March twilight of the Kaposia parking lot, Augustus IronHorse had asked Barb StandingBull the question to which he had already known the answer, but did so with the knowledge that uttering it would ultimately commit him.

"Will you go with me to California?"

***

As their flight landed in San Diego, Barb offered her hand to Gus, who grasped it with an almost unbearable sweaty tightness until the 727 taxied to a stop, the sound of dozens of cell phones being turned back on and seat belts clicking open filled the cabin, and he loosened his grip. At the baggage claim, where they expected to meet Alistair, they found instead a small welcoming party. All cotton candy smiles, toting a bouquet of daisies and carnations, Isadora skipped forward, Alistair close behind, as Amanda and her husband waited reservedly beside the carousel.

"You're my Uncle Augustus, aren't you," she exclaimed. "I could tell because you have a choker just like Uncle Al. I'm Dora. These are for you, Aunt Barbara."

StandingBull accepted the flowers and a bear-sized hug from the elated girl, as Alistair and Gus embraced.

"Good to see you, Brother," Trigg said.

"You, too," Gus said, and pointed at Alistair's choker and then at his own. "Looking good!"

Dora peered up expectantly at IronHorse, who, seeing her bright cherubic face, dropped the carry-on bags, knelt on one knee, and opened his arms to receive their niece's zealous hug. Then she grabbed an index finger and, bouncing on her toes like a playful kitten about to pounce into another adventure, said, "Come meet Mom and Dad!"

Amanda offered a less enthusiastic greeting than her daughter, but as genuine as Alistair's, and introduced her husband Javier. With dimples as deep as Dora's, he shook their hands, saying how happy that he was to meet them.

"My mother, my sisters, my cousins, they've been cooking all day. They're excited to meet you and welcome you to the family."

Amanda gave a weak, nervous little laugh as she involuntarily smoothed the nonexistent wrinkles from the arm of her blouse, a habit unconsciously adopted from Helen, whose hands could never remain idle during moments of unease.

Her busy hummingbird fingers flitted from the fabric and then hovered to adjust her perfectly aligned gold necklace as she said, "I hope you're hungry and love chilies."

"Yes to both," Barb replied, her mouth watering at the thought of the kinds of savory, spicy dishes that she had so often craved lately. "I can't wait."

IronHorse retrieved their luggage, and, as they trooped outside to where Alistair had pulled up in the Garcia's van, Barb heard Dora turn to her mother and say, "Uncle Augustus looks a lot like Grandma Helen."

The open-hearted hospitality with which her Garcia in-laws met Gus and Barb soon loosened Amanda's remaining misgivings, and, by the end of the evening, she found herself quite charmed with Barb's amiable personality and voracious appetite for all the Mexican delicacies that Javier's grandmother kept bringing her. With every plate, bowl, and saucer, the old woman whispered something in StandingBull's ear, and, with very little understanding of the Spanish language, Barb would nod agreeably, as she feasted upon chicken with a sumptuous chocolate mole, pork tamales, and warm corn tortillas.

In the backyard, the men had gathered, chatting, smoking and laughing as they passed a quickly vanishing bottle of agave. Javier's unassuming wit and good humor, complemented with the fine tequila, soothed IronHorse's frayed nerves and allowed him to temporarily forget the trip's primary purpose. At a point in the night when Alistair was out of earshot and the alcohol had saturated some of Garcia's filters, he said to Gus, "He was a real son of a bitch."

"Who?"

"Old Man Trigg. Or, as I was always required to address him, Lieutenant."

The reference stung the back of Augustus IronHorse's neck; a thirty-five-year-old razor burn splashed with bile he had not spilled since childhood.

"I know it isn't right to speak ill of the dead, especially not my own wife's father," Javier continued, looking at Gus apologetically, while seeming to, at the same time, ask for permission to continue.

IronHorse nodded, took another swig from the bottle, and said that he understood.

"He didn't accept me from day one. Amanda tried to prepare me with some gentle warnings, but I don't think either one of us expected what we got. Right away, he had a burr up his ass because I hadn't served in the military, and then when he met my older brother who did a tour in the first Iraq war, he played it down … like Thomas had just told him that he had returned from Boy Scout camp with a wood carving badge."

Javier's square jaw tensed as he spoke, and IronHorse felt the empathetic ache beside his own ear.

"At our rehearsal dinner, Trigg asked my father if he and my mother were illegals. Can you believe that shit? On the eve of our fucking wedding! Because I love Amanda, I put up with it, kept myself from slamming a fist into his mouth on numerous occasions. I even managed to refrain when Isadora was small and Trigg targeted her. Amanda and I want her to have the benefits of being bilingual, and the poor little girl came crying to us, saying that Grandpa was mad at her for speaking—get this—Mexican. The old prick claimed that it wasn't American."

Garcia could see angry heat rise into IronHorse's face as his fists pressed to his knees and he willed himself not to punch the empty air, to battle the ghost of their shared foe.

"I'm sorry, ,an. It's upsetting, and I didn't mean to unload on you. You have your own demons when it comes to Trigg," Javier said, suddenly feeling as if perhaps he had gone too far and should throw water on the blaze he had set before it defied containment. "What it comes down to is that I get why you ran all those years ago, and why you stayed away, but I'm glad you're here now, and that Amanda is having an opportunity to know her brother, and Isadora, her uncle. You and Barb bring something good to this family, something that balances out a lot of the past bullshit."

Javier Garcia clasped IronHorse's shoulder and Gus returned the gesture, saying,

"Thanks, Brother. Lately, I'm finding that my family grows bigger every couple of months, and, despite myself ... I like it."

At midnight, Alistair drove Gus and Barb to his house so that IronHorse could sleep off the tequila, and Barb her one too many tamales, all knowing that the next day's visit would demand much more of them.

***

Helen Trigg was tired. All she wanted was to sleep, but strangers kept coming. They carried trays of bland food for which she had no appetite, spoke to her about things in which she no longer had any interest, and asked her questions to which she seldom knew the answer. Why couldn't they just let her go, let her sleep, let her dream? There, in the only clear peaceful place left to her, she could see him, and she was happy. Why couldn't all the outsiders, with their sympathetic, singsong urges to eat, to move, to stay awake, go away, and allow her the only thing that she desired.

***

Late in December, pneumonia had almost taken Helen, but, although it profoundly weakened her, it had, in the end, offered her no mercy. Watching the decline of their mother carved Amanda's temples with permanent worry lines, and threaded gray, then white into Alistair's hair. As January drew to a close and Helen Trigg's mind seemed to slip away by miles rather than the previous inches of her pre-illness condition, she attempted to sit at the edge of her bed one morning, without assistance, convulsed, and fell in the throes of a seizure. Subsequent tests revealed the inoperable brain tumor.

In the wee hours, during the sleepless night that followed, Alistair had whispered prayers of thanks, not to his father's god, as he had been taught as a child, but to the universe, as he had taught himself. He burned sage and sweet grass and cedar, and chanted sounds that were of his own making, his own pure ache, from a place void of dogmatic perfection, until his mind had never felt clearer, sharper, more serene, and the lingering torment of imminent loss gave way to realistic relief. At dawn, he had called Augustus.

***

Now, as they turned up the winding drive of the Buena Vista Senior Care Center, he glimpsed his older brother's face in profile, silhouetted by the glaring morning sun, and for one jarring breath, he saw a man that he did not know. Then thin clouds streaked across the sky, IronHorse's familiar features solidified in the diffused light, and Alistair exhaled. When the car was parked, for several minutes, they stayed in the comfortingly close, uncomplicated quarters, as if a protraction would somehow better prepare them.

"I should warn you," Alistair said. "She hasn't known who I am for over a week, so she probably won't—"

IronHorse raised a hand and shook his head. "It will be what it will be. I have no expectations."

Alistair Trigg nodded, but grew graver at the thought of the reunion's high probability of pointlessness. Whose sake had he been pleading for when he had begged IronHorse to come to California? It wasn't for their mother. Maybe it wasn't for Gus, either. Had his encouragement for his brother to come before it was, as he had perhaps too dramatically put it, too late, been rooted in his own need for closeness, for comfort, for companionship? Maybe Alistair's nature was at fault; he had always positioned himself as the fulcrum of any social scale, forever attempting to balance, to harmonize, to bring a satisfying resolution to those around him who were at odds with one another. The most passionate of diplomats, he loved nothing more than reconciliation, a laying aside of past differences, forgiveness, and happy endings.

This time, however, he suddenly had the skewed feeling that his nature had set them all up for something far worse than decades of separation. In a clutch of panic, he almost started the car, almost drove away before anyone's life could become more tilted, but before he could put the notion into action, Augustus IronHorse got out of the car and opened the back door for Barb StandingBull.

"Come on," Gus said. "It'll be all right, Alistair. I've got you … and I know you have my back. And Barb, well, my Barb is everyone's rock. So no matter what happens, we're covered. We'll be fine."

Alistair sighed, climbed out, and followed them inside.

In a bright, sunlit lobby, several of the center's residents sat, some engaged in a sequence of instructed chair exercises, while others watched a large screen television as a perky blond on the screen announced that she would like to solve the puzzle. Beyond, in the dining room, several tables were occupied with people playing bridge, gin rummy, and five hundred. At another table, a man sat in a wheel chair, engrossed in a crossword. When he saw Alistair, a broad grin spread across his dark brown face, and he waved, calling, "Hey, Al! How's it hanging, son?"

One of the bridge players shook her snowy head with a disdainful little jerk and a cluck of the tongue against ill-fitted dentures, which only drew the jovial man's unwanted attention.

"Don't get uppity, Lucille," the man in the wheel chair scoffed, a gleam in his eye. "I saw you peeking at Grace's cards last hand!"

In a huff, Lucille threw down a pair of kings, as, from behind her trifocals, Grace offered him a conspiratorial wink.

"Al, bring that beautiful lady over here and introduce us."

"Harmless," Trigg whispered under his breath, as they walked over to where Alistair's elderly friend waited.

"Sam, this is my brother Gus and his wife Barb."

"Sam Spencer," he said, shaking IronHorse's hand, and then appropriating Barb's fine-boned fingers. "It's a pleasure to meet you."

With a roguish glint, he planted a loud, theatrical kiss atop the delicate knuckles.

Alistair drew up a chair and made friendly small talk about the warm weather, March Madness, and how the Padres might be shaping up for the season.

"So, Sam, if Gus and I were to go to Helen's ward for a while, do you think you could manage not to woo my sister-in-law? Too many visitors at once frightens Mom, so Barb volunteered to stay here."

Sam folded up the cross word book, and chuckling, said, "I can't make any guarantees, Al. I *was* voted Valentine King last month, you know. The ladies love me. But since Gus looks like he might be able to outrun me, I promise not to work my full range of charm on his lovely lady. Just decaf coffee and conversation."

"I appreciate that, Sam," Alistair said, offering the chair to Barb. "And so does Gus."

With concerned reluctance, Barb leaned towards Gus and whispered in his ear as she slipped an arm around his waist. "I'll be right here, if you need me. Remember, I'm here for you," she reassured before she let go and sat down across from the gregarious senior citizen.

Now that he was here, Augustus IronHorse no longer shared the tense apprehension of Barb and his brother. Instead, he found himself in a state of absolute calm—a dreamer realizing that he controls the dream—and as he kissed Barb's cheek and walked down the hall behind Alistair, towards the locked double doors of the dementia ward, he felt free of everything that bound him to the past, right down to his very identity. With each step, another layer peeled away, another aspect of himself, until they reached the closed door of the room he must enter, and he stood before it a nameless, faceless being, solidly planted within the present. He was simply one, meeting another. A stranger about to happen upon a stranger.

Alistair quietly pushed the door open and they stepped inside.

The woman asleep in the bed did not stir, her shallow breath barely raising her frail chest. Augustus IronHorse could only stare at the aged husk of a creature whose gaunt appearance surpassed her age by decades, and whose features were so ravaged by time that, had Alistair not brought him here, he would never have known her. The skin of her arms sagged waxen, as if slowly melting, and the once dark, lustrous hair now lay limp along her skull in thinning patches of ash and steel. Behind her closed lids, sunken eyes seemed to disappear into the void of their sockets, and her full lips had become pale cracked borders of a mouth that no longer served much purpose. And yet, as she slept, a faint smile, both lovely and ghastly, formed, vanished, and then reappeared, and Augustus IronHorse couldn't help but wonder at her peaceful whereabouts, the origin of the obvious happiness she had found within her unconsciousness.

Alistair motioned to the Queen Anne's chair at the foot of the bed, and IronHorse sat, still cushioned in a state of self-unawareness, while he objectively observed the surroundings as if the woman tucked between the crisp white sheets had been specially selected for his compassionate, yet detached, assessment; an example of the facilities fine care. The spotless floors, the air free of the insidious odors of elder neglect, the wide clean window that offered a view of groomed flower beds and a songbird bath and feeder, the woman's washed face, combed hair, manicured nails, everything spoke of her children's good choices and what the woman's choices, right or wrong, had afforded her.

From his place of protective impassiveness, Augustus IronHorse thought it all satisfactory, and, nodding to himself, turned his attention towards an arrangement of framed photographs that adorned the beige wall beside where she slumbered. He studied each one: Javier and

Amanda's wedding; the golden apple of Isadora's third school year; Alistair's UC Berkley graduation; Randall, Helen, their adolescent children in suits, ties, floral dresses; and looking at each one as if glimpsing the paper advertisement models that smile from behind the glass of a newly purchased picture frame, he sat within the shielded bubble.

But eventually, he caught sight of a shiny silver rectangle, less worn than the others, and Augustus IronHorse stared at a black and white of a boy with a bicycle propped against one hip, shoulder-length hair tied back in a tail, white T-shirt, jeans, ragged canvas high-tops, and a defiant expression tinged with pure animosity. Confronted by his own thirteen-year-old face, the bubble burst.

***

"The housing bubble burst," Sam Spencer explained, as Barb sipped a second cup of coffee. "My condition wouldn't let me stay. Too many stairs and the bathroom wasn't large enough for a wheelchair. I finally had to sell, and didn't get what my place was worth. Damn shame, too. I worked hard my whole life believing that owning a home was part of the American dream, part of investing in your future, setting up for retirement, blah, blah, blah!"

He scratched his thin halo of tight gray curls and shrugged. Grace, who had joined them after the card game, nodded sympathetically and patted Sam's dark hand with her own milky white one. As if she thought the physical gesture needed further explanation, she said, with shy pride, "Sam and I are dating."

StandingBull couldn't help but smile at the notion of the eighty-something couple and at the beautiful endurance of the human capacity for love. Whatever constituted octogenarian dating, she hoped that she and Augustus would see their elder years together, hoped that their commitment to one another would remain strong despite the absence of children and grandchildren, hoped that their health would grant them as much time as possible.

"I'm lucky, though," Sam said. "My children are good to me. My daughters found Buena Vista, and my son out east helps pay for it. My girls come every week and bring their kids for a visit."

"Sam's granddaughter plays the cello," Grace said. "She performed here last month. It was marvelous."

He grinned, and then said, "Course little Katie—that's Grace's grand girl—she plays piano and sings like an angel."

"Do you and Gus have children?" Grace asked, and Barb could see that the kind old woman sought her inclusion in the joys of parental satisfaction.

But it was the question with which Barb StandingBull had never found solace, and when placed in the position, a strange guilt clamped down on her, as if she had, in her choice to stay childless, committed a biological crime. Time and again, she listened to herself explain the reasoning, though the information seemed too personal, and, as she revealed it each time, she harbored an underlying resentment towards all the well-meaning inquirers who had inadvertently drug forth her confession.

This time, Barb just ran a finger around the rim of the empty coffee cup and shook her head.

Grace saw the younger woman's hint of melancholy, and in a soft consoling voice, ventured, "Because of the blindness?"

"No," StandingBull said, trying to temper the annoyance she heard creeping into her tone. "Diabetes. It's high risk."

Sam threw in with a matter of fact manner that she could appreciate,

"Diabetes sucks! It took my damn legs, which took my damn house. Ten years ago, it took my kids' mother. It sure has it out for us black folks."

"It's no friend to Native Americans, either," StandingBull said, a sudden surge of anxious sorrow flooding her veins as the concerns that plagued her more with each passing year rushed to the forefront.

Where would she and IronHorse be in twenty or thirty years? Who would help them in their old age? Who would come to play the cello for them? Who would bring them school pictures, share report cards, sing lovely songs? In their final moments, who would sit beside them? Which one of them might die alone? For Barb, Helen Trigg's mental and physical state had sharpened the edges of the questions surrounding her own mortality, and, try as she might, StandingBull could not evade the stalking entity that fed upon her doubt and fear. It caused disquieting qualms whenever she mulled over her life and began to assess what she had gained, what she had lost, and what, when she was most honest with herself, was lacking. The presence loomed large behind her, a raw, too real reminder of absence, and sometimes, when no one could hear, she crouched in its shadow and cried.

"It's wonderful that you and your husband came all this way to see Mrs. Trigg," said Grace, and Sam agreed. "She wasn't in the special ward when she first arrived. We played cards together a few times. It seems that her illness progressed so quickly. It is a merciless disease, too."

StandingBull reddened with self-deprecating shame. Was a childless woman any worse off than the mother who no longer could recognize her sons and daughters?

"Alistair tried to prepare Gus," she said soberly. "She may not even know that he's here."

Grace reached out and patted Barb StandingBull's arm, and, with maternal sweetness and the wisdom of her years, said, "She'll know that someone she loves is here. She'll know."

***

The wind whipped through Helen's hair as they raced through the Carolina foothills, she bumping along in the dented side car, he steering the old WWII Harley motorcycle he had rebuilt around the larger ruts while maintaining a reckless speed. She shrieked with excitement and reached to clutch his leg.

"You're crazy," she screamed, and he smiled in the secure knowledge that the spirited girl didn't truly want him any saner.

He finally squeezed the brakes when the clearing came into view, and he pulled off the dirt lane, the tall weeds and wildflowers brushing across Helen's laughing face like a capricious lover. He spread the moth-eaten Army blanket atop the warm earth and she blushed a young girl's self-conscious blush before she beckoned for him to sit with her.

From far off in the distance, muffled voices that did not belong vibrated everything around them, and as if the world were formed of a fine powder, the scene shifted, distorted, and fell away. For now, he was gone again, and, although she often tried, keeping her lids closed to what lay beyond would not bring him back, so Helen took the ragged breath of the very old, the very ill, and opened her eyes.

But this time, he sat before her, hunched forward, elbows on knees, head hung. She blinked, and he was still there, so she spoke his name.

"Jimmy ... you're here."

Startled, Augustus IronHorse looked up to meet sharp, liquid brown eyes, so brimming with love and unrestrained joy they seemed to belong to one still freed by youth. A shaky hand, veined with purple, reached for her hair, self-consciously smoothing it.

"Billy should have told me you were coming. Why didn't your father call, Jimmy?"

He looked older to her than she remembered him, but still so handsome.

"Who is your friend?" she asked, her adoring gaze drifting momentarily away from IronHorse to Alistair, and then quickly back again.

Gus hesitated. He hadn't expected a thing from her, not recognition, not absolution, not explanation. He had only harbored the smallest hope that, if he could see her one last time in this life, he could free himself, and, with clear conscience, close the door behind him. He hadn't needed words, or embraces, or acknowledgements, and yet, now, in his mother's confusion, she had given him something much greater, and he suddenly didn't want to lose the fragile connection to it. She smiled in a come-hither manner as she paid tribute to the man she so obviously had never stopped loving, the man who had been his father.

"You've always had such a way with people … not shy like me. Remember when we met? You walked right up to MariJo and me. I thought you had come over to talk to her. She was the pretty one; the one the boys always were flirting with, but you smiled at me instead. Do you remember what you said, Jimmy? You said that you hoped that I could dance in heels that high because a Cherokee girl as pretty as me shouldn't be sitting in the corner. We went out on the floor and two-stepped. MariJo was so jealous because you really can dance. And handsome … so very handsome. I still can't believe you chose me."

Both Alistair and Augustus sat mesmerized by their mother's nostalgia; Trigg captured by the fact that it was the first time he had ever heard her willingly reference being Indian, as IronHorse continued to realize the deep well of adoration she had boarded over for half a century. All that had been lost to him as a boy suddenly became tragically clear to Gus. He had been so young when Jimmy went to prison, and had spent most of his days with Grandpa IronHorse while Helen waited tables during her waking hours, and worked in a motel laundry most nights. He had never witnessed her bitter tears of longing and regret. He hadn't noticed her shifting from the horrible crippling love she had for her imprisoned husband to a kind of salvation she thought she could find in hating him. As a boy, Gus had filled the empty space left by his father with his grandfather, too innocent to realize Helen's life had its own vacant spot. Now, as he heard the tenderness in her voice, saw the light in her eyes, Augustus IronHorse wondered if his mother had sacrificed the love of her life to improve the life of her son. Lieutenant Randall Trigg must have seemed like some answered prayer: an up-standing, well-respected white man who wanted to marry her, despite her divorce, her ethnicity, and a child that was not his blood. She made the head choice, buried any feelings that still tied her to that laughing young girl in Jimmy IronHorse's motorcycle sidecar, and reshaped her heart into a practical tool that would construct a decent existence for herself and her son.

"I've missed you. It feels like forever since I saw you last. Please don't stay away so long, Jimmy. You know what it does to me … when I think I've lost you. I love you, Jimmy. I always will."

Augustus IronHorse met his mother's suddenly somber look, and, nodding, reached out to touch her blanketed foot. Like wind scattering the lovely cloud shapes she had been seeing, his touch brought a confused expression to Helen's face, and she stared blankly.

"Who are you?" she said as she fearfully drew her leg back.

Alistair moved to her side, attempted to console her, told her who they were, but she weakly shook her head.

"You need to leave now," she demanded with as much strength as her feeble voice could manage. "I'm tired. I don't want any dinner."

Helen Trigg slammed the doors of her eyelids shut, and when she finally opened them, the strangers were gone. Never again did she find her beloved sitting at the end of the bed in the beige-walled room with the framed pictures of people she did not know, but one early morning, many uncounted months later, she closed her eyes for the final time and found him there. Offering a strong rough-skinned hand, he gently helped her into the sidecar as first light rimmed the distant mountains. She touched his leg, nodded for him to fire the bike's engine, and they departed. Racing, the wind now forever at their backs, Helen and Jimmy flew upwards towards the brilliant, blazing light of the sun.

***

Barb StandingBull's return home left her reflective, and, after their farewells, with promises that Isadora could come in the fall to witness her first snow, a flight spent beside a very quiet Gus, and post-travel indigestion, while unpacking and sipping ginger tea, she thought of Katherine TwoBears, and their life-long on-again-off-again relationship. Katherine had given birth to her first and only daughter, Barbara, three weeks after Dan StandingBull's surprise exit, and, with a botched C-section guaranteeing the future, Katherine would have been justified in giving the baby her family name. Instead, with the tragic hopefulness and poor planning of youth, she gave the girl the StandingBull surname, as if it would draw Dan home to claim what had been marked as his. But when the bronco busting rodeo Romeo stayed absent, she grew restless with the need to find him—or least find *someone*. She left the infant StandingBull among her TwoBears relations, and promised she would come back to Pine Ridge when she found who she was looking for.

In the six years Barb spent in the loving care of Daisy and Isaac TwoBears, she was fed, clothed, and taught the invaluable lessons of their Lakota culture, lessons she might have missed on the road with her mother, but Katherine's choices still occasionally cast unpleasant shadows across Barb's sunny childhood.

"Why am I a StandingBull?" she had once asked Grandma Daisy when all the TwoBears cousins had come for a feast. "I want to be a TwoBears like everybody else."

Daisy had tried to dissuade her daughter, knowing that their family would be the only ones responsible for raising the girl, but in her usual stubborn form her Kat had veered away from Daisy's advice.

"It's your father's name," Daisy told the child, keeping a neutral tone despite the resentment that rose every time she thought of Dan.

"I never met him, so why should I have to call myself *his* name," the petulant child reasoned. "Besides, a dad who takes off shouldn't be called StandingBull; he should be called RunsAwayBull."

Daisy took Barb into her wonderfully safe embrace and whispered into the silken crown of her sweet granddaughter's head that she agreed, saddened with how early, and how often, children must decipher adult's bad decisions.

"StandingBull is a strong name, one that goes back many, many winters to the time before our people had first and last names. Each member of our tribe earned his or her name from a vision, an experience, a particular personal characteristic, or, in some very special cases, one might bestow his or her own name upon another they deemed worthy," her grandmother had told Barb. "As a boy Crazy Horse was known as Curly because of his wavy hair. The name Crazy Horse belonged to his father, who gifted our great warrior his name, then taking the name Worm for himself. There are wonderful stories and teachings attached to what our ancestors were called, and though I'm sorry that I do not know the history of the StandingBull name, I believe that I can say without doubt that the man to whom it originally belonged must have had a very powerful experience to have earned such a title. For some, like your father, the name carries too little sway over their actions in life; it's nothing more than a surname, shared with anyone born or married into that family, but it doesn't have to be that way, Granddaughter. Live a life worthy of whatever sacrifice your ancestor made in earning the name StandingBull. That is how the old ways can become new, how our traditions can live on, how we can stay strong."

When Barb turned seven, Katherine came home, not with Dan StandingBull, but with Tony, a fat, red-faced beer distributor headed for Minneapolis.

"We're going to stay with your Uncle Chick," Katherine told Barb when the child grew distraught about leaving her grandparents. "You like Aunt Victoria and your cousins, don't you? There's great schools in Minneapolis, much better than here on the res. I promise, you're going to like it in the city, and you and I will see each other every day. Won't that be good, my girl?"

But Barb StandingBull did not like the city, nor did she see her mother every day. In fact, two months after their arrival, Tony was replaced by a sullen bass player named Eddie, and Katherine headed east, again leaving her little StandingBull among TwoBears. Although their house was already full and Barb slept in a sleeping bag at the foot of three crammed twin beds that belonged to her female cousins, the one bathroom made life in a house with seven people often complicated, and Barb felt swallowed whole by the Minneapolis public school system, Victoria and Chick treated her as their own, and Isaac still claimed Barb as his "favorite sister."

"I might harbor a grudge towards Mom, had she left me in the care of people who didn't love me," Barb said to Gus one evening, as they sat on the couch, Finnegan, Siegfried, and Roy all cuddled between them. "But I can't say that. She irritates me with all her flightiness and her moving target brand of mothering, but she has never done anything to intentionally hurt me."

"I guess I would have to say the same of Helen," IronHorse admitted. "She really loved my father … I know that now. I spent much of my life thinking that she loathed him, and, by extension, didn't care much for me, either. It must have been a little piece of hell every time she looked at me, thought of Jimmy, and how she couldn't make a life with him. I think she let me run away, go back to North Carolina, back to Grandpa Billy, back to the mountains, back to where she fell in love with my dad … well, I think she let me go home because she couldn't."

Barb laid the small piece of brain-tanned leather that she was beading aside, and reached for another threaded needle. Her impaired vision had been the necessity that caused her to invent new methods of organizing beads and stitching the thick leather, but the needles, with their almost imperceptible eyes, remained a problem until Seattle's steady hand and keen focus came to her assistance. He declined the buck-a-needle offer, but Barb kept a tin that was quickly filling with dollars, and when the boy least expected it, she would secretly slip it his direction. Barb located the coil of waxed thread with the short, sharp length of metal at the end, and took it from the antique wicker sewing basket, the basket that had once held Helen's secrets.

"Our mothers weren't all that different, were they?" StandingBull mused.

How is Old Katherine these days? Texas treating her right?"

"She seems to be thriving," Barb said, as she slid a couple more pale yellow beads onto the needle. "Dad, too."

The title still seemed a bit awkward to Barb. Dan StandingBull had never filled the role, but now that Katherine, after over thirty years ,had reunited with the Lakota cowboy, now Texas ranch manager, Barb felt nudged towards the word. By a strange twist of fate, Katherine TwoBears had found herself stranded in Waco one weekend and happened upon Dan StandingBull grinning over a stack of pancakes from the opposite end of a Denny's lunch counter. Thrice divorced, with several children and grandchildren, Dan rekindled his and Katherine's flame. Now she lived in a rustic ranch hand's cottage, a lone TwoBears among StandingBulls.

"We would have done better than the whole lot of them," Augustus said, as he rubbed the nearest cat's soft belly. Barb's needle slipped, a single drop of her blood staining the buttery deer skin.

***

April's full moon rose, spilling its magical, milky light into the kitchen and onto the center of the round oak table. Augustus IronHorse found Barb StandingBull there, a tiny pair of beaded moccasins in front of her. He picked one up, admired the precise way in which she had sewn the numerous rows of pale yellow, light blue, spring green, and white beads, and said, "They're beautiful. You do amazing work. Who are they for?"

Barb smiled. When she had cut the leather and sorted the colors, she herself had not known, and had simply followed the feeling that compelled her hands forward. But Javier's grandmother knew; she had known before anyone. With every delicious morsel she brought, the old woman had shared the special phrase that Garcia women had been saying to their daughters and granddaughters for generations: "For the little stranger who you soon will meet."

Life provided such unplanned, petrifying pleasures. It delivered so many opportunities to know how little one ever truly knows. In its web, all the unanswerable questions, all the little mysteries of how and why and when dangle like dewdrops that evaporate if one reaches to touch them. Who could inquire the reason behind some gifts? Who ever should?

Barb StandingBull rose, the moon a glowing halo behind her. She had almost seen forty winters, and Augustus almost fifty. Logic, practicality, and the pills in her nightstand drawer had lost their credibility; everything was in *Wakan Tanka* now, as it always had been. And though many challenges lay ahead of them, a lack of love would never be one of them.

She took IronHorse's hands and laid them on her belly.

"The moccasins are for our baby."

~32~

Beneath the Paint

From their introduction, that odd afternoon when the spiders had drawn them into the same seductive web, Evan Rubinfeld had painted her likeness. Racing back to the studio apartment to transfer the memory of her alarming beauty onto canvas, he had worried that Desiree Stark had been as illusory to his reality as the insects. Working feverishly through the night, dawn's first light found the joyous artist shaken to the core by his own tangible creation. The first of what would soon become a series depicted her among pines, mist and muted morning light woven into the silken garment that clung to her, the many spiders that wove it suspended from the green-black bows. Her lips, two dewy rose petals, like her dark telling eyes, spoke not of the captured, but of the captivating. They wrapped their beloved in this glistening fragile garment; they and her one within the act of ensnarement. Her hair, lifted by something unseen, seemed to slide through the trees' prickly needles, as if they, too, desire to groom the lovely woman. And though the thin, intricate white web lines covered in the most modest of ways, the young artist's heated yearning shown through. It was the first, the one he had once thought his best, but sitting beside his muse, a cold cup of coffee between them, he thought of the strange, secret sketches, the ones tucked in a hidden slot of the portfolio, and he knew that the assessment was wrong. He knew now that he must reveal all, must ask for permission, and, perhaps … for forgiveness.

"What is it that you have to ask me?" Desiree Stark said, as a disconcerting rush of paranoia constricted the question in her throat.

Evan Rubinfeld shook his head, saying, "Not here. There's something I need to show you first."

Quickly, she gathered her packages, he, the weighty binder of his life's work, and they fled the café, a crow's caw echoing all around them like some dismal overture of a Greek tragedy.

They had left the small apartment's window open and were met with unwelcoming cold. Desiree shivered, and Evan grabbed one of his flannel shirts from the rumpled bed and encircled her in it, but even after he had closed the window, shutting out the damp night air, she felt the chill of anticipatory unease tightening every muscle. He felt it, too; the tension of what had to be said, the difficulty of how to say it, and what might result.

"Sit down," he said smoothing the quilt that had entangled their naked bodies that very morning, and that now somehow caused him to be self-conscious at asking her to receive what he had to say, seated upon the place where they had made love.

She sat, and Evan cleared the coffee table of a book of impressionist painters, a lidless tin box of brushes, knives, and linseed oil-soaked rags, and a pizza carton. He then laid the portfolio in the center like a lawyer readying to present Exhibit A.

What had provoked him to, at the last minute, slide the rudimentary pencil sketches into the portfolio before leaving for the gallery appointment? They were mere moments caught upon scratch paper; ideas for future blank canvases, not gestated enough for outsiders to see. So why, when the gallery owner had nodded appreciatively at the planned contents and then asked if he had any more, had Evan, against all better judgment, against the stone in his stomach, against the very trepidation shackled to their origins, slid the zippered pocket open and let the sketches out?

"We will include these in your show," the owner had stated, the point so precisely annunciated that the young artist could only nod at the obvious fact that one was contingent upon the other.

He knelt, the narrow table between them, and said, "Desiree, these drawings, they're like nothing I've ever done before. They're … well, they're a little frightening to me; frightening in how they came to be, frightening in that I haven't much recollection of drawing them, but, most of all, they're damn scary because of how good they are. That's what bothers me the most, because, as I watched the gallery owner thumb through my work, I could see that he liked it, thought it was acceptable … perhaps even acceptable enough for a place or two on his walls, but when he saw these sketches, it was like witnessing a drug rushing through someone's veins, like seeing the professional, cynical mask shatter and glimpsing this pure unadulterated excitement beneath it."

In that moment, it had been like a drug for Evan, too, a sweet, warm narcotic flood that dulled the edgy fear's dangerous cut as luxurious thoughts of success — and fame and money — numbed him, but no sooner had he stepped outside the gallery's door, than a stiff wind of reality whipped grit at all the unseen lacerations.

"I should have shown them to you. I should have left them here. On a very deep level, I feel like I betrayed you, Desiree."

She shifted, frowned, looked down at the still unopened portfolio. She presumed that the sketches featured her, and couldn't quite fathom why he seemed so rattled. Early on, she had agreed to his painting her, had felt flattered when he asked, had loved the way in which he represented her. She found more beauty upon Evan Rubinfeld's canvas than she had ever discovered in the mirror. Though sensuous, all had been executed with the utmost taste, and she looked upon each with a sense of pride, not only in the man who loved her, but in herself. With every stroke, with each pigment, the artist had drawn an exquisiteness, a goodness and purity, into her image, which displayed for Desiree everything she had never seen within herself. It was as if his brush was a key, and he had unlocked the secret, sacred contents of Desiree Stark's soul.

"Evan, I gave you permission. You know that you have my blessing to exhibit any of the paintings of me," she said. "Why would these drawings be any different?"

As answer, he unzipped the nylon cover, slid the half dozen pencil and ink sketches out, and laid them in a row. He tried to read her reaction, even as she tried to conceal it. With everything literally on the table, Evan Rubinfeld asked the question he had been delaying for weeks too long.

"Desiree," he said in preparation of accepting and honoring any answer. "May I share these with the world?"

More naked than the carefully concealed nudity, she saw her most terrible secrets pictographically revealed upon six rectangles of wrinkled paper, and, willing the primal scream trapped in her chest to remain there, she shifted her sight quickly between each, as if counting the enemy, as if looking for her best escape. Straining for words, some soothing sound to stop the inner shaking, she heard herself dumbly ask, "You drew these?"

It seemed like such a cruel trick; that he might have forged them out of imagination, but far crueler if he had not.

"Yes," he said, as though he hadn't noticed the oddness of her inquiry or the bizarre way in which she seemed to have just arrived in their conversation. "But they're a bit of a mystery to me … like I drew them in a kind of dream."

During a late winter blizzard, Evan had risen from bed, and, somewhere between clear consciousness and hazy half-sleep, he moved from beneath the warm cocoon where Desiree lay, unaware, and stared out the window into the slurry of blackest night and swirling white. Above the wind's mournful whine, the rattle of the loose eaves, and the antique radiator's hiss, he heard a baleful howl, and although his bones tingled, he pressed his nose to the frosty glass. From out of the whirling white a not-quite canine face emerged, mouth twisted into a fanged snarl, eyes like diamonds cutting the glass between them. Ice and snow and mangy fur fused into something born from the storm, something wild and ancient, something juxtaposed against and challenging to the civilized cement and concrete city. Wind and flecks of frozen blindness roared down the empty canyon of apartment buildings and the animal was suddenly gone. Evan had turned from the window with the molasses-slow movement that dreams sometimes impart upon the dreamer, and, with all the paranormal power that lies buried within the vision of the periphery, he glimpsed her. He did not recall procuring paper. His mind held no memory of either the pencil or the pen dancing madly across the blank space. Even when he awoke with the sketches beneath him like some homeless man's news-scribbled, make-shift sheets, their origins seemed unclear. Everything about them had disturbed, had excited, had screamed for secrecy, although he couldn't say exactly why, and, while Desiree slept, he had hidden them away. But in the weeks that followed, their presence called to him, and he would awaken in a cold sweat, the faint sounds of scratching claws, beating wings, scurrying legs all posing the question, "Who do you love ... her or us?"

"They are unusual," Desiree said, and wiped her palms against the bedding as she leaned away from the almost photographically clear collection of phantasmagorical images.

"You probably are questioning my sanity right about now, aren't you?" Evan said, and looked away from her unreadable face.

"No," she said too quickly, and then added, "I believe that you have an amazing imagination."

She placed a tentative finger against the edge of the closest drawing, as if the paper might lunge forward and slice her flesh.

"Are those feathers?" she asked, examining herself reclined in sleep, one coal-black wing spreading from her shoulder, covering her naked body from breasts to thigh. "Like a bird?"

Encouraged by her assumed interest, he rearranged the sketches, pointing out the way her lip curled over large canine teeth and how her feet curled as mud-spattered paws in one, and the eight thin black legs that transmuted from her long hair in yet another, and all the while Desiree felt the shriek beating the walls of her chest, as she calmly nodded what the artist thought was pending approval. She watched him closely, carefully, continuing to compliment his imaginative qualities, even going so far as to commend him on utilizing elements of "old forgotten Indian fables," until, at last, the scream within her was silenced. In a time of science, cynicism, and an utter disregard for the unexplainable, where better for ancient magic to hide than in plain sight.

"Show them," Desiree Stark, a daughter of many forms and faces said. "Show them all."

***

She strolled through the gallery door as if infused with the crackling power of an electrical storm, and all eyes turned from her oil, acrylic, and watercolor likenesses. Hush fell like a wake behind the crisp click of her high heels against the Italian tile as she moved with statuesque grace and an almost defiant dignity. A fitted black dress hugged each curve, yet left much for an imaginative mind. She wore her hair, shiny as obsidian, swept up, elegant tendrils falling free, brushing her long neck and framing her lovely high cheek bones. The cut glass beads of the earrings that nearly caressed her bare shoulders caught the light as she moved, throwing tiny sparkles of vibrant reds, oranges, and yellows, luscious licks of fire. Evan Rubinfeld's words fell in mid-sentence when he saw her approach, and he felt every cell of his body respond, metal to magnet. She took the artist's arm and kissed him lightly on the cheek, and, as if witnessing life's imitation of art, some mystical merger between dimensions, some onlookers smiled approvingly, while others softly applauded.

They worked the room together, the break-out artist and his breathtaking subject matter, Desiree sipping pinot grigio through a demure gracious smile, Evan elaborating about technique, inspiration, and future ideas yet unpainted, until the gallery owner took Evan aside and Desiree was left alone to take a private tour. Beneath the perfectly aligned lighting, behind the protective illusion of the velvet ropes, the paintings were even more fantastical, more conducive to tricks of the eye. She stood for a long moment, the velvet barrier between her two selves lightly pressed against her thigh, as the great ebony wing seemed to ruffle as if a wind had passed over the sleeping bird woman.

"My favorite," the deep, warm butter voice said, so close behind she felt breath against her skin. "Yours, too?"

Desiree Stark slowly turned to face a man in an expensive silk shirt, tailored black pants, and boots crafted from the hide of some unrecognizable, possibly reptilian, creature. His hair was cut short and slicked away from a flawless face, that, if anyone compared long enough, they would, within its lines, see Desiree's similar features.

"It's gratifying to know that I had my hand in these masterpieces," he said, as he lifted a strand of her hair with his index finger and then let it fall. "On every level."

She glared at him, hatred so potent she suddenly feared that she might crush the crystal wine glass she held. He liberated it from her grasp and set it on the tray of a passing server. With his cleanly shaven chin, he pointed left and then right, at the six paintings Evan Rubinfeld had named "Beneath the Dream."

"May I take this phenomenal display as your proclamation of true paternity? It is a wonderfully wicked way of waving it in the faces of the delightfully dull twenty-first century public. Look at them."

He scanned the crowd derisively, and offered a dry flat chuckle.

"How easy they are! What amusing little toys! It brings me such joy to make them sit and stand and run and, when I'm feeling particularly malevolent, march. Many of them believe that a list of names on a social media site constitutes friends. Even more are still convinced that they live in a democracy. Most think that dollars denote worth, love is measured by sex, and levies are the answer to floods. And yet with all these fanciful thoughts, they stare at your half-naked image and tell themselves the feathers, the fur, the creepy-crawly legs are only figments of brilliant Mr. Rubinfeld's artistic genius. Funny, isn't it, Desiree, what one can make one's self believe or disbelieve? But you have figured it out … you have figured them out. Confess to the deaf man … then neither of you has to carry the weight of your crime."

He looked passed her then, raising a brow in a comically surprised gesture. "Speaking of the witless masses, Leonard Stark has arrived!"

"My father," Desiree growled, matching his conceited stare. "You are speaking of my father!"

"Am I?" he whispered, the coldness in his tone aiming for control, aiming for cruelness.

But, unafraid, Desiree kept staring into the deep, bottomless pools of his eyes and she saw the increment of weakness there. Having detected it, feeling the shift of power, she drove her words into the hairline fracture forming in his ego.

"I am Leonard Stark's daughter. *He* is my father!"

She whirled then, turning away from the man and the paintings, and hurried forward to greet Leonard. When she dared to look back, he was gone, a single black feather tucked like a calling card in the frame of his favorite.

The exhibition closed a month later with Evan Rubinfeld having sold several individual pieces, and with a pack of interested buyers waging a bidding war for acquisition of the "Beneath the Dreams" series. The delicious drug flowed through the artist and gallery owner, each floating higher, losing a little more sight of earth, with every new, more exorbitant offer, until the anonymous collector called. Four times greater than the next highest bid, the nameless benefactor dealt them the overdose. Offer accepted, the pleased patron hit a smart phone's end button with a crooked beak and took wing into the twilight. The steel and concrete of Minneapolis rose from beneath, the city's cold foolish fingers forever reaching towards the unattainable, and trickster flew higher, forever luring it.

33

Wanted

"Ever been to Iowa?" Evan Rubinfeld asked as Desiree Stark handed him her garment bag and he laid it in the back of the shiny SUV hybrid.

"No, but it will be nice to get out of the city and take your fancy new ride on a road trip. And a dawn wedding, that's going to be beautiful."

"What do you think of it, their choice to marry?"

Desiree shrugged, smiled, and then adjusted the bag so that the contents did not wrinkle beneath the pile of sketch pads, charcoals, and portable easel that Evan had placed among their travel belongings. Since the Minneapolis show and the lucrative windfall that had purchased his vehicle and rented the larger apartment where he and Desiree now lived, Evan had hit an artistic dry spell conjoined with the desolation of a deep, debilitating depression. For Desiree, the sight of the tools of his talent tucked between suitcases felt like a superb step towards recovery.

"I'm happy for them," she said as he shut the rear door and they climbed inside. "They have as much right to love and commitment as anyone else."

"Absolutely," he said, carefully exiting their parking area, swerving to miss a large mud puddle. "Maybe I shouldn't admit this, but I think it's very romantic."

"Really?" Desiree grinned, truly astonished by the confession. "So you're a wedding guy, huh?"

"Not necessarily. I guess I find it compelling when two people have to struggle a bit to have what comes more easily for others. You have to agree, Dez, it's been no cakewalk for them."

He was a compassionate man, she mused, who had obviously given great thought to the situation, as he did with so many events that involved the inalienable right to pursue life's happiness. When he could, Evan Rubinfeld found empathy, and even when the condition was one unfamiliar to him, he almost always managed a level of sympathy so sincere it was sometimes difficult to tell what he had and what he had not actually dealt with in his scant twenty years.

"Your soft, gooey center is showing," Desiree Stark said, as she stroked his thick, wavy hair with her fingers for a moment, "And I find it irresistibly sweet."

***

Augustus IronHorse had plotted their course south along 169 based on Barb StandingBull's current, frustratingly frequent, restroom requirements, and, as he exited into Mankato, he groused, "I'm still amazed by the idea that a peanut-sized fetus can cause a woman to have to pee so often."

"Hurry! Hurry!" Barb said, while wiggling miserably from side to side.

Executing a Steve McQueen-inspired turn, IronHorse whipped the Mustang into the lot of a fast food restaurant, roared up to the side entrance, and squealed to a stop, causing several people to gape. Barb jumped out, oblivious to the stares and frowns, yanked the telescoping white cane into position, and rushed inside. Gus grinned broadly and gave one particularly pinched-faced critic a comical little finger wave that allowed his middle digit to linger up in the air just a second or two longer than the others, saying through closed teeth, "That's right, take a good look. It's not every day that you get to spot a couple of wild Indians with such a fine pony!"

Mankato always put IronHorse on edge. The historical residue of the place descended upon him, a sticky pollen of past atrocities that inflamed him. The town, the state, the nation, they had all done a fairly adequate job of burying facts, cleaning up details, washing their collective hands of nastiness, but, despite their efforts to leave the events of December 26, 1862 in an unmarked grave, the surviving Dakota people remembered. Because they remembered, their children, and their children's children, remembered, refused to forget, refused to silence the death songs of their murdered ancestors, and other tribes learned the history, re-told the egregious account of the largest mass execution in American history.

In violation of treaty, the scheduled annuities promised to the Dakota bands of southern Minnesota went unpaid; corrupt governmentally appointed white Indian agency superintendents and traders stole the trickle of cash and goods that infrequently arrived; starving native families were told that, if they were hungry, "they can eat grass or their own dung"; and Dakota warriors, led by Little Crow, declared war. By the conflict's conclusion, much blood—settler, soldier, and Dakota—was shed, the surviving Dakota were forcibly removed from their homeland, and the Great Emancipator, Abraham Lincoln, signed the order that thirty-eight Dakota prisoners of war be publicly hanged.

Augustus IronHorse had seen the copies of the old news photographs of the massive circular gallows and its dangling Dakota victims, displayed before a crowd of thousands that had reportedly cheered and applauded the gruesome spectacle, and he often wondered about the tricky psychological transition made by the participants as they moved from a celebration of the birth of their lord and savior on one day to a deadly mob mentality the next. What explanation, if any, had they given to their children, as they brought them out on such a cold winter's outing? Had they lifted the smaller ones onto their shoulders for a better view? Did tiny pale hands, wrapped in new woolen mittens, cling to cherished mementos of the previous day: a carved horse with wheels to let it run, a rag doll with corn husk stuffing, or something rarer, something imported from a far-off European homeland, a small velvet bag of shiny glass marbles?

These were the thoughts that blew through IronHorse's brain each year when he and Barb went to the Mankato powwow, each time they passed through on their way to South Dakota, during his stay in the city while attending a conference at Mankato State. Although he resisted them, they howled in, flattening reason, clearing way for anger.

Gus watched the man that he had just flipped off, a man who bore the solid jaw, ruddy complexion, and light hair and eyes of some genealogical Germanic Nordic combination, trudge across the parking lot, and, knowing that Barb did not condone these little exhibitions of what she called "inappropriately placed rage," he suddenly hoped that the man hadn't noticed the rude gesture. He rolled down the Mustang's window. The man had the rear doors of a full-size SUV open and was doling out happy meals while reminding his pint-size lunch crew that napkins, not the car's upholstery, were meant for their grubby little paws.

"Hey, sorry, man. Didn't mean to pull in here so recklessly," Gus shouted.

The man gave Gus a frosty, ambivalent look, and IronHorse's offending middle finger twitched a fraction of an inch off the steering wheel, but Gus reined in the reaction, took his hand out of range, and gripped the gear shift.

"My wife's pregnant. We have a bathroom crisis every ten miles. Didn't want to sacrifice the Mustang's seat ... you know what I mean?"

The man's expression softened and he said, "I understand. Mine's pregnant, too. This time, twins. Talk about a lot of stops!"

Gus gave him an empathetic nod, congratulated him, and rolled up his window, as the father's attention was caught by the sound of ice and cola hitting the pavement just outside the open rear door, followed by the wail of one child and the angry reprimands of another.

Gus took Barb's empty water bottle from the cup holder and filled it from a gallon jug that was in a cooler behind the passenger seat. It would mean another pit stop in Blue Earth, but the doctor had told her to stay hydrated, and Barb was taking all her recommendations with the utmost seriousness. She counted the carbohydrates of every mouthful of food. She wore a pedometer throughout the day and had Gus read the results each night before bed. She swore off all red meat that might contain antibiotics or hormones. She questioned the origins of all fish, produce, chicken, and eggs. Pregnancy was Barb StandingBull's full-time job, and, so far, she was proving quite good at it. In support of her commitment to their unborn child, Gus had joined her in many of her vigilant, health-conscious choices, but as the aroma of French fries tickled IronHorse's taste buds, he wondered if he had enough time for a clandestine trip through the drive-through. Barb returned, chatting with a woman whose grand-scale baby bump could only link her to the family with the now corn syrup-coated car interior. In an affectionate ritual often demonstrated among the sisterhood of the pregnant, the women gave each other a brief A-frame hug before Barb climbed into the car, dashing Gus' plans of a secret snack.

As she clicked the seat belt closed, she said, "Our daughter thinks that her father should be allowed a cheeseburger."

"Really? Our son gives me permission?"

"Yes," Barb said matter-of-factly. "*She* does!"

"Well," he said, steering into the drive-through line, "Whatever the case turns out to be, I'm taking the kid up on the offer."

As they slowly cruised towards the exit, Gus caught a last glimpse of the disgruntled family man wrestling a squirmy toddler under one arm while the mega-pregnant mother went to work with a wad of wet wipes to combat the soda, ketchup, and globs of orange American cheese off the howling child whose dining disaster had required that he be stripped down to nothing but a diaper, which sagged dangerously heavy in the rear. Man, was life going to change. Was he ready? Probably. Was his pony ready? Maybe not. He gave them a friendly horn tap and, in mock surrender, the woman waved the sheets of stained wipes in their direction and mouthed, "Good luck."

With one happy empty bladder, one happy full stomach, and a few more hours to go, they hit the road once more.

"This is a long way to go for a wedding. Why did they choose Iowa?"

"They didn't choose it as much as it chose them," Barb replied. "Minnesota wasn't an option. If they're going to make it legal, it's got to be the Tall Corn State."

Gus slowed behind a wide-load trailer carrying a fertilizer application implement that looked like some long-legged insect just landed straight out of a futuristic, machine-dominated hellscape. The trio—tractor, trailer, and TerraGator—tossed copious clouds of gritty dirt in their diesel-perfumed wake.

"Well, if they hadn't asked us to stand up with them, and if I didn't consider them family, I would have thought twice about attending. I don't drive my pony on gravel roads for just anyone, you know"

"I know, Gus," Barb said with the tired exasperation earned from her years of witnessing his meticulousness when it came to the Mustang, while still leaving pants and socks and pairs of boxers on the bedroom floor, and the lid flipped open on the toothpaste. "They know, too. Anybody who's ever known you … *knows!*"

***

They had promised Seattle that, when they reached their destination, they would let him practice his amateur driving skills on some of the less traveled back roads. The soon-to-be fourteen-year-old wanted a learner's permit, and had negotiated a savvy deal with his uncles, who insisted upon an end of the school year grade point average of at least 3.5 in order for them to give permission. The industrious, highly motivated teenager had bled, sweat, and cried through a final algebra exam, and had actually performed a little happy dance when Jack received a letter informing that Seattle Bordeaux had a cumulative GPA of 3.8 and had earned a spot on the honor roll.

"What is the speed limit on a gravel road?" the boy inquired, this being his umpteenth question since their departure.

"That depends," Isaac TwoBears said.

"Depends on what?"

"On whether or not you see a county sheriff up ahead."

From the van's driver seat, Jack shot him a disapproving glance.

Catching the vibe, Isaac put aside comedic for cautionary, and said that steering a vehicle along unpaved roads was serious business and mandated full attention, a good eye for deer that might leap from a ditch, and slow speeds depending upon the condition of the gravel. Bordeaux, who had virtually no experience when it came to operating a car outside the city, nodded his approval.

This was a life-changing trip, and, as they exited off 35W and merged with the moderate flow of west-bound traffic on 90, shared anticipation road like a fourth passenger, too expansive for the capacity, ever pushing against Isaac's neck muscles, ever pushing against Jack's right foot, and ever pushing Seattle's young mind towards more questions.

Bordeaux would be meeting many of Isaac's family for the first time, and, due to the event which would bring them all together, he couldn't net the fluttering nerves that kept taking the speedometer above the limit. Beside him, TwoBears set his phone's GPS with new coordinates, checked, then rechecked the event schedule for any missed details, and opened an email from a cousin who would be unable to attend but sent much love and support as, all the while, he bounced a knee so energetically that his partner finally lifted a hand off the wheel and halted it.

"Relax. Everything will go smoothly," Jack said, as much to himself as to Isaac. "No worries. Let's enjoy this … embrace it. It's special and sacred. I love you."

TwoBears smiled, closed his eyes, and felt the cords of his neck slacken. This was the reason he had chosen Jack. It was the reason he had asked him to come on this most important journey. It was, in these increasingly common moments, when Isaac felt himself able to safely relinquish the burden of all responsibilities with the knowledge Jack would handle the slack, the reason that TwoBears knew, without a fragment of doubt, that Bordeaux was the one with whom he wanted to spend the remainder of his life.

***

As the sky faded from indigo to a washed denim, quickly approaching cornflower, as gauze clouds splashed with pale pink, lavender, and apricot drifted at a ceremonious pace, and as all the ragged, perfect beauty of the stretch of prairie swayed in its simple splendor, a groom waited, Augustus IronHorse beside him. The guests shifted expectantly in their white wicker seats, redwing blackbirds trilling a prelude to the processional, and then the first chords floated soft and sweet from the singer's guitar, as she sang the Fleetwood Mac lyrics.

"For you, there'll be no more crying."

The groom turned, the old farm house's screen door opened, and the intimate gathering of friends and relatives rose.

"For you, the sun will be shining."

The groom's future descended down the wooden steps of the front porch.

"And I feel that when I'm with you, it's all right…I know it's right."

Across the lush, dewy grass, everything he'd ever wanted approached.

"The songbirds keep singing like they know the score."

Peter Gustafson lifted his weathered hand from the bride's arm and, as he retreated, saw his only daughter look at Leonard Stark and mouth the words.

"And I love you, I love you, I love you, like never before."

This was the special moment that Peter had watched his Mag-pie create in play, over and over throughout her childhood: a white tea towel bobby pinned to her blonde curls, a bundle of blazing star, golden rod, cone flower, black-eyed Susan, and wild indigo almost too much for her little arms to manage, as she smiled a missing tooth grin at the family's German Shepherd, and told him that he could kiss the bride, which had always caused the dog to wag his tail and lick her face gleefully. But when Maggie turned twenty, a sullen young local farmer's son with a bad attitude, a fancy truck, and no sense of honor drove Peter's daughter to Vegas and convinced her a quick version was the way to go, depriving Maggie of her dreams of white wicker on the green lawn of the farm where she had grown up, the five acres of prairie in full June bloom, her mother's satin and seed pearl wedding gown, and her father walking her down the steps of the old front porch. Not this time, Peter thought, as Maggie said that she took this man, and he watched a tear escape from the corner of Leonard's eye. *This time she chose right.*

Peter Gustafson put an arm around the mother of his children, his wife for forty years, the beautiful redhead who had asked him to marry her all those summers ago. Had she not been the intuitive woman that she was, had she not possessed the courage to step outside the traditional courtship box, had she waited around for Peter to feel worthy of her and live down the humiliation of being exempted from the military and Vietnam because of asthma, where would he be now? He still wasn't sure he felt worthy, but it wasn't for lack of his Ruth's trying. She laid her head against his shoulder and offered him a tissue.

"Leonard is like your father," Ruth had instructed their daughter. "He may not think himself good enough, Maggie. Perhaps he believes asking you to become a mother to his children is too much to ask. Maybe no one has ever truly made Leonard feel wanted. He loves you; it's crystal clear. Ask him, sweetheart … I know that he will say yes."

So, the evening of Leonard Stark's birthday, Maggie Gustafson had asked, and, as a very wise woman had predicted, Leonard Stark said that he would marry her.

Now, as the big blue stem, buffalo grass, Indian paint brush, side oats, butterfly weed, prairie rose, and spider's wort glistened diamond-like before them, and the dragonflies, swallowtails, and hoppers buzzed electric, the Justice of the Peace pronounced Leonard and Maggie husband and wife. As the guests applauded their kiss, Augustus IronHorse stepped aside so that Oscar and Owen, who stood beside him, could join their father, and beside Maggie, Barb StandingBull did the same, Desiree flowing forward in a light-as-air matching floral sundress. Together, the newly formed family of five swept down the green grass aisle.

***

Family, friends, and anybody interested in a feast and a giveaway, showed up outside of Porcupine at the old TwoBears place. Aunties, uncles, and countless cousins piled into whatever vehicles might weather the trip and headed out from Pine Ridge, Oglala, Wounded Knee, and Rapid City, bound for Old Grandma Daisy's sendoff. They came rolling up the dusty road with huge bowls of macaroni and greasy cardboard boxes, lined with whatever paper could be found, piled high with fry bread. Someone had whipped up a big batch of stew, and when asked if the chunks of meat were beef, the cook just grinned and said, "Sure, let's call it that."

Isaac and Jack, with the help of several young men, built a fire pit while some older folks instructed on the proper way to roast the large slabs of buffalo that Isaac had bought and kept on ice since Sioux Falls.

"So you Minneapolis braves run that bull down with your minivan there?" a cousin jabbed.

As he had since he was a boy, Isaac TwoBears took the good-natured ribbing, and replied, "Kunsi wanted some buffalo for her feast and I see I'm the only man who brought it."

"Well, Cousin, you Two Spirits sure can hunt."

Isaac added, "And we can gourmet cook it once we drag it back to our lodge."

Seattle helped a group of boys arrange sawhorses, oil drums, and planks of wood, metal signs, and the actual top of a metal kitchen table thats legs had rusted off into makeshift banquet tables. A scrawny mutt dog ran from here to there, hoping for some scraps. People kept arriving, carrying covered dishes of whatever meager rations they could manage to pull together. Everyone wanted to bid Daisy TwoBears a respectful farewell.

From a central spot, just beyond the screen door, the old woman sat, enjoying the blur of activity around her, not because it was for her sake, but because she was watching the community coming together to make the occasion happen. She would miss Pine Ridge. She had been born not ten miles from the very spot where she now sat; Isaac and she had raised their children, some grandchildren, a few nieces and nephews, and several foster kids here in the dwelling that had somehow always managed to squeeze within its walls a few more. She would miss the view of vast windswept ancestral land where she greeted the day each morning, and the world of sound that rarely contained anything but natural nurturing noise: wind, thunder, the distant bark of a dog, the soft snorts of the horses that grazed behind the house. Although her home would be condemned had it been sitting anywhere but on a reservation as impoverished as this, Daisy would miss it, too. Her dear departed Isaac, like he had with his broken-down cars, always figured a way of keeping a roof, though often leaky, over their heads. The original cabin had seen many additions over the decades: a battered mobile home had provided running water and extra places to sleep, a lean-to had been attached on the trailer's rear as the family grew, and, during powwow season, when relatives were passing through, even the old cars, left like rusting carcasses in the tall grass, became cramped accommodations for anyone without another option. Life here had been hard, never short on deprivation or sadness. Daisy had attended more funerals than she cared to count, and, at eighty years of age, she had almost out lived the reservation's average rate of mortality by thirty years.

But despite the violence, the addiction, the disease, and the sobering numbers of suicide, Daisy TwoBears had witnessed much goodness here, too. Over the course of her life, she had been a part of the resurgence of Lakota spirituality and the ceremonies and traditional rites that lay the foundation of their people's culture. She had lived long enough to see her husband, their sons and grandsons, receive the skewers through the flesh of their chests and backs, and then commit themselves to tearing loose from the sacred Sun Dance cottonwood. Along her forearms, Daisy carried rows of scars as silent symbol of her own offerings given during those most holy of days. Her decades here contained memories of great kindness and bravery and love, and, as she scanned the people filling the space beyond, she could match a face to many. She saw the woman who spent every weekend organizing groups of res kids for games of basketball or baseball or dodge ball; any physical activity that brought them together, out of alcoholic households, into fresh air, towards better mental and bodily health, and away from isolation and the thoughts of suicide that haunt it.

Daisy nodded to the young man who had pulled the woman who had killed both his parents in a drunk driving accident from her burning house, and then ran back into the flames, saving the woman's infant and toddler as well. Across the way, tossing a partially deflated football with Seattle, was the fifteen-year-old boy whose father grazed his horses on Daisy's land and had found her when she had fallen that spring. A patch of ice had taken her down fifty yards from the house, breaking her wrist, cracking a rib, and spraining an ankle. Unable to get up or even crawl, Daisy TwoBears had laid on the frozen earth, stared into an impossibly blue sky, and did the only thing she could do: she waited. After seven hours, with the sun setting, the temperature decreasing along with her hopes of being discovered, she had closed her eyes and thought of how good it would be to see her dear sweet husband in the spirit world. But as she had begun to drift off, happily resigned to her slippery fate, the boy, out hunting jackrabbits, ambled up to check on the family horses, and found the old woman lying there. Upon hearing of his mother's fall, Chick TwoBears made a decision.

"Next time, you may not be so lucky, Ma. We both know you can't rely on Jake; tribal cops got him in the drunk tank more than he's out of it."

The truth about her youngest child, spoken out loud, had felt colder and harder than the icy ground that had broken her brittle bones, but Daisy could not deny it. Jake couldn't seem to care for his children, their mothers, or, most of the time, himself. Even Daisy's injury and her need for help hadn't overpowered the thirsty illness that lured Jake across the border into White Clay, into another malt liquor can's lightless bottom, into another blackout, into another arrest.

"Kat's all the way down in Texas," Chick had reasoned. "Now that she's finally landed StandingBull after forty years, she's not coming back to the res."

Daisy had sighed. All the nieces, nephews, and foster children she had cared for in her long lifetime of mothering were scattered to the four winds, and she began to dip a reluctant toe into the frigid waters of reality.

"Come to Minneapolis, Ina," Chick had gently urged. "I'll take care of you. I'm your son. I'm the oldest. Let me have this honor."

Jack Bordeaux came to stand beside her chair.

"Mrs. TwoBears," he said, as he offered her a soft-skinned, yet strong hand. "Would you like me to help you outside? Your place at the head of the table is ready."

"Call me Kunsi," Daisy said, clutching his arm with her good hand. "That means Grandmother. As my little Isaac's partner, you are now my grandson, too."

"Thank you … Kunsi," Bordeaux said, trying the Lakota word on for size, which made the old woman grin a missing-toothed smile of satisfaction.

Daisy greeted friends and family, her faded vision taking as many candid snapshots of as many beloved faces as she could, storing them away in the place of pure pleasure where she kept all beautiful recollections, all the while knowing with the bitter, biting certainty of old age that it might be her last opportunity. Despite months of healing, still unsteady on her feet, Daisy let Jack guide her into a lawn chair beside her cousin, Frank LittleFire, who quieted the crowd and prepared to offer a prayer of gratitude. Silence fell, except for the ever-present whisper of a plain's wind and, somewhere in the distance, the distinct, high-pitched keen of a hawk. The old words of thanks, in the language of the oyate, the people, their language, their people, past, present, and future, rode the force of the fast-moving afternoon air, taking all that listened under strong, unbroken wings.

Tomorrow, with her grandsons, Daisy TwoBears would leave Pine Ridge. She would leave behind her house, along with most of her other earthly belongings, with no expectations attached. She would leave the chipped white mug from which she had drunk a million mornings' coffee, a cast iron skillet that had fried a thousand strips of bacon, the rusted wood stove that had cradled a thousand logs' fire. She would leave behind seen and unseen bits of her self: a strand of white hair, the salt of sixty years' tears, the echo of her words; the stuff of dust, of time, of memory, the minute human imprint that bound her with the imprints of her ancestors that bound them all to the land itself.

"I will come to the city," she had told her eldest son. "But my bones will rest on Pine Ridge. Promise me that. Give me your word."

With shaky hands, Jake placed a plate of food in front of Daisy, and then turned away before she could notice the tears in his bloodshot eyes. He wanted to apologize, wanted to say that he wished he could have been a better son, but his hunger couldn't be fed at this feast, and the ever-thirsty ache silenced anything that he wanted to tell anyone. He avoided all faces, following the progress of his own ragged sneakers as he made his way through the clusters of people, some turning away, others glancing with a knowing pity that alluded to lives of being both on and off the wagon and the pain of both, until he reached the house and ducked inside. At the kitchen sink, he found his oldest daughter washing dishes, his granddaughter drying. He slumped against the doorframe where Daisy had marked the growth of her children, his finger blindly rubbing a notch in the wood, wondering if it had once belonged to him. Engrossed in a mother/daughter moment, Tawny confessing to Delia that she thought the Ojibwe boy from Minneapolis was "smoking' hot," Delia teasing that her boy-crazy thirteen-year-old better keep her legs crossed, they didn't notice Jake right away, and when they did, both seemed embarrassed to find him at the perimeter of their private moment.

"Since, after tomorrow, this place belongs to you," Jake said, still pressed against the scarred door frame, leaving the short distance between himself and his child and grandchild vacant. "Can I stay here a couple of days?"

Delia put hands to hips, a posture that Jake had witnessed Daisy assume time and again, and said with the calm, kind assertion of her grandmother, "House rules still stand."

"I'd expect no less."

For a moment, pride leaked in like something clear, cool, and foreign, but then the thirst told him he had no claim on good feelings for the girl he had taken so little part in raising, and resentment clouded him, as the old tug of war between wanting this roof over his head and wanting what was in White Clay started all over again.

"Pilamaya … appreciate it," he muttered, turning to leave, but before he could slip away, gentle hands grabbed a shoulder, and he looked back to see Tawny.

"Please, Grandpa TwoBears," she said, the plea framed with such formality it tugged the man's softer sinews with how little the girl knew him, but how much she seemed to want to. "Stay home … with us."

And for this night, for these strong women, for the fragile feeling of being wanted, he would try.

34

Where Butterflies Land

Jack Bordeaux reclined against the high-gloss purple slats of the porch swing, crossed his long legs at the ankles, and swigged from the tall glass of iced jasmine green tea. He had an hour before everyone arrived, and this, having become a form of daily meditation, was what he needed most right now.

From inside, the muffled clatter of pots and pans, the whir of a mixer, and Isaac's somewhat off-key singing only seemed to add to his sense of peace as he studied a pair of hummingbird's hovering around the red trumpet vine flowers that formed a solid tangled wall of old and new growth at the far end of the porch. On each side of the front steps, butterflies clung to the climbing morning glory's pale blue petals, their delicate motion fanning memories into Jack's quiet thoughts, reminding him of how he had gotten here. He closed his eyes, drifted back to Minnehaha Falls, back five seasons, back to the stomach-twisting, palm-sweating, mouth-parching sight of Isaac TwoBears down on one knee, and back to the question that had seemed almost anti-climactic when uttered by a lover from such a docile, dramatic stance.

"Will you buy a house with me?"

For a long, uncomfortable, cramped knee joint minute, Jack had simply stared, and then, tugging Isaac's arm, he had said, "Please, get up."

Embarrassed, Isaac apologized, said that he had gotten too caught up in the moment, brushed off his jeans, and told Jack just to forget it. But when he tried to retreat down the trail, Jack had grabbed him by the elbow.

"Wait just a damn minute! You can't assume the proposal position, ask me a crazy question like that, then just tell me to forget it. What the hell, Isaac?"

Encouraged beyond what Bordeaux had intended, Isaac launched into his well-thought-out plan, the one he had been hatching for several months. It had birthed itself one afternoon as he had left Jack's apartment, found the usual street he took to the freeway closed due to a water main break, and detoured a few blocks into an unfamiliar neighborhood. There, as he usually did when houses or architecture or landscaping caught his eye, Isaac slowed, admiring a few older two-story stuccos that had been renovated to their original grandeur. As he approached the end of the block and the dilapidated Victorian, its realty sign lilting to one side, half obscured with dingy, gray snow banks, TwoBears' ten-miles-per-hour pace slowed to a complete stop.

Warped and broken boards gave the wrap-around porch a droopy, crooked-toothed frown, an eye patch-like sheet of plywood on one front window only augmenting the neglected house's pity-inducing state. A fat red squirrel scampered along the branch of an enormous oak, leaped onto the roof, and scampered towards the fireplace chimney, taking all the guess work out of who currently occupied the address. The cement driveway, hefted aloft by the extremes of Minnesota weather and several trees' powerful root systems, looked as if a small quake had occurred beneath it. For most people, the word condemned might have come to mind, for many impressionable children, the word haunted, but for Isaac, as he climbed from the truck, saw the solid construction of the foundation, admired the original leaded glass in an upstairs window, and trudged through hard-crusted snow and broken branches to the rear garden where he found the remains of a rotting gazebo, the word *home* emerged.

"It would require a great deal of work, but I think the bones are good, and I bet we could negotiate a decent price. We could fix it up, the three of us, really make it our own. Seattle wouldn't have to change schools and it's still in walking distance of Oscar and Owen's. What do you think? Want to go see it?" TwoBears had said excitedly, not failing to notice Jack's lukewarm response, but still hopeful that he could sell the idea. "Before you flat out refuse, at least see it, and then you can take your time, think about it."

Hadn't Jack been the one to say that they should throw their moccasins to the other side and cross the river together? Were this house and the commitments that came with it what lay on the far bank? Essentially, they were already cohabitating, just at two locations, which, if Jack admitted it, had become tedious. As if Isaac had been reading his thoughts, he joked, "Wouldn't it be nice to wake up and not have to wonder in which closet you left your favorite shirt, which of our kitchens had the last slice of cheesecake in the refrigerator, which couch, at which location swallowed Seattle's missing geography text? How many times in the last year have we freaked because I went to my front door to pay the pizza guy and found that my wallet was in Saint Paul, on your nightstand, or you got to work after leaving your apartment only to find that your cell was beside my bathroom sink? Wouldn't one base of operation just be less complicated ... more comfortable?"

Reluctantly, Jack had agreed to go see the old Victorian, but as they left the falls and drove towards St. Paul, he felt the familiar weightiness of all his past uncertainties return to press discomfortingly against his temples. By the time they reached the ramshackle house, the tension headache caused Bordeaux to squint, shake his head, and ask Isaac if he had ever seen the movie "The Money Pit."

"As I recall, the couple ends up hating one another."

"Yes, but only for a while," TwoBears had replied optimistically. "And it has a happy ending."

In the weeks that followed, Jack had avoided the topic. As promised, Isaac did not push.

During an odd early May snowfall, Bordeaux, in some subconscious need to cling to that which had robbed him, drove to Minneapolis and parked outside Paulette's apartment building. He hadn't seen her in over a month and he sat in the van, struggling to decide if he should go inside or just leave well enough alone. No news had served as good news, and stepping into the depressing space that had been the birthplace of so many demons and the tragedies they had played out upon this stage he had once been forced to call "home" suddenly seemed too regressive, too self-abusive, too pathetic, for such a gray, cold spring day.

He started to reach for the key when she came slowly out the front door, a cane clutched to the hip that she had broken, a cumbersome bag over one shoulder. As she moved to the railing and carefully began to descend the three concrete steps, Jack jumped out of the van and called to her, "Wait, Mom, let me help you!"

Paulette peered out from under a faux fur trimmed hood. Her face looked puffy, but her eyes were clear; she had cut back on the beer since the heart attack, but salt was still a problem, and she had informed the cardiologist that food stamps bought far more white bread than whole wheat and ground turkey cost twice as much as the seventy percent lean hamburger. What did a doctor who drove a Mercedes home to dinner each night know about stretching food dollars?

"Where are you headed? Can I give you a lift?"

"Sure," Paulette said, as she let Jack take her free hand and assist her down the final step. "I need my blood pressure pills. Renee's never around when I need her."

Mother and son rode to the pharmacy, making the kind of small talk indicative of cordial, distant relatives. How was Seattle? Did Renee find a job yet? Had Clayton called her lately? How were things at the university? Would Jack graduate soon?

The return trip included similar, simple conversation, until the van was parked in the same spot from which they had exited twenty minutes earlier, and Paulette unhooked the harness, but did not reach for the door handle.

"How is your ... do you call him your boyfriend?" she asked. "You still ...?"

"Yes," Jack said. "Isaac and I are still together."

"He live with you?"

Despite the uncomfortable feeling that tied itself to the unprecedented direction their chat had taken, Jack suddenly heard himself inexplicably pouring everything out about the house, about the idea of a mortgage, about the seriousness of it all. He told her that he was afraid. He told her that he was worried. He told her that it was what he wanted.

When he had finished, she grinned a hardcore little smile of motherly contempt.

"This man has been with you a year?"

"Yes."

"He ever screw around on you? He ever hit you?"

"No."

"He wants to buy a house with you? He wants to raise a kid with you?"

Jack nodded.

"That's more than any man ever offered me," Paulette Bordeaux said, as she got out of the car and lifted her cane onto the curb to support herself.

Jack moved to help her, but she waved him off, saying, "Leave off, kid. Quit being the fool. Go get yourself what this old woman ain't ever going to have."

Jack watched the lacey flakes fall and stick in the coat's black acrylic fur that framed his mother's face, and, for a moment, as she turned at the door and gave him a thumbs-up, the closest thing to maternal affection he had received in years, Paulette appeared almost soft, almost loving, almost beautiful.

***

Like the rarified May snow, Jack and Isaac's happiness was short lived, melting away quickly when the realtor told them that the house had been taken off the market because the grandson of the deceased owner had decided to restore it for his family. In the weeks after, Jack and Isaac would drive passed, watching for signs that restoration had begun, and wistfully commenting each time that it must not have been meant for them.

One morning in late July, Jack, in an effort to shed the few extra pounds that Isaac's gourmet cuisine had added to his waist, laced up his running shoes and hit the streets, his path reflexively taking him towards the Victorian. Still untouched, it stood in disrepair, but summer had adjusted aspects of the property with its wild, unrestrained adornments, and Jack couldn't help but stop along the sidewalk, drawn by the solid wall of green and red scaling over the brown, brittle knots of the previous year's trumpet vine, the morning glories that must have seeded themselves, generation after generation, and the butterflies. There had been so many, gliding from flower to flower that he blinked several times, trying to focus where wings ended, and petals and leaves began.

Jack glanced around the empty street, and then walked up the cracked stepping stones to the porch, where he slumped onto splintering boards, put his head in his hands, and exhaled the great disappointed breath of a marathon's last finisher. Once he had made his decision, he had wanted this house as much, if not more, than Isaac, and, with every slow pass he had made down the maple and oak lined street, he had felt a sense of unreciprocated love. The feeling might have lessened, had he seen someone—anyone—caring for it, but it was apparent that no one had been here, a situation which only compounded Jack's frustration.

As he sat, he allowed himself to imagine a life within these walls. He imagined the inviting glow of the fireplace. He imagined Seattle bouncing a basketball on the driveway. He imagined the sun setting through the windows of his and Isaac's bedroom. He pictured the three of them around a big kitchen table, eating pancakes and bacon on a Saturday morning. He could see himself mowing the grass around the gazebo and weeding a vegetable garden where Isaac could grow those heirloom tomatoes that he always bought at the farmer's market. He concentrated on all the lovely things he knew a life inside this house could hold, until it felt so real to him he almost pulled his hands from his face, rose, and tried to open the front door to the home that should be his.

The faint sensation of something brushing across his bare arms drew him from the fantasy, and he looked up and saw that several butterflies had landed on his skin as if there might be something sweeter there than the surrounding flowers. The sight startled him. He had no memory of one ever touching him, let alone so many at once, and he held his breath, remaining very still, not wanting the small miracle to conclude. They sat for a few moments longer, slowly opening and closing their colorful wings, until, somewhere, in the far off recesses of Jack Bordeaux's mind, he heard the soft metallic tinkling of a wind chime, and then the butterflies were gone.

Isaac waited at the bottom of the garage apartment stairs, and when he spotted Jack jogging up the alley, he ran towards him, waving his cell phone frantically, yelling, "Why haven't you picked up? I've been calling you for an hour!"

Panting hard, Jack stopped, not sure that his already pounding heart could withstand whatever Isaac was so wound up about, saying, "I left my phone at your place. What's wrong?"

"Not wrong, baby!" TwoBears laughed, grabbing Jack and kissing him full on the mouth. "Very, very right! Realtor called. Grandson thinks the Victorian is too much work. Wants to sell quickly. It's ours, Jack!"

And then the two grown men were hugging and laughing and jumping around, bumping fists, and howling like carefree boys.

***

Jack rocked slowly back and forth, the porch swing making the perfect little creaking sound that all good porch swings should. He sipped the tea, ran a palm over the excellent paint job he and Seattle had done on the wooden slats. Color. Everywhere they had included bright color. From the turquoise bathroom tiles to the lemon yellow kitchen walls, from the emerald green shudders to the apricot bird bath, they wanted their life full of glorious, vibrant color. It had been a year of hard work and cramped living when Isaac's house sold and he moved into the apartment, and a few moments of sticker shock as they chose fixtures, flooring, and furnishings, but they muddled through it, along with the help of many of their soon-to-arrive guests. And Isaac's "guy" connections. When Seattle's room needed new wiring, Isaac said, "I know a guy." When some new pipes were required under the kitchen sink, Isaac knew another guy. The bathroom tile had required one of his guys, too, but that "guy" had shown up as a petite, curvy blonde named Courtney, who had kept Seattle's full, teen hormone-driven attention all afternoon. Gus had helped paint. Leonard had assisted with the reconstructed gazebo. Clayton had come from Stillwater with a tiller and dug their garden plot. Chick and Victoria helped with their move and the unpacking. Barb, hugely pregnant through much of the process, provided countless dozens of cookies for the laborers and a twenty-four- hour hotline of moral support when Jack and Isaac let exhaustion pull them into a squabble and needed a calm reminder of how much they loved one another.

Isaac came out on the porch and Jack slid over so that he could join him.

"The potato salad is done. Seattle finished it up by adding a crap load of diced dill pickle, so beware."

"You did put him in charge."

"True enough," Isaac said, planting his feet and taking up the slow rhythm of the swing. "I guess my parents will appreciate it. It'll remind them of their carpet."

Jack chuckled and offered Isaac his glass. He took it, drank, and handed it back.

"Ready for the whole ram-damn crazy clan to converge upon our peaceful domicile?" Jack asked, as he slid an arm around Isaac and massaged his shoulder.

TwoBears leaned into his touch and just smiled.

***

The house, once silent, dark, and neglected, now overflowed with laughter and loved ones who had come to appreciate its restored beauty and to celebrate its new family's good fortune. Grandma TwoBears sat in the shade of the gazebo, her namesake, Daisy Marie IronHorse, cuddled on her lap, the baby drifting off to the sweet sound of her great grandmother's Lakota lullaby. Beside them, Barb hummed along and waved an eagle feather fan that Isaac had given her to cool the oldest and the youngest guest.

Before her departure from Pine Ridge, many people had asked Daisy TwoBears if she would miss "Indian country," upon which the old woman had pondered the question, a lifetime of accumulated contemplations pulling her away from a simple "yes" or "no." Was Indian country limited to the hodge-podge patchwork of reservations and reserves that the United States and Canadian governments allotted or was it a concept less managed by Departments of Interior than by the souls of the people themselves, the physical's futile attempt to bind the metaphysical? Her mother had said it best on the gray autumn morning the St. Anthony Indian School's bus pulled up outside the tribal office building, and a tearful Daisy BadMoccasin had clung defiantly to her mother's faded flour sack skirt in refusal of the nun's firm order that the waiting children board. Lowering onto her knees, Daisy's mother had taken her daughter's wet cheeks and tilted her face until their eyes met, and, with a love that would carry the little girl through the anguished, isolated years of their separation, she said in low Lakota tones that traveled beneath all others' detection, "They can not take you from where you live."

With that sweet breath of possible salvation, Daisy had believed that her mother had formulated a bold strategy to spirit her away, to defy the orders of the Indian Bureau, to run and hide, but Jerusha BadMoccasin didn't rise, did not, in full flight, tuck her fledgling beneath a protective wing. She took a hand, moist with her daughter's grief, pressed her long fingers into the dusty ground, and painted the smears of earth against Daisy's palm.

Ina maka does not belong to us … we belong to her. You were born of my body, but she is mother of all, and wherever you go, wherever they take you, whatever they tell you, this is truth. They can only take you from me. They can not take you from our mother."

After pauses so drawn out that the ones who had asked usually assumed that elderly Mrs. TwoBears had either not heard or had floated off into whatever had lit the sudden sparkle in her milky eye, Daisy would chuckle dryly. While the gnarled thumb of one hand traced the heart line, the head line, the life line, the forever remembrance of her mother's warm, gritty touch, she would say, "Indian Country … is that here? Is it there? Is it nowhere? Is it everywhere? Isn't it all of them?"

Most cleared their throats, as if that were answer enough to what seemed like an unanswerable question. Others patted the crescent moon curve of Daisy's shoulder, a universal gesture for calming agitated infants and addled old folks. A rare few had grasped the elusive thought-thread, and Daisy and her philosophical co-conspirators would clasp hands in the secret grip of some enigmatic fraternal order.

Daisy bent close to the sleeping babe in her arms and whispered into the delicate shell of tiny ear. As if "Indian country" was as baffling and bemusing a concept to her as it was to her great grandmother, the baby's eyes flitted back and forth beneath closed lids, her petal soft mouth curling into the same soothingly lopsided smile once worn by Jerusha BadMoccasin.

Delicious, savory smoke rose from four charcoal grills. The older children shouted and laughed as they played volleyball under the great twisted oak. At a picnic table, Paulette Bordeaux and Victoria TwoBears sipped lemonade and felt each other out for the latest local native gossip. In the kitchen, Maggie Stark delivered the cake that she had decorated for the occasion: a lovely white-frosted house complete with real pictures of Isaac, Jack, and Seattle tucked between the green icing shutters. Clayton arrived with his family and four huge watermelons. Renee, who had brought Paulette, said she had to work, but popped in long enough to sample the potato salad.

"Awesome!" she had announced, scooping a second spoonful. "Lots of pickle, just the way I like it."

Isaac grimaced. Seattle grinned. Later, Jack's sister Ronnie came with one of her daughters, which lead to the potent, painful pangs of a first crush for Owen Stark and much teasing fuel for Oscar.

Early evening, as the party wound down, Chick helped Daisy and Paulette into the back seat of his and Victoria's car and drove them back to Minneapolis, Gus placed their infant daughter in the stroller and he and Barb walked home, and the other guests washed dishes, folded up borrowed lawn chairs, and extinguished the remaining embers of the house warming cookout, before bidding Jack, Isaac, and Seattle goodnight.

Around midnight, an hour after Seattle had fallen asleep in the quiet cool of his sky blue room, he woke to the sound of music softly drifting up the staircase and into the moonlit space that surrounded the bed. Compelled by the wonderfully strange way that it made him feel, he got up and quietly moved down the hall. He slid a hand over the banister as he found the stairs more by touch than sight and descended the first flight. He stopped at the landing, lowering himself onto a step and, hidden from view, he looked up at the gift that Isaac had given to him and Jack.

In the landing's tall, narrow window, the one that had captured TwoBears' attention with its original leaded glass at the top, hung the hand-made wind chime in all its stained glass and steel glory. The ghostly light of the moon spilled around and through a trio of vibrant, multi-colored butterflies. For a moment, he imagined what the world might look like if one peered through a single wedge of wing. Green was the color and scent of their freshly cut lawn grass, the tiny, newly-formed tomatoes and peppers in the garden, the ivy that had begun to crawl the latticework of the gazebo. Red was the taste of Uncle Isaac's cherries jubilee, the vivid geraniums they had potted on the porch, the shy smile of the beautiful girl who had danced passed him at the last powwow. Yellow was the happy, lively lemon of their kitchen and the taste of hot, buttered popcorn on their family movie nights. He loved blue best, the calm, cool way it made him feel, the way it could pull his attention to the sky with nothing more than its alluring shade, and how it made him think of all that might be beyond it. Sometimes, the mere sight of a certain kind of blue could make him feel relieved of every thirst, every need, that you've ever known.

Yes, Seattle Bordeaux loved the color blue best, but he wanted to look—to live—through them all.

Below, one song ended, another began, and he heard quiet laughter, quiet movement that drew him to the top of the second flight. Unobserved, he perched on a step and tucked knees against chest. Through the carved rungs of the open railing, he watched them dance. Eyes closed, they held one another, and tenderly swayed. Captured by the tranquility of his uncles' faces and the hauntingly beautiful, almost sad strains of the music, the boy lingered until the sweet lyrics came around again.

"Tangerine," Seattle whispered through a smile. "Tangerine."

And somewhere, in the bluest of the blue beyond, a butterfly softly landed.

About the Author

 Amy Krout-Horn, Oieihake Win (Last Word Woman), has resided in two worlds: the world of the sighted and the world of the blind. She has been a writer in both of them. She is the co-author of *Transcendence* (All Things That Matter Press 2009), which received the National Indie Excellence Award 2012 for visionary fiction, and author of the autobiographical novel, *My Father's Blood* (All Things That Matter Press 2011). Her works are included in the anthologies *Unraveling the Spreading Cloth of Time: Indigenous Thoughts Concerning the Universe* (Renegade Planets Publishing 2013) and *When Spirits Visit* (Renegade Planets Publishing 2016).

A staunch advocate for social and environmental justice, she writes and lectures on native history and culture, diabetes and disability, and humanity's connection and commitment to the natural world. For more information, visit her web site at http://www.nativeearthwords.com

ALL THINGS THAT MATTER PRESS

FOR MORE INFORMATION ON TITLES AVAILABLE FROM
ALL THINGS THAT MATTER PRESS, GO TO
http://allthingsthatmatterpress.com
or contact us at
allthingsthatmatterpress@gmail.com